GODSLAUGHTER

GODSLAUGHTER

Louis N. Jones

Dove
Publishers

Godslaughter

Published by
Dove Christian Publishers
P.O. Box 611
Bladensburg, MD 20710-0611
www.dovechristianpublishers.com

ISBN: 9780998669045

Printed in the United States of America

Dedicated to my Lord and Savior Jesus Christ

"Write the vision" Habakkuk 2:2

Think not that I am come to send peace on earth: I came not to send peace, but a sword.
Matthew 10:34 (KJV)

Therefore go and make disciples of all nations, baptizing them in the name of the Father and of the Son and of the Holy Spirit, and teaching them to obey everything I have commanded you. And surely I am with you always, to the very end of the age.
Matthew 28:19-20 (NIV)

"Watch out for false prophets. They come to you in sheep's clothing, but inwardly they are ferocious wolves."
Matthew 7:15 (NIV)

PROLOGUE

St. Mary's County, Maryland
Wednesday, 1:14 am

The road appeared just like any other country road; one lane in each direction, faded striping, lined with lanky loblolly pines on both sides, and illuminated only by the moonlight, when and if the moon bothered to show up. It was miles removed from any major highway, and the only sound was the *swish-swish* of a 13-point buck moving majestically through the woods. As the brown-coated animal approached the road, they could hear the faint drone of an automobile in the distance. Hearing no other sound, the buck quickly crossed the road before the automobile's headlights came into view.

The car's engine slowed, and the car, with Maryland tags, came to a stop on the side of the road near an opening in the trees. Three other sets of headlights were visible farther down the road and were slowly approaching.

With the car's engine still running, a man climbed out of the driver's seat and pushed open a wrought-iron gate stretched across the opening in the trees, revealing an unpaved driveway that led deep into the woods. The man got back in his car and drove down the driveway. One of the approaching cars, with Pennsylvania tags, followed the first car into the gloom of the woods. The second car, with Delaware tags, was not far behind. A final car, with Maryland tags, rolled just past the gate, then stopped. The engine and the lights switched off. A man, roughly six-foot seven tall, got out.

The man, wearing an Army combat camouflage uniform that meshed with the late summer foliage, walked to the mouth of the driveway and poised himself against a tree, making himself almost impossible for passers-by to see unless he revealed himself. And he would do just that if some poor inquisitive soul dared to figure out what was going on at the end of that driveway.

What was there was very nondescript. The driveway ended abruptly at a bank of trees, and a narrow, almost invisible trail led to a circular clearing a few yards beyond. The clearing was a 25-foot diameter patch of dirt dotted with a few tufts of grass and a mixture of fresh and decaying leaves. At the center of the clearing sat a bunch of smooth stones arranged in a circle, with ashes in the center. Tiki torches stood at 5-foot intervals along the edge of the clearing. To the casual observer, it appeared to be a camping site. But this was private property, converted to function as a clandestine meeting spot that, due to the natural canopy formed by the curve of the tree branches above, was invisible even to flyover aircraft.

Three white men and three black men climbed out of the three cars that had parked at the end of the driveway. Each carried a folding chair. Using flashlights, they trudged along the path until they came to the clearing. One man lit two of the torches using a cigarette lighter, but left the others untouched. They arranged the chairs around the circle of stones and sat down.

They remained silent for a moment, listening and looking around to ensure there were no interlopers or eavesdroppers nearby. The site was fairly remote, with no dwellings or other buildings within a half mile. But their paranoia and need for extreme secrecy demanded that they be extra careful and vigilant.

Satisfied that no other human was anywhere within earshot, one of the black men, the leader of the group, broke the silence. "I have an update on Gary Walls."

The other men leaned forward in interest.

"The Southern District, Georgia sector reports that Mr. Walls was located. He has been taken care of." There was a menace in his voice.

Another man, wearing a gray suit, answered. "That's good news."

The leader nodded. "Indeed it is. If Mr. Walls had told anyone else about us, we might have had to go dark. And that, gentlemen, is not an option." He looked around at the other men, the orange glow from the Tiki torches flickering on his face. "I hope we're on the same page here."

The other men nodded.

"Good. Our man in the Georgia sector is working to locate any other preachers Walls may have told." The leader looked at the man in the gray suit. "What about the preacher he talked to at the conference?"

The man with the gray suit gave the leader an assured smile. "The plan is in place. Roth's going to take care of that tomorrow, during the rally."

"Make sure Roth knows to do it before the preacher talks to any media. We don't want him blabbing to any news stations about what he knows."

"Don't worry. Once we take care of this, the Maryland and D.C. sectors should be sound."

"Good." The leader looked at another man. "Any news from the Pennsylvania sector?"

The Pennsylvania sector leader said, "Nothing to report."

"Delaware sector?"

The man representing Delaware said, "Nothing to report."

"So, after we take care of the preacher, we can confirm that there are no loose ends in this district?"

The men nodded again.

"Good. We can't afford for anyone to find out about us. It was a huge mistake bringing Gary Walls into our fold to begin with. My team is working on tightening up vetting procedures so that this does not happen again. Gentlemen, I'll stress again that in order for us to accomplish our mission effectively, society at large cannot know we exist. Our adversaries cannot win this war if they have no idea who they are fighting against. Even if we have to silence more people, we cannot give the dogs any trace of our scent. I hope we are clear on that." The leader removed a bulging folded envelope from his jeans pocket and handed it to the man with the gray suit. "Hand this to Roth on the way out. Make sure he doesn't botch this."

The man in the gray suit scoffed while taking the money. He motioned toward the driveway, where the tall man was keeping guard. "Roth is the most ruthless enforcer in this country. When have you ever known him to botch anything?"

"He's also the most expensive," the leader pointed out.

"Well, you get what you pay for. Trust me, at the rally tomorrow, Pastor Benjamin Lyons will be handled, and no one will have a clue what happened."

The leader nodded gently while maintaining a steady gaze at gray suit. "Seems dangerous and ill-advised to do this so publicly, when a clandestine approach might be more effective."

The man in the gray suit looked away. He hated to be second-guessed, especially when he was confident his plan would work. He parted his jacket to put the envelope in his inner jacket pocket. As he did so, he revealed a security access badge hanging on a lanyard around his neck. The badge was labeled with the words *Senior Pastor, Harbor Christian Cathedral.*

The man with the gray suit closed his jacket. "As I explained before, this has to look as if it is connected to the rally, which will throw any suspicion off us in case Mr. Lyons told others about us. This'll work. Trust me."

CHAPTER ONE

Benjamin Lyons
11:16 am, Wednesday
Freedom Plaza,
Washington, DC

The preacher stood behind the red oak pulpit and looked out over his audience. As he prepared to speak, his heart felt both elation and disappointment. He and his pastor's coalition had been planning this Rally for Racial Reconciliation for over three months. Several suburban white churches and several urban black churches had agreed to come together to sing, preach and pray, presenting a united front against racism. He quickly estimated there were over 500 people in the crowd standing shoulder-to-shoulder on the concrete plaza in the blazing sun on an eighty-degree day. A few witnessed the event from the fringes. Some stood on the steps of the Wilson Building, the seat of the District of Columbia government, directly across Pennsylvania Avenue from the south side of the Plaza. Others filed in and out of the Marriott Hotel on the north side of the Plaza, stopping long enough to see if the event would interest them and then either staying or moving on. Despite his rally having been scheduled for a weekday morning, Pastor Ben Lyons was pleased with the turnout.

However, Pastor Lyons was not happy about the lack of news media. He saw only one reporter with a tripod-mounted camera close-by. He wasn't sure how many print reporters were there, but there didn't appear to be many. He had sent out press releases and called media contacts weeks before the event, trying to draw attention to societal racism. Pastor Lyons was disappointed there had been no requests for on-location interviews. He knew that without substantial press coverage, events like this were not as effective. *Maybe I would have drawn more media had I held this event on the Capitol grounds instead of the Plaza*, he thought. From his vantage point on the Plaza, he could see the Capitol dome, even though it was fourteen blocks away.

Knowing he would probably get only 15 seconds of coverage on a local station during the C block, he would press on. He pulled a cotton handkerchief from his pants pocket and wiped the sweat from his bald, dark head. He saw he had the crowd's rapt attention-they had been waiting to hear from the man who had championed this cause of racial unity ever since his 17-year-old son disappeared in a Birmingham suburb two years before. Speculation from residents was that a white police officer killed his son in a racial profiling incident, then disposed of to cover up the crime and avoid the ire of the city's black residents. No evidence had ever come forth to support this theory, but Pastor Lyons felt in his spirit that the theory was likely correct.

Pastor Lyons adjusted the microphone, the clunking noise ringing loud over the speakers and the constant roar and drone of nearby traffic. Several pastors, both black and white, stood behind him on the raised platform, fanning themselves under a green tent. Feeling their energy, he started his speech. "First of all, I want to thank all of you for being here today. It warms my heart to know that so many of you are willing to come together to present a united front, to show our elected officials, our communities, our families and our churches that people of different racial backgrounds can lock arms together, despite the continued racial animosity that exists in our country."

His remarks earned a few amens from the crowd. He looked over briefly and saw that the news crew was recording his comments on camera. Pastor Lyons couldn't see what station was recording him. He hoped it was the AP, or maybe Reuters, which gave him the chance of getting broader coverage beyond the local channels.

He acknowledged a few key individuals who were there, men and women who had helped him to organize the rally. He gave shout-outs to several who weren't there — his wife, who was at his upper northwest Washington church preparing a luncheon for rally organizers, several D.C. Councilmembers, the mayor, a few other prominent pastors. For good measure, he threw in the reps of the National Park Service, with jurisdiction over Freedom Plaza.

Pastor Lyons continued. "We stand just across the street from the hotel where Dr. Martin Luther King wrote his 'I Have a Dream' speech, and this plaza is named in honor of him. It is unfortunate that although we have made a few strides in the area of race relations, the—"

They were the last words out of his mouth before something slammed into the outer corner of the pulpit and shattered a chunk into splinters. A few seconds later, Pastor Lyons jerked back and then fell backward on the raised platform.

The crowd stood shocked for a moment. Someone yelled, "He's been shot!" Then, chaos broke loose. Amid screams, shouts, and confusion, some spectators dropped to the ground. The rest of them scattered in various directions, causing traffic to screech to a halt on Pennsylvania Avenue and on 15th Street to avoid hitting them. Spectators spewed into the street as fluid as water, knocking down the green metal barriers that surrounded the Plaza, some tripping and falling over them. The pastors standing on the platform ran to the rear and crouched down behind it. A few bravely ran up to the platform to attend to Pastor Lyons. They could see the jagged hole in his jacket just above his waist, and the widening pool of red moisture surrounding it.

A few spectators ran up the steps and inside the Wilson building, which alerted the guards inside to the melee. "Somebody's shooting," the spectators yelled. The lieutenant in charge of the guards quickly sprang into action. Using an active shooter scenario, he ordered the building shut down, and sent word through the building's intercom that all employees should shelter-in-place, at least until they can determine there was no greater threat. He ordered another guard to dispatch police and an ambulance to Freedom Plaza, although myriads of people had dialed 911 on their cell phones.

Two police officers, who were already in the area, sprinted to the Plaza, guns drawn, to see what was going on and to mitigate any threat. After seeing the officers and deciding there was no longer an immediate threat, the people that stayed at Freedom Plaza gathered around the pastor and prayed. The pastor had slipped into unconsciousness. A woman cradled his head in her lap and rebuked whatever demons interrupted a peaceful event with sickening violence.

A man knelt next to the pastor, his head nodding as the woman prayed, his hand laid on the pastor's shoulder. His actions appeared genuine and caring to everyone around him, but were as fake as the knockoff Gucci loafers he wore.

Just hours before, this man had changed into a black suit from the gray suit he had worn earlier that morning in St. Mary's County.

Wynn Delano
Two hours prior
Freedom Plaza

The assignment editor had called him earlier that morning on his day off. "Windy, get down to Freedom Plaza. Pastor Lyons is giving some sort of rally down there. I'll shoot you the NR."

Wynn Delano, a one-man-band reporter at local station NewsNetwork 10, had only been at the station for a year, not long enough to ruffle feathers by refusing to work on his day off. And besides, all the station's other reporters were across town covering the aftermath of a violent storm that had blown through in the early morning. Wynn was often assigned to do filler stories that aired after sports, stories not important enough to merit airing during the coveted A block. Wynn knew that almost every producer in town thought Pastor Lyons to be a blowhard using his son's disappearance as an opportunity to gain publicity for himself and his church. Most producers had decided not to accommodate Pastor Lyons' media hogging any longer. But one producer for NewsNetwork 10's dinnertime broadcast was a member of Lyons' church. The producer assigned Wynn just so he could save face, although the story stood almost no chance of airing.

Wynn arrived at Freedom Plaza and parked his black Ford Escape in the prohibited parking spots along the northern neck of Pennsylvania Avenue. According to the news release that his station had sent to his cell phone, the rally was scheduled to start at ten; at least three hundred people were already present and watching the stage hands as they installed sound equipment. A group of nattily dressed men and two women stood off to the side of the platform and appeared to be in an impromptu meeting. Wynn saw Pastor Lyons among the group and was tempted to approach and get comments from him before the rally began but decided against it. He was probably too busy and things were too hectic right now. If need be, he could always pull Lyons to the side afterward. Best to see how the event would progress.

Wynn checked himself in his car mirror, hoping that his carefully coiffed black hair, peaches-and-cream skin, and his boyish good looks would one day win him an anchor position, or, at least, the attentions of one of the lovely young corporate ladies he had seen walk past his vehicle.

Wynn popped out of the vehicle and surveyed the Plaza for a moment. He walked to the rear of the SUV, popped the hatch, and pulled out his camera, tripod, and a fistful of cords and microphones. He approached the Plaza, walked up three steps to the Plaza floor, and found an abutment, raised higher than the floor, where he could set his tripod and record the events without worrying about people walking in front of his camera.

Just as he had set up, a multi-racial choir of about 40 singers took the stage. Wynn pointed the camera toward them, found a good angle, and let the camera record. He hadn't been to church in almost four years, but from the looks of it, he would get plenty of church today.

Celia Rayburn
Six minutes before the shooting

"So, did I get the job?"

That was always Celia's last question at interviews. If she had absolutely no chance at getting the job, that question would make interviewers squirm, which was her sign she should not expect a call back. But if the interviewer was engaging and encouraging, she figured she might have a shot.

The interviewer responded with, "Well, you were better than the last two candidates. We still have a few more interviews to do before we can decide who gets the job."

Ambiguous, but at least it wasn't an outright denial. Celia thanked the interviewer, expressed once again her interest in the job, and stood to leave.

Her interview had taken place at a corner table in the food court of a sixteen-story office building directly across the street from Freedom Plaza. The manager of the pizza place had no office in the booth where he served pseudo-Italian fast food, so he would meet potential employees in the dining area. Celia didn't mind people buzzing around while she was being interviewed. Having come from a family of five siblings, she was used to such distractions.

Celia took the escalator downstairs to the lobby and headed for the Pennsylvania Avenue exit. She felt confident the pizza place guy would call her back and offer her the job. Her ace in the hole was mentioning that she had worked in her father's restaurants in Detroit and Canada.

When Celia left the building, she saw that the rally that had just gotten started when she entered the building was in full swing. The message of racial unity resonated with her and struck a personal chord. She was a twenty-six-year-old African American woman who, five years ago, married Justin Rayburn, a white man four years her senior. In Celia's old Detroit neighborhood among her peers, marrying outside of her race was an act akin to voting for a Republican.

Celia stopped for a minute, adjusted her purse on her arm, and watched the goings-on. Her parking meter wouldn't expire for another thirty minutes, so she still had enough time to hear the words of the preacher, who had just started his speech. Her silk-linen white suit, the only one she owned, was sharp and professional, yet still lightweight enough for her to survive a few minutes in the heat, although she despised wearing it with a passion. She would have preferred to wear ripped blue jeans and a crop-top, but knew it wasn't proper. Besides, the suit covered the blue-ink lace-and-rose tattoos on her upper arms. She didn't want some stick-in-the-mud potential employer to write her off because of her ink. Her uptown salon had styled her hair into a bob with rose-colored streaks that shone in the sunlight and danced in a slight breeze around a face the color of Ceylon cinnamon and eyes big and round with full eyelashes. She would have preferred her naturally curly blowout Bohemian look.

Celia watched as the pastor's words were cut short with a grunt and a sonorous dull, cracking sound, as if someone had taken a sledgehammer to an old rotten oak tree. Bits and pieces of the edge of the pulpit catapulted into the air, and suddenly the preacher was on the ground. There was no sound other than the crashing of wood and the muted thud as the bullet hit Pastor Lyons body.

Despite the chaos and screams and scattering of several people from various directions of Freedom Plaza, Celia stood transfixed, shocked, unable to believe or register what she was seeing. *Did she just see a man get shot?* She felt the urgency and fear as people ran for their lives. There was no sound of gunfire, and she saw no apparent assailants, but the confusion and uncertainty of what was going on compelled her to move. She rushed back inside the office building and stood in the lobby, watching the scene through the floor-to-ceiling windows. At least ten people gathered around Pastor Lyons' body, and several people ran up the steep stairs to the Wilson Building to promptly alert the D.C. Protective Service guards inside. And just ahead of her, there was a cameraman, standing on an abutment, who was intently recording everything around him, seemingly unconcerned about his own safety.

The sounds of sirens blared in the near distance over the noise of traffic. Celia watched as two D.C. police cruisers charged the wrong way down 15th Street and screeched to a stop on the western edge of the Plaza. Two officers got out of each cruiser, and they immediately squirreled to a far corner any remaining people still on the Plaza. Within three minutes, an ambulance and ten more police vehicles pulled up. Swarms of officers in Crayola blue shirts blocked off streets around the Plaza. One officer shooed the camera-man away from his vantage point just at the edge of the Plaza and stretched yellow crime scene tape around the perimeter.

An office building security guard came to the window and stood beside Celia. "What's going on?"

"A minister got shot over there."

The security guard uttered a vulgar phrase that meant, "No kidding?" He walked out of the building, but a canvassing police officer ordered him to go back inside. The security guard quickly obeyed and stood next to Celia, watching as U.S. Park Police officers arrived, adding to the throng of cops. About fifteen police vehicles and 40 police officers, some holding assault rifles, were now milling around.

"This city," the security guard huffed. "Always something."

Despite the seriousness and the fact that a minister was shot, Celia's mind now drifted to other concerns. *Lord, how angry will my husband be if I come home too late?*

***

Wynn Delano

This was Wynn's big opportunity to get out of the C block dungeon. This story just turned from an insignificant fluff piece to the biggest catch in D.C. at the moment. *A shooting of a high-profile D.C. pastor, and he had caught it live on camera.* And he was the only reporter on the scene. He had already called his producers at the station and texted one of his contacts at D.C. Police's public relations office, trying to get some inside information on what had happened. Now he needed to talk to some witnesses, the ones that hadn't scattered away, and get their perspective. And he needed to do it quickly. He had to get this story on the air before the other stations found out about it.

Using his camera, he rolled back the footage and watched it again, trying to catch any details so he could craft more compelling questions for witnesses. As he watched the moment leading to the shooting, something caught his eye, something strange, maybe inconsequential, but suspicious.

Only thirty seconds before the shot was fired, a man, standing on the dais behind Pastor Lyons, looked up and to his right. Wynn froze the footage. Yes, the man was looking upward toward one of the hotel windows. No, this didn't look like a momentary glance at something that had just invaded his peripheral vision. Nor was he looking at a bird flying overhead. Wynn slowed the footage and saw the man glancing furtively around as if to see if anyone was paying any attention to him. From what Wynn could see, all eyes were on Pastor Lyons and no one seemed to notice the man's strange behavior.

The man's next move told Wynn that something was amiss. The man gently took two steps back and moved to the left, away from the pulpit and several feet away from Pastor Lyons. Several seconds later, the gunshot found its target.

Wynn continued to watch. After Pastor Lyons hit the ground, the man stood there, watching. Even as everyone else scrambled away, he stood there, for more than a few seconds, with no sense of surprise or danger. Then he ran off the platform and hid behind it. Due to the chaos on the Plaza, casual witnesses would not have noticed his hesitation and his delay in retreating, but Wynn saw it clearly. This guy was as dubious as a three-dollar bill.

A few seconds later, a beefy police officer ordered him

behind the yellow police tape stretched around the block. It was not a problem. Wynn had gotten enough footage to fill out his story. He gathered his equipment and moved outside of the crime scene tape, looking around for the man he had seen in the video. He spotted him, standing on the other side of the Plaza, behind the crime scene tape, talking with a group of men and a woman as they watched the EMTs prepare Pastor Lyons for transport to the hospital.

Wynn ran this over in his mind. This was his chance. Being on the air before the other stations was no longer a concern. He now had an angle the other stations did not have. He was certain this man knew the shooting was about to happen and moved out of harm's way. The other stations could only report what had happened. Wynn had a suspect.

He grabbed his equipment and hauled it to the other side of the Plaza. He set up the equipment just a few yards away from his suspect and set the camera to record. He then approached the man, who had been eying him since he rounded the corner to the side of the Plaza where he stood.

"Hi," Wynn said to the man, ignoring the others in the group. "I'm Wynn Delano with NewsNetwork 10. May I speak with you for a minute?"

The man, wearing a crisp black suit as if he had prepared to go to a funeral, nodded affably. "Sure." He moved a few yards away from the group, closer to the camera, with Wynn following.

"Again, I'm Wynn Delano." He extended his hand. "Your name is?"

The man reluctantly shook Wynn's hand, then hesitated. "Um, I'm Jonathan Newberry."

"It looks like you were close to the pastor. I wanted to get some on-the-air comments from you about the shooting." Wynn removed his notepad from his pocket. "Would that be okay?"

"We were friends, but I wouldn't say we were close."

Wynn noticed the man's use of past tense. *We were friends.* Was he so sure that Pastor Lyons was already dead? "No, I mean you were standing right next to him," Wynn clarified.

"I'd prefer not to comment." Jonathan avoided eye contact with Wynn. "My friend has been shot, and I'm not in any mood to make any comments at this time." He looked to the right and saw that the EMTs were moving the pastor on a stretcher toward the ambulance.

"I understand that, but there is some footage on the video that makes you look rather suspicious. I'd like to ask you about before I turn it over to the police."

Wynn hoped his bluff would work. He had no intention of turning the footage over to the police, and such a thing would have to be handled by his bosses, anyway. It surprised him that no cops had requested his footage, even though he was recording. But in this age of video-enabled cell phones, umpteen people probably caught that shooting on camera. Maybe the cops had all they needed from other people's footage.

Jonathan's eyes finally turned to Wynn. "I need to get to the hospital to see about my friend. Can I speak to you there? I should be in the waiting area."

Wynn could tell he had gotten this man's attention. "Do you know what hospital?"

"GW, I believe."

"Not a problem. I'll meet you there." Wynn pulled a card out of the cardholder in his pocket and handed it to Jonathan.

Jonathan glanced at the card, then moved away. "I'll see you there."

"Thank you." Wynn watched as Jonathan joined the group again as they gathered near the ambulance.

Wynn needed someone else to comment. He looked across the Plaza, remembering earlier seeing a petite black woman with rose-colored streaks in her hair standing not far away from where his camera had been perched. The woman was pretty and was professionally dressed, and he was instantly attracted to her. Now he had a reason to approach her. He needed someone like that in his life rather than the Emo women he usually hung out with.

Wynn gathered his equipment again and walked to the other side of the Plaza, near the office building where he had seen the woman. If she was still there, he might kill two birds with one stone: get a comment for his story, and get her telephone number. If he did that, it would be a relatively successful day.

As Wynn rounded the Plaza, Jonathan Newberry did not take his eyes off him.

Celia Rayburn

The urgency of danger seemed to have passed, and there was nothing else to see, so Celia decided to get home before her meter expired and a D.C. parking control officer slapped her car with a pink love note. As she walked out of the building, a man approached her directly, as if he had every intention to speak with her and no one else.

"Did you see that?" Wynn asked her.

"See what?" Celia responded, thinking how rude of this man to ask questions before he introduced himself.

"Pastor Lyons get shot."

"Yeah. I was looking right at it."

"Would you be willing to be interviewed on camera?"

"Who are you?"

"Oh, I'm sorry." Wynn was a little miffed that he still had to introduce himself, even though he had been filing stories on the air for the station for a year now. Maybe she wasn't local, or maybe she didn't watch the news. Wynn gathered his equipment on his left arm and extended his right hand. "I'm Wynn Delano, a reporter with NewsNetwork 10."

Celia shook Wynn's hand. "Celia." She intentionally left out her last name.

"Celia, would you be willing to give an interview on camera about what you saw across the street?"

Celia quickly agreed. Being on the news would give her a readily confirmable alibi on why she was getting home so late. Plus, the exposure couldn't hurt her job prospects.

"Cool. Give me a minute to set up." Wynn found a spot directly in front where he could interview Celia against the backdrop of Freedom Plaza. Once he was set up, he motioned for her to come over and had her stand in front of the camera, her back to Freedom Plaza. Wynn pulled a notepad and pen out of his pocket, switched on the camera, and started his interview.

"Please state your full name," Wynn asked.

"Okay. Celia Rayburn."

"Can you tell me what you saw over there, Celia?"

Celia recounted everything she had seen from the moment she walked out of the office building following the interview. Wynn periodically interrupted with questions to get more detail. When the interview was done, he switched off the camera and nodded his thanks.

"Appreciate it, Celia." Wynn offered his business card. "You know, I'd really like to thank you by taking you to dinner."

Celia scoffed at first, but then checked him out. He was decent looking. Not the most handsome man she had ever seen, but since she was certain she would be in divorce court with her husband within a year, she would entertain his interest. A dinner wouldn't hurt. She momentarily wondered what it was about her that attracted so many white boys.

"I'll call you," Celia said, intending to control the communication so her husband didn't discover.

Wynn had heard that before. He knew he would never hear from her again. "Not a problem. Call me anytime, day or night."

Celia heard a siren and looked back at the Plaza. The ambulance, with Pastor Lyons inside, was speeding away to the hospital. Some police officers were milling about while others were talking to the witnesses who had not run away. She watched as Wynn dismantled his equipment and made his way back over to the Plaza, hoping to speak to an on-site police supervisor about what had happened.

Celia, feeling as if there was nothing more to see, headed back to her car, knowing she would have a whopper of a story to tell when she got home.

CHAPTER TWO

August 2012

They had been legal adults for several years, but both twenty-one-year-old Celia Wise and her sister, 23-year-old Meagan Wise, had, only now, defied their parents' conservative values and celebrated at the Loris Nightclub in downtown Detroit.

Meagan Wise had just landed a job as an on-air reporter at a local Detroit television station. The achievement was especially noteworthy because it was unheard of for such a young candidate with no prior experience to be hired as a reporter in a big city market. Yet, Meagan had prepared years for this, starting from her childhood days when she would mimic mentor-in-her mind Carole Simpson, studying her voice, cadences, and mannerisms.

Meagan had heard her parents say many times that the Lord had blessed her, and they planned to have a fellowship celebration at their church for her. That was fine, but Meagan wanted to party. *Really party.* So, with her younger sister in tow, she stepped out on a hot August Friday night wearing the sexiest red dress she could find and walked into the Loris Nightclub at 10 pm like she owned the world.

Celia, two years younger, eight inches shorter, and much more introverted than her older sister, had never been in a nightclub before now. This was not only due to her more reserved nature and the Christian values that were a mainstay in her family home, but she could not legally go to a nightclub until she had turned 21. Nonetheless, she was so proud of her sister that she readily agreed to hang out with her, knowing she might not see her sister as frequently once her busy career kicked off.

A few men sized up the two beautiful women immediately after they walked in the noisy club. Within an hour, several men had propositioned Meagan, and she soon accepted an offer to dance from a tall man who looked to be ten years her senior. While Celia sat at the table alone, a handsome guy approached her.

"Hi, I'm Justin." He pointed to her nearly empty Moscow Mule sitting on the table. "Can I buy you another drink?"

Celia smiled and nodded, which Justin took as permission to fetch her a drink. When he turned to go to the bar, Celia checked him out. Besides his deep voice, his perpetual tan, unruly brown hair, square face, prominent cheekbones, and lanky frame gave off the vibe of a schoolboy fresh out of puberty, although he had to be at least 21 years of age to get into the club.

After ordering a Mule and a Jack Daniels from the bar, Justin sat and took in Celia's round face, big, round eyes, and bushy curly brown hair. "May I ask your name?"

Megan had warned Celia never to give her real name in a club, just in case a creepy stalker guy wanted to track her down. Maybe that was Meagan's experience, but Justin seemed safe to her. "I'm Celia."

"Pretty name for a pretty girl."

"Thanks."

"You know, this is awkward for me. I don't go to clubs often," Justin admitted.

"Neither do I." Celia sipped on her drink.

"You from around here?"

"Born and raised in Detroit. What about you?"

"No, I'm not from around here. I'm from Baltimore."

"What brings you to Detroit?"

"Automotive conference. My employer sends several of us every year. One of those boring things you have to endure in exchange for getting a free trip out of town and a nice hotel room." Justin shifted in his seat. "A couple of guys wanted to come out to the club to unwind a bit, and so here I am. It was either that, or sit in a hotel room by myself watching *Sons of Anarchy*. What about you?"

"Celebrating with my sister. She just got a great job."

Justin looked around. "Who's your sister?"

Celia directed his attention to the center of the dance floor. "That's her in the red."

Justin nodded, staring, for a little longer than he should have, at the woman in the red dress grinding and bouncing against a man that looked old enough to be her father. Justin returned his attention to Celia. "Doesn't look like she's going home alone tonight."

Celia drew back and frowned. "What does that mean? Are you saying my sister is a ho?"

Justin held up his hands as in surrender. "Not saying that at all."

"Sure sounds like it."

Justin stumbled over his tongue a few times, trying to justify his flip comment. After failing miserably, he said merely, "I apologize. I didn't mean any offense."

"My sister is an upright, Christian woman," Celia added. "She's having a bit of fun, but she's not going home with any man tonight."

"Pardon my question, but if she's a Christian woman, what's she doing here?"

"Christians can enjoy good music and dance just like anybody else." Celia knew how much her parents would give her a good tongue-lashing if they heard her say that.

"Just because you're a Christian doesn't mean you can't have fun."

"Well, I hope you forgive me for putting my foot in my mouth." Justin's lips curled into a smile. "I really am a great guy if you get to know me. And just so you know, I'm not here on the prowl. You seemed like a nice young lady, and I wanted to talk to you. No strings attached."

"You expect me to believe that?" Celia scoffed. "Guys don't come to clubs just to 'talk' to girls." She made air quotes as she said the word *talk*.

"Well, like I told you, I don't really go to clubs, so I don't know what they do or don't do in clubs. But I'd be lying if I told you I wasn't hoping for a friendship out of this."

"Why do you want to be my friend? You don't even know me."

"There's something about you," Justin said without a bit of hesitation.

Celia scoffed.

"No, really, that's not just a line," Justin continued. "There's something innocent, fresh about you. I mean, even the way you dress. All these other girls got everything hanging out, but you show up with a pair of conservative black slacks and a blue blouse. I mean, you could be just at home at church in that outfit. When you see that kind of purity in a nightclub like this, it makes you kind of curious."

Celia scoffed again. "Translation: I can't have my way with all these bad girls in this club, but a goody-two-shoes like her I can have my way with."

Justin lowered his head. "You really got me pegged all wrong. Why don't you let me take you out to dinner, so I can prove it? Again, as just friends."

Celia couldn't avoid being attracted to this man's confidence and irascible charm. But she would need to talk to this man more before deciding on any dates with him. So, there in the club, they would continue to talk until 1 am, a conversation which ended with an exchange of numbers and promises to keep in touch.

***

After calling his producer and updating him on the situation downtown, Wynn Delano headed to GWU Hospital and parked in a public underground lot in a building across the street from the hospital. Knowing that due to patient privacy rules he could not record any footage inside the hospital, he left the camera equipment inside his SUV, took only his notepad and pen, and walked across 23rd Street to the entrance of the hospital emergency room. After checking in with the security guard, Wynn walked through the ER waiting area, passed through a set of double doors and found the visitor lounge area, where he found a sizable number of dignified-looking people standing around talking in three separate groups. He noticed Jonathan Newberry in one group and stood to the side until Jonathan noticed his presence. Jonathan excused himself from the group and walked over to Wynn.

"What did you want to ask me, Mr. Delano?" Jonathan asked, annoyed that Wynn had followed up on his request to meet him at the hospital.

Wynn motioned his head toward the lounge area door. Both men stepped out into the corridor. Wynn waited until the corridor was clear before he spoke. "I need you to explain something to me. Just before Pastor Lyons was shot, I saw you glance up at something, and then move a few feet away from the pastor. Now, someone looking at that might think you were trying to avoid getting shot yourself. But I'm certain that's not the case. So, what happened?" Wynn flipped his notepad to an empty page and held his pen ready to write.

Newberry scoffed, and his eyes darted back and forth before he answered. "That's simple to explain. The sun was in my eyes, and I was trying to get to a spot where the glare wouldn't be in my eyes."

Wynn knew immediately that was a lie. As a reporter quasi cameraman, he had to study the sun's position in the sky to capture the most effectively lit footage. He knew that the sun was above Newberry's head, and slightly behind, but not in a position to shine glare directly into his eyes. Nonetheless, he jotted down Newberry's response and then went on to the next question.

"You also didn't seem surprised that Pastor Lyons was shot. You just stood there for a few seconds, almost as if you knew it was going to happen."

Newberry stood there for a moment, giving Wynn the blankest of expressions. He finally drew near to Wynn just a hair short of violating his personal space. "Are you accusing me of something, Mr. Delano?"

Wynn dared not answer that question as affirmatively as he wanted to, for Newberry was close enough to sucker-punch him. Instead, he responded, "I'm not accusing you of anything. I just want answers."

"Why is that important?" Newberry was close enough that Wynn could smell the mint of his chewing gum. "You report that Pastor Lyons got shot, and that's it. Why am I so important to your story?"

"Because if something looks suspicious, it's my duty to report it to the cops," Wynn answered with as calm a voice as possible. "It keeps our relationship with the police tight in case we need something from them. Now, if I am misreading the situation, I would just as soon keep the footage out of the cops' hands."

"So, the police don't have it?"

"Nobody has it but me."

"Hmm." Newberry removed his smartphone from his pocket and punched and swiped while he spoke. "Well, like

I said, I was trying to avoid the sun. And the reason why I did not respond with panic, like so many others did, is because I did two tours in Ramadi during the Iraq War." Newberry looked up from his phone at Wynn. "I'm used to people being gunned down around me. My first instinct is to swoop in and try to save my fallen comrade, and that's what I did."

"Hmm, I see." Wynn finished taking notes, and then looked up at Newberry. "I guess that's fair. I mean, why would a preacher be involved in getting another preacher shot, right? I mean, preachers can sin just like anybody else, but usually, their sin is getting horny, not committing homicide."

Newberry's eyes narrowed. "Any other questions for me?"

"How's the pastor doing?"

"Not sure. If you stick around for about 15 minutes, I may be able to get some information for you."

"That would be great. Thanks."

Newberry headed back to the lounge area. Wynn flipped the notepad shut. He still didn't believe Newberry's story, and that made him want to put on the mantle of an investigate reporter. Wynn had another two hours before he had to turn in his footage for the early afternoon newscast. He intended to stick around and talk to some other witnesses before he left and then head back to Freedom Plaza to talk to investigators and prepare for a live shot for the afternoon newscast.

Newberry walked into the lounge but did not rejoin his conversation group. Instead, he retreated to a far wall out of earshot of the others in the room and dialed a number on his phone.

A voice with a German accent answered, "Hallo."

"This isn't done," Newberry said. "He's still alive. And a reporter caught the whole thing on video."

"What reporter?"

"His name is Wynn Delano, out of News Channel 10. He has some footage that may incriminate me. I need you to take care of it."

"Where is he?"

"He's here at GW. I can text you a link to his online profile. You may be able to catch him on the way out of the hospital if you get here in time."

"On my way."

"Don't do it anywhere near the hospital."

"Don't worry. It'll be handled."

12:16 p.m., Wednesday

Celia's apartment was on the 10th floor of a luxury sixteen story high-rise in Silver Spring, a city in Maryland at the upper northeastern edge of the District of Columbia. The neighborhood was downtown Silver Spring, just over the D.C. line, boasting a large shopping and dining district. The one-bedroom apartment cost $1700 per month and had a great view of downtown Silver Spring. It was the only apartment she had lived in since leaving Detroit five years before and was a far cry fancier than any flat she had rented in the Motor City.

Yet she still dreaded coming home because of who was waiting for her inside.

When she inserted the key in the door, she hoped—prayed—that he wasn't at home. Her hopes were dashed when she opened the door, and a strong smell of skunk weed assaulted her nose.

Celia rushed inside, dropped her purse on the carpet, and headed for the kitchen just to the right of the door. She grabbed the aerosol air freshener from under the kitchen counter and sprayed liberally around the living room and in the outside corridor near the door. Lord, she couldn't stand that smell. She quickly closed the door and headed to the bedroom.

Justin Rayburn lay on the queen-sized bed, a joint smoldering in the ashtray on a nightstand next to the bed. He wore only a pair of dingy, wrinkled boxer shorts. A daytime talk show was playing on the flat screen TV affixed to the wall across from the footboard of the bed. As Celia entered, Justin never took his eyes off the TV.

"J, I thought I told you, you can't smoke in here," Celia's voice trembled slitghtly. "This is a non-smoking building."

"Who are these people to tell me what to do in my own apartment?" Justin's defiance rode on a very smooth, deep voice.

"It's *my* apartment," Celia said with an edge that on any other day would have earned her a smack in the face. But thanks to the effects of the weed, Justin was much too mellow now. It was a different story when he had three or four boilermakers in his system.

"How'd the interview go?" Justin feigned interest.

"Might be a possibility."

"What took you so long?"

"Something happened downtown. Somebody shot a preacher speaking at a rally. I saw the whole thing."

Justin grabbed the remote and switched channels. "Nothing on TV about it."

"It's probably gonna air on Channel 10 tonight. The reporter interviewed me."

"Why d'you do something dumb like that?"

Celia was used to Justin criticizing her, but this time, it especially bugged her. She had told him she saw a shooting, and all he could think to do was to call her dumb. Maybe she was, for thinking that Justin would care about her enough to ask how she was doing. "Don't be dramatic. I just told him what I saw."

"Like I said, dumb."

"Dumb how?"

"Snitches get stitches."

Celia scoffed. "I wasn't snitching. I don't even know who did the shooting." Celia turned toward the door.

"Where are you going?" Justin asked.

"To make lunch," Celia responded. "And to put something out for dinner, if you don't mind."

Getting no further response from Justin, Celia kicked off her shoes, left the room and headed to the kitchen. The kitchen was a lot smaller than she desired, with only a stove, a refrigerator, and six feet of faux oak counter space spilt in half by a stainless-steel sink. It was a kitchen made for people who didn't cook often. However, Celia didn't see it as an issue when he first rented the apartment. There were so many restaurants nearby, she knew she wouldn't spend much time cooking.

She opened the refrigerator and found one package of chicken legs, the only thing edible in the fridge except for a carton of milk and two half-drank bottles of beer. Food was scarce these days. Justin had been unemployed for several months after losing his job as a car mechanic because he couldn't stop getting high. They were two months behind in rent, and Justin's meager unemployment payments weren't helping much.

Celia's attempt to find employment was the last-ditch effort to get money flowing into the house before they got evicted. At least, that's what she wanted Justin to believe. But Celia's real plan was to make enough money to get as far away from Justin as humanly possible.

Celia switched on the kitchen radio, hoping the smooth sounds of singer Jill Scott would infuse pleasure into what had been a challenging day.

***

It may have been the chaos of the event, or the uncertainty of what had happened, but no one at the hospital would go on record with Wynn. His statement from Jonathan Newberry and the on-camera interview from Celia would have to do. He could always get more from the Metro police PIO.

He needed to get back to Freedom Plaza to meet the production truck and prepare for a live shot teaser before the afternoon newscast. His producer had been hounding him to get the footage to the station quickly, as other news stations had now heard about the shooting and were likely headed downtown for their own live shots.

Wynn, confident he had gotten as much information from the hospital as he could, left the ER just before 2:00 pm. He walked a block to the public parking garage, retrieved his SUV, and headed out of the garage into ever-increasing weekday traffic. He had only an eighteen-block drive from the hospital to Freedom Plaza, a route that would take him past the White House and the Ellipse. But in city traffic, it could take almost a half-hour to get there.

Making the left turn from 23rd Street onto Virginia Avenue, he was barely five blocks from the hospital when he heard the familiar chirp of a police siren behind him. In his rear-view mirror, Wynn saw the red and blue light bar flashing from inside the vehicle, but the car didn't appear to be a standard marked police cruiser. Nonetheless, he pulled over into a metered parking space directly across from the US State Department. The police car stopped behind him and to the left, blocking off one lane of Virginia Avenue.

The man who got out of the police car was not a uniformed cop, but had a badge around his neck. *Maybe he's a detective*, Wynn thought. The man approached Wynn's vehicle and leaned down. "Good afternoon, sir. You know why I pulled you over?"

"Not a clue," Wynn said.

"You made an illegal left turn back there."

That struck Wynn as strange. "I didn't see any signs saying I couldn't."

"You must have missed it. License and registration, please."

Wynn knew it was no point arguing with a cop. Since he was on the clock, he'd let the station's lawyers fight for him. He fished his wallet out of his rear pocket and handed the officer his license and registration card.

"Be back in a few minutes." The officer walked back to his vehicle and got inside. As Wynn looked back, he could see another shadowy figure sitting in the passenger's seat. Wynn figured it was another cop.

Wynn faced forward, checking his watch. He had no history of moving violations, so he fully expected a warning. He hoped it came quickly, so he could get to Freedom Plaza.

Suddenly the police car switched off its light bar and shot off. Wynn watched it pass by him and head straight down Virginia Avenue. "What's this guy doing?" he said aloud. "He has my license and registration." He continued to look down the road to see where the police car was going. It had registered much too late that when the car passed by, the second person was no longer in the car.

He heard his unlocked passenger down open. By the time he could turn toward it, a menacing-looking tall man was sitting in his passenger seat, pointing right between Wynn's eyes the largest bore barrel of a gun he had ever seen. "Give me all the tapes you recorded today." His accent was thick German.

"Back there," Wynn responded, shaking and without an ounce of hesitation.

The tall man reached for the camera bag on the rear seat. He rummaged through it and found several HDCAM videotapes. "Which one did you use to record the shooting today?"

"It's still in the camera," Wynn pointed again to the rear

seat.

The tall man dropped the camera bag at his feet, then leaned back, the gun still pointed at Wynn's head.

"Drive."

***

It was 5:30 pm when Justin suddenly announced, "I'm going out for a minute."

Celia knew what that meant. He was headed to a bar, where he would hang out for a few hours and then come home drunk, if he came home at all. Celia almost wished he *wouldn't* come home. When he stayed out all night, the buzz would wear off, and she stood little chance of being beaten because of the least little thing she said. She tried to convince herself that when he stayed out all night, he was just sleeping it off in his car or on a park bench somewhere. It couldn't be that he was with another woman, because who, other than her, would want a drunk, unemployed stoner? These were the things she told herself to make herself feel better. But her woman's intuition never stopped nagging her, and it told her he was likely hanging out with some woman who was as much a loser as he was. But it also meant that between his episodes of intoxication and womanizing, he had little interest in her, which was all right with Celia.

At 5:58 p.m., Celia reclined in her living room on a modernesque aqua leather couch she had bought from a nearby furniture store during her more lucrative days. She favored pastels, as everything else in the living room was white or pink. She switched the flat screen TV to channel 10 and watched the teaser while she enjoyed fresh-out-of-the-oven barbecue chicken and some canned green beans. Celia was disappointed to see that the teaser did not mention the pastor's shooting.

Celia grabbed the remote and switched to another channel, and then another, and then another. All the other local channels had the pastor's shooting as the lead story and were working the angle that the shooting was likely a hate crime in response to the racial unity aspect of the rally. Some channels had obtained cell phone footage from attendees at the rally.

Celia turned back to channel 10, hoping that maybe they would cover the story later. She eventually watched the entire half hour telecast, but there was only a passing mention of the Plaza shooting from the anchor. No footage, no interview. Her fifteen minutes of fame dwindled to nothing.

Celia grabbed her purse and pulled out her phone and Wynn's business card. Within five minutes she had accessed several TV and print news sites on her phone; all of them listed the Plaza shooting as one of their top stories. On NewsNetwork 10, only an AP report, but no footage or interview.

Celia read all the stories and pieced together a few facts. Police were investigating the shooting as a hate crime due to several threatening racial messages left on the pastor's voice mail and social media accounts. They guessed that the shot likely came from a sniper in one of the buildings surrounding Freedom Plaza and that the bullet that had struck the pastor was from a military grade weapon. This wasn't a casual drive-by from some street hood. This was a carefully calculated assassination attempt.

But the best part of the story for Celia was that the pastor was still alive. In critical condition, but alive. She prayed, as she had done several times that day, that the pastor would recover from his injuries.

Then she looked at Wynn Delano's business card. She thought about calling him, if only to discover why NewsNetwork 10 had no footage of the shooting. At least, that would be her excuse for calling. She knew that after discussing the reasons for the lack of coverage that Wynn would segue the conversation into a more personal one. Then, she could decide if she wanted to risk cheating on her husband and go out with this guy.

After a few minutes, Celia thought the better of it and decided not to call, at least not now. She had no desire to sneak around Justin, although she was certain he was sneaking around her. No, first things first. Get enough money, then an apartment away from Justin, then the date with the forlorn news reporter.

Celia slipped the card back into her purse, hoping that within a month, she could put that card to use.

***

November 2012

It was three months later when Celia decided that her relationship with Justin was serious enough to warrant his meeting her parents. One November evening, Celia picked up Justin from the airport and drove to her parents' modest Alpheus Street home for dinner. They parked on the street outside of the house, after which Celia felt the need to prep Justin before they entered the house.

"Okay, you remember what I told you about my parents, right?" Celia said.

Justin removed his seat belt. "Yeah. And I should be sweating bullets right now."

"It'll be okay." Celia brushed a speck of lint off her black polyester coat. "Just remember that they are very straight-laced. They probably won't like you, but I'm not doing this because I want to get them to like you. I just want to give them the opportunity to formally meet you, but no matter what they say, remember that I love you and that the decision to be with you is mine."

"I'll remember that, babe."

"Having said that, please don't say anything that'll set them off."

"I'm sure they are not that bad, Celie."

"Are you kidding?" Celia took the keys out of the ignition and shoved them into her brown Coach purse. "Think of the most judgmental Christian you have ever encountered. Multiply that by 100, and you have my parents."

"Don't worry. I'll keep my abundant arsenal of four-letter words to myself. And I won't tell them that I strangle chickens after midnight."

"I'm serious, Justin." Celia leaned over and kissed him on the cheek. "Just be good."

"Best behavior."

When they got out of the car, Justin looked around. Men sitting on stoops of run-down houses eyeballed him, their breath vapor emitting furiously in the 30-degree chill. "You grew up in this neighborhood?"

"Yep." Celia walked around to his side of the car.

"Why is everybody staring at me? They've never seen a white boy before?"

"Usually if a white boy is in this neighborhood, he is either a cop or looking for drugs. They're trying to guess which one of them you are. You grew up in BMORE. You know the deal."

Celia and Justin walked through the gate and approached the front door. Before Celia could get her hands on the door knob, the door swung open, and standing there just beyond the threshold was a thin, ebony-skinned woman with black tresses hanging to her shoulders.

"Baby!" Marjorie Wise's ebullient greeting made it seem as if she hadn't seen her daughter in years; in fact, they had seen her the day before. Marjorie stepped forward and gave her daughter a hug; Celia was grateful that her adult years had not robbed her of appreciating her mother's embrace.

After the hug, Celia enthusiastically looped her arm with Justin's and almost shoved him in front of her mother. "Mom, this is Justin."

Justin got an identical greeting, then Marjorie swept them in the house and shut the door behind them. The living room was small but cozy, well-furnished, with several family photos and knick-knacks neatly hung on walls and arranged on table tops. After Marjorie took their coats, Justin's attention went to a large photo hanging on a nearby wall.

Marjorie noticed his interest. "That's my family at Tiger Stadium, the last game the Tigers played there. Celia was only seven years old in that picture. She was such a tomboy." Marjorie leaned forward and pointed out Celia in the photo.

Justin cut an eye at Celia and smiled. "She's so cute."

Celia rolled her eyes.

"Celia's father was a caterer for the team back then," Marjorie noted. "We took this before the game started. There's Selig, Archer, and Moehler. There's my husband, and my daughters Rosalyn, Meagan, and Hope, and my sons Brian and Lance."

"Pretty large family."

"Yes, and they've all been a blessing. None of them have been in jail or been arrested. None of them are on drugs. It's through God's grace and mercy that I was spared from that kind of headache."

Celia sensed a preaching spell from her mother coming on, so she quickly interjected. "Where's Dad?"

"I'll give you one guess."

"In the kitchen?"

"Where else? Putting the final touches on his chicken."

Celia elaborated. "Dad makes great charbroiled chicken. He's planning to open his own restaurant."

"It smells great," Justin said.

"I'll tell him you're here." Marjorie excused herself and disappeared into the dining room, headed toward the kitchen.

"Your mom seems nice." Justin wrapped an arm around Celia.

"I'm glad you like her," Celia stated. "I hope they feel the same about you after dinner."

A few seconds later, Marjorie walked in with her husband. George Wise was, similar to his wife, tall and thin. His salt-and-pepper closely cropped hair revealed an age on the east side of 50. Many had mistaken them for brother and sister, which the Wises explained was due to God drawing them so close together they almost looked alike.

George Wise wiped his right hand on the side of his dad jeans and extended it toward Justin. "I'm George."

"I'm Justin." Justin almost winced at how firm George's hand-shake was. *Was this guy trying to squeeze my hand off?* "Nice to meet you."

"Same here." George looked past Justin at his daughter. "Hey, Pookie."

"Hey, Daddy." Celia practically ran to him and embraced him.

Justin observed their long hug and knew that Celia and her father were close. *Daddy's girl.* At that moment, something ignited within Justin, a spark of jealousy that caused him to dislike Celia's father even before he got to know him.

During dinner, Justin would regale the Wises with stories of growing up in Baltimore, being descended from Scottish immigrants who fled to the ports of Baltimore during the Great Irish famine. He would try to impress them with his strong family ties—his mother and father were office workers in Leesburg, his sister was married with two children and living in Locust Point, his cousins, aunts, and uncles were many and scattered between Maryland and Virginia; just for good measure, he even threw in a mention of his uncle, who was a pastor in Columbia, Maryland. The Wises listened intently during dinner, saying little, reserving their questions until Marjorie had served the chocolate cake for dessert. It was then that George Wise would begin what appeared to Celia as a thinly veiled interrogation.

"So, Justin, what church do you attend?"

Celia had prepared him for this question, so he confidently answered, "Walk in the Spirit Church in Baltimore." It was the name of a church he had attended twice in his teens but had not been to since.

"Your pastor's name?"

Justin made up a name; he doubted that George Wise would check. "Pastor John Mitchell."

"When the last time you attended?"

Justin made up another lie. He wanted so badly to impress George if only to please Celia. "A couple of weeks ago."

"What did the pastor preach about?"

Now that question Justin was unprepared for. He cut an eye at Celia, who had picked that moment to pop a morsel of cake into her mouth and avoid his gaze.

"Uh, well…"

Both George and Marjorie leaned forward, eagerly awaiting his response.

"Actually, I was helping a deacon with some things downstairs, so I didn't hear the message."

George and Marjorie looked at each other. They knew a lie when they heard one. Celia's downcast expression was as big a tip-off as anything. Marjorie stood and cleared empty plates from the table. Celia looked up and managed an uncomfortable smile, as she thought the questioning was over.

But George was not finished.

"Tell me what your beliefs are, son."

To Justin, this seemed like an easy question. "Well, I believe in Jesus."

"What about him do you believe?"

"Well, I believe He is the son of God."

George merely looked at Justin, waiting to hear more. When Justin handed him a confused look, George would not relent. "Well, you believe. The Scripture says that even the devils believe and shudder. Tell me about your faith, son, and the outworking of it."

Justin swept a hand across his forehead and again glanced at Celia, hoping she would say something to bail him out. To his surprise and chagrin, Celia didn't utter a word. Knowing anything he said theological would likely draw more questions from George, Justin finally broke down.

"Sir, I gotta be honest with you. I haven't been to church in years, and I don't have a lot of faith. To tell you the truth, I'm not even sure God is real."

Celia's head popped up as if it were on a spring. *Not sure God is real.* He could have said anything but *that.* She glanced over at her father, whose face had become blank. She quickly tried to deflect. "Daddy, how's the progress going with opening the restaurant?"

George turned to his daughter with the same blank expression. "Going fine, honey. There's a place closing over on 8 Mile next week, so that looks like a good possibility." George rose from the table and, without another word, headed into the kitchen, leaving Celia and Justin staring at each other wondering what had just happened.

A half hour later, while Justin relaxed in the living room, George and Marjorie summoned Celia upstairs to their bedroom. Once she arrived, George shut the door behind her. "Pookie, what are you thinking?"

"Dad…"

Marjorie chimed in. "This man doesn't even believe in God. What are you thinking getting yourself hooked up with this man?"

"Mom, he's a good man. He doesn't believe in God now, but I'm sure he'll change." Celia walked past her parents and sat on the edge of the bed. "Things are complicated for him right now. He's been through some stuff, and he's just doubting right now."

"I'm not sure I want my daughter dating a man who doesn't believe." George quieted his voice so it didn't travel. "And a liar to boot. We taught you better than that."

"Yeah, I know, Dad. Being unequally yoked."

"Exactly. So why would you go against what God wants for your life?"

Celia looked down, trying to fashion words to answer her father. She noticed the Bible sitting on the nightstand and glanced away from it. "Dad, Mom, you know I love you, right?"

Marjorie wasn't having it. "Uh huh. But?"

"Maybe your beliefs aren't all there is of God."

George furrowed his eyebrows. "What's that supposed to mean?"

"Daddy, you used to take me all over the country to broaden my horizons, so I wouldn't think that the ghetto was all there was to life. Maybe the way we believe isn't all that God has for us. Maybe we can find God in people who don't necessarily believe the way we do."

George had learned over many years not to lash out at his daughter when she said things he thought were ridiculous. Instead, he sat next to her and kept his voice calm. "Pookie, is this what Justin is telling you?"

"No, Dad. I find Justin to be the most caring, considerate, compassionate person I have ever known apart from you and Mom. I mean he's more loving than many so-called Christians. He's such a great guy. How can loving him be wrong?"

Marjorie knelt before Celia. "Honey, the scriptures declare that even the devil disguises himself as an angel of light. Honey, the man is deceptive. He outright lied to us."

"He did that to impress you guys, Mom."

"That doesn't make it right," Marjorie retorted.

"Okay, maybe he didn't give you the greatest first impression. But if you get to know him..."

"I would say the same to you, honey." George reached for his daughter's hand and held it lovingly. "I know you like this guy, but it's only been three months. Don't make any major moves with Justin for at least a year. Take that time to get to know him. *Really* know him. Then come back to me after a year and tell me if you feel the same way."

Celia looked in her father's eyes for the first time since she had entered the room. "What if I still feel the same after a year? Will you give him your blessing then?"

"We'll cross that bridge when we come to it." George gently

patted Celia hand and stood. "But honey, I walk in the spirit. And in the spirit, I'm just not feeling this dude. And I'm praying that within a year, the Lord will help you see what I see. In fact, I don't think it will take that long."

"Maybe he'll surprise you, Dad."

"Maybe. Just maybe."

***

With Wynn's vehicle parked along the side of a remote road in Rock Creek Park, the tall man, still seated in the passenger's seat, flipped through a notepad he had retrieved from Wynn Delano's blazer pocket. Ignoring the flecks of red moisture on his hands and on the notepad, he tore out the pages, one by one, crumpled them and stuffed them in his pants pocket. But there was one page he left intact.

The tall man reached for his cell phone and dialed. After four rings, the man answered, "Officer Kirsch."

"I need another favor."

"Name it."

"I need someone located. She may have seen what Wynn saw. I need to tie up any loose ends."

"Less I know the better. Give me the info."

The tall man squinted to read Wynn Delano's undefined penmanship. "Celia Rayburn, Silver Spring, Maryland, telephone number 301-999-5674."

"Give me an hour."

The tall man ended the call, then slid into the driver's seat and guided the vehicle back onto the road toward upper Northwest. He needed to get rid of the body of Wynn Delano, who lay stuffed in the cargo hold of the SUV after meeting a deadly fate from a bullet in the center of his forehead.

***

George and Marjorie Wise
Forest Hill, Toronto
8:24 p.m.

With his stomach pleasingly overstuffed from another of his wife's fabulous dinners, George Wise headed toward his study just down the corridor from the living room. On the way, he opened a door, walked into the garage, and checked the garage side door to make sure it was locked. He then headed to his study.

He checked his postal mail at once upon arriving. Amid the voluminous pieces of junk mail and bills was a statement from Royal Bank addressed to his daughter in care of him. He sat at his desk and gently opened the envelope. He pursed his lips and gently shook his head as he read the numbers on the statement. He ran his hand over his closely cropped gray speckled hair as if trying to assuage a nonexistent headache.

Seconds later, his wife, Marjorie, walked in. She flipped on a light switch. "Honey, what have I told you about reading in the dark?"

George did not respond to her comment, although he was proud he could still read so clearly in the dark at fifty years of age. Instead, he said, "Honey, come over here and look at this."

George watched his wife as she walked over. Marjorie stood just over George's shoulder and peered at the statement. "Only $218.00?"

"That's right."

"She had almost ten grand last year."

"Should I be worried?"

"Maybe she has another account?"

"When she calls tonight, I'll ask her. And if I find out Justin is bleeding her dry..."

"Now, George, please don't go prodding into her affairs.

You know how proud and independent Celia is."

"Marge, I can't just sit back and do nothing."

"That's *exactly* what you'll do." Marjorie's eyes widened, her voice sharp. "If Celia needs our help, she'll tell us. The last thing I need is for your trigger-happy self to go down to Maryland and catch a case."

The desk telephone rang, the one attached to the number for family only. George knew it was Celia, calling them faithfully as usual once per week. He answered quickly. "Hey, Pookie." He put the call on speakerphone so Marjorie could hear.

"Hey, Daddy."

George noticed her voice was devoid of the usual spirit. "What's wrong?"

"Nothing," Celia lied. "How's everyone?"

"Everyone's great. Your mother's here, too."

"Hey, Mommy."

"Hey, sweetie."

"You wouldn't believe what I saw today."

George and Marjorie answered together. "What?"

"I was in downtown D.C. today, and this pastor who was leading a rally got shot."

Marjorie drew in a sharp breath and covered her mouth "Oh, my God. Are you okay?"

"Yeah, Mommy, I'm fine."

"Is he dead?"

"No. The news said he was alive."

"Thank Jesus for that," George chimed in. "And you saw all this happen?"

"Yeah. I was right across the street. It wasn't like in the movies, where somebody gets shot, and blood and guts fly all over the place. He was just giving his speech, and then he just fell like somebody gave him an uppercut."

"What were you doing in downtown D.C.?"

"Meeting a friend for breakfast," was the quickest lie Celia could come up with. She hoped it worked.

It didn't. George knew something was going on. He shot his wife a disappointed frown for forbidding him from prying any further. "Pookie, are you sure you're okay? It must have been scary to see someone shot like that."

"Yeah, it was scary. But I'm okay. It reminds me of that time you took me up near Runners Mill, and we went hunting, and you shot that deer."

"And you cried for two days and would not eat any of the meat."

"The funny thing was, I didn't cry for that pastor. I don't know why. Why would I cry for an animal, and not a human being?"

While George searched his mind for an answer that would never come, Marjorie broke in with, "Sweetheart, maybe if you knew this pastor, you'd feel differently."

"But why should that make a difference? The man gets shot, and I feel nothing."

"Maybe you're distracted by something." George hoped his subtle hint would draw something out of her about what was going on in her life. If this girl was okay, then he was a Chinese bamboo salesman.

Celia quickly skipped the subject. "How's business?"

"Business is great. We got a write-up in one of the local papers. We were one of the 10 best charbroiled chicken restaurants for Millennials. How's that for a ringing endorsement?"

"Wow, that's great, Dad," Celia said with barely detectable sarcasm. She could not understand how her father became a self-made millionaire off of his special organic recipe for charbroiled chicken. She cared little for the chicken herself, but with an average 1.2 million in sales at each of his restaurants around Ontario and in Detroit, there were a lot of customers who begged to differ. *Must be all those Millennials.*

Not that she was complaining. Once her father struck it rich, he moved the family 250 miles away from Alpheus Street to the tony Forest Hill village of Toronto. That allowed Celia to spend a few months in the splendor of wealth before she eventually hit rock bottom with Justin.

"Thanks, hon," George replied. "Speaking of Runners Mill, we might be opening up another location there soon."

"Dad, isn't that a little far? It's like a two-hour plane ride."

"I know, but it's a great opportunity. Rent is dirt cheap, and a good location right across from a Mickey D's. But enough about me and my business. Are you sure you're okay?"

"I'm fine, Daddy. Really."

"You know I'm here if you need anything."

"I know."

"Okay, Pookie. Well, we have to hang up now. Me and your mother are going to turn in early. She's joined a morning prayer group, and they pray at 4 in the morning." George rolled his eyes at his wife.

Marjorie clicked her teeth at him and said to Celia, "No distractions, no TV, no cell phone. Good time to pray, sweetie."

"Good time to sleep, too." George smiled.

Celia laughed.

Marjorie gave George a playful punch on the shoulder. "Okay, sweetie. Talk to you later."

"Bye, Mom. Bye, Dad."

Immediately after hanging up the phone, George's smile morphed into a frown. He turned to Marjorie. "Something's going on with her."

"Well, you can't blame her for inheriting your pride," Marjorie commented. "She probably won't tell us unless she absolutely has to. Until then, we are not going to butt in. We have to trust her. It's her life." She gave George a peck on the cheek and then left the room.

Muttering quietly to himself, George said, "Yeah, well if I find out that Justin is not taking care of my baby, it'll be *his* behind."

Chapter Three

On the Run

Celia Rayburn

After talking to her parents, Celia enjoyed a bath in the apartment's Jacuzzi tub, then settled in the bedroom to moisturize with Mānuka honey and shea butter and catch the ten o'clock news. Justin had not yet returned home, and she was thinking this would be another one of his overnighters. It was fine with her, as she had another interview the next morning, and she didn't need any drama with Justin to affect her focus on getting a job.

Unfortunately, the ten-o'clock news had no added information on the Plaza shooting, so she watched another half-hour, then went to bed. She felt strange yet relieved that she didn't have the typical concerns about where her husband was at this time of night, but it didn't matter. Including the $218 she had in her checking account, she had squirreled away some money now and then from Justin's unemployment checks. She hoped to have enough money to hire a divorce attorney. She was determined to do this on her own and not ask for money from her parents.

Celia turned off the TV, checked a few emails on the laptop next to her bed, and slid down under luxurious sheets. Before she closed her eyes, she remembered past times with Justin. After a year of dating, Justin and Celia got married in a ceremony that her parents reluctantly paid for, only because it was traditional for them to do so and they didn't want their daughter estranged from them. But before she moved to Maryland with her husband, her father gave her a piece of advice which she never forgot:

Make sure you have your own. Don't mix anything of yours with his. Trust me, in this day and age, that's the best way to go. Keep your own bank account. Get the apartment or house in your name. Never let him have that much control over you. I would say that no matter whom you married. Let him prove himself before you start bringing everything together.

That was the one piece of advice she kept. To her knowledge, Justin had no clue about the checking account because the statements went to her parents' house in Toronto. The apartment they shared was in Celia's name, which was not an issue for Justin, since he was so smitten, he would do anything she asked.

My, how times had changed.

Celia went to sleep remembering those times and trying to put out of her mind the monster that her parents had warned her about and that Justin had suddenly become.

***

A crash coming from the living room jerked her awake. At first, Celia thought it was Justin in one of his drunken tirades. But when the walls thumped and shook, and she heard another crash along with grunts and screams, terror struck Celia's heart.

She jumped out of bed and ran toward her bedroom door, forgetting she had nothing on but panties and a T-shirt. As she cracked open the bedroom door, she heard another huge thump, then a crashing of dishes and glass. Another groan and a scream rang out, this time from a voice not her husband's.

Knowing there was a fight going on, Celia backed up and grabbed a baseball bat from the corner of her walk-in closet. She hated her husband, but she would not let him get beat up, either. She walked out of the bedroom and turned the corner, the bat poised, ready to strike whoever her husband was fighting.

A tall man, dressed in a white T-shirt, blue jeans, and a ski mask, stood near the living room window, his back to her and about seven yards away. He knelt over Justin with his right boot on his head. He reached behind his back and pulled a pistol from under his shirt. Celia's heart went cold, and she froze, hoping that she was only having a nightmare.

The tall man aimed. Celia saw a flash and heard a small crack, like a faraway firecracker, not loud enough to register much beyond her apartment. Justin's bare feet, slashed and bloodied from the glass on the floor, jerked, and then lay limp.

Celia suppressed the urge to scream as adrenaline kicked in. She knew she could not traverse the distance between the bedroom door and the attacker, across broken glass before he turned the gun on her. Instead, still holding the bat, she made a mad dash for the open front door, just three yards ahead of her, and did not look back. As she ran into the hallway, she heard the crunching of glass behind her, a sign that the gunman was coming after her. She screamed as loud as she could to draw attention and picked up speed running down the hallway. Just as she reached a corner, she heard a loud clang against a fire extinguisher just inches from her and felt the pressurized chemical spray out against her side. She turned the corner just before another bullet thudded into the wall just over her head.

Celia shoved open the fire exit door and ran down a flight of stairs to the ninth floor. She continued to run down the hallway, finding herself quickly running out of breath, as she hadn't run like this in years. She took another corner, found another fire exit, and then ran back upstairs to the tenth floor. Directly across from the fire exit was the trash chute room. She opened the door and squeezed herself into the narrow room, shut the door, turned off the light, and then plastered herself against the wall so the door could be opened part way with no one seeing her.

Her heart was beating so fiercely she could literally feel the blood pumping through her head. The brilliance and the stupidity of hiding in this trash room quickly became clear to her. The gunman, if he were still pursuing her, would likely not think she had returned to the tenth floor. But if he found her, she had no escape. She gripped the bat, closed her eyes, tried to pray the fear out of her trembling body, and hoped that the gunman had given up trying to find her.

***

2:30 a.m., Thursday

She hadn't fallen asleep, but she hadn't realized that she had been in the trash room for almost two hours. Celia was too petrified to take one step out of that room. Twice, she felt spiders crawling on her naked feet, but she didn't care. What if the gunman was still standing around somewhere, waiting for her to show her face? Whenever she heard footsteps in the hallway, she squeezed her eyes shut and hoped that it was just someone coming home from a late shift.

What had her husband gotten into that someone wanted to kill him? Thanks to her father, who had owned plenty of guns during his time in Detroit, she knew enough about guns to know the attacker's was not a typical street model. It was a pricey one, with a suppressor. Professional quality.

But then Celia had a frightening thought. What if the gunman was after *her*? She had just seen an attempted murder earlier in the day. But how would the assailant have known anything about her, especially to have found her address so fast?

Celia hoped that the police had arrived by now. The fight in the apartment was loud and likely would have alerted the neighbors enough to call the authorities. But her apartment was down the hall and around the corner from where she was now, so even if they were there, she wouldn't have heard them. For a murder to have just taken place on her floor, things were eerily quiet.

She still had the bat with her, although it had dubious value against a professional quality handgun. But she couldn't stay in that trash room forever. Fortunately, no one had to dump any trash in the wee hours of the morning, or they would have felt the business end of a baseball bat from a frightened, half-naked woman.

Pulling her resolve together, she finally peeked into the hallway to see if everything was clear. She had no idea what time it was, or how long she had been in the trash room, but she deduced that a man who had just murdered someone would not be still hanging around on the tenth floor all this time. That logic emboldened her, and she stood, shook the numbness out of her legs, and gently, gradually, opened the door. She poked her head out and looked down both ends of the hallway. No one in sight.

She grabbed the bat and then gently walked out into the hallway, heading toward the corner. Once she turned the corner, her apartment would be ten doors down. She leaned against the wall and poked her head around the corner. She breathed a sigh of relief. Several police officers stood around behind a strip of crime scene tape. She left the bat behind and walked down the hallway toward her apartment. She was only ten feet away when the officers noticed her.

The officers noted that she was barely dressed. One of them said, "Ma'am, are you okay?"

"No." Celia's sobs choked the words, and she was barely comprehensible. "I live here. That's my husband in there."

One officer wrapped his jacket around Celia, while the other went inside to gather clothes, shoes, and her purse. The officers would not allow her inside, not only because of the gruesomeness of the scene, but because the medical examiner on site would take no chances she would inadvertently contaminate the crime scene. She changed into jeans and a pair of flats in the hallway. Because Celia was the shy and silent type, she knew none of her neighbors, but that didn't keep them from standing in the hallway next to their doors, gawking at her with feigned concern.

A young, handsome, black detective approached her from somewhere behind her front door. "I'm Detective Williams. And you are?"

Celia wrapped her arms around herself. "I'm Celia Rayburn. I live here. I was here when all this happened."

"Why d'you leave?" Williams reached into his inner jacket pocket for a pad and pen.

Williams did not get an answer. When he looked up, he saw that Celia was staring at the lifeless body of her husband, still crumpled on the floor near the living room window. Williams motioned to a uniformed officer standing outside in the hallway. With a few head and hand gestures from Williams, the officer had received his instructions.

"Mrs. Rayburn, if you don't mind, I'll have this officer take you to our station house. We need to get a little more information from you about what happened."

Celia nodded slightly and forced her eyes shut, squeezing out tears.

The officer drove Celia five miles away to the County District police station. During the ride, she checked her smartphone and saw it was almost three in the morning. Upon arrival at the station, the officer led her to the reception area, where she waited for 30 minutes. Another officer, this one wearing a navy sport coat, slacks that didn't quite match the coat, and a button-down white shirt with no tie, came out to greet her. She had seen him milling around with the other cops at her apartment.

"Hi, I'm Detective Liskey." His white face was thick and square, his smile muted, his thinning hair gray, except at the roots and at the temples, where it settled into a grayish-brown. An impeccably groomed full mustache curled beyond the edges of his lips, and blue eyes greeted her. He wanted to be friendly, but he knew the woman in front of him was probably a wreck.

Celia shook his hand, which was large and rough, but she said nothing, her mind caught in a torrent of thoughts and emotions. She went with the detective through a door, on the elevator to another floor, through another secured door, and into a room filled with brand-new cubicles. Other than the detective, there were only two employees present. They walked into a small conference room. Detective Liskey directed her to a chair at the conference table. He sat diagonally across from her at the end of the table.

"Mrs. Rayburn, I'm going to be working your husband's case. First of all, I'm so sorry for your loss."

Celia nodded sullenly but said nothing. Now that the threat of being killed was not imminent, it had just registered that Justin was dead, and a deep woe came over her.

"Are you able to answer some questions for me? I know it's early in the morning, and you're probably very tired, but the quicker we get the information we need, the better chance we have of catching your husband's killer."

Celia nodded her consent. She doubted she could get any sleep, anyway.

"Great." The detective reached for a pad and pen on a satellite table and set them in front of him. "Why don't you tell me what happened?"

The question triggered her memories, awful and graphic.

She could only see the tall gunman reach for his pistol and fire into Justin's head. The memory sickened her, and she felt nausea enveloping her. Even though she grew up on the rough streets of western Detroit, she had never seen anyone shot. Yet in the past 24 hours, she had seen two people gunned down. It was too much for her to take, and she stood to her feet.

"Where is your bathroom?" Celia's face grew pale.

The detective frowned. "Out the door, to your right."

Celia gathered her purse and hurried out the door. She found the ladies bathroom quickly. She pushed open the door, headed to a stall, slammed the stall door behind her, dropped to her knees, and vomited. After she had finished, she fell back against the stall door and burst into tears. Her own tears surprised her since there were many moments, after Justin had left her black and blue, that she wished he was dead.

A female officer came into the bathroom and knocked on the stall. "Miss, are you okay?"

"Yes." Celia's voice cracked. "Just give me a minute, please."

"Of course."

Once Celia heard the bathroom door open and close again, she reached into her purse, found tissues, wiped her face, tossed the tissues in the toilet, and retrieved her cell phone. She debated on whether she should call her parents at this hour. Her parents had been worried about her ever since she moved to Silver Spring. A call to them to tell them that Justin had been murdered was just the ticket they needed to board a plane and drag her, kicking and screaming, to Toronto. And that was not an option for Celia. She prided herself on being the most independent sibling of the family. She insisted on making it on her own, even as some of her other siblings clung tightly onto Daddy's wallet. Not her. *Mama may have, Papa may have….*

She put the phone away, sat on the bathroom floor for a few more minutes to gather herself, then she left the bathroom and returned to the conference room, where Detective Liskey and the female officer who had checked on her in the bathroom were waiting.

"I'm sorry." Celia returned to her seat. "I needed a moment."

Liskey nodded. "I understand." He scribbled a quick note, in handwriting even he had trouble understanding. *Check to see if Justin had any active life insurance policies.*

"So, what happened was this." Celia recounted her entire day, from the job interview to the moment where she returned to her apartment after Justin was shot. Liskey listened carefully, asking a few questions here and there, clarifying other points. His notes were sparse, and Celia wondered how he would remember it all. Then a quick glance at the camera on a far wall answered her question.

When Celia had finished, Liskey reared back in his chair. "Describe this guy to me."

"Tall, about six-five. White dude. Wouldn't say he was skinny, but not exactly muscular. I never saw his face. He had a black ski mask on."

"What was he wearing?"

"Jeans and a T-shirt."

"Shoes?"

"Black boots, I believe."

"Any other distinguishing characteristics? Tattoos, jewelry, anything?"

"Not that I noticed."

"And you're sure you don't know of anyone who would want to kill your husband?"

Celia shook her head. "No, I don't."

"Drug debt, maybe?"

Celia hesitated.

Liskey explained. "We found marijuana on your husband's person and in the nightstand next to your bed."

"That was my husband's. I don't do drugs, and I have no idea where he got his drugs from."

Liskey jotted another note. *May be a drug hit. Check.*

"Anyone else have a key to your apartment?"

Celia thought. "No, not that I know of. Well, there's my Dad, but he lives in Toronto."

"Have you spoken to your parents since this happened?"

"No, I haven't."

"Hmm." Liskey asked her about twenty more questions before he flipped his note pad shut. "Do you have some-place to stay?"

Celia could think of at least two girlfriends who would take her in, but she wanted to be alone. "I can just go to a hotel."

Liskey stood. "Why don't you do that? Get some rest, and I'll give you a call when the medical examiner clears your apartment."

Celia's face turned sour. "Wait, you don't expect me to go back to my apartment, do you? I can't go back there. What if that guy comes back? Don't you guys have witness protec-tion or something like that?"

Liskey took a seat and gave Celia a serious glare. "Well, I can put you in touch with the States Attorney for assistance. But I wouldn't count on relocation."

"Why not?"

"There's no continuing threat. I know the guy shot at you, but there's no sign he plans to *continue* coming after you. He wore a mask, and you can't identify him, so it's unlikely he's gonna pay you another visit. Unless you know something we don't."

Celia's sighed. "That guy shot at me. He wanted to kill me. I'm not going back to that apartment."

"Well, then you'll want to get to a hotel," Liskey stood again. "I'll touch base with patrol and have an officer stationed outside your hotel until your apartment is clear. Then, the officer can go with you to your apartment and get whatever belongings you need. And, if you don't have any friends or relatives in town you can stay with, it might be a good idea to visit your dad in Canada for a while. I assume if we catch the guy, we can depend on your testimony at trial?"

For Celia, the thought of testifying struck the wrong chord. She was from western Detroit, and in that part of Detroit, you didn't testify against about anything or about anybody if you wanted to stay alive. But she was not in Detroit. She was in metro D.C., and something had killed her husband. What type of woman would not do everything possible to bring her husband's killer to justice, especially since he had also tried to kill her, and would likely try again? She could never sleep again at night with this guy running the streets.

"Yeah, I'll testify."

"Great. I'm going to send Officer Fairchild back in, and she'll have some paperwork for you to fill out, and then she'll see about getting you a hotel room." Liskey handed her his card. "If you need anything, don't hesitate to call anytime."

"Thank you." Celia took the card and watched as Liskey left the room. Cops in Montgomery County seemed more cordial and relaxed than those in Detroit, she noticed. But then again, Montgomery County didn't have to deal with over 300 murders per year.

She again looked at her cell phone, debated calling her father, then again decided not to. She would see what options were available to her first. But with only $218 to her name, things didn't look good.

***

Detective Liskey got Celia a two-day voucher for a hotel in nearby Bethesda, which meant she didn't have to give her name or use her credit cards. And with a patrol officer situated right outside the hotel, Celia felt safe enough to at least try to get some sleep.

But sleep came sparingly. Every door closing, every bump in the hallway, every kid who dropped something on the floor above, forced her eyes open. By the time she finally decided to just stay awake, it was ten a.m., and she had awakened about five times during the night, and she knew she would be awakened again when room service came by.

Just after she got up, she peered out her room window and saw that the police cruiser that had driven her to the hotel was still there, parked on the street, near the front door, within shouting distance of her window.

Celia showered again after still smelling the lingering stink of the trash room on her. She stuffed her old clothes in an overnight bag she had brought with her and changed into a fresh pair of jeans, white sneakers, and a T-shirt. She checked herself in a mirror and ran a brush through her hair. Fortunately, her round face showed no signs she had barely slept.

All dressed up, with nowhere to go, she thought. She didn't feel comfortable leaving the hotel, at least not yet. Her scheduled 9 a.m. job interview was an afterthought, and her car was still at the apartment. At least if she had the car, she could drive somewhere—anywhere—to put things in perspective, clear her head, and figure out her next step.

Turning on the TV didn't help. She would stare at the screen but barely pay attention to what was going on. Her mind kept replaying the events of the earlier day. Even when she was in Detroit, she had never experienced as much violence in one day. And to see her husband brutally murdered in front of her was something she knew would haunt her for many days and weeks to come.

Her sympathy for him was almost palpable. She wished she could have stopped it. He was horrible to her, but he didn't deserve to die in that way. He may have fallen off the rails, but he didn't seem to be into anything that would get him targeted by a professional killer.

Celia tried to counteract the negative memories with pleasant ones. She remembered when Justin came home early from work one Thursday and surprised her with a weeklong cruise to the British Virgin Islands. He had just received a promotion to supervisor of an eight-man team of engineers, and he wanted to celebrate. They had been married for a little more than a year, and the trip was like a second honeymoon. She had never been more in love with her husband than during that trip and had never been more convinced that her parents were wrong about him.

For the first two years of the marriage, Justin was a doting husband who never went a day without kissing her or telling her he loved her or squeezing her tight in his arms, which she loved. He would often send her texts with sweet, off-the-wall comments expressing his affection for her. They often spent their evenings doing the things she loved — shooting pool at the Dave & Busters in the nearby Ellsworth Place mall, watching old sitcoms on TV, or going for cheeseburgers and fries at the Five Guys. Celia was a simple soul who didn't go for a lot of fancy things, but she was still excited when Justin splurged on her occasionally, such as when he bought her a pair of $900 black Louis Vuitton open-toe pumps on her birthday.

Justin even wanted to have a child with her, but Celia urged him to wait until they had bought a house, which they planned to do soon. But the house-buying plans went down the drain when Justin came home one day and announced that he had lost his job.

That was news difficult for Celia to hear, but she did not despair. If Justin was talented enough to get an $81,000 job, he could get another one. She constantly tried to encourage him. But it did not stop Justin from going into a deep depression, which he dealt with by smoking pot and downing occasional shots of vodka. It didn't take long for Justin to develop an addiction, which kept him from getting almost every job he applied for.

Justin eventually found a job at a mom-and-pop auto mechanic shop in Hyattsville, but his addiction to pot continued, and his drinking worsened.

The first time he smacked her was on their third wedding anniversary. Justin had promised to take Celia out after work to dinner and then to a performance of *Annie* at the Warner Theatre in downtown D.C. However, Justin never made it home in time, choosing to hang out with co-workers at a bar, and getting so tipsy he forgot the time and didn't arrive back home until 11 p.m.

When Justin got home, Celia was so angry she snapped at him, and their resulting argument was vicious and loud. When he had run out of words to challenge her, Justin slapped her so hard she spun and hit the floor.

Justin immediately apologized, and Celia, after some sweet talk from Justin, forgave him. After all, maybe it was her outburst that caused him to strike her like he did.

And that was her mentality throughout the next two years. Whenever Justin hit her, it was because she had provoked him to uncontrollable anger. Justin's abuse was not his fault; it was hers. When Justin lost his auto mechanic job because the boss could no longer tolerate him coming to work high or hung over, she told herself that he was just a little frustrated and would be okay once he worked through all his problems. And she had convinced herself of this until he started to stay out all night. And that was when she realized that her relationship with Justin was quickly expiring.

It is amazing that in this day, a woman can tolerate a relationship with a man that beats her, but not one that cheats on her, she heard someone say on a talk show one day. The description fit her snugly. She was *that* woman. And even to this day, she struggled to understand why.

Celia reached for her purse and took out her phone. Eventually, she would have to tell her parents about this, and since she literally had nothing to do except stare at the TV all day, now was as good a time as any.

***

The tall man pulled the black SUV to a curbside parking space directly across the street from the hotel. The police car was parked three spaces ahead of him, its engine running. He could see a uniformed officer inside. It made sense. This was definitely the right place.

He rolled up his tinted windows, switched on the air conditioning, and pulled his binoculars and fully loaded Sig Sauer pistol within immediate reach. His eyes, covered with a pair of large sunglasses, alternated between watching the front door of the hotel, watching the cop car, and examining the laptop computer sitting on the seat next to him. On his laptop was a cell phone GPS tracking app, which had tied onto Celia's cell phone signal and had led him directly to this location.

Now all he needed to do was wait for her to emerge. The moment she did, it would be over in five seconds.

CHAPTER FOUR

You can run, but you can't hide

Celia tried to call her father's cell phone first, but he did not answer. No surprise. George Wise was always so busy during the day trying to keep his ten charbroiled chicken restaurants prosperous and relevant. Marjorie Wise was almost as busy teaching high school history, but fortunately, Celia had called her while she was on break in the teacher's lounge.

"Sweetie, is everything okay?" Marjorie asked, not accustomed to getting calls from her daughter outside of their regular 8:30 p.m. time.

"No, Momma." Celia's words trembled as the tears fell again.

"What's the matter?"

It took several seconds before Celia poured the words from her mouth. "Justin. Somebody killed him."

"What? Oh my God, Celia." Marjorie could hear the grief in Celia's voice. "What happened?"

"Somebody broke in the apartment last night and shot him. Then he tried to shoot me, but I ran out."

"Oh, my sweet Jesus. Where are you now?"

"I'm in a hotel. The police are guarding me."

"How long will you be there?"

"Maybe a couple of days. I have to go back to my apartment and get my stuff and the car. But I'm done with the apartment."

"Where will you go?"

"I don't know, Momma."

Marjorie's voice sharpened. "What do you mean you don't know? You can always come here. You know that."

"Yes, I know that, Momma. But I have to try to figure things out for myself."

"Baby, you know when your father hears about this, he's not going to accept that."

"I know, Momma. I need you to hold his leash."

"I will do no such thing. Not this time. You just told me your husband got killed, and they tried to kill you. Now, we moved out of Detroit to try to get away from that nonsense, and now you're in D.C. in the middle of it. If your father can figure out how to get you back up here, he's got my blessing."

Silence. It was Celia's default response whenever her mother dropped knowledge she couldn't dispute.

"Do they know who did it? Or why?" Marjorie asked.

"No." Celia left out the details of the professional nature of the hit. She didn't want them to worry. Celia had enough worry to go around.

"Justin's parents?"

"I haven't called them yet. That was gonna be my next phone call. But I'm sure the cops already told them."

"Sweetie, if you won't move back home, at least let us send you some money so you can find someplace safe."

Celia agreed. After all, $218 wouldn't last her two minutes in this town. "Okay."

"We'll send it to your account."

"Thanks, Momma."

"So, honey, let's pray together. Times like these you definitely need protection from the Lord."

"Okay," Celia responded through a cloud of doubt. *Why would God protect me and not protect my husband? Why would God allow a preacher to get shot?* The more she thought about it, the more she wondered about the value of faith. If a preacher, a man of God, gets shot, then why would she think God would protect her? Nonetheless, she switched the phone to her other ear and listened as her mother prayed.

"Father God…."

***

Detective Frank Liskey returned to Celia's apartment building and spent most of the early part of the morning interviewing Celia's neighbors and getting the security footage from all the building's seven cameras. He returned to Headquarters just in time to meet his partner, Detective Ramon Williams, who had just returned from a visit to the chief medical examiner's office in Baltimore. Ramon's dark, crisply tailored suit hung well on his five-foot nine-inch frame. Clean-shaven, with a broad nose, thin lips, and brown eyes augmented by wide glasses, Ramon was one of the few African Americans in the department to make it to detective status. He could think of only six others in the entire department, and only one other in Major Crimes where he was stationed.

"The ME knocked it out of the park this time, buddy." Ramon settled into his cubicle, directly across from Liskey's. Both men had adorned their cubicles with various tchotchkes along with greeting cards, cartoons, and random Post-it notes with memory-aid scribblings. Ramon handed Liskey a Kraft folder full of papers, then ran his hand across his head.

"What's this?" Liskey asked as he opened the folder.

"Oh, just the name of our hostile."

Liskey looked at Ramon for a moment to figure out if he was serious, then looked at the papers in the folder. "Isaac Roth."

"Yep," Ramon smiled. "No fixed address, though. The

guy was an illegal from Germany who was kicked out of the United States about five years ago."

Liskey read the file. "Weapons possession. So, he's back in the country?"

"Looks that way."

"How'd they find this out so quick? No way those forensic tests are back already."

"Me and one of the guys at the ME were talking. He used to work for the bureau a few years back. He remembered a federal case a few years ago that involved some tall white guy with a Sig. He said he remembered that because the guy was so meticulous, he didn't leave any evidence behind, not even a hair. Not a lot of six-five white guys walking around the country dropping people, so he kinda sticks out like a sore thumb."

"Let's see if we can get a picture of this creep."

Ramon turned to his computer, and within five minutes had pulled up a photo of Isaac Roth from ICE databases. He printed out two copies and then gathered near Liskey's computer to look through the apartment surveillance camera footage. They search for almost an hour before they saw something of interest.

"There's our guy," Ramon pointed out, noticing on the lobby feed a tall man, wearing a skull cap, walking across the lobby toward the elevators. Liskey noted the time: 12:05 a.m.

"Guy walking around with a black skull cap at midnight when it's 75 degrees outside," Liskey shook his head. "That should have been a dead giveaway."

"How'd he get in? Isn't that a secured building?"

"Looks like he slipped in when someone else went out," Liskey noted. "And there's no security guard in the lobby."

They continued to search the feeds until they found something else.

"That's him leaving out a back door at 12:32 a.m." Ramon

took careful notes. "What's that in his hand?"

Liskey paused the feed and craned his head toward the computer screen. "Looks like a laptop."

"That it does."

"He didn't come in with it."

"No, he didn't."

"Celia made no mention of a missing laptop."

"She wouldn't have known. They kept her out of the apartment."

"Question is, did he get that laptop from the scene, or did he get it from somewhere else? There's no camera coverage on the tenth floor to check." Without waiting for an answer, Liskey pulled his cell phone from his pocket and dialed Celia's number.

Celia answered on the second ring. "Hello?"

"Mrs. Rayburn, this is Detective Liskey. How are you?"

"Not bad for a hunted woman."

"You'll be okay. Do you own a laptop?"

"Yeah."

"Do you have it with you?"

"No, it's still in my apartment."

"Where in your apartment?"

"On the nightstand next to my bed."

"On the nightstand next to your bed?" Liskey repeated her statement primarily so Ramon could hear, then looked up at him.

Receiving his cue, Ramon quickly grabbed a set of keys from his desk and left.

"Yes? Is something wrong?"

"Do you know of any reason why someone, other than you and your husband, would be interested in your laptop?"

"No. I just use it for Facebook and emails."

"Okay, can you check those from your cell phone?"

"Yes."

"Okay, check to see if there is any unusual activity on any of those accounts. If there is, give me a call back. You still have my card?"

"Yes, sir."

Liskey hung up and looked more closely at one photograph of Isaac Roth. The mug shot staring back at him was of a white man, long of head and square-jawed, bald, and clean-shaven except for a modest mustache, bluish-green pupils, and a broad nose with a ridge traversing his nose about halfway down to his nostrils. He compared the photo to the camera footage of Roth walking in and out of the building and could see a resemblance, although the camera footage was fuzzy, and Roth had turned his head to avoid any direct shots of his face. And he had a witness statement that the perpetrator was wearing blue jeans, a white T-shirt, and a ski mask, which would fit what he saw in the camera footage. Whether he had enough to file charges was iffy. That would be the call of the assistant state's attorney.

Liskey got on his computer to issue a BOLO for Isaac Roth. In his notes, he noted Roth as a person of interest and asked that the BOLO be kept off the air and off social media. Cops only. No media. He didn't want Roth to get wind they knew about him. That would likely force him into hiding, back under whatever rock he crawled out from under.

Then, he picked up his desk phone and dialed. After a few seconds, he said, "ASA McPherson, please."

***

The tall man knew he would risk detection if he stayed parked outside the hotel much longer. He looked at the laptop and refreshed the screen. The laptop's Wi-Fi connection had dropped, so he didn't know if Celia's phone was still in the hotel or not.

He grabbed hold of a duffel bag from the back seat.

Straining, he pulled it to the front seat and stuffed both the laptop and the pistol inside. He then switched off the engine and looked around. There was another hotel a few yards up the road. The right room would give him a perfect vantage point.

He started the SUV and drove past the police car to the end of the block, turned left, and found another street parking space near the rear entrance of the second hotel. Grabbing the duffel bag, he got out of the truck and walked around to the front of the hotel, strolled through the lobby without saying a word to the front desk clerk, and pressed the button to summon the elevator.

The front desk clerk looked up at him and, finding nothing particular to interest her, went back to surfing through Instagram on her cell phone. After all, he looked like a normal guest, not someone who was about to use the hotel to murder someone.

***

Five minutes after he arrived at Celia's apartment, Ramon called Liskey on his cell phone. He only needed to say a few words. "No laptop. And crime scene never saw it."

"Thanks, man," Liskey said. "Come on back. ASA McPherson is on the way."

Immediately after talking to Ramon, he dialed Celia.

"Mrs. Rayburn, Detective Liskey again. It looks like your laptop was stolen."

"By who?"

"By the person that killed your husband."

"Well, it looks like he got into my cloud account."

"What's in your cloud account?"

"Nothing. I don't put any pictures or anything up there. My husband used it sometimes to track—"

The realization choked off Celia's words. Liskey realized

the same thing.

Detective Liskey stood and held the phone to his ear while heading over to the walkie-talkie charging station. "Celia, I want you to listen to me very carefully. As soon as I give you these instructions, turn off your phone and do not turn it back on for any reason. I want you to lock both locks to your room. Then, pack everything you have and wait for Officer Fairchild to come and escort you downstairs. Do not open the door for anyone except Officer Fairchild. She'll knock on the door three times, pause, and then knock once. Are we clear?"

"Yes, sir." Celia started frantically packing even as she spoke.

"We're going to bring you to Headquarters and then arrange for another hotel."

"Okay."

"Turn your phone off. Now! And take out the chip. He can still track you with that chip still inside."

Celia didn't need to be told twice. She turned off her phone, almost tempted to dump it in the melted ice water she had in the room. Instead, she took out the chip, put it back in her purse, and finished packing, frantically, occasionally dropping items on the floor and having to pick them up. Her entire body trembled, and fear had her almost at the point of collapsing. As soon as she finished packing, she pulled her bags into the bathroom, locked the door, and waited for Officer Fairchild to arrive.

***

One reason Isaac Roth was such a high-paid assassin is because he could pick any lock, anywhere, anytime. It didn't matter if it was mechanical or digital; Roth had tools in his bag that would let him in any door in a matter of seconds. It was a skill he had picked up from his days in the *Jagdkom-*

mando.

He had listened through the door of Room 317 and knocked to make sure the room was empty. Using his lock picking tools, he craftily unlocked the door and, looking both ways down the hall to ensure no one had noticed him, entered the empty room. Roth walked straight to the window and parted the vertical blinds. He had a clear view of the front of Celia's hotel. Perfect.

Within five minutes and several swift but calm movements of hand, Roth had his 9-mm submachine gun out of his bag, suppressor screwed on, magazine slapped in, mode set to single-fire, laptop open and connected to the hotel's Wi-Fi, almost ready. He opened the window as far as it would go, which was only three inches, but enough to fit the barrel through. He pulled a chair near the window, sat down, and kept his gun trained on the front of the hotel, ready to take out his target if she should step one foot beyond the door.

To his surprise, the police officer waiting outside got out of her cruiser and ran toward Celia's hotel. Maybe they know something, Roth thought, but it didn't matter. They had no idea where he was, and he would stay right there until Celia showed her face.

And if he had to kill the cop too, so be it.

***

Three knocks. Two-second pause. One knock.

"Mrs. Rayburn, it's me, Officer Fairchild."

Celia, carrying her overnight bag in one hand and her purse in the other, hurried out of the bathroom and unlocked the front door. The officer motioned her out of the room.

"Okay, it's probably nothing, but we need to be safe." Officer Fairchild pressed the button to the elevator. "We are going to go out to my vehicle, and we will head to the station. Stay behind me at all times."

It's probably nothing? Celia noticed that Officer Fairchild disengaged the safety on her weapon and was wearing body armor, so this was more serious than anyone was telling her. When the elevator arrived, Celia was beyond nervous. Her hands shook, despite the items she was holding in them.

As the elevator door opened on the basement level, Officer Fairchild barked something in her shoulder-mounted walkie-talkie that only she understood. As they got off the elevator, people in the basement looked curiously at them. Celia wondered why they found her so interesting.

When they turned the corner and walked toward a rear door, she discovered why. There were two squad cars outside, their emergency strobes flashing red and blue all over the rear alley. Two uniformed officers were standing just inside the door. Celia's heart relaxed.

Officer Fairchild led Celia out the rear door and almost threw her into the waiting squad car parked near the rear door. The car drove off quickly, followed by another squad car. Celia felt like a high-powered official being whisked away by the Secret Service. Officer Fairchild stayed at the door, watching to make sure no other cars followed the squad cars.

Two officers approached Officer Fairchild. "We good?" one of them asked.

"Yes, we are." Officer Fairchild said proudly, then followed up with, "Anything unusual?"

"Not a thing," said the second officer. "If he was here, we probably scared him away by now."

"Hmm." Officer Fairchild headed toward her squad car. As she got in, she looked around one more time, then thought, with astonishing clairvoyance, *No, he was here.*

***

The tall man cursed to himself, frustrated at the number of police cars that had suddenly emerged from an alley at the rear of the hotel. Somehow, they must have known he was nearby and slipped Celia out the back door. He looked over at the laptop sitting on the bed, frowned at his own stupidity, and then gently pulled the barrel of the gun from its perch on the windowsill. He carefully and methodically disassembled the weapon and stuffed it back into the duffel bag. He would have to go after the target another time, which he trusted would be soon.

Just before he walked out the door, he grabbed the laptop and slammed it over his knee, snapping it in two pieces held together only by a few wires. He stuffed the broken laptop in his bag and walked out, leaving only a few shards of plastic strewn on the floor.

***

Detective Liskey allowed Celia to spend a few hours in the headquarters sleeping quarters to rest while he planned his next strategy. Ramon stayed at Celia's apartment building, canvassing residents to see what they knew about Isaac Roth. Had they seen him before? If so, under what circumstances?

He hunted around in his email for the ballistics report from the Crime Lab. The bullet was a .357 SIG, bullets typically used by military or law enforcement. Liskey guessed the killer used a military or police grade weapon, most likely a Sig Sauer 226 or similar, but he could never know for sure until they found and tested the killer's gun.

Meanwhile, Liskey punched around in a few law enforcement databases and tried to discover as much as he could about Isaac Roth. Given the lack of information he found, he suspected the name Isaac Roth was probably an alias. If that were the case, then all he had were photos and fingerprints from Immigration and Customs Enforcement to get intelligence on Roth. He emailed the photo out to a few local, state, and federal police contacts, hoping someone had encountered him before. By then, the BOLO was out there, in the hands and laptops of cops in Montgomery County, Rockville, D.C., Prince George's County, Arlington, Alexandria, Fairfax County, and every other jurisdiction in the D.C. area. He knew someone would spot Roth eventually.

He hadn't called his wife since his 8 pm to 6 am shift officially ended. He needed to call her now.

"Hey, sweetie." Marian smiled as she answered his call.

"Hey."

"Everything all right?"

"Yeah. Just a little tired."

"Caught a case?"

"Yep. Guy got shot in downtown Silver Spring in his own apartment."

"So, I guess you won't be home anytime soon."

"Probably not. But this case I caught has got me scratching my head."

Marian Liskey knew not to ask any further, and her husband did not want her to. Discussions of work were off-limits in their relationship, primarily because the conversations were not balanced. Detective Liskey's job in Homicide could be depressing and frightening, while Marian's career as a wedding planner was usually joyful and relatively stress-free. Rather than regale and worry his wife with his killer-of-the-day news, he kept silent about his job unless something happened that directly affected his wife. As a sixteen-year veteran of the force, ten years as a beat cop, he had seen all too many marriages among colleagues break up, mostly due to the stress of police work. Liskey had no intention of taking that stress home with him. Being married to a cop was stress enough.

"Don't scratch too hard. You lose what little hair you have left." Marian grinned.

That was what he loved about his wife. She knew when to take him seriously and when he needed a little levity to obliterate the heavy cloud enveloping him whenever he dealt with the coldness of men's hearts.

"When will you be home?" Marian asked.

"I have a little follow-up to do, but probably not before the midnight shift gets in."

"Well, you need to have a talk with Graham. He's been acting up in school."

Graham was Liskey's ten-year-old son from his marriage to Hazel Wims, his ex-wife. Hazel ran off with a younger man and Liskey hadn't seen her since. Liskey and Marian had decided not to have their own kids until later so they could focus on Graham. But Liskey hoped to have a child with Marian one day, and Graham was giving him a lot of practice in child-rearing.

"I'll speak to him."

"Great."

"But I need to ask you something."

"What?"

"Do you think we can accommodate an extra guest tonight?"

The tall man

The two-story Craftsman-style house sat several yards off a rough-paved road in the Arlington neighborhood of Baltimore. In front of the house was an impeccable lawn and a walkway that looked as if it were made of hardened sugar. Sitting on the porch, reading *A Tree in Brooklyn* in the light of the quickly setting afternoon sun, was a white-haired septuagenarian whose diminutive stature could barely be seen above the railings surrounding the porch. Only the occasional creak of her rocking chair gave away her presence.

A black SUV rolled up to the curb, barely affecting the idyllic quiet of the neighborhood. The tall man got out, and with his duffel bag in hand, walked up the driveway toward the left side of the house. He nodded politely at the woman, whose social security checks were being supplemented handsomely by his monthly envelopes of cash for the rental of her basement apartment. The woman peered at him over the top of her half-moon glasses, nodded back, and then went back to reading.

The tall man walked past the porch to the side of the house, walked down ten steps, and unlocked the basement door. As soon as he was inside, he shut the door, shutting off all daylight to the apartment. In the dark, he made his way to an end table, switched on a lamp, and then tossed his bag on the floor next to a sleeper sofa. Other than those two pieces of furniture and an 18-inch color flat screen TV sitting atop a gunmetal gray two-drawer file cabinet, there was nothing else in the room.

He grabbed a remote from the end table, switched on the TV, sat on the sofa, and thought for a moment. He needed to strategize. A small army of cops had quickly pulled Celia out of the hotel room, so they knew he was on to her. She likely had more security around her than a sitting United States president in Iraq. He couldn't go at her directly, not if he wanted to avoid his first stint in prison. Trying to kill her while there were cops around with heightened attention would not be smart. He didn't avoid arrest by being stupid, especially with his body count.

Options? Wait until things died down, since the police couldn't guard her forever? *No.* This had to be done quickly. Find out about Justin's funeral and try to get her there? *No,* since there was no guarantee she would be there, especially if she was under guard.

He needed another way to get to her, draw her out in the open, get her away from the cops. And he knew just the thing to do. But he would need more money.

He pulled a satellite phone out of his bag, then pushed the bag under the bed. As he straightened, his eye caught an image on the TV screen. A pretty blonde anchor reported about a Baltimore archbishop who had been elevated to cardinal. As the archbishop's face took up half the screen next to the news anchor, the tall man sneered and quickly shut off the TV.

He walked outside, around to the back of the house, and approached the alley. He looked around and, seeing no persons outside, made his call.

A voice that sounded mechanically manipulated said, "Yes?"

"No success." The tall man spoke with a hint of a German accent. "I need to regroup."

"What do you need?"

"Another five thousand dollars."

"Why?"

"I need to go to Canada."

CHAPTER FIVE

Isaac Roth

Detective Liskey was about halfway through a roast beef on rye when his computer chimed. He checked it and saw he had received a new email. He looked at Ramon, who was reading a newspaper in the cube across from him. Liskey balled up a napkin and playfully tossed it at Ramon, partially to get his attention, and partially to invalidate Ramon's impression that Liskey was "too serious." Once Ramon looked in his direction, Liskey said, "Might have something here. Got an email from the feds, Atlanta field office. Gotta call this agent."

Ramon ignored the napkin, which had bounced off his head and settled on the desk behind him. "Roth?"

"Looks like it."

"Dial him up, man." Ramon folded the paper and set it on his desk while Liskey dialed the number and activated the speakerphone. After a few rings, a man answered, "Special Agent Josh Collins."

"Agent Collins, this is Detective Liskey with Montgomery County Major Crimes. I'm on the line with Detective Williams."

"You guys are homicide, right?" Agent Collins' voice was sharp, young, vibrant.

"Yeah."

"Didn't think there was such a thing."

"Why do you say that?"

"Didn't think you guys get any murders in that part of town."

Liskey rolled his eyes, sending Ramon into a silent laugh. "We're too close to D.C. to be that kosher, bud. Now, if this were Montgomery County, Pennsylvania, then you'd be talking."

"Well, maybe I can help with this one. Isaac Roth, right?"

"Right."

"Yeah, we had some intelligence on this guy about six years ago, back before he got deported. This guy is no joke."

"Why do you say that?"

"You remember Fax Hoffman?"

"No."

"Representative from Georgia? Was collared for that racketeering case a while back?"

Liskey paused, searching his memory. "Oh, yeah. He got off for that, didn't he?"

"Yep. And you know why?"

"You couldn't seal the deal."

"And you know why we couldn't seal the deal?"

"Why?"

"The one lone witness was shot dead the night before the trial."

"The shooter was Roth?"

"We believe so. But we never could pin anything on him, except not having his papers. So, ICE shipped him back overseas. You sure you want to be dealing with this guy?"

Liskey scoffed. "Do I want to be dealing with a German killer? No, but I don't have much of a choice."

"Well, let's get one thing straight. He ain't German. He's Austrian. He just lives in Germany. His parents live in Vienna, and they don't want anything to do with him. He was once in the Austrian special forces and then did some contract engineering work for a rail company. His wife divorced him after his son committed suicide back in '95. Word has it he never got over that, and he started his killing career by murdering a couple of parish priests."

"Why would he do that?" Liskey asked.

"Don't have all the details, but I hear his son may have been abused by one of the church officials, which led to his suicide. According to his profile, they believe he's murdered over 200 people around the world. Yet, nobody can tie a case to him."

"Why?"

"He's extremely careful, almost obsessively so. He avoids close-quarter contact with his victims. He likes to kill them from far away so as not to leave any evidence at the crime scene, except for a bullet. I guess he made an exception in your guy's case. He wears gloves religiously. He shaves almost all the hair off his body so he doesn't leave any hair fragments. He rarely eats or drinks while working. If he uses a bathroom, he will clean it afterward just to avoid leaving any trace. He uses scrubbed weapons and rounds, and he uses a different weapon and round for every hit. He's well trained, and he is no joke. He covers himself so well that he could probably come into your building right now, sit two feet away from you, look you in your eyes and drink a cup of tea, and there's nothing you could do about it."

"Hopefully that changes. Roth was in a fight with my vic, so hopefully something'll turn up; blood, spit, something for DNA." Liskey took a quick sip of cola out of a coffee cup on his desk.

"That'll be a few days. He'll be in the wind by then."

"Naw, I don't think he's finished. It looks like he's coming after my witness."

"You got a witness? What'd he see?"

"It's a *she*, the victim's wife. She saw Roth kill her husband. And now it looks like he's coming after her."

"What was her husband into?"

Liskey sighed. "Not much that I could see. He liked to

get high, so he may have had a few drug debts. We checked out the girl, and she is squeaky clean. No priors. No insurance policies she can cash in on. A bit quirky, but that ain't a crime. The neighbors said they argued quite a bit, though."

"Well, there has to be something she's not telling you."

"How do you figure?"

"Word on the street is that Roth ain't cheap. He charges twenty large and up a head. Hard to believe someone would pay Isaac $20,000 to enforce a $200 or $300 drug debt."

Liskey looked at Ramon as his eyes widened. "Does seem like overkill, pardon the expression."

That tidbit of information obliterated Liskey's theories about the motive for Justin's killing. Most killings in Montgomery County were domestic, drug-related, or gang-related. He agreed that five figures a head was not cost-effective enough to be a drug hit, and Roth didn't seem like the type that would be a street-level enforcer.

That left only the domestic angle. Did Celia pay someone to kill her husband? No, that made little sense. Why pay someone five figures to kill her husband when plenty of people would have done it for much less? *No.* Roth was contacted when there was a need for someone with professional savvy who could kill and leave the police guessing for years. Roth handled killings that were worth a lot more to his clients than five figures. This wasn't a mere street murder or a crime of passion. If Roth was involved, it was something deeper. *But what?*

"Gotta press that girl, man. If Roth is chasing her, she or her husband was into some serious stuff," Agent Collins said.

"Alright, Agent Collins. Anything else for me?"

"Just keep us posted, man. We may have another open case tied to this guy."

"Will do. Thanks." Liskey turned to Ramon as he hung up the phone. "What do you think about that?"

Ramon picked up the newspaper he was reading and turned it back to the front page. "You read the Post this morning?"

"No." Liskey tried to stay away from newspapers. His job was depressing enough.

"They're saying that the pastor's shooting in D.C. yesterday may not have been a hate crime. They now think it was a professional hit."

Liskey could tell what Ramon was thinking. "I don't think Celia's situation and the pastor's are connected."

"You sure? Didn't you say Celia saw the pastor's shooting yesterday?"

"She did, but so did 500 other people. And Celia wasn't even on the Plaza, but across the street. Why would the shooter target her, out of all those other people? And how would he know where to find her so fast?"

Ramon shrugged his shoulders. "Maybe he followed her."

"So, he's bold enough to shoot a prominent pastor in the middle of a plaza in broad daylight, and then he plucks a random girl, follows her home, waits until after midnight and then attacks her in her apartment?" Liskey dismissed the thought even as he said it. "Doesn't make sense."

"Let me work it." Ramon began a half-twirl in his chair toward his desk. "I'll call Park Police and D.C. Police. Couldn't hurt to look into it a little."

Liskey nodded. "You do that." He grabbed his sport coat from the back of his chair and stood. "I need to tell you something, and you have to promise me you won't tell the sergeant."

"You know I'm a rock, Lisk."

"I'm not gonna turn Celia over to victim services," Liskey whispered.

Ramon wasn't certain he heard Liskey correctly. "What?"

Liskey jerked his head toward the break room and walked

in that direction. Ramon followed. Upon arriving, Liskey looked around to make sure no one else was listening and said to Ramon, "Me and my wife are gonna put Celia up in one of my spare bedrooms."

Ramon lowered his voice to match Liskey's tone. "Why would you do that, Lisk? You don't even know this girl. There's no real evidence that Roth is still chasing her. And even if he was, why would you put your family at risk?"

Liskey lowered his head and looked down at his shoes. Since he was a kid, this was his gesture whenever he couldn't adequately explain himself. "I don't know, Ramon. I just got a gut feeling this is not gonna end up well for Celia. If she stays with me, we can keep an eye on her. She's off the books, so even if Roth is trying to find her, there's no way he's going to succeed."

Ramon shook his head. "I don't know about this, Lisk. Too risky. I mean, what if the ASA needs to get in touch with her? How are you gonna explain that she's at your house?"

"I don't imagine the ASA will need to talk to her until we are close to getting Roth. And Ramon, this is not gonna be forever. Maybe a day or two until I can work some other things out."

"Lisk, are you serious?" Ramon leaned away and remained quiet while two detectives passed by the hallway outside of the break room. Once they had passed, Ramon continued. "There's a high-paid assassin who just killed this girl's husband. Who knows what they were into? You really want your family exposed to that?"

"I don't think this girl is all that, Ramon." Liskey closed his eyes and shook his head. "I don't think she has a clue what's going on."

"Well, Lisk, your secret's safe with me, but I don't know, man."

"I know, man. But I'm just going with my gut on this one."

Liskey called it a gut feeling.

He had no idea it was the gentle urging of something unseen but powerful.

***

Celia was at first hesitant when Liskey extended an offer for her to stay with his family for the night. Not that she felt Liskey had improper motives, but Celia was always an independent sort who felt uncomfortable depending on a stranger, even if it was a cop. But when she thought about it, at least Liskey's home would lessen the sense of isolation she would feel if she stayed at a hotel. Besides, having a sixteen-year veteran detective protect her, as opposed to a less-experienced beat cop, made her feel that much safer.

Hearing Isaac Roth was a professional assassin made Liskey much more careful when handling Celia. In case the killer was lurking nearby watching, Liskey had Celia crouch down in the back seat of a cruiser inside the headquarters garage. He then had a beat cop drive Celia to his house in Bethesda, while he followed in his car, making sure no one was following the cruiser. When he was confident no one was following them, and they were safe, Liskey sent the beat cop back to the station, and he and Celia walked inside the house.

The inside of Liskey's split-level home was thick with the savory smells of roast beef. The living room looked well-lived in, with barely an inch of wall space not covered with something, whether it was a bookcase, or a family picture, or a framed landscape print, or a piece of furniture. Marian Liskey walked from the kitchen to the living room just in time to greet her husband and their guest.

Liskey smiled broadly. "Celia, this is my wife, Marian."

Celia took one look at the round face woman with the gray-streaked shoulder-length hair, a hint of freckles, and the bright, inviting smile, and knew she had found an instant friend. Celia extended her hand. Marian would have none of it.

"We do hugs here, sweetheart."

That was fine with Celia. After everything that had happened, she needed a hug or two. She would revel in her mother's hugs if she were home. And Marian's mannerisms reminded Celia of her mom. She walked willingly into Marian's embrace.

"You just make yourself at home, dear." Marian parted from the embrace and briefly held Celia in front of her with both hands. "I'm so sorry about your husband."

"Thanks." Celia looked down sullenly.

"Well," Marian cut an eye to her husband, "dinner will be ready shortly. I'll show Celia her room." She walked over, kissed her husband, and then led Celia to the staircase just beyond the far living room wall.

Once Celia got settled in her room, she ruminated about how her life had fallen apart so fast. Just 24 hours before, she was relaxing in her own posh apartment. Now, she was in a stranger's home, on the run from a maniac killer. What frustrated Celia more than anything was that she did not understand why she was being chased. She couldn't identify the man that had killed her husband because he was wearing a mask. Except for his height, she wouldn't be able to spot him if he sat down at the table with her. The killer knew this. Why was she such a threat?

She also wondered if Justin was into a lot more than she knew about. Maybe those overnight stays held secrets that were more diabolical than she imagined. They had been pressed for money lately, so he was apt to do something illegal that would have eased their financial woes.

"Oh, Justin, Justin," she said aloud, closing tear-moistened eyes. She wanted to pray now, but couldn't, because she wasn't sure if God was playing a cruel joke on her. For years, she avoided leaving Justin because she feared he would come after her and make her life hell. Now, her husband was dead, and she was still on the run, with no money, living the same life she would have had if she had left him.

But would she have left him? Perhaps having a job would have enabled her, and allowed her to hide, but there were other obstacles to overcome. Chief among them was that she was too proud to admit to herself and reveal to her parents that her marriage was failing. The last thing she wanted to do was put the words *I told you so* in her parents' mouths.

But also, being with Justin had taught her it was possible to love and hate someone simultaneously. Despite the evil manifested through him, Celia knew that deep down was the wonderful, giving, and compassionate man she had married. She loved him, even though he became a monster. And it was those loving times she remembered and became the basis for her mourning rather than the cruel times. If she wrote his obituary, there would be no mention of the slaps and the bruises, and the harsh words and threats would be buried with the casket.

Celia had no appetite, and if she could do so without offending the Liskeys, she would pass on dinner and just stay in the room. But she suspected that Marian had made a special dinner for her, and she didn't want to disappoint her. She walked into the adjacent bathroom with her purse, aiming to freshen herself up before dinner.

***

During dinner, despite her husband's death and her obvious pain, Celia was a witty, engaging conversationalist, talking fondly of her parents in Canada and her brothers and sisters, all of whom had achieved success in both family and career. It surprised Liskey to hear that at one time, she wanted to be a cop herself. Back in the day, she played cops and robbers with her siblings in the parking lot of Southwestern High School, and then her father took her to a remote county road in Ontario and showed her how to fire a gun for real, despite protests from her mother.

Once dinner was over and both Graham and Celia were settled in their rooms, Liskey engaged the home security system and then sneaked down to his lair in the basement, knowing his wife would spend the next 45 minutes primping and prepping for bed. He had received a call from Ramon during dinner, but since he left no urgent-marked message, he waited until now to return Ramon's call.

His basement office was the only demarcation of Liskey's work life and his home life. It was almost the spitting image of his cubicle at work, with police bulletins, photographs, and law enforcement posters plastered on the walls. A lone desk with a laptop computer and a telephone sat in the corner of the room. Liskey sat at his desk, pulled out his cell phone, observed that it was 11:03 pm, and dialed.

Ramon answered. "Hey, Lisk."

"You at home or the office?"

"Home."

"Sorry to bother you. Can this wait until tomorrow?"

"It can. But since you called."

"What's up?"

"I spoke with the D.C. detectives investigating the pastor's shooting."

"What d'you find out?"

"They got someone on camera they think shot the pastor. They got him walking out an alley door of a hotel across from Freedom Plaza with a duffel bag five minutes after the shooting."

"How does that connect to our case?"

"The guy they caught on camera is a white guy, over six and a half feet tall."

"You're kidding?"

"Nope. The shooting in D.C. and our vic's shooting? They're *definitely* connected."

***

Celia knew she would never return to her apartment. Even if they caught Isaac Roth, she could never escape the memories of what had happened in that living room if she continued living there. And since they were behind in the rent, they would probably be evicted anyway. So, rather than enjoy the comfortable, plush bed in the Liskey's guest room, she paced around, thinking about what her next move would be. Without a job or very much income, she didn't have many choices. Fortunately, her thoughts were not complicated by the need to arrange a funeral for Justin; his parents had agreed to make the arrangements, and since she was technically in hiding, she couldn't do much to help. She doubted she could even attend the funeral without putting herself, and maybe Justin's family members, in danger.

After dinner, Marian had run out and bought Celia a disposable cell phone so she could make calls without fear of being tracked. Liskey had taken her regular phone and turned it over to their Computer Crime office, hoping that they could use the phone to track Isaac Roth's location. The first call she made using the new phone was to her parents, although it was three hours after her regular 8:30 p.m. call time.

Her father answered the call on the first ring. "Hello?"

"Dad, it's me."

"Thank you, Jesus." George Wise's voice was deep and flecked with the accent of the learned. "Honey, are you okay?"

"I've been better."

"We've been trying to call your cell, but we got no answer."

"I'm not using that phone anymore. This is my new number. For now."

"Your mother told me what had happened. I'm so sorry."

Celia knew her parents were not mean and spiteful people. But their expressions of sympathy for her didn't quite ring genuine. It seemed as if none of this surprised them. She responded with just "Thanks, Dad."

"Where are you?"

"I'm in a detective's home for the night. He and his wife. His name is Liskey. We're going to regroup tomorrow and see about getting me someplace permanent."

"Honey, let me come back there and bring you home," her father pleaded. "You don't have to stay long term. Just until you get on your feet."

That was looking like Celia's only choice. Either that or hang out in hotel rooms or cops' guest rooms until whatever time they caught her pursuer and brought him to trial.

George Wise interpreted her silence to mean she was at least thinking about it. His daughter could be a stubborn and proud sort, so if she would even consider it, it was a small victory.

"So, do you want me to book a plane ticket and come down there?" George repeated, his pushy salesman tactics evident.

"Let me think about it, Dad," Celia told him, although her mind was already half made-up. Having the extra protection of her father would make her feel safer. George Wise may be a big businessman, but he was no punk. She recalled when she was ten, her father came home to his Detroit home and discovered a burglar. Her father confronted the burglar, snatched the pistol out of his hand, and beat him within an inch of his life. That incident made him a hero in Celia's eyes. It also cemented his commitment to protecting his family by investing in his own guns. This gave George a reputation in the neighborhood as someone you didn't want to trifle with.

"Don't think too long," George retorted. "I'm not trying to lose my baby girl."

Celia heard his voice crack, and that put things in a new perspective for her. He seemed genuinely afraid for her. Being in Canada would be more comforting for him than for her.

"I know, Dad." She fought back the tears. "Let me talk to the detective tomorrow and see where we go from here. I'll call you back tomorrow morning."

"Can I count on that?"

"Yes, you can."

"Wonderful. Have a good night, and I'll talk to you tomorrow. Love you, Pookie."

"Love you too."

Celia ended the call and undressed for bed. Unless there was a major objection from Detective Liskey, she would honor her father's wishes. It was time to go back home.

***

3:10 a.m., Friday

Three hours of sleep was all he needed, and he was ready. A pair of khaki shorts, white sneakers, an Orioles cap, and a Norman Rockwell T-shirt later, he looked like any man headed out to vacation.

The tall man known as Isaac Roth walked upstairs from the basement and placed a note on the old lady's dining room table. The note explained that he would be out of town for about three days on business. He said nothing else, and the note was not signed.

He went back downstairs, grabbed his duffel bag, turned off all the lights, and headed outside to the SUV. Before starting the engine, he checked in the glove compartment to make sure his passport was there. It was; a brilliant fake that identified him as Nash Applewhite, with passport stamps from Mexico, China, and Ireland, although he had been to neither country. It set him back $1000, which he dismissed as the cost of doing his business.

He reached down into his duffel bag and removed the disassembled parts of the 9-mm machine gun, and the Sig P226, and several clips for each, and put them in a rolling suitcase he had bought earlier. The only things left in the duffel bag were a change of clothes, a pair of binoculars, handcuffs, keys, two ampules of a white liquid chemical, a burner phone, his satellite phone, a box of random electronics, another pouch containing his lock-picking tools, and something that resembled red-orange clay in a clear plastic package.

The tall man looked around before he started the engine. At 3:15 am, the neighborhood was as still as a deep underground cave. With stop offs and meal breaks, he estimated he would reach the Canadian border by noon. He programmed his portable GPS to the address he had found in the contacts on Celia's laptop before he destroyed it. He started the truck and pulled away, hoping, in 72 hours, to return to this spot with one more notch in his belt and $15,000 richer.

CHAPTER SIX

A possible lead

7:46 a.m., Friday

Celia padded downstairs, her hair in a ponytail, her petite body dressed in jeans and an orange T-shirt. Walking into the kitchen, she saw Detective Liskey sitting at the kitchen island talking to Graham. Graham's dark brown hair with bangs, pasty skin and dimples made him look almost like his stepmother.

Both Liskey and Graham turned when they heard Celia enter, and they stopped their conversation.

"I'm, sorry, I didn't mean to interrupt." Celia backed out of the kitchen.

"No, no, no," Liskey stopped Celia's retreat. "We need to talk." He turned back to Graham. "Please try your best. Can you do that?"

Graham turned away, sighed, and then nodded reluctantly.

"Okay. Go and get your things for school. Your mom's gonna drive you."

Graham hopped off the stool and hustled past Celia toward the living room, making eye contact only briefly with Celia as he passed. Celia moved into the kitchen and sat on the stool that Graham had vacated.

"Is he your only child?" Celia nodded toward the living

room.

"Yes." Liskey stirred a cup of coffee in front of him. "But not with Marian. I was married before."

"I'll bet he's a handful."

"You bet." Not one for personal chit-chat, Liskey cut to the chase. "Are you sure you told me everything about what happened downtown yesterday morning?"

Celia thought for a few seconds about why Liskey could be asking. "Yes, I did."

"You left nothing out?"

"No."

"You didn't know the pastor at all?"

"No."

"You weren't connected to the rally?"

"No."

Liskey sighed, then leaned forward toward Celia. "Well, we found out that your husband and the pastor were shot by the same guy."

Celia's mouth dropped, and her head stretched forward in disbelief. "What?"

Liskey would not repeat himself; he knew Celia had heard him. "We showed a photo of the shooter to D.C. and Park Police. They compared it to camera footage of the hotel across the street from Freedom Plaza. The same guy that shot your husband left the hotel, with a duffel bag, five minutes after the pastor was shot. They think he used one of the empty hotel rooms."

"Well, why is he after me?"

"You tell me."

Celia's voice escalated. "I told you I don't know!"

"Hmm," Liskey said with a hint of skepticism. To diffuse the tension, he pointed to the coffee maker in the middle of the island. "Would you like a cup?"

Celia nodded, exasperated. "Please."

Liskey got up, grabbed a mug from a cabinet, poured her

coffee, and set the mug in front of her with a spoon, dairy creamer, and a sugar bowl. He took one sip of his own coffee, then continued. "Well, this would have to be an incredible coincidence. Either that or the fact that you witnessed the pastor's shooting may have something to do with it."

"But why me?" Celia responded. "There were, like, a million people down there. I wasn't the only one who saw it. Why would he pick me?"

"Well, that's what we're going to look into." Liskey shrugged. "I mean, we don't even know for sure that he's still after you. He may have tried to kill you because you were in the room when your husband was killed. He had a mask on so you couldn't I.D. him. For all we know he's out of the country by now. But to be on the safe side, we're gonna keep you in protection until we catch him."

"What if you never catch him?"

Liskey had no answer. "We'll cross the bridge when we get to it. But we'll catch him. We don't give up." He dared not mention Roth's pedigree and frighten Celia even more.

He also hated to acknowledge that without a continued threat of danger to Celia, Liskey could not protect her indefinitely. The state's attorney would not sign off on it. At some point, Celia would have to fend for herself, maybe sooner than later once he gave an update to his sergeant and the assistant state's attorney about the progress.

It was one reason he went outside of policy and brought Celia to his own home. The likelihood that Celia would receive protection when there was no arrest, and no credible evidence that Roth was still pursuing Celia, was slim. But Liskey knew better. This case had enough questions that he would do his best to keep Celia safe until he had answers.

"So, what's going on today?" Celia asked, putting a lot more sugar in her coffee than Liskey thought was reasonable.

"You'll stay here," Liskey responded, drinking the last of

his coffee. "Marian will be here. She works from home. I'll get a patrol officer to keep an eye out. But nobody except me and my partner knows you're here, so you should be safe."

Celia nodded doubtfully.

"Trust me," Liskey retorted. "I wouldn't have you here if I thought there was any real danger. I wouldn't put my family at risk. Unless this guy is Jesus Christ in the flesh, he won't find you here."

Celia seemed more confident now, but she knew there was never any way she would be safe, no matter what Liskey said. Now that there seemed to be a connection between Freedom Plaza and her husband's murder, this thing was a lot deeper than she realized, and it felt inherently dangerous to her.

***

The moment Liskey got to his desk, he read an email from Weirick in the Computer Crime Unit. *Call or stop by. Something you may need to know.*

Although Weirick was just two floors down from him, Liskey had no intention of stopping by. He picked up the phone and dialed Weirick's extension. When Weirick answered, Liskey said, "You got something for me?"

Although Weirick was twenty-eight years old, his voice carried an innocence and naiveté of a kid barely past middle school. "I checked out the cell phone you gave me and contacted some of my buddies at the phone company. They pulled some archival packets off their routers from the past 48 hours attached to the phone's IMEI, stripped the IP addresses and MAC addresses and sent them to me."

"English, Weirick."

"I found information that told me who's been tracking the cell phone."

"How can you do that without a subpoena?" Liskey

asked.

"IP addresses are not exactly private information," Wei-rick explained. "I wasn't asking for a phone call or other data that might be private. I just wanted to know who and what had been talking to Ms. Rayburn's cell phone. That's what I told them and they believed it."

Liskey let out a muddled laugh. "So, what d'you find?"

"I looked up the IP addresses and found that they are registered to the Recli Hotel chain. I called the IT department at Recli and asked them to do me the courtesy of telling me which router in their system handles that IP address. They looked it up and said that the router was located on their property at 88901 Wisconsin Avenue."

Liskey frowned, slightly confused. "Celia's hotel?"

"No. Different hotel. Ms. Rayburn's hotel was down the street. Same block, but further down."

"So, are you telling me that Isaac Roth was right down the street from Celia, at another hotel?"

"I know her laptop was. Can't verify it was Roth holding it."

"That would have to be the coincidence of coincidences if it wasn't. What if her phone somehow hooked into the Recli Hotel Wi-Fi system, since they are so close by?"

"I thought about that. But I can tell by the MAC address of the equipment accessing the network. Based on that, it wasn't a cell phone. It was a laptop wireless network adapter."

Son of a bitch, Liskey thought. Roth was right on Celia's heels, and he never knew it. If he hadn't pulled her out of the hotel when he did…

"Any way you can pull more of that data, find out where that laptop has been other than the hotel?" Liskey inquired.

"I can try."

"I want to know if he took the laptop home, or anyplace else where we can catch him."

"I'll work on it."

"Thanks, Weirick. I know you're pushing aside days of casework to accommodate me. I owe you." Liskey hung up the phone and then dialed Ramon Williams. Ramon picked up after six rings.

"Where are you?" Liskey asked.

"Running late."

"Meet me at the Recli Hotel on Wisconsin. I got a lead."

***

Thirty minutes later, Liskey and Ramon walked into the Recli Hotel, an eight-story gray masonry behemoth that could have passed for a high-end apartment building if it were not for the identical double-paneled white drapes at every window. It was a short walk to the reception desk, which was decked out in faux mahogany. The detectives exchanged no greetings or pleasantries with the college girl at the desk, but Ramon merely showed his badge and said, "We'd like to speak with your general manager."

The college girl nodded and quickly dialed a number on the phone. "Rick, two police officers are here to see you." She hung up five seconds later. "He'll be right out."

"Thanks." Ramon turned and look around the lobby.

Almost at once, a 40-ish man who resembled the character George Costanza from *Seinfeld* sprang out of a side door and came to meet the detectives, his hand outstretched. "Rick Harper. I'm the general manager." After handshakes, Rick said with the panache of one used to dealing with detectives, "Let's talk in my office."

Rick's office was basically four walls, no windows, with an oak veneer wraparound desk occupying two of the walls. Papers, notepads, and books covered every square inch of the desk. A velour couch was against the third wall, and Rick motioned the detectives toward it. The detectives complied, finding the couch well-worn, and their behinds several inches below their knees.

Rick sat at his desk. "What can I do for you?"

Liskey spoke first. "We're investigating a homicide. There's a person of interest that may have been in this hotel." As if on cue, Detective Ramon pulled a photocopy of an FBI wanted poster from his jacket pocket and handed it to Rick. "Have you seen the man in this picture in your hotel?"

Rick studied the photo, then shook his head. "No, he doesn't look familiar. But my front desk clerks and my housekeepers may have seen him. It says his name is Isaac Roth. I can look to see if he checked in."

"Don't bother," Ramon chimed in. "He wouldn't use his real name, or any alias he's used before."

"Actually, I'd like to show this photo to all of your staff, and maybe also to some of your guests," Liskey asked.

"Uh, I think that's okay." Rick looked up from the photo. "But I'd like to consult with my general counsel first."

"Sure," Liskey said. "And while you're speaking with him, you may want to mention that I will also need the room numbers of all your current guests who were checked in yesterday any time before noon. I will also need to look at your surveillance footage and maybe inspect some rooms."

***

"I saw this guy."

The next-shift front desk clerk took another look at the photo to make sure she knew what she was talking about. Once certain, she handed the photo back to Ramon Williams. "He came through the lobby yesterday. I remember him because he was tall and kinda intense looking. He had a big bag in his hand. I thought he was someone that maybe had checked in the night before."

Ramon stood with the clerk and Rick in the manager's office. She was the fourth staff member interviewed once the hotel's general counsel gave the okay.

"What time was this?" Liskey asked.

"Around noonish." The clerk inflected her voice almost as if she were asking a question.

"Where did he go?"

"Took the elevator. Not sure what floor."

Liskey turned to Rick. "We're gonna need the video feed of the front lobby around that time."

"My security people are working on it," Rick assured.

Liskey turned back to the clerk. "How big was this bag?"

"I don't know. Like a regular duffel bag. But it had a lot of stuff in it."

Ramon chimed in. "Sounds like the same bag he was carrying during the Freedom Plaza hit."

Liskey nodded. "Probably tried to take her out the same way he did the pastor." He sent the clerk back to her duties, then spoke to Rick privately. "Gather all of your housekeepers, maintenance people, custodians, and anyone else that was on shift yesterday, in the conference room."

Twenty minutes later, four purple-uniformed Latina ladies sat in the conference room next to Rick's office. Five additional hotel personnel waited outside. All looked nervous to see cops and eschewed their normal conversation among themselves.

Liskey quickly set their minds at ease by telling them he was not from ICE. He held up the photo. "I need to know if either of you saw this man in the hotel yesterday. He is about six-foot four and was carrying a black duffel bag. ¿Viste a este hombre en el hotel ayer?" He handed the photo to one lady, who looked at it, shook her head, and passed it to the next.

The second woman stared at the photo, then lowered it and regarded Liskey. "I saw, yes." She spoke with a heavy Spanish accent.

Liskey straightened, like a dog about to get a treat. "Where?"

"On my floor yesterday. I saw him walking down the hallway."

"What floor?"

"Three."

"Was he just walking?"

"He was going to the stairs."

Rick was leaning against a wall, listening. Liskey turned to him. "I need to inspect every room on that floor where the windows face east. Let's start with the empty ones."

***

11:45 a.m., Friday

Feeling a need to reassess his strategy, the tall man stopped at a shopping center in Cheektowaga, a town near Buffalo. His initial plan was to stop here, ditch the SUV, kidnap a family man in a vehicle with Canadian tags, and force him to drive across the Canadian border with him in the trunk. He would ensure compliance by recording the man's driver's license information, and then pretend he was sending the information to a third party who would kill his family if he didn't comply. But the more he thought about it, the more the plan seemed far-fetched to him. There were too many fail points, and he dared not risk at any point being locked in a trunk with no idea what was going on. No, it would be better to deal with the border himself. But first...

He parked in a distant parking space in a Walmart parking lot. He fished his smartphone out of his pocket, accessed a browser, and spent an hour checking law enforcement and media sites. There appeared to be no mention of him. Police had no leads in the murder of Justin Rayburn and the attempted murder of Benjamin Lyons, at least not any they would report publicly. But that was enough to be considered public enemy number one, so he was confident law enforcement had no idea he was involved. Otherwise, his photo would be on every TV screen and on every social media feed in the country.

Crossing the Canadian border was a risk. He had no doubt his fake passport would do the trick. But if a border officer were to detain him for a secondary inspection, he would be in trouble. Experience taught him to do everything possible to avoid suspicion at the border so they would not refer him for a secondary inspection, which would involve pulling him over to the side and undergoing more extensive questioning and maybe a check of the vehicle and his belongings. It was a risk he'd have to take.

The tall man stuffed his phone back into his pocket and started the SUV. As he looked up, he saw a man stuffing groceries and toys into the trunk of his car, with a boy, about eight years old, excitedly looking on. The tall man focused on the boy for a moment, allowing his mind to momentarily abandon his murderous mission. He remembered earlier, better days in Vienna, with his wife and twelve-year-old son, in a high-rise apartment overlooking St. Rupert's Church. Though the times were pleasant, the memories were not, for his wife and son were no longer with him. All because of a rogue priest.

1997
Vienna, Austria

The tall man stood just outside the 15th century Romanesque Gothic cathedral, embarrassed that he still looked at it with some measure of affection. His baptism, confirmation, and first communion were here. He met his wife and married her here. His son would later receive the same sacraments. But that was where it ended. He would have to tuck his memories away for safekeeping in a corner of his mind, for they could not co-mingle with the future he was about to author for himself.

He walked around to a side entrance, one he knew was always unlocked. The special forces had trained him to kill quickly and get away even more quickly. But this was personal, and he could not let this man meet his maker without knowing exactly why.

The side door creaked open, and he walked inside. Down the rustic hallway was the entrance to the sanctuary and the apse, which let in streams of midday sunlight through its dome of stained-glass windows. He looked around and, seeing no one, headed across the sanctuary to the left side and to the door of the sacristy. The priest was inside, preparing for 12:30 mass, as usual. He reached back, removing from his waistband a fully loaded Glock with a suppressor. He held it in his right hand, the gun down against his side, as he pushed the door open with his left. The squeak of the door startled the priest, who was removing his vestments from a closet. When he saw the gun and the man standing there with it, he dropped the vestments on the floor and stood silent as the man approached.

"Alexander, what are you doing?" the priest said in shaky German.

Alexander Koffler raised his gun and pointed it directly at the priest's head. He said only one word before cocking the hammer of the weapon. "Jonas."

The priest sighed. "You must understand, Alexander. I meant no harm to your boy."

"The courts may have found you innocent, but I know what you did." A lone tear streaked down his cheek. "I know the truth. The things you did to him, you get no absolution. He's dead today because of you."

"Alexander..."

"My wife is gone because of you."

"Alexander, let's talk about this."

Alexander's right arm stiffened, and his finger pulsed nervously on the trigger. "This is the only justice I have left, and even this is unfair."

"How so?"

"My pain will carry on. Yours is about to end."

"Please, Alexander, I..."

Those were the priest's last words before a faint crack rung through the sanctuary and his body fell to the floor atop the vestments he had dropped. Alexander stepped close to the fallen priest and shot him again, ensuring he was dead.

Somehow the murder of one man didn't seem like justice. His son was gone, and he didn't blame just the priest. He blamed God — the same God that allowed his chosen vessel to abuse his innocent son. He decided, not long after that moment, that hurting God would be the balm that would soothe the pain of losing his son. And since he couldn't slaughter God, the next best thing would be to slaughter as many of God's people as he could. Killing this priest had given him a taste for murder, and he would not shed a tear, nor lose one wink of sleep.

He walked as calmly out of the sanctuary as he had walked in. On the way out, he inadvertently looked up at a statue of Jesus, his arms outstretched, the nail prints visible on his hands, his eyes seeming to stare directly at Alexander.

Alexander looked away in disgust.

It was at that moment that Isaac Roth was born.

***

The tall man shook the thoughts from his head and pulled the SUV out of the parking lot. Within fifteen minutes, if all went well, he would be across the border and well into Canada.

***

The tall man had just driven through Buffalo, New York

and had crossed the Peace Bridge into Canada. As he arrived at the border station, five cars were in line ahead of him. He observed them, noting how a border patrol officer checked them for only two to three minutes each before he sent them on their way into Canada. No drug-sniffing dogs, no search of the vehicle, no bomb detectors. Just a check and stamp on the passport and they were on their way.

When it was his turn, he pulled up to the booth slowly, stopped, and handed his passport to the border patrol officer inside the booth. He looked at the officer only until the officer checked his passport, then looked at the road ahead of him. The officer studied the tall man for a moment and then punched something into his computer. The tall man noticed that the sun was orange and low in the sky, and it would be dark soon. Only 120 miles to go to his destination.

"Where are you coming from?" the officer asked, keeping his eyes on the screen in front of him.

"Washington, DC," the tall man answered, trying to disguise his accent.

"Long drive."

"Indeed."

"What brings you to Canada?"

"I'm visiting relatives."

"Where?"

"In Hamilton," he lied. The tall man dared not them where he was really going.

"How long will you be in Canada?"

"A couple of days, maybe three."

"Any guns or other weapons in the vehicle?"

"No."

Four more minutes had passed before the tall man recognized that his border clearance was taking longer than usual. He looked at the officer, who looked back to him briefly before returning his attention to something on his computer screen. Sensing something was amiss, the tall man looked ahead. About 50 yards ahead of him was a toll booth plaza with two empty lanes.

The officer stepped halfway out of the booth and pointed to a group of covered parking bays just beyond and to the right. "Sir, if you could pull into one of those parking spaces over there. We just need to check a couple more things, then you'll be on your way."

He was being referred to secondary. *Not good.*

He caught movement behind the officer and saw three more officers headed for the exit door. One of them was holding a sniffer dog on a leash. Something was *definitely* wrong.

It was now or never.

The tall man nodded and slowly pulled the vehicle out of the border booth, angling to the right as if he were following the officer's instructions. Instead, he turned back to the left, straightened, and then slammed on the gas, escalating to 20 mph as he headed toward an empty toll bay. Ignoring the red stop light in front of him, he shot through the toll bay at almost 30 mph, crashing through the yellow and black striped toll gate and sending it careening back until it snapped off and hit the pavement. The tall man gunned the gas and skidded until the vehicle was flying down Queen Elizabeth Way at sixty mph. He looked back and saw three border services agents running for their cruisers to pursue him.

The tall man charged down the road, weaving around other vehicles until he noticed a grove of trees alongside the road a mile away from the border. He turned wildly off the road, mowing through tall grass and lurching through brush and shrubbery until the trees thickened, the wheels spin on wet ground, and he could go no further. He left the vehicle in drive and opened the rolling suitcase. He urgently removed the guns and clips and stuffed them into his duffel bag, along with the GPS, which had bounced off the center console onto the floor. He stepped out of the SUV, grabbed a stick from the ground, and jammed it between the pedal and the front seat, causing the wheels to continue to spin and kick up mud and leaves in a spray behind the truck. For the first time, he heard sirens in the distance.

The tall man grabbed the duffel bag, locked the truck doors, closed them from outside, and ran through the woods in an unknown direction. Ignoring the branches whipping against his legs and the pools of muddy water which sopped through his shoes, he kept running as fast as he could, tripping a few times over fallen tree trunks camouflaged by piles of rotting leaves. Finally, he reached a clearing, and about twenty yards ahead of it was another road. He stopped, looked in all directions, including upward, making sure he was in sight of neither man nor machine, then scurried across the road, running until he was hidden once again in another grove of trees. The sirens were louder now.

The tall man ran faster, the heavy duffel bag he was carrying stripping him of endurance, his breathing becoming more labored, the scrapes on his legs becoming more painful. But he refused to rest, but pressed on, knowing he had only a few more minutes to get out of the area before Border Services and the RCMP set up a perimeter and trapped him inside.

He reached another clearing, looked around again, then trudged through the tall brown grass until he reached another grove of trees, this one narrower than the others. In three minutes, he was on another road, a single lane, barely paved road with more farmland across from it.

The tall man crouched back into the woods and watched, allowing himself only that moment to rest. Fortunately for him, only a minute had passed before a car, driving slowly to avoid potholes, came up the road. He pulled his pistol out of his duffel bag, waited until the late model Dodge Dart was almost in front of him, and stepped out into the road directly in front of the car. The car screeched to a halt, with the front bumper just a foot from his legs.

The tall man pointed the gun directly at the man in the car and walked around to the driver's side. The driver, whose fear made his skinny face look a few shades lighter than normal, watched the tall man through the driver's side window with widened eyes. The tall man made a rotating motion with his left hand. The driver obeyed, rolling down his driver's side window.

"You know how to get to Burlington?" the tall man asked, not waiting for an answer. He hopped into the back seat of the man's car, pointed his gun at the rear of the driver's seat, and crouched down low. "Drive. Now."

The driver guided the car along the road, trying to keep his jittery hands steady. When he reached the Niagara Parkway, he turned left, not sure where he was going.

"Here's what I want you to do." The tall man shifted so he could lie on the back seat and still see everything the driver was doing. "I want you to get me to Burlington. Stay off Queen Elizabeth. I don't want you to stop for anything, even if you must go to the bathroom. If you see any roadblocks, tell me at once. Don't do anything stupid, and you'll live through this. Do you understand?"

"Yes, the driver said, his voice clipped and shaky.

"Good. Because if you don't follow my directions when I say, and exactly as I say, I will kill you. Understand?"

"Yes."

"Good."

After a few minutes of driving, the driver found the courage to speak. "Sir, can I make a suggestion?"

"What?"

"You can just take the car and let me out. I'll mind my own business, and I'm not going to be any harm to you."

"Keep driving."

"Sir?"

"I said keep driving."

"I don't want to die, sir. I have a family."

"And you will see your family again, today, if you get me to Burlington without any problems."

The tall man was not bluffing. He had every intention to keep his promise. He was not sadistic. He only killed those someone paid him to kill unless someone interfered. Like Celia's husband.

Celia's parents? Well, they would have to be the exception.

Chapter Seven

A troubling development

Celia found Marian a doting and caring host, which put her more at ease about staying at the Liskeys' home. For breakfast, Marian made bacon-cheddar scones with fresh strawberries on the side. With a wife that cooked like that, Celia wondered how Liskey was not fatter than he already was. They ate on the rear deck, which overlooked a spacious and manicured lawn surrounded by a white picket fence. The morning cool was still lingering, and Marian wanted to enjoy it before the hot weather set in later that day.

Small talk dominated most of the first part of their breakfast. Celia couldn't help but notice that Marian had some type of accent. She couldn't name it, not that she was any good at that sort of thing. But she couldn't resist the urge to ask.

"Miss Marian, what country are you from?"

Marian smiled at her question, forcing her cheeks almost into dimples. "I was born in Melbourne, Australia, but moved here when I was ten."

"I thought maybe it was England."

"Well, you're close. My family has roots in Britain through my mother. My father is Irish. What about you? Were you born in Detroit?"

"Born and raised. My dad was born in Rocky Mount. He moved to Detroit in the '50s with his parents. He met my mother during a baseball game at Briggs Stadium, and the rest is history. I spoke to them last night, and they want me to move back home."

"Are you going to?"

"It might be the safest place at this point. I'll have to come back down here for Justin's funeral, but I think it's the best place to be right now. But I'm in my feelings about it."

"Why?"

Celia took a deep breath. "My parents can be very judgmental sometimes. They didn't want me to marry Justin because they thought he wasn't good enough for me. But then again, I don't think anybody would have been good enough for me, except the boy that *they* liked."

"What boy was this?"

Celia laughed at the memory. "Clarke Sanders."

Marian smiled at her, then craned her neck forward. "What was wrong with Clarke?"

"He was okay, except his idea of a good date was to talk about Scriptures the entire time."

"What's wrong with that?" Marian said, half-jokingly.

"Miss Marian, c'mon." Celia gave Marian her best *are-you-serious* look. "You go on a date, you talk about one another, you get to know each other. You don't go into long talks about First Timothy 4 and 5. I mean, don't get me wrong. I'm a Christian, and I like the Bible, but that was just a little too much."

Marian's chortle-laden smile pushed her cheeks upward until they thinned her eyes. She wanted to know more about Justin Rayburn but wasn't sure what questions about him would trigger memories that would intensify Celia's grief. She continued the conversation with a much safer topic.

"So, I assume your parents are Christians?" Marian asked, realizing just as the words escaped her lips that talking about religion may not be that safe either.

"They're not just Christians. They're hyper-Christians." Celia seemed to pipe up at the topic. "They read nothing but

Christian books. They only watch Christian movies. They always have their TV tuned to TBN. And if it isn't gospel or praise music, to them, it comes straight from hell. My mom even gets up at 4 in the morning to pray."

"Is that why you have mixed feelings about returning home?"

"No, it's not that. I grew up with that. But I guess coming home, especially like this, gives my parents the satisfaction of being right. They thought marrying Justin would screw up my life, and now they get to gloat."

"But why?" Marian leaned forward. "You didn't screw up your life. Your husband was murdered. That doesn't mean *you* are a screw-up."

"They'll say I screwed up because I married the wrong man. They'll think he was into something that got him killed, and that's gonna prove to them that he wasn't the one for me. With everything that's going on, I'm not sure they were wrong."

Marian's voice became softer. "You don't believe that, do you?"

"I don't know what to believe anymore." Celia reached back and rubbed the back of her neck for no apparent reason. "Two days ago, I was at home getting ready for a job interview. Now my husband is dead, I'm in hiding, and I still have no idea why."

Marian leaned back. "I'm sure my husband's working to get answers."

"I'm sure he is. But what if I don't like the answers? Could I live knowing my parents were right, and I was wrong?"

"Why couldn't you?"

"Because it means that maybe I'm not a good judge of character, or a good judge of anything, or that maybe I don't make the best decisions. And that's an ugliness about myself that I hate to acknowledge sometimes. But my parents will remind me, without fail."

"Or maybe they'll have compassion, given your situation." Marian plucked a scone from the table and popped it almost like she would a Tylenol.

"Maybe they will." Celia's eyes went up and to the right. "I just hope that Detective Liskey finds out my husband is innocent, so I don't have to hear them say I told you so."

***

Liskey had been drawn to detective work because of the glory and the glamor, only to find there was no such thing. It was all drudgery and monotony. Hours spent on reviewing surveillance footage. Days waiting for forensic reports. Shift after shift interviewing people and pulling together small clues he hoped would lead to a big revelation. And now, nitpicking through empty hotel rooms, hoping to find a clue that would lead him to the killer. Room 301, 307, 311, *nothing*. None of the housekeepers nor the guests he canvassed knew what room the killer had been in. It was a shame that privacy laws and concerns made hotel owners skittish about putting cameras in hotel corridors. If cameras were installed in the corridors, Liskey's job here might have been done two hours earlier.

But he pressed on to Room 313 while Ramon Williams checked out Room 317. Walking in the room, with Rick standing by in the corridor, he followed the same routine he had done with the previous rooms: slip on a fresh pair of latex gloves; open the curtains to allow the maximum amount of light inside; check the waste baskets for debris; inspect the bathrooms to determine if they had been used; examine the windows for anything unusual. He was just about to check the night stand and dresser drawers when his walkie-talkie chirped.

"Liskey, I got something in 317."

Way to go, Ramon, Liskey thought. It was well past lunch,

and he wanted to get out of there and check out a new ko-sher carry-out down the street. He left the room and walked down two doors to Room 317, where he found Ramon standing just to the right of the bed. He approached Ramon, then followed Ramon's gaze to the floor beside the bed. Lis-key squinted, then kneeled to inspect Ramon's find.

It was a *U* key that had apparently popped off a laptop, surrounded by a few plastic shards.

Liskey stood and glanced at the foot of the bed. "Looks like the bed has been sat on, too. Was that you?"

"No, sir."

LIskey briefly looked at Ramon and then walked back into the hallway where Rick was waiting.

"Call your boss and your general counsel," Liskey advised. "We're going to have to process this room for evidence. Our man was in here."

***

An hour after the tall man abducted the driver in Fort Erie, they had arrived in Burlington. The tall man instructed the driver to find a fairly secluded road, and, after driving around for another fifteen minutes, they found a worn asphalt road surrounded by tall brush and trees, with the closest house about a fifteen-minute walk.

"Pull over," the tall man ordered.

The driver pulled the car to the side of the road, the brush scraping along the bottom of the vehicle. The tall man sat up in the seat, looked around and, satisfied, continued to point his gun at the driver.

"Hand me your cell phone and your driver's license."

The driver quickly fished through his pockets, produced a small flip phone and his license, and handed them to the tall man. The tall man stuffed the license in his duffel bag but kept the cell phone in his hand.

"Now leave the keys and get out."

The driver sniffled. "Oh God, please don't kill me."

"I said get out. And walk to the other side of the road."

The driver, almost in tears now, got out of the car and walked to the other side of the road, hoping that a police car would happen by.

The tall man got out of the car, leaving his duffel bag in the back seat. "Keep walking."

The driver turned and walked through the brush. When the driver was no longer visible, the tall man climbed in the driver's seat, slammed the door, and pulled off. About a minute later, he slowed down and tossed the cell phone out of the window into the brush.

He drove quickly out of the area until he reached an industrial zone. The success of his next effort would depend on how quickly he found a target. He had little time before that driver found a house with a telephone and reported his car and license stolen.

The tall man continued to drive, drifting, but not so slow as to draw suspicion. He scoped the warehouses and commercial buildings, scanning quickly, head moving from side to side, until he saw the ideal target—a lone 1998 Ford, parked in a remote parking space next to a warehouse. It likely belonged to a worker who would be inside for many hours before he noticed the car missing. *Perfect.*

He parked next to the car and shut off the ignition. The tall man looked around and, certain no one was looking, reached into his duffel bag and grabbed a ring full of shaved keys. He twisted three Ford keys off the ring, put the rest back into the duffel bag, and got out of the car, once again checking around for lookie-loos. With the gun in his waistband, he grabbed the duffel bag and dashed around to the driver's side of the vehicle. He smiled when he found the door unlocked. *Stupid Canadians.*

The door of the Ford was open and the duffel bag in the

back seat within five seconds. The tall man cringed when he got inside. The car reeked of cigarette smoke and other foul odors not identifiable. Fortunately, he would have to deal with it only another 45 minutes.

The tall man shut the door and jiggled one of the shaved keys in the ignition. It didn't work, nor did the second key. The third key took some jiggling, but he finally got the ignition to turn. The car started and idled roughly. A plume of smoke rose from behind the car.

He reached again into his duffel bag for the GPS, setting it on the passenger seat. The tall man put the car into drive and headed out of the parking lot. His strategy was to stay away from major highways and busy roads. They probably had his face on every law enforcement computer in Canada. The fewer eyeballs on him, the better.

His next stop would be in Toronto and on the front doorstep of 97 Connery Road, the home of George and Marjorie Wise.

***

Detectives Liskey and Ramon waited outside Room 317 while a lone crime scene investigator, the only one on duty, swept the room for clues and dusted for fingerprints. Liskey hoped that he could lift a fingerprint. That would establish Isaac Roth's presence in the room, along with the piece of the laptop. He hoped that would be enough evidence to prove that Roth was tracking and following Celia, which would get the assistant state's attorney to sign off on extended protection for Celia. He couldn't keep Celia in his house forever. If his sergeant discovered she was there, a report would go in his file. It wouldn't be the first one, and probably not the last, but the more he could avoid ticking off his bosses, the better.

While waiting, Liskey shot the breeze with Ramon.

"How's that girl you've been seeing?" Liskey asked.

Ramon sighed. "I don't know if that's gonna work out."

"Why do you say that?"

"She's just into me because of my job. I'm just a badge to her."

"Hmm." Liskey looked down at his own faux leather shoes, noticing a scuff he hadn't seen before. "She seems like a sweet girl."

"She is."

"Cute."

"Very cute."

"But no keeper?"

"She ain't into me, man."

"And you've been on how many dates? Two? Three?"

"Two."

At first, Liskey grinned, then it turned into a full-blown chuckle.

"What's so funny?" Ramon wondered aloud.

"You young people are so impatient. You want everything right away." Liskey reached into his mind for a relevant memory. "I remember the first partner I had when I was promoted to detective. He was a young buck, only been on the streets for a few years. He was about 25 or 26 years old. He got a promotion because he had dirt on one of his bosses. He was assigned to me, and we caught a case over in Kemp Mill. Some guy beat up his girlfriend and put her in the hospital. The guy was nowhere to be found when we arrived at the scene. So anyway, later that day we got a tip from the guy's cousin. He said the guy was planning to come back to the house at some point to get some money he had left there. Since we didn't know the exact time he was planning to be there, we had to sit on the house until he showed up. We staked out that house for 14 hours."

Ramon shrugged. "I've done longer. Heck, when I was in Iraq, we did two to three times as much."

"Yeah, but my partner was still fresh. It drove him crazy to sit there for 14 hours. I told him that this is what the job entails. If you want to get your man, sometimes this is what it takes. You gotta put the time in. Very little is gonna come to you in a couple of hours. Same with this girl, man. You gotta put the time in."

"But Liskey, c'mon," Ramon argued. "Two dates, and all this girl wants to talk about is my job."

"It may be fascinating to her, yes. But a lot of relationships start with something superficial like that. For guys, it's how the girl looks. For girls, it's the kind of car he drives, or his job, or maybe even a nice pair of shoes. There's always something that draws interest. That's what attracts them. But once they get to know you, they may find something that keeps them, makes them fall in love with you. That's what you hope for. That's why you have to be patient before you make that determination."

Ramon's eyebrows dipped toward his nose. "Isn't that stringing her along, though? By the end of five dates, she might think the relationship is something special when it ain't."

"You gotta manage that. Let her know you're just hanging out right now. Nothing serious."

"So, I guess you don't believe in love at first sight, huh?"

Liskey scoffed. "I do. But that type of love doesn't sustain a relationship. I mean, I'm no expert on this kind of stuff, but—"

Ramon interrupted with, "Well, you and Marian have been married for a few years, so you must know something about it."

"Funny you mention that, 'cause when I first met Marian, I wasn't sure I was all that attracted to her," Liskey admitted. "I didn't think she was ugly, or anything. She just didn't stir me like I thought a woman would."

"Yeah, but you told me you thought she had a man at the

time. You met her in the men's department in Blooming-dale's at White Flint. She was checking out men's suits."

"That wasn't the only thing she was checking out." Liskey clicked his tongue and lightly elbowed Ramon. After Ramon finished laughing, Liskey continued. "But the point is, we went on a couple of dates, and I wasn't feeling it at first. But after a while, she grew on me. I think that's the best thing, to have a woman just sneak up on you like that."

"Well, I hope to have what you have someday," Ramon said with no small amount of admiration for his partner.

"Yeah, but you don't want to wait as long as me, either." Liskey felt the vibration of his cell phone in his jacket. He reached for it, continuing to talk while he checked the caller ID. "I was thirty-five when I first got married. You're a kid. You don't want to rush, but when you find a good woman, you don't want to delay it, either."

Ramon watched Liskey's phone. "Who's that?"

"Sarge." Liskey answered the call. "Hey, boss."

Within ten seconds of the call, Liskey's face fell.

***

Celia felt comfortable enough to walk around the back yard of the Liskey home while Marian was inside returning business phone calls. The back yard reminded her of her parents' back yard, which was only slightly larger than this one. That was one perk of returning to her parents' home—she would enjoy a lifestyle she never would have imagined in Detroit and was volumes above what she had enjoyed with Justin before his downfall.

Celia had been to visit her parents several times during her four-year marriage to Justin. The first visit was a few months after her parents had moved to Toronto following two years of record profits from their chicken business. She recalled her shock as she got out of the cab at her parents' new house and thought she had the wrong address. There was no way her parents were wealthy enough to afford the house at the address they had given her. How loaded were her parents that they could move from a three-bedroom detached house off of Grand Boulevard to a French-European style two story home, a former embassy, with Palladian windows facing the street?

She recalled being blown away when she walked through the covered courtyard and into the foyer, ushered by her smiling and proud father. George Wise eagerly led her on a tour, starting with his private study, then to a master closet as big as her old bedroom, and a master bathroom almost the same size as the closet. Celia's astonishment was pasted on her face as she walked through the master bedroom, through a door to the rear covered patio, then through another door to the living room, the dining room, the breakfast nook, the pantry, the kitchen, and a guest bedroom and bathroom. The second floor had three more bedrooms, each with their own bathroom, a covered porch, and a media room and a game room. After being flabbergasted and more than a little impressed, Celia wondered what her empty nester parents would want with a house that big.

Maybe that's why they wanted her to come home, she thought. Maybe they were feeling the loneliness of such an empty house and wanted—needed—their sons and daughters to come home. Justin's death was just the latest opportunity in a year's long quest to bring Celia back home again. Celia was George Wise's favorite, and he was almost heartbroken when she moved out of the family home while in Detroit.

But the more Celia thought about it, the less it mattered why her parents wanted her back home. It made sense. Justin was the only reason she was in Maryland. She had made few friends in her four years in the state. Justin was not only her husband, but he was also her life. Given that the relationship had dissolved into abuse, he had probably planned it that way all along. Since nothing was holding her here, she might as well head to Toronto and live like a princess.

Her father was waiting for a call from her, so she decided to dial him now and give him the good news. Her phone was in the kitchen, so she headed back into the house, through the dining room, and into the kitchen. There was no sight of Marian; she guessed Marian was downstairs working.

Celia's phone was on the kitchen island counter. She picked it up and noticed a missed call. A 240 area code. No one in the area knew her telephone number except Liskey, so she promptly dialed the number back. After two rings, Liskey answered.

Before she could say hello, Liskey said, "Celia, I need your parents' names, address and telephone number."

"Why?" Celia asked.

Liskey had no time to explain, but he knew he couldn't force the information out of her, so he said, "We heard from the Canadian border police. Your husband's killer skipped the border into Canada. We think he may be headed for your parents' house, likely looking for you."

"Oh, my God."

"Celia, I don't have a lot of time. I need that address."

"Uh, 97 Connery Road, in Toronto."

"How many people live there?"

"Just my mom and my dad."

"I need their work addresses, too."

"Those were on my other phone. I don't remember them by heart. But you can look my dad up. He owns Wiseman's Grill. His name is George Wise. My mom is Marjorie."

"Where does your mom work?"

"She's a schoolteacher, but she transferred to a new school, and I don't know which one."

"Okay, now I need the telephone numbers, cell and home, if you have it."

Celia recited the information to him, then said with a

trembling voice, "I need to call them."

"No!" Liskey's voice was sharp, almost a shout. "Do not call them. Let us take care of that. We'll have special instructions for them. Stay off the line, and I'll call you when I know something."

"Oh, Lord." Celia drew a long breath.

"Celia, don't fall apart on me," Liskey said. "We're gonna do everything we can to protect your family. We gonna dispatch Toronto police to that address now. Just stay there and wait for my call."

Celia answered "yes" but had mind up her mind that if she hadn't heard from Liskey within the hour, she would call her dad anyway. It was one thing to put her life in limbo, but another for this nutjob to put her family in jeopardy.

If he did anything to hurt them, it would turn Celia into an entirely different person.

CHAPTER EIGHT

Canadian Taken

2:37 p.m., Friday

Within ten minutes, two Toronto police patrol cars, one unmarked, had pulled up to the curb in front of 97 Connery Road, a huge European-French Tudor-styled home on a tree-lined street directly across from a parkette.

The tall man sat on the other side of the parkette in a stolen plumbing van marked *Tobin's Mechanical*. He watched the goings-on through the driver's side window from the cargo area. He had dumped the Ford a half-hour earlier and stolen the van directly from a fleet lot from among thirty other vehicles. It would likely be hours, if not days, before the plumbing company realized it was missing. He had arrived at the parkette only a few minutes before the police arrived, but he had enough time to briefly case the house.

He watched three police officers emerge from their vehicles and fan out around the house, while two officers approached the front door. Based on their uniforms, their bullet-proof vests, their everyday clothes, he guessed these weren't ordinary police. Probably a task force of some type. That made the tall man smile. He was respected and feared enough to earn the attention of the city's elite. It would have been insulting for a rookie beat cop to search for him.

A minute later, the front door opened, and the tall man

watched as a slim man with short gray speckled hair spoke to the officers for a few seconds before inviting them inside. The other three officers, one of whom had migrated to the rear of the house, stood guard outside.

Too volatile, the tall man thought. His plans foiled again, he had to come up with a new scheme. He fished his smartphone out of his pocket, pulled up an internet browser, and looked up the name "George Wise." A guy with enough money to afford that house would be mentioned on the internet.

Within two minutes, he had found an article titled, "Detroit Man Takes on Church's." He continued to read, discovering that George Wise was once a chef who had worked at hotels and three-star restaurants before opening his first charbroiled chicken place, called Wiseman's Grill, offering a healthier, organic charbroiled chicken without affecting taste. Wise intended to take over Church's Chicken's market share. As his flagship location in Detroit, though successful, never grabbed Church's market share in Detroit, he opened stores in Ontario. Once expanding to Canada, his stores blossomed, and business publications were touting him as the next Colonel Sanders.

The tall man read further, learning more about the father of his target. He learned that George moved to Toronto to better manage his business and to escape his violent Detroit neighborhood, much to the chagrin of Detroit civic and church leaders, who decried that yet another successful black man who could help the city of Detroit with jobs and opportunities was running away. George ignored the criticism, believing he had a right to move wherever he wanted and that he owed nothing to Detroit, especially since Canada was more receptive and supportive of his business.

The tall man looked up from the article to check what was going on. The cops were still there. None seemed to have noticed the van or paid it any attention. He looked back down at his phone, reading something which heavily piqued his interest:

> *The move to Canada also uprooted one of Detroit's best teachers. Wise's wife, Marjorie, resigned from the history department at Detroit Technical High School, and now teaches at Havenhill Secondary, near the Forest Hill neighborhood of Toronto. Marjorie Wise came in second in a survey of the best teachers in Michigan in an independent poll conducted last year.*

He punched Havenhill Secondary in the browser and came up with an address only a ten-minute drive away. He looked up and saw a lone BMW parked in the Wise's driveway, leaving enough room for another vehicle to park. A couple that prosperous could afford more than one car. Marjorie Wise was likely not at home, but at Havenhill Secondary, preparing a generation for the challenges they would face in this crazy world.

He started the van and drove off, heading toward Havenhill.

***

In the living room of 97 Connery Road, two detective sergeants were giving George Wise the most harrowing news he had ever heard in his life.

"We believe your daughter is the target of a professional hit." Jim Peeks, one of the detective sergeants, spoke as matter-of-factly as if he were ordering a pizza. "The hit man is now in Canada, probably trying to find you so he can use you as leverage to fish your daughter out of hiding."

"Why is she the target of a hit?" George asked, wiping his brow.

"We don't know," Peeks said. "Information is a little

sketchy because it's coming from outside agencies. But we need to get you out of here and take you and your wife to a safe location. Where is your wife now?"

George looked confused. "She's at work."

"Where does she work? We'll send someone to get her."

"Uh, she works at Havenhill."

The other detective sergeant stood up and walked out the front door to tell some of his fellow officers to rush to Havenhill.

Peeks then addressed George. "Okay, I need you to go upstairs and get whatever clothes and belongings you and your wife will need for three days. Any prescription medicines or anything else crucial. The only exception is any electronic devices that communicate with the outside world. Those won't be allowed in the safe house. Do not worry about food or drink. And I will need the keys to your house."

George Wise stood and sighed. "This is crazy."

Peeks just looked at him.

George tried another appeal. "Sir, you should know that this house —"

"We know about that," Peeks interrupted. "I hope you don't mind that we don't trust it's enough to keep you safe."

George gave the officer a troubled frown. "How did you know about that?"

Peeks smiled. "A colleague of mine, when he was a constable, guarded this house in the '80s when it was owned by Trudy Bellerose."

"Oh." George Wise knew the history. Trudy Bellerose was a filthy rich, eccentric, and paranoid former actress who had bought the house during her heyday in the 70s. Believing her riches were in jeopardy and that unknown forces were out to get her, she had a fortified safe room constructed below the house, with entrances from the master bedroom and the basement. Bellerose passed away five years later, and the house served as a diplomatic mission until George bought it.

George tried again. "I have a meeting tomorrow with city leaders to discuss possibly partnering with some of the school lunch programs." George hoped for a compassionate response.

"You'll just have to postpone it."

"Sir, this is my business we are talking about here."

"Sir, I should hope the safety of your wife and daughter are the priority."

Frustrated, George said, "I know. I just...." He sighed again. "I was hoping I could just slip out for a quick meeting."

Peeks drew closer to George and looked at him sternly. "That won't be possible. You have to understand the seriousness of this situation. This guy that's chasing your daughter is the real deal. He's wanted by Border Services, RCMP, and about three or four agencies in the United States. We're not sure what he knows, whom he knows, or how he knows it. To be safe, you and your wife will need to disappear for the next few days. And we need to notify any other relatives you have in the area."

"No one," George told the detective. "All of my kids live in the U.S." With that, George disappeared down a hallway just off the living room, headed toward his study.

Jim Peeks walked outside just as a patrol car, its light bars flashing, darted down the street toward Havenhill. He spoke to the other detective sergeant. "Have a couple of unmarked units sit on this house, front and back. I'm heading to the Home Hardware to get a few of those outlet timers, put them on the lamps in the bedroom and living room to make the house look lived in, y'know. And make sure the officers we sent to Havenhill get Mrs. Wise's car and bring it back here."

"You think Isaac Roth will actually show up here?" the

other detective sergeant asked.

"If he's smart, he won't," Peeks said. "But, better safe than sorry."

***

2:50 p.m., Friday

Havenhill Secondary School, a two-story Gothic style structure veneered in gray limestone, sprawled across two city blocks. The tall man guided the van around the school twice, scanning all the exits, before he parked the van directly on the street, at the rear of the school, across from a rear door.

He sat there for a moment, looking at the school. It would be his first time entering a school since that horrendous day, the last day he saw his son alive. The memories seared him like a hot iron. He had thought to keep his son home from the academy that day, as the boy seemed groggy and out of sorts. Thinking the boy likely stayed up past his bedtime, he made him go to the academy anyway and then promised to pick him up that afternoon after his shift as an electrical engineer at a rail technology company.

Two hours after he dropped off his son, the boy committed suicide by somehow climbing to the roof of the five-story academy building and jumping off.

His first grief-stricken reaction was guilt, which soon morphed into anger and rage. After burying his son and enduring two weeks of mourning, he went into a seedy neighborhood in Vienna and inquired there about buying a gun on the black market. A week later, he held in his hands a 9 mm Glock, definitely a step down from the assault weapons he was trained on in the Jagdkommando.

He shook off the memories. Time was of the essence.

He got out of the van and walked around to the front of the school. He walked in the front entrance, his pistol and silencer taped under his shirt in his waistband and handcuffs in his rear pocket. A security guard signed him in. No metal detector. Obviously, school shootings weren't much of a concern here, he thought.

Around the corner and a few yards to the left was the main office. The tall man entered and smiled at the woman sitting at a desk behind the counter. The name tag on her desk read *Mrs. Bernbaum*. There was another woman in an office to his left. The nameplate just to the left of the door read *Vice Principal*.

"Hi, I am here to see Marjorie Wise." The tall man made no effort to disguise his accent.

"She's in class right now," Mrs. Bernbaum told him with a smile. "And our teachers are not allowed to receive visitors without an appointment."

"It's an emergency." The tall man cut an eye over to the left, where the vice-principal had emerged from her office.

Mrs. Bernbaum's smile gradually faded as she looked at him. "I can give you her office extension. You are welcome to leave a message, which she can return once she gets out of class. Are you a relative or friend?"

The tall man did not answer the question. Instead, he turned to leave.

After the tall man left, the vice-principal whispered to Mrs. Bernbaum. "That guy looked pretty intense."

"And he smells like he's been in the woods all night."

"Hmm." The vice-principal picked up the phone. "I'd better call the student resource officers, tell them to make sure this guy leaves the premises. I got a weird feeling about that guy."

***

"Where's Mrs. Wise's class?"

A sixteen-year-old kid, who barely knew his socks from his shoes, was all too eager to give this stranger the information he was asking for. "Down the hall, Room 123D."

"Thank you." The tall man continued quickly down the corridor, the walls lined with red recessed lockers, the floor glistening white. He passed another hallway, this one leading to a door at the rear of the school. He saw no security guards, or anyone else. A few doors down, he had arrived at Room 123D.

He peered inside the classroom through the window in the door. The teacher was striking, thin, swarthy, long hair down just beyond her shoulders, streaked with gray. High-heeled shoes, form-fitting gray slacks, and a white blouse completed her outfit. Fifteen students gave her their rapt attention as she lectured from the blackboard.

The tall man opened the door and poked his head inside. "Miss Wise?"

Marjorie turned toward him, as did the rest of the class. "May I help you?"

"I'm Mr. Smith. I'd like to talk to you about my daughter. Mrs. Bernbaum said I could just stop by." A closed-mouth smile accompanied the tall man's request.

Marjorie's frown registered both confusion and annoyance. *Why would Nadine Bernbaum send someone to interrupt my class? And I thought I had met all the parents at the start of the school year.* "I'm sorry, Mr. Smith, but you'll have to wait until my class is over. Perhaps I could meet you at the office?"

The tall man's smile disappeared. "It's very important."

Marjorie turned back to the class. "Please read page 69. I'll be back in a minute." Marjorie walked out to the hallway just as her cell phone buzzed inside her purse, tucked away in her desk drawer.

Marjorie faced the man and spoke to him in a tone she

would use with one of her misbehaving students. "Mr. Smith, if you want—"

She could barely get the words out before the tall man had his pistol out, the tip of the silencer pressed under her chin. "Shut up. Don't say a word unless I ask you a question. If you do, I will kill you. If you don't do exactly as I say, I will kill you. Do you understand? Blink if you do."

Marjorie stood frozen and blinked, her body feeling palpitations.

"Turn around and put your hands behind your back."

Marjorie's tone was friendlier this time. "Sir, if I could—"

Before she could finish, the tall man's bony knuckles connected with her left cheek, sending her reeling into a locker with a loud clang. Marjorie held her cheek in pain and looked at the tall man with tears in her eyes.

"I told you, don't say a word. That was your warning. There won't be another..."

Marjorie quickly nodded her understanding.

"Turn around and put your hands behind your back."

Marjorie quickly obeyed. The tall man removed the handcuffs from his back pocket, slapped them tightly on Marjorie's wrists, then grabbed her arm and led her down the hallway. Besides the muffled voices of teachers lecturing in their classrooms, the hallway was quiet and clear. The tall man picked up his pace, tugging Marjorie along, her high heels dragging on the floor.

The tall man heard the cough of a radio behind him. He pivoted, shoving Marjorie to the floor. A uniformed Toronto police officer, serving as a school resource officer, had just turned the corner from another hallway and happened upon the scene in front of him. The tall man waited, watching as the officer's eyes widened and his shoulder twitched. The officer was about to go for his gun.

The tall man fired, producing a sound like a plastic soda bottle bursting. The bullet crashed into the officer kneecap, sending him careening to the floor howling in pain. Marjorie screamed.

Not waiting for any other officers to show up, the tall man reached down, pulled Marjorie to her feet, and ran down the corridor, turning right at the hallway leading to the outside door. Marjorie alternated between running, stumbling over her shoes, and being dragged down the hall. When they reached the rear door, the tall man kicked the crash bar, forcing the door open. He stopped, looked around outside and, seeing no threats, jerked Marjorie down a flight of stairs and onto the concrete sidewalk leading to the street. One of her shoes fell off her feet and tumbled into a tuft of grass. The plumbing van was parked just a few yards away.

A young man and a woman came jogging out of an alley. They stopped, their brains in a fog, not believing what they were seeing, and not knowing what to do about it, especially since the man was holding a rather large gun. The tall man sized them up quickly and, certain they were no threat, pulled Marjorie toward the van. He opened the rear door of the van, tossed Marjorie in like a sack of laundry, and then grabbed a bundle of wire, intending to tie Marjorie's feet, and secure her to the cargo area of the van. But he heard sirens in the distance and quickly decided against it.

Instead, he gave Marjorie another warning, slammed the door, and then climbed into the driver's seat. He glared once again at the jogging couple before he started the van, did a U-turn, and raced down a side street in the opposite direction from where the sirens were coming.

***

"Son of a—" Liskey angrily kicked over a wastebasket that sat along the wall just outside of Room 317. Ramon, who had been inside the room finishing up a conversation with the evidence technician, came running out to the hallway.

He found the wastebasket tumbled over, some of its contents strewn out on the carpet. Liskey was standing there, looking at it, cell phone in hand, already feeling regret.

"Lisk, you okay?" Ramon studied Liskey's distressed face.

Liskey looked blankly at Ramon. "Sarge just called. Isaac Roth's got Celia's mother."

"What?" Ramon exclaimed loudly. "What the—"

Liskey explained. "Roth found out where she worked. He went to the school, pulled her out of the classroom, handcuffed her, and then shot a cop on the way out."

Ramon shook his head. "Whoa."

"I may not have probable cause on my case, but between Toronto and D.C., they got enough to put this guy in prison for the rest of his cursed life."

"I don't know about that, dude. D.C.'s in the same boat we are. None of us can connect this guy to the shootings with any certainty."

"Well, he messed up. After he shot that cop, they're not gonna let him get out of Toronto in one piece, that's for sure."

"So, no trace of the guy?"

"None."

"It's Charlie-tango, that's for sure."

"So, now everybody's waiting to see what this guy's next play is. He didn't abduct that woman just because he was lonely."

"Probably using her to draw out Celia."

Liskey leaned back against the wall and let out a long breath. "I still don't know what this guy's story is. He's going after good, honest, hardworking people. I can understand if they were into some dirt. But to go after a pastor, and then a housewife, and then a school teacher? That baffles me."

Ramon, who had long been used to Liskey being the voice

of wisdom between them, now had wise words for Liskey. "Yeah, but keep in mind. Celia's the only thing connecting all those people. I still think there's something that's not being said."

Liskey reached down and gently picked up the trash from the carpet and returned it to the wastebasket. "Listen, why don't you go and see Justin's family, give them an update on the case. Also, why don't you try to find out if there's anything about Celia and Justin that Celia's not telling us."

"Roger that. What are you gonna do?"

"I'm going to go home, press Celia again. Maybe the knowledge of her mother being in the hands of a homicidal lunatic will loosen her resolve and get us the information we need."

***

It was 4 p.m. when Liskey arrived home. He found the living room empty but heard the TV in the family room. A quick trek across the dining room and he was in the family room, where Marian had convinced Celia to watch a 60s era movie with her. Liskey smiled. Marian had gotten her new friend to do something she got Liskey to do only once — while they were dating. He hated those old movies and would have no part of them.

Marian looked up and smiled when he entered. "You're home early today."

"Maybe," Liskey shifted his eyes to Celia, then back to Marian. "Honey, where's Graham?"

Marian noticed the intense look in his eyes and knew something was wrong. "He's down the street at Travis' house."

"Can you give us a minute? I need to discuss with Celia some details about the case."

"Sure." Marian stood and walked over to Liskey. She

kissed him, then left, affectionately dragging her hand along Liskey's shoulder as she passed him.

Celia looked up at Liskey. Something about his demeanor told her this would not be a pleasant conversation. She braced herself for whatever was to come.

Liskey sat on the love seat across from Celia. He reached for the remote, paused the movie, and took a sip of a sweating glass of Coke that Marian had left on the side table. "Hello, Miss Celia."

Celia managed a quiet "hey."

Liskey took a breath, then spoke. "We heard some news from our counterparts in Toronto. It looks like Mr. Roth has kidnapped your mother."

"Oh, sweet Jesus!" Celia's body slumped, and she turned to look toward the floor at nothing in particular.

Liskey felt embarrassed at having failed Celia even though he had nothing to do with it. "She was in class teaching. Mr. Roth walked in the school, coaxed your mother out of class, and then handcuffed her and marched her out a back door. He shot a cop on his way out."

Celia's head moved steadily from side to side. "Oh, my God."

"He was..."

Celia interrupted with, "What about my dad? Where is he?"

"He's safe. He's on his way to a safe house somewhere in Toronto."

"Does my dad know about Mom?"

"I doubt it. And we want to keep it that way for now. We don't need him going off the deep end."

"Sounds like you know my dad well."

"But the problem is that we don't know where Roth is. Nobody does. They got BOLOs in every district up there, but until we find him, we don't know what his next play is."

Celia banged her fist on her thigh, not caring about the

pain. "I should have gone up there when she first asked me. Maybe if I had done that…"

Liskey stopped her with, "Now, don't start blaming yourself for this. What you need to do is be one hundred percent truthful with me."

"What are you talking about?" Celia snapped. "I've been—"

"Celia, this kind of guy doesn't go around committing murder and kidnapping for nothing. He's a professional killer. He's getting paid a lot of money to do this. And unless this guy tips his hand somehow, the quickest way we're going to find him is to find out who's paying him. If he makes contact with whoever's paying him, we may be able to find out where he is. So, I need you to tell me *everything* you know about this."

Celia was on the verge of tears. "I've told you!"

"Tell me again. Maybe there's something you missed."

"Tell you what?"

"Start from the beginning. Tell me about that day. Everything. Step by step. From start to finish. Don't leave anything out."

"Jesus." Celia sighed, reached up to dry a tear, then recounted her day from the moment she woke until the moment she saw the murder and ran for the safety of an office building lobby. When Celia talked about her interview with the reporter, Liskey stopped her.

"Hold it. What was this reporter's name?"

Celia thought for a moment. "I don't remember. I think his card is in my purse."

"Why don't you get it for me?" Liskey ordered.

Celia stood, gave Liskey a disgusted face, and left. Five minutes later, she returned with the card and gave it to Liskey.

"Wynn Delano," Liskey read. "So, what happened next?"

"Nothing." Celia gave Liskey a sharp attitude. "He asked

more questions, then he was done. He asked me on a date. He said the interview would air that evening, but it never did."

Liskey leaned forward. "What do you mean 'it never did'?"

"It never aired. Just a reporter talking about the shooting, but no interview."

"You mean a news channel had a reporter on site of a major event, and there's no on-air news coverage of the shooting?"

"I didn't see any. Of course, I didn't have a chance to check the next morning."

"Hmm." Liskey leaned back. The pastor's shooting occupied a huge block of time on almost all the evening newscasts. Why would NewsNetwork 10 have a reporter on site, but air no coverage? Liskey ruminated on that for a moment, then returned his focus to Celia. "So, what happened next?"

"I drove home."

"Where did you park when you were downtown?"

"On the street, about a block away. I even got a parking ticket."

"Where is it?"

"The car?"

"No, the ticket."

"I left it in my car. I'm surprised you guys didn't search it already."

"We need a warrant for that. Unless you're giving us permission to search the vehicle."

"Sure. I've got nothing to hide. I keep telling you that." Celia wiped at another tear running down her eye.

Liskey looked away. Celia's tears were getting to him. He knew it. There were perps in the interrogation room that would turn on the waterworks under hard questioning, and Liskey would never bat an eye. But here he was, feeling a strange empathy for this girl. Her tears seemed genuine. He would not have lasted long in the homicide business if he couldn't tell the difference.

Liskey believed Celia. But he knew his partner wouldn't, nor would any other cop. He decided to check out the news reporter and find out what he saw. If he confirmed Celia's story, at least he would feel much better trusting this woman staying in his house with his family.

****

Thirty minutes later, Liskey was back in his cubicle at Headquarters, much to the chagrin of his wife and son. While Ramon was in Leesburg meeting with Justin's family, Liskey was determined to talk to the reporter and run out this dangling string on his case.

Out of respect for his fellow cops in D.C., Liskey needed to call the lead detective on the pastor's shooting before he interviewed anyone that might be connected solely to that shooting. A quick check of a police database and he had the detective's name and number. He dialed, hoping the detective was not working the midnight shift.

The call was answered quickly. A deep voice said, "MPD. Anderson."

"Hey, this is Detective Frank Liskey with Montgomery County Homicide. How's it going?"

"Can't complain, partner. You the lead on that Silver Spring shooting?"

"Yep."

"Surprised we ain't been talking much, since we're both chasing the same suspect." Anderson's words mixed with chuckles.

"How about that? Any more leads?"

"Naw. Just a name and a face. And we wouldn't even have that if it wasn't for you guys. So, you got my gratitude for that. We just need to connect him to that scene. We know he did the shooting from Room 1010, but we got no physical evidence. Not even GSR. Nothing."

"I'm told he's very meticulous."

"More like he broke into that room just after a couple had checked out of it and then rolled out just before the housekeepers cleaned it. We can get him on breaking and entering, but that's it."

"You hear about Canada?" Liskey asked.

"Yeah, man. Got an alert on it about fifteen minutes ago. Shot a cop, too?"

"Yep."

"That's gonna freeze both our cases. If the cops up there got any cojones at all, that guy ain't gonna make it out of Toronto alive." Anderson let out another chuckle.

"Yeah. But I got another matter."

"What's that, buddy?"

"You heard of a reporter named Wynn Delano?" Liskey asked.

"Can't say I have. What's his deal?"

"He interviewed my witness for a story about the Freedom Plaza shooting, but it never made it on the air. You ever hear of such a thing?"

"It's been all over the news for the past few days. It's even gone national. Hard to believe any local station wouldn't want to hop all on it. What's the station?"

"NewsNetwork 10."

"Not the top news market, but big enough to have covered this. Was he there when it happened?"

"He might have gotten some of it on tape."

"Really? How did we miss that?"

"So, you wouldn't mind if I talked to him?"

"Naw. As long as I can tag along."

"You bet. Thanks, dude."

"No problem. Call me and let me know where to meet you."

After hanging up with Anderson, Liskey dialed Wynn Delano's cell number from the card, but the call went straight to voice mail. Liskey dialed NewsNetwork 10's main number, then hung up, thinking it would be better to visit the station in person, show his face, present his badge. If Wynn Delano was there, he could speak to him face-to-face and discover where things led.

Chapter nine

Celia had no desire to finish watching the movie. She had no appetite, although Marian had prepared lasagna and tried ardently, though unsuccessfully, to get Celia to eat. She sat in the family room, seemingly catatonic, although occasionally she would dip her head into her hands and weep. Though her body seemed still, her mind was active, as she constantly thought about her mother and father and what sin she had committed that would cause such an evil to befall them. She had decided that if Roth wanted to trade her mother for her, that she would gladly make the exchange. But if Roth killed her mother, it would practically kill her, too.

What did this man want? Why was he attacking her family like this? After coming up with more questions than answers, she finally decided this was an unspeakable act with no reason or purpose. Her mother was in the throes of pure evil—a man who would slaughter Celia's husband, gun down a prominent pastor, and then come after her with a relentless vigor. It made her feel overwhelmingly feeble. Even if she had all the weapons in the world, she could do nothing now but wait to see what card Mr. Roth would play. And Celia hoped he would play it quick, because the thought of her mother in Mr. Roth's control made her heart ache and her body tense.

She sat there for over two hours, with the only light coming from the paused visage of Cary Grant on the TV screen. Marian came in periodically just to check on her, until it became clear, based on Celia's failure to acknowledge her, that maybe it would be best to leave Celia alone. This was not grief, but it was awful close.

Celia knew her father felt the same way. He was likely angry enough to literally tear up the town looking for his wife. Celia knew her father well enough to know that with Marjorie, he feared nothing and would stop at nothing to protect her and his children.

When Celia was growing up, George Wise's reputation in the neighborhood was that of a friendly, fair, but stern man who would quickly become dangerous if anyone threatened his family. Folks in the community knew that George Wise kept guns in the house and that he had a concealed pistol license. The teasing, horseplay, and bullying heaped upon other kids, George Wise's kids were mostly exempt from. But George was fair. If his kids caused any trouble, and then tried to get out of it by playing the *my daddy has a gun* card, George would make sure that his kids were disciplined according to the offense.

If only she could talk to someone from her family. Her father was squirreled away in some safe house, barred from any contact with the outside world. The telephone numbers of her brothers and sisters were in her old phone, which was now in the evidence room at the Montgomery County police headquarters. She regretted not remembering the numbers, and she hated that all her siblings had unlisted numbers to cut down on telemarketing calls. She wondered if they had heard what was going on. But she knew where each of her siblings lived, and she had tossed around in her mind going to visit one or more of them. She doubted they knew anything going on, and she needed their support more than anything.

But Frank Liskey was her pipeline of information from

Canada, and she didn't want to do anything to cut off access from him if she needed him. And if Roth broke his silence by requesting her in exchange for her mother, she would need the detective more than ever.

The feelings of isolation and uselessness swept through her and chilled her to her bones. There was nothing to do but sit and wait. She knew that. But even as she settled on that plan of inaction, her mind activated words from her past, jogging a remote area of her memory:

Wait on the Lord: be of good courage, and he shall strengthen thine heart: wait, I say, on the Lord.

It was not in a Bible study or church service where Celia first heard those words. Her mother had whispered those words to her when she was sixteen years old and trying out for a highly coveted spot on the cheerleading squad at her high school. When she did not make the team and fell into a depressed funk, Marjorie whispered Psalm 27:14 to her. She said nothing else, allowing the scripture to take hold and heal her wounded heart.

The next year, Celia tried out and made the squad. Her mother whispered the words again. Only this time, Celia got the message. There was no sense in being discouraged about something she couldn't control. Wait on the Lord, and He would bless her in due season. But waiting, her mother later explained, was never done silently. She had to sing, worship, and pray, because she believed something would happen, and worship created the atmosphere for the blessings to come. Celia was sure that wherever her mother was, she had a song in her heart.

Celia hadn't prayed regularly in a few years. The busyness of D.C. city life had choked the desire out of her. To her, prayer seemed ineffectual and a total waste of time, because whenever she prayed, nothing happened. Now, it was the only thing left to do.

Celia broke herself out of her stupor and fell to her knees in front of the coffee table. There was no prayer closet here like her father had in their home in Detroit. But this room, meant for family leisure time, had now become her prayer closet.

Celia looked upward, closed her eyes, and prayed earnestly, asking God to protect her family, and especially her mother. And she also prayed for Isaac Roth, that he would listen to the voice of God and abandon his murderous ways.

But mostly, she prayed for understanding on why a contract killer would seek a suburban housewife who had done no wrong to him or anyone else.

***

Liskey pulled into the parking lot of the NewsNetwork 10 studios in Falls Church, Virginia. As he got out of his car, another man got out of a late model Ford Taurus. Detective Anderson was a beefy fellow whom Liskey knew he would not want to get into a fight with. The D.C. detective wore blue jeans and a white polo shirt, his badge hanging around his neck, his short hair and goatee framing a face with thick eyebrows and almost squinting eyes. The two detectives met in the middle of the parking lot, exchanged introductions, and shook hands.

"Thanks for calling me," said Detective Anderson.

"No problem," Liskey replied. "Like I told you on the phone, not sure where this will lead, but I have to play it out."

"I'll let you take point. If I need to chime in, I will."

Liskey nodded, and they both headed into the building.

When they walked into the lobby, they found a square receptionist desk with a huge backlighted number 10 on the wall behind it. The blonde sitting behind the desk was trying not to be rude to the rotund security guard flirting with her. There was a waiting area to the left of the desk, inside a small alcove with a brown leather couch and a 30-inch monitor playing the live 6 pm newscast. When the security guard saw that the visitors were cops, he quickly stood, moved a few steps away, and tried much too late to look professional.

"Hi, my name is Detective Frank Liskey. I'm with—"

Before Liskey could get out another word, she said, "Yes, hold on" and was on the phone.

Two minutes later, a man wearing a gray suit emerged from a side door and approached the detectives. "Detectives, my name is Lawrence Hensley. I'm the general manager here. Thank you for coming so soon."

Liskey gave a confused frown. "I wasn't aware I was invited." He looked at Anderson. "I never called ahead."

"You're from missing persons, correct?" Lawrence asked.

"No. I'm from Montgomery County homicide." Liskey presented his badge to Lawrence and gestured to Anderson. "This is Detective Anderson, D. C. Police, CID."

Lawrence looked at the badge for a second, pasting the same confused look on his face that Liskey had on his. "Wait a minute, you're here about our reporter, Wynn Delano, right?"

"Yes, we are. But why did you think we were from missing persons?"

Lawrence cut an eye at both the receptionist and the security guard, then used his access badge to open the side door and beckoned the detectives inside. Once they were just inside and the door closed, Lawrence said, "Mr. Delano was sent out on assignment two days ago to D.C. He reported in a couple of times since then, but we haven't heard from him since."

"The Freedom Plaza shooting?" Anderson asked.

"Yes. When a reporter is on assignment and doesn't report in within a reasonable period of time, our policy is to exercise due diligence to find out where he is. We've contacted his emergency numbers. We've been by his house. No luck. That's when we filed a report with the D.C. police, and they called us back a couple of hours ago saying they would send a detective over. That's whom I thought you were."

Liskey tossed a look over to Detective Anderson. Anderson caught the non-verbal cue and pulled his cell phone out of his jacket pocket. "Let me check with missing persons, see if they have a file open." He dialed his phone and then stepped to a remote corner of the room.

Liskey pulled a pad and pen from his pocket and took notes. He didn't want to wait until Missing Persons showed up since he was pressed for time. "You said you went by Delano's house?"

"Yes. I went myself."

"What happened?"

"I knocked. There was no answer. His SUV wasn't in his driveway."

"Wasn't he sent out in a news van and with a crew? What happened to them?"

Lawrence seemed annoyed at the question. "We only use a van and crew with major stories. The Freedom Plaza thing wasn't major to us when we assigned Delano to cover it, so he used his personal vehicle..."

Liskey interrupted with "Wasn't major? A shooting of a prominent pastor in the middle of downtown Washington?"

"No, detective, you don't understand. We assigned him to cover the pastor's rally. He just happened to be there when the pastor was shot. When he told us what had happened, we sent a crew to the scene. By the time they got there, Delano was gone."

"What kind of car did he have?"

"A Ford Escape, late model, black."

Liskey continued writing. "Mind giving me Delano's home address?"

"Uh, no." Lawrence pulled a cell phone from his pocket and punched up the address. He gave it to Liskey, then asked a final question. "Detective, may I ask how Montgomery County is connected to this?"

"He's connected to a case I am working." Liskey left it at that.

***

About an hour later, Liskey and Anderson's vehicles pulled up in front of Delano's house on 41900 Yuma Street in northwest Washington, D.C. The detectives got out of their cars and gave the house a visual once-over. It was a boxy split-level home separated from neighboring houses by about five yards of lush, healthy lawn and bookended by shrubbery. The driveway leading to the garage was empty. A dog's chew toy lay astray on the front lawn. The street was quiet, and the sun was unforgiving, heating the air to 85 degrees even in the early evening.

Liskey approached the house, opened the storm door, and knocked. Anderson stood a few feet away, checking windows for any movement while Liskey knocked. Liskey expected to hear a dog's barking, if nothing else, but heard no sound. He knocked four more times before he concluded that Delano was not at home. He reached into his jacket pocket, pulled out one of his business cards, found a pen in his other pocket, and jotted a note on the rear of the card. *Call me ASAP regarding someone you interviewed.* It was just the right information to leave Delano curious enough to call him as soon as he read the card.

Liskey knelt and opened the mail slot, tossing the card inside. He felt a blast of cool air through the mail slot from the air conditioning in the home. But although the air was refreshing, the stench was revolting and nauseating.

Liskey quickly closed the mail slot and stood. He knew that smell. As a homicide detective, he had smelled it often, and eventually got used to it, although it still repulsed him, especially during the first few minutes of a crime scene investigation. *It was the smell of death.* But he had to be careful; he recalled the story of one cop who broke into an apartment after getting complaints about a putrid smell, only to find that the person who owned the apartment was on vacation and hadn't dumped the trash before he left.

Since there was no vehicle, no dog, and no other evidence that Delano was there, Liskey hoped the smell was from rotting trash. But he doubted it.

He turned to Anderson. "Something stinks in there."

"Think it might be a body?"

"I'm almost sure of it."

A woman, in her sixties, with a brown and white beagle on a leash, headed toward them from next door. Liskey turned toward her, allowing her to see the badge hanging from a lanyard around his neck. When the woman saw the badge, she took in a deep breath.

"Officers, officers." She stopped within three feet of the detectives. The beagle sniffed around Liskey's ankles. "I'm so glad you're here. I'm Doris Phillips, Mr. Delano's next-door neighbor. I've been trying to reach Mr. Delano for a few days now, and I haven't been successful. I think something's wrong."

"What makes you say that?" Liskey said.

"Because this is his dog," Doris told him. "Mr. Delano sometimes leaves his dog with me when he's at work, just so the dog doesn't always get lonely. But usually, he's back home after work. But I've had his dog for three days, and I haven't heard from him."

"Do you have a number to reach him?" Liskey asked.

"I do, and I've called it. There's no answer, and he hasn't

returned any of my calls."

"You said *usually* he's back home after work. Not always?"

"Occasionally he hangs out with buddies after work. But that's it."

"Does Mr. Delano own this house?"

"He does. Bought it about a year ago."

"Is there any place you can think of where he might have gone?"

Doris thought for a moment. "Well, he has no wife, no children. I think his family lives in upstate New York. Maybe you should check his job. I'm just really concerned. I would have called the police by tomorrow if you hadn't shown up today."

"We'll look into it, ma'am. Would you be willing to give us Mr. Delano's cell phone number?"

"I sure can. I just need to go into my house and get it." Doris walked toward her front lawn.

"One more question, Miss Doris."

The woman stopped and turned.

"Has anyone been by this house in the past few days?"

"Not that I know of."

"Thanks, Miss Doris."

Liskey watched until the woman had disappeared into her home. He turned to Detective Anderson.

"You married, detective?" Liskey asked.

"Five years and counting."

"Well then, you may want to call her, tell her you'll be late getting home. I'll bet my next five paychecks you just caught a murder."

CHAPTER TEN

Dead Ends

After a quick visit to Headquarters and a stop at the A&W for carryout burgers and fries, three plainclothes detectives loaded George Wise and one rolling suitcase of his belongings into the back of a conversion van. The van's windows were tinted so dark he could not see out of them. One of the officers rode in the back with him, and the other two sat up front, shielded by a curtained metal grate. George wondered if he was being protected, or were the cops protecting him from others. Except for the relatively plush seats in the back, the vehicle could have doubled as a perp van.

George made chit-chat with the officer throughout the 2-hour trip to wherever they were going. Once the van arrived at the destination, the two officers got out and opened the doors for George and the third officer to exit the vehicle. George looked around and noticed an idyllic paved country road adorned with two houses. The safe house was a typical white siding ranch with a single-car garage and a wide front yard bordered with 6-foot tall trees. The area did not look familiar, and George noticed no street signs to clue him in on their location. Between a clearing in the trees, he noticed a body of water in the distance.

"Detective Hall, where are we?" George asked the cop who had ridden with him in the back of the van.

"Nottawa," one cop answered.

"Is that Lake Huron over there?"

"Yep."

"Nice."

"It's Sergeant Peeks' getaway house."

George nodded approval. *Better to be hid in the boonies than some hole-in-the-wall over in Regent Park.* "Is my wife here?"

Detective Hall diverted his eyes. "Let's go inside."

George wasn't sure he liked that response. But he picked up his suitcase and followed the detectives inside the house. The modest living room was furnished with a black leather sofa and love seat, a marble coffee table, and bookshelves lining almost every inch of the walls.

George scanned the bookshelves. "Lot of books."

"Yeah," Detective Hall motioned George to a seat on the couch. "Peeks and his wife do a lot of reading. They don't do much TV."

George smiled as he sat. He was not a big fan of TV either. "I can relate." Returning to the matter foremost in his heart, he asked, "Where's my wife?"

Detective Hall whispered something to the other officers, and they walked out the front door. George watched them until they left, and then turned back to Detective Hall, his eyes beckoning the detective for a response.

Detective Hall sighed and plopped down on the loveseat.

George frowned and squeezed his eyes shut. "Please don't tell me she's dead."

"No," Detective Hall quickly reassured him. "She's not dead. Well, actually, we don't know."

George added a look of confusion to the pain already on his face.

"Isaac Roth kidnapped her from the school about two hours ago."

"Aw, no!" George got up from the couch and paced the room, crying out "No!" and "Jesus!" almost every three seconds, his head hung back, his mouth agape. He banged the soft part of his fist against the the wall in an area not covered by a bookshelf. He ran his hand firmly across his head before he looked up at Hall and asked, "What happened? I thought you guys were going to pick her up."

"Isaac Roth got there before we did. He just walked in the school and pulled her out of class. He shot a cop on the way out."

"Oh, Jesus, Lord!" George turned to the window and hung his head. His mind racing in a million directions, he had to focus on something positive, as he did not believe that God would bring him this far in life just to have his wife killed by a madman. "So, if he was going to kill her, he would have done it at the school, right?"

Detective Hall was pleased that George had gone through his initial shock and grief reaction. "Yeah. He's probably using her as leverage to get to your daughter. But don't worry. Your daughter is being protected in Maryland. He won't get to her as long as she does what she's told."

George scoffed. "You sure about that?"

"What do you mean?"

"Celia is my youngest, and she's also the most headstrong. She's not one to follow directions. If she hears about her mother, she'll do whatever it takes to save her mother. As would I."

Detective Hall stood. "Well, I can't stress strongly enough that both you and your daughter allow the authorities to take care of this."

"Yeah? What if I decide to walk out of here right now?"

"We won't stop you. You're not under arrest. You're not incarcerated. We're doing this for your family's protection, and I hope you respect that and help us to keep you safe."

George held back his pending vitriol. "I know, and I appreciate that. I know you guys are doing your best."

"Thank you for saying that." Detective Hall nodded.

"How's the cop?"

"Got shot in the knee. Probably not gonna walk right

again for the rest of his life."

"I'll pray for him. We'll let God decide whether he walks right or not."

"I'm sure Constable Olson would appreciate that. I'll pass the word." Detective Hall let a few seconds of awkward silence go by before he spoke again. "So, the house is yours. Just a few ground rules. We advise that you do not communicate with the neighbors. Stay on the property. One of our people will make sure you have food and everything else you need. There's a TV in the master bedroom down the hall. There's also a telephone there, but it'll only work for calling 911. Again, we advise you not to try to contact anyone in your family right now, not even your children who are out of town."

"Is there a computer? I need it for my business."

"One of our detectives will bring you a laptop with a secure, encrypted connection."

"Encrypted. Goodness." George reached down for his suitcase. "You'd think with all these precautions and security, this guy must be a regular Chester Wheeler Campbell."

"Who's that?" Detective Hall asked.

"Sorry. Local reference. Old school Detroit. But anyway..." George started toward the hallway. "I'm going to go lie down for a minute. I have a serious headache."

"Anything I can do?"

"Just find my wife. And keep my baby Celia safe, whatever you do."

***

Liskey sat in his car, relaxing in the air conditioning, listening to his Neil Diamond greatest hits CD, waiting for Detective Anderson, who was sitting in his own car, to get approval for a search warrant.

While waiting, Liskey touched base with Ramon. Justin's

parents had nothing new to add; to hear them tell it, Justin was about as squeaky clean as the pope. They blamed Celia for not being as supportive as she could, for being an arrogant, pompous, preening daddy's girl so used to being kept she couldn't fathom getting a job to help while Justin struggled.

It was another hour before Detective Anderson stepped out of his car. The sun had set, the street lights were on, and there was still a blue haze in the sky. Liskey glanced at his dashboard clock and saw that it was 8:45 p.m.

Liskey got out of his car and met Detective Anderson at the edge of the lawn.

"No dice on the warrant," Detective Anderson reported. "Probable cause is weak. We need more. All we got is a missing guy and a stinky house. None of that proves a crime."

Liskey frowned. "So, are you saying we both go home and let this guy rot inside his own house?"

"No. I'm saying we gotta get something more."

"Like, wait until this guy starts smelling up the entire neighborhood?"

"In that case, it's a public nuisance, and we can break the door down." Detective Anderson's sharp tone revealed his annoyance. "Until then, I get Missing Persons down here, have them canvass the neighborhood, put out a BOLO on his car. This is their case, anyway."

Liskey had nothing else to say. It was Anderson's jurisdiction, and he knew the system and politics in this town much better than he. He watched as Anderson got on his cell phone and dialed someone at D.C. headquarters. Shortly after, his own phone rang. He stepped away from Anderson and took the call from his duty sergeant. The three-minute conversation with the duty sergeant produced both scoffs and stern head shakes from Liskey.

After he hung up, Liskey eagerly moved back over to Anderson to share the latest news he had received. "Guess what?"

"What?" said Anderson.

"Delano's vehicle was found."

"Really? Where?"

"In Toronto, in some woods about a mile from the border."

Anderson's eyebrows went up.

"Yeah. Isaac Roth was driving Wynn Delano's vehicle when he skipped the border.

"Well, I'll be…"

"And they found blood in it. A lot of blood. And it ain't Roth's."

Anderson dropped his head and breathed out loud.

Liskey gave him a smug smirk. "You think you got enough PC now?"

***

11:04 pm

The plumbing van sat in an empty parking space on Roxborough Avenue in East Hamilton, a city at the western point of Lake Ontario about 42 miles from Toronto. The tall man had been sitting in the driver's seat for hours, waiting patiently for night to fall and for foot traffic to die down. It was finally time to make his move.

He got out of the van, opened the rear door, pushed the muzzle of his gun against Marjorie's cheek, and warned her that if she resisted, screamed, or did anything out of the ordinary, he would execute her on the spot.

Something about this man made her believe him.

The tall man grabbed Marjorie's forearm and snatched her out of the van with such force that her other shoe came off. He pulled her to her feet and wrapped his arm around her waist as if he were a jealous lover. With his bag on his other shoulder, he looked around and then guided her down a dark street between an elementary school on one side and a neat row of well-kept bungalows on the other. She reluctantly walked down the street with him, hoping that someone would notice them and call the police, but at this late hour, it seemed as if no one was out. Finally, the tall man saw *him*.

The 19-year-old, whose only mistake was to own a conversion van and to be just getting home from work when the tall man happened by, climbed out of his van, turned, and saw the muzzle of a gun just inches from his face.

Within two minutes, the tall man had the keys to the conversion van, had forced both the 19-year-old and Marjorie through the side door of the van, had threatened them both with death if they tried to escape, and then began the hour-long journey back to Toronto.

On the way back along the lonely highway, his mind drifted again. He had never killed anyone while in the Jagdkommando special forces, which was why he held on to the Glock for about two months before he finally had the nerve to use it. His wife, who was pierced by their son's suicide and received no support from her increasingly distant husband, one day packed a suitcase full of her belongings and left the home, never to return. Now, having lost his entire family and allowing bitterness to take hold, it was much easier for him to do what he had been contemplating. Twenty years of entrenched Catholicism could not stop him now. No amount of *Hail Marys* or *Glory Be* prayers would soften his heart. There was a priest who had taken indecent liberties with his son, and he would not forgive that. His son could not live with the tormenting effects of that encounter, and the priest would have to pay. With his life.

It was this moment that turned the mild-mannered Alexander Koffler into Isaac Roth, an assassin with a particular hatred of anything having to do with God.

Focus, focus, focus.

Returning his mind to the present, the tall man sped up, hoping to get back to Toronto before anyone spotted the plumbing van or realized that the 19-year-old was missing.

***

Once he arrived back in Toronto, the tall man climbed into the back of the van and ordered the teen to call whomever he lived with, using the tall man's his satellite phone, and tell them that if they wanted the teen to live, they would have to call the Hamilton Police emergency line and tell them that a tall white man had just dumped a plumbing company van on Roxborough Avenue and that he was walking up the street with a well-dressed shoeless black woman.

It was a credible ruse. He knew the police were looking for a plumbing van. Once they found the dumped van in Hamilton, it would draw a huge police response to the area. That much he was certain of.

What was less certain was whether the second part of his plan would work. He sat, with his two captives in the rear of the conversion van, watched and waited.

***

Two doors up and across the street from 97 Connery, an unmarked unit sat in the driveway of a brown brick Georgian style house. The two plainclothes constables inside enjoyed a vantage point where the car blended in with its surroundings, yet they could still observe 97 Connery without binoculars. Alongside a street at the rear of the house, another unit sat, its officers paying close attention to any movement around the perimeter of the house.

The two constables on Connery knew that because they

were the lowest among the rank and file, they would have to do things that seasoned cops hated, such as sitting on houses in quiet neighborhoods for hours looking for criminals that likely would never show up. At least that's what Rick Denton thought as he yawned for the umpteenth time and only occasionally lifted his eyes to look at 97 Connery Road. He spent the rest of the time surfing on his smartphone in-between binges of high-calorie snack food and 7-Eleven coffee.

His partner, Jimmy Markell, on the approaching side of twenty-five, threw his head back into the headrest and let out a breath so hard it sent an empty potato chip bag on the dashboard into a pirouette. "I hope our relief gets here on time. I am *so* ready to get out of this car."

"Well, like our bosses say, it's part of the job," Rick stated. "Heck, I did security at a power plant for a year before this. This was a cake walk compared to that. At least on these stakeouts, you get to see a cute girl every now and then."

"Not on this one. All I've seen is silver foxes."

"Better than being at the power plant looking at guys in hazmat suits all day. You know what they look like with those suits and masks on?"

"What?"

"You ever see those old episodes of Star Trek? The classic ones with Spock in them?"

"Yeah. My dad tried to get me to watch them. Said they were the best Star Treks." What Jimmy left out is that he thought they were boring. He was a kid firmly ensconced in the Star Wars generation.

"You ever see the one with the salt monster?"

"The what?"

"The salt monster. This creature that kills people by sucking all the salt out of them."

Rick's cell phone rang the whistling part of Maroon 5's *Moves like Jagger.*

Jimmy sat up straight. "Must've missed that one."

"Well, you should see it. That's what those guys at the power plant look like when they wear those suits." Rick punched the screen of his phone and put it to his ear. After saying "hello", the conversation seemed to consist of Rick responding with *uh-huhs* and *okays* for three minutes before he finally said, "Roger that" and ended the call.

"The boss?" Jimmy guessed.

"Yep." Rick slipped the phone into his side jeans pocket and started the car. "They're pulling us off the stakeout. Somebody down in East Hamilton just saw Isaac Roth dump a plumbing company van down there. Said he left the van there and was walking up Roxborough Avenue with his arm around some shoeless black lady who didn't look like she was happy to be with him."

"Marjorie Wise."

"Yep. HPS has got road blocks set up. They don't think he left the area. They're getting an assist from OPP. They think they'll have him within the hour."

Jimmy nodded. "That's good news."

"Good news for them, and good news for us. We get to go home an hour early."

"Well, let's get outta here before somebody changes their mind."

"Roger that."

Rick put the car in gear, pulled out of the driveway, and made a right on Connery. At this late hour, it was virtually a ten-minute cruise back to the station house.

The tall man, waiting in the van on the other side of the parkette, watched them drive off.

He smiled.

***

It took another two hours for the warrant to be processed

and Anderson to arrange for Second District officers and the Mobile Crime Lab to meet him at the scene. While several curious neighbors gathered outside to watch, Anderson started positioning the officers around the house, ordering two to cover the rear and one on each side. He, Liskey and the two remaining officers would enter through the front door, while the crime scene technicians would wait outside until everything was clear.

Once the men were in position, one officer banged on the front door and yelled, "Police! Search Warrant!"

After they got no response, the officer tried twisting the door knob and was surprised to find the door unlocked. He kicked it open, and an odor worse than 40 dead rats assaulted his nostrils. He drew back, and then, deciding he could not enter, stepped away from the front door, his hand covering his mouth and nose. Anderson and Liskey looked briefly at one another before Anderson mouthed the word *rookie*.

Anderson and Liskey stepped in front of the officer and took the lead. With their right hands near their still-holstered service weapons, they entered the house, breathing through their mouths as much as possible to avoid the smell. Another officer headed upstairs, while Liskey and Anderson quickly searched the main floor, clearing the living room, the kitchen, the dining area, and the garage. Once the officer upstairs had yelled downstairs that the upstairs was clear, Liskey and Anderson set their sights on the closed basement door.

Anderson pulled the door open and flipped on a light switch just beyond the door. They slowly headed down the carpeted stairs, finding themselves in a wide room furnished only with a black leather couch, a 60-inch flat screen TV hanging on a wall, a cocktail table, and an elliptical machine in a far corner. Seeing nothing unusual within view, while noticing that the smell grew more intense, Anderson and Liskey split up, with Liskey going to the right toward another section of the room with two closed doors, and Anderson turning left, walking down a hallway toward another set of rooms.

Liskey drew closer to the doors in the far section of the basement, noticing that one door was larger than the other. He guessed that the smaller door was to a closet, and the larger door led to a bathroom. The smell was getting stronger; though he was breathing through his mouth as much as he could, he could almost taste the odor on his palate. He was certain that the source of the odor was behind one of those doors.

Liskey pulled open the closet door first. He found only a few boxes and files; the closet was barely big enough to hold anything else. Leaving the closet door opened, he headed over to the bathroom door. He hesitated for a moment, preparing himself mentally for what he might find. Bathroom crime scenes, for some reason, tended-to be the most gruesome.

Liskey placed his latex gloved hand on the bathroom door knob, turned, and gently pushed open the door. Before the door was fully open, Liskey saw the man, lying on his side on the floor, lodged between the toilet and the bathtub, his body decomposing and turning hues of red and green. Liskey could not see the man's face, as it was turned toward the tub. He called for Anderson, not knowing that Anderson was already headed toward him.

Anderson approached and looked at the scene. "That your man?" he asked.

"Can't tell," Liskey said. "Never seen him or spoke to him. Don't want to go in. The entire floor's covered with blood and maggots."

"I'm gonna get the MCTs down here." Anderson reached for his walkie-talkie and summoned the mobile crime technicians down to the basement. He looked at the body for a few more moments, then said to Liskey, "We're gonna let the MCTs do their thing, man. I'll give you a call once we ID the guy, and I'll give you any other information I get. Why don't you go on home to your wife?"

Liskey nodded. Two murders, two attempted murders, and one kidnapping, all somehow connected to Freedom Plaza, and he was no closer to establishing the link than he was before. The discovery of this body in the basement of Wynn Delano's home just left more questions than it resolved. Isaac Roth held all the cards, and he was still in the wind.

***

1:00 am, Saturday

Marjorie Wise awakened to almost stifling heat, her entire body soaked with sweat. She was still in the van, lying on a cushioned back bench, the only one in the van, her legs numb and draped over the arm rest.

Her last memory was of the tall man producing a syringe, seemingly out of nowhere, and injecting her in her stomach with a thick white liquid. She could recall getting drowsy a few minutes afterward, and then nothing.

Now, her feet were tied, and her wrists were handcuffed and secured with a rope to the bench. Her gray slacks and white blouse were damp but intact. The 19-year-old boy was no longer in the van. She wondered what happened to him. Did the tall man kill him? Maybe he let him go. Marjorie seriously doubted the latter.

As she looked out the front window, she could see a wall just beyond the front of the van, with several storage units and a Schwinn bicycle hanging on two hooks. She thought the bike looked a lot like her husband's bike. She thought no more of it until she noticed that the ice chest and the box her new microwave came in also looked similar to hers.

Wait.

Was she in her own garage?

Marjorie turned her head and looked out the side window. There was no mistaking it now. George had just erected those metal shelves a year ago to hold all his files. The banker's boxes inscribed with his handwriting were a dead giveaway.

Marjorie pulled on her restraints to loosen them but found them well-secured and tight. It was impossible to move from her position the way she was restrained. She tried not to panic. The next instinct was to scream, but if her abductor were nearby, he would hear it before anyone else would, and he didn't look like the type to be trifled with. The area of her stomach where Isaac Roth had stuck the needle was still a little sore. She wasn't sure why she was in her own garage, and that confused her. Then again, maybe she was dreaming. Perhaps she had never awakened from whatever Roth had injected into her. She closed her eyes and shook her head, trying to wake up. When she opened them again, she was still there, in a van that was not hers, in a garage that was.

She lay there and tried to catch her breath. All the windows of the van were closed, and the air inside was thick and hot. She could not fall asleep again, so she had no choice but to lay there and occupy her mind with thoughts. She wondered about her husband. Was he in the house? Did he know what had happened? Did he know she was out here? She was asking questions where neither a yes nor a no answer would have made sense.

She wanted to believe that her daughter's troubles in Silver Spring had not visited her all the way up in Toronto. But if this wasn't about her daughter, then it had to be about money, pure and simple. It was a rather convoluted robbery. She imagined her abductor had rifled through the house, taking all her expensive paintings, her Tiffany jewelry, and her Hermès bags. But if that was his intent, why did he need her? Her purse, with her money and keys, was still at the school. Marjorie's mind spun trying to sort it all out. Or it might have been the drug. She couldn't tell which.

Then she heard a sound. A door opening and closing. She wasn't certain whether to be hopeful or frightened. Was this a rescuer? Or was it her abductor coming back to finish whatever he started?

The driver side door of the van opened, and a rush of 85-degree air found its way to her. Compared to the heat in the van, it felt like air conditioning, and it immediately comforted her. But it vexed her spirit when she saw the tall man climb into the driver seat and glare back at her. A syringe of white liquid was in his hand.

"What is the password to your computer?" The tall man asked with an intense stare that suggested he'd better get a good answer.

Marjorie did not understand why he wanted the password to her computer, but she knew he wasn't trying to play digital Solitaire. "Why do you want my password?"

That wasn't the answer the tall man wanted. He pulled himself out of the seat, stepped over the center console, and reached back for Marjorie, grabbing her by her neck. He squeezed hard enough to constrict her airway, but not hard enough to choke her. His hand was large and rough, and Marjorie gasped for air while his fingernails were like talons digging into her skin. Her widened eyes moistened.

"I'm going to ask you again. What is your password?" The tall man loosened his grip slightly, just enough for her to talk.

Marjorie strained to recite the date of her marriage to George. "J-u-l-y-0-9-1-9-7-3. The 'J' is in caps, and the '1' is an exclamation point."

The tall man released his grip and watched her as she coughed and wheezed. After she had caught her breath, he said, "Time to sleep again."

With no more warning than that, the tall man jammed the needle into her stomach. Marjorie howled as the needle pierced her flesh, and she felt a burning sensation as the drug coursed through her veins. She felt him tugging at her clothes, but didn't stay awake long enough to register what exactly he was doing.

***

Liskey awoke in the dark on his living room couch. He checked his watch—three a.m. He had come home an hour before, and his mind was spinning with so many thoughts he had to lay down on the couch to process them all. But his weary body had overridden his thoughts, and soon he had fallen asleep. It was only the uncomfortable position of his head against the arm of the couch that awakened him.

Content to table his thoughts until the morning, Liskey got up from the couch and padded wearily toward the dining room. Along the way, he noticed that the patio door leading to the deck was slightly cracked open. At first, he blamed Graham, as this behavior was typical for him. But when he approached the door to close it, he noticed a lone figure outside sitting on the deck, staring into the dark. He knew it wasn't his son because Graham and pitch-black darkness were not great bedfellows. And though his wife could be contemplative, sitting in the dark was not her cup of tea.

Liskey opened the door wider and stepped outside. "Celia?"

Celia barely moved, although a twitch of her finger told him she was awake.

Liskey walked around Celia and perched himself against

the deck fence, facing Celia. Celia looked up at him. She acknowledged his presence at least—that was promising. He didn't want to tell her the news, fearing she might further withdraw. But Liskey had no choice. This girl had information proving a link between herself, the pastor, and a now-dead news reporter. He took a deep breath, the only sound other than the crickets in the backyard and the hum of the air conditioning compressor.

"I found Wynn Delano, the reporter you talked to," Liskey started, trying not to look as grim as he felt. "He's dead. He was killed in his own home."

Celia let out a breath that, to anyone else, would have sounded like relief, but to Liskey was a peculiar exasperation. She turned her head away and twisted her lips.

Liskey knew he needed to tread lightly from this point. Celia had received enough bad news over the past few days to send anyone over the edge, and she was as close to it as he had ever seen. He would have felt better if Celia yelled and screamed and threw his precious china against the wall. But her silence showed that she was a ticking bomb ready to blow.

"Celia, this guy has got two bodies on him now. No telling how many more." Liskey kept his voice quiet and smooth. "I want to save your mother, and I want to save you. But the only way I can do that is to know exactly where this guy is. If we knew whom he was working for, we might be able to track him down through his employers. But to find them, we have to know everything you know about this case, even the things you may be ashamed of telling. Even if it's illegal. I'm a homicide cop. I want to solve your husband's murder. I don't care about any skeletons in your closet."

Silence hung between them for almost a minute. Celia took a breath, and Liskey prepared for her to say something that would be instrumental to the case.

"Y'know, my mom is one of the greatest individuals I

know." Celia's face was barely visible in the darkness. "She's a loving woman, she loves God, and she loves her family. She never misses a Sunday service, even when she isn't feeling well. If I could be half of what my mom is, I would be happy. I adore my mom, and I would do anything for her. If this Isaac Roth wanted to trade my mother for me, I'd take that offer in a heartbeat. *Yes*, I would die for my mom."

Celia stood to her feet and drew close enough to him so Liskey could see her pained expression. "It insults me when you think I would sacrifice my mother just to hold some secret to save myself. It hurts me that you think I would hold on to important information when my mother's life is at stake. As a detective, I thought you'd be smarter than that. I thought you'd know better than to try to squeeze blood from a turnip."

Liskey was unapologetic. "Celia, I have to press for information, because it makes no sense that you, the pastor, the reporter, and Isaac Roth are not connected in some way."

"I'm telling you all I know!" Celia's voice came out in a blast, and Liskey thought it might have carried into the neighbor's yard. Calming down, she said, "If you can't accept that, then I don't know what to say to you." She stood and walked down the deck stairs to the yard. She walked closer to the picket fence and stared out into the woods.

Liskey took one more look at her, and then went inside. He closed the patio door but left it unlocked. Liskey knew she was right. It was no longer a matter of her saving herself. Now her parents were involved. If Celia knew something, she would have told.

But there was one person—one person—tied into this mess he hadn't spoken to yet. He walked back into the living room, got on his cell phone, and dialed Detective Anderson. He got no answer, which he expected after 3 in the morning, but he left a message.

"I need to talk to Pastor Lyons as soon as possible."

CHAPTER ELEVEN

The Lyons Den

7:08 a.m., Saturday

Marjorie awakened with numbness all over her body. She could tell by the sunlight streaming through the garage door window and bouncing off the front wall that it was sometime in the early morning. It seemed as if she had slept only a few minutes. Then, as she shifted, and the coolness of sensation came back to her body after the numbness wore off, she noticed she was wearing only her panties. She looked around and saw shards of her clothing strewn on the van floor and her shoes nowhere to be found.

Why had he stripped her naked? Maybe he had mercy on her, and he cut her clothes off to keep her cool in the swelter of the van. Maybe he had perverted intentions. Or, it could have been to add to her humiliation. Whatever it was, the shame of her nakedness paled compared to the fear she now felt. She was too groggy to find weakness in her restraints, and she was still soaked with sweat even though she was wearing almost nothing.

Marjorie lay quiet for a minute and tried to think. Somehow, some way, she had to escape. With no answers to any of her questions, and with no idea how to change her circumstance, she remembered God, and the many scriptures, Bible study lessons, and sermons that told her that God was a deliverer. She remembered the bondage of Israel and knew if God could deliver them, He could deliver her from the clutches of this maniac. Her first prayer would be for forgiveness, for waiting this long to call upon Him. But she also knew God may choose *not* to deliver her, in which case she needed strength to withstand whatever was to come.

She closed her eyes and prayed, for forgiveness, for her family, for herself, and finally, for the man who had suddenly snatched her freedom away. With nothing else to do, she focused on God and hoped that for whatever rhyme or reason she was laying there in that van, she would come to understand it, even if she would never accept it.

***

At 10 a.m., Detectives Liskey and Williams pulled up behind Detective Anderson's unmarked Ford Taurus at a Crittenden Street address in Washington. They stepped out of the vehicle and ogled the massive two-story Tudor-style house. Liskey guessed the house had at least seven bedrooms. *Nice.* It was moments like this that Liskey wished he had been a pastor instead of a cop.

Detective Anderson walked up to Liskey and Williams as they admired the house. He turned and waved at an unmarked unit parked just across the street from the house. The two shadowy figures inside waved back.

Before Anderson could say a word, Liskey asked, "So, Pastor Lyons lives here?"

Anderson nodded.

"Passing the collection plate has been very good for this guy," Williams said.

"Tell me about it." Anderson sighed. "If I had more of a gift of gab, I'd be carrying a Bible instead of a gun." Anderson quickly switched subjects. "So, I'm gonna allow you full access to the pastor, but I'm wondering what you want to know from him that wasn't already in our WACIIS reports."

Williams spoke first. "In your interview with the pastor, he says he believes that he was shot because of the work he does in the city. I guess that doesn't add up for us, because if that is the case, why would the suspect target our witness' husband, and kill a reporter, and go across the border to kidnap her mother? If his motive is to stop the pastor, how do all these other people, none of whom allegedly knows the pastor, fit in?"

Anderson nodded. "I can see where that would be a little confusing." He checked to make sure no one else was in earshot, then lowered his voice and continued. "Frankly, I don't think this guy is telling me the whole story. It's one of the reasons why I'm letting you do this. Maybe you can get something out of him I can't."

"What do you think he's hiding?" Liskey asked.

"I don't know. His answers to me were very clipped. He seemed very uncomfortable with me asking questions. Doesn't seem like the type of guy that's grateful I'm trying to find the SOB that almost killed him."

"Speaking of which," Williams interjected, "according to your ballistics report, the round was a 308 Winchester."

"Yep."

"At a range of 468 feet?"

"Yep."

"How is this guy home already? A gut shot, at that range, with a 308?"

"I know," Anderson said. "He should have been a half of him on each side of Pennsylvania Avenue. But the bullet barely pierced him. Almost like he was wearing a vest, but he wasn't."

Liskey shook his head. "This case just gets stranger every day."

"Well…" Anderson looked toward the house. "He's in there. I'm gonna sit this one out. If he didn't say anything to me, he's probably not gonna say much while I'm in there. Maybe he'll like your ugly mugs better."

Liskey scoffed. "Yeah, right."

The detectives headed, single-file, up the brick walkway toward the house, admiring the spherical hetz midget shrubs lining the walkway. As they neared the door, it opened, and a brawny gray-suited man, whose head barely cleared the top of the rounded doorway, emerged. He stood in front of the door until he eyeballed the badges hanging around the detective's necks. Liskey noticed a slight bulge at the waist beneath the man's suit jacket. He guessed the man was probably private armed security, but without a badge in sight, Liskey didn't want to take any chances.

"You're here to see Pastor Lyons?" the man asked. Without waiting for an answer, he stepped aside and allowed the detectives to enter. Liskey and Williams found themselves inside a foyer with Purpleheart floors and a large, ornate chandelier overhead.

Ramon Williams headed farther inside, but Liskey lingered. Liskey looked down at the bulge in the man's waist. "You got a permit for that?"

The man gave Liskey a mean look and remained silent.

"Did you hear my question? Do you have a permit for that gun?"

The man spoke, his voice deep and menacing. "You're kidding me, right?"

"Do I know you?"

"I don't think so."

"Then why would I kid with you? Give me the gun."

"Are you serious?"

"Yes. Give me the gun."

"Come on, man—"

"Look, either you give me that gun, or show me a permit, or we're gonna have a problem."

Williams stepped closer and eyeballed the man, waiting

for him to comply, and ready to act if he didn't.

The man, not wanting to tangle himself up with real police and arrested for unauthorized concealed carry, reached for the gun and handed it to Liskey, handle first. Liskey took the gun, removed the clip, and put both the gun and the clip in his pocket.

"When you get a license for this, see Detective Anderson. He'll give it back to you. Now, where's Pastor Lyons?"

The man looked to the top of a winding staircase leading to a second level. Following the man's gaze, the detectives saw another man, thick, bald head, the lights from the chandelier dancing on his dark skin. He slowly but carefully walked down the stairs, his injury evident in his measured steps and the mild wincing with each step. When he reached the bottom of the steps, he fixed a smile on his face to override appearing to be in pain.

"Are you the detectives from Montgomery County?" Pastor Lyons asked as he approached them.

Liskey gave a slight nod and extended his hand. "Detective Frank Liskey. This is Detective Ramon Williams."

After they shook hands, Pastor Lyons nodded to the security guard. The guard turned and walked somewhere down a hall on the right side of the staircase, while Pastor Lyons led the detectives to the left side, revealing an ornate living room that looked as if it belonged to a head of state. The detectives admired the tall vaulted ceilings, the marble fireplace, and a Persian rug that looked as if it cost more money than Liskey made in six months. Pastor Lyons directed them to sit on a plush brown salon sofa with tassels, while he, grunting in pain, sat across from them in a similar armchair. On the coffee table in front of them was an array of doughnuts and croissants, along with silver-plated pitchers of tea and coffee.

"Please help yourself," Pastor Lyons offered.

Ramon Williams spoke while Liskey helped himself to

a cup of tea. "You still need security? You know the man that tried to kill you is in Canada, and the Mounties are not gonna let him out of the country alive."

Pastor Lyon's eyes narrowed. "I have other security considerations."

Pastor's Lyons' statement caught Liskey as he was taking his first sip of tea. "What security considerations require you having unlicensed armed security in your home?"

Pastor Lyons smiled and looked down for a moment. When he looked back up, he ignored the question. "I understand you have some questions to ask me about what happened downtown."

Liskey played with the lemon in his tea, causing it to bob up and down. "Yes, and we appreciate your willingness to talk to us."

"What's on your mind?"

"Well, quite frankly, this case is baffling me. There is one victim, a TV reporter that was at the Freedom Plaza rally. Then there was the husband of a young lady who was at the Freedom Plaza rally. All killed by the same guy who shot you. I guess I'm trying to connect the dots. Did you know either victim?"

"I did not."

"Perhaps if I hear, in your words, what you think happened that resulted in your getting shot, it might put some things into perspective for me."

Lyons looked back and forth at the detectives. He stood and walked over to the fireplace, staring at nothing. "Are you a religious man, Detective Liskey?"

The question came out of left field, and Liskey was not expecting it. He looked over at Williams as if his partner had any insight into the meaning of the question or how to best answer it. Finally, Liskey asked, "How is that relevant to what happened at Freedom Plaza?"

Pastor Lyons turned back to them and spoke distinctly.

"There is a Scripture in the Bible. It says, '*But the natural man receiveth not the things of the Spirit of God: for they are foolishness unto him: neither can he know them, because they are spiritually discerned.*' I asked the same question of Detective Anderson, and his answer led me to believe that he was not a religious man, nor a spiritual one, if one wanted to toy with the meaning of the word 'religious.' So, I knew what I had to say to him would be foolishness, because he did not have the spiritual capability to perceive as rational what I would have told him. So, I ask the same question of you, Detective, and also of your partner. Are you a man of faith?"

Detective Liskey hesitated, not because he was uncomfortable with the question itself, but because he was uncomfortable with where it might lead. He had no desire for further conversation around that topic, as he was sure he would not measure up in a conversation about faith. The earth had traveled around the sun twice since Liskey went to church regularly, and he prayed only when things got rough and it seemed the right thing to do. Marian went to church as much as she could and often unsuccessfully tried to coax Liskey to come with her.

Liskey outwardly blamed the unpredictable nature of his job for not attending church, and there was truth to that. But Liskey knew the main reason was that he had seen so much evil and death in his job that he couldn't believe in a God that would 'make everything all right,' according to countless sermons he had heard. In the church, God was a rescuer, a deliverer, a healer, a balm in Gilead. Yet in the world outside of Sunday services, people were being maimed and killed. Kids, pregnant women, people just walking down the street minding their own business, people worshiping in churches. Dead. Sometimes over a little money. Other times, over passion. Sometimes, for no reason at all.

Yes, Liskey was a man of faith, but about as weak a faith as anyone could muster. Several weeks before his last regular day at church, one of his colleagues was the lead on a case of a church deacon that had been shot and killed during a carjacking as he took a group of kids to a church outing at Six Flags. A man who lost his life because he owned a BMW. A man who believed, more than most people, that God had his back. Liskey didn't see the point of going to church, although he still believed, in an intellectual sense, that God was there and was taking care of him in some unknown way. But if push came to shove, Liskey had more confidence in his Glock than in his faith.

"Yes, I am a man of faith," Liskey answered, harkening back to the days when he was never over three days removed from his last church service. He hoped Pastor Lyons did not probe deeper.

"Explain to me what that means."

Liskey again looked at Williams, who seemed content to be silent, at least for this part of the conversation. Liskey resented his silence.

"I believe in God. I believe in Jesus."

"So does 70% of the United States population. What is unique about your relationship with God?"

Liskey squirmed like a child with his bladder full. "This isn't about me, sir."

"Well, it isn't about me, either." The pastor headed back toward his chair. "But if you're not in the right frame of mind, and I tell you what I have to tell you, you will leave here with nothing valuable, but only the impression that I'm some kind of fool."

Finally, Williams spoke. "Why don't you try us? We're trying to save lives, and the longer we delay, the less our chance of doing that."

Pastor Lyons leaned on the back of his armchair and studied the two detectives for a moment. He could see a sincerity in Liskey's eyes that, although he was uncomfortable with questioning about his faith, revealed that he understood the realm of the spirit. No telling how long Lyons would wait before finding a cop in this city anywhere close. At worst, he would be no better off than he was now, holding onto a dreadful secret that no one would take seriously.

But the pastor insisted. "Tell me about your relationship with God."

Something tempted Liskey to walk out and try to go at the pastor another way. Maybe one of his colleagues, who was no stranger to a Bible study, could come back and be more competent at faith talks with the pastor. He looked at Williams, who seemed overly content at watching him squirm.

Then he remembered. Isaac Roth had Celia's mother in his grasp. *Tick tock tick tock.* No time to do anything except humor the pastor.

Liskey hung his head, refusing to meet the pastor's gaze. "I haven't been to church in a while..."

The pastor interrupted. "How long?"

"Maybe a couple of years. But I do believe in Jesus, and I, uh... I'll be honest with you. I'm not sure I have much of a relationship with God. My wife does, and she goes to church. I do pray with her sometimes, but..."

"When you pray, do you believe that God answers prayer?"

The answer flashing in Liskey's mind was a stark "Not always," but he feared to utter it in case he turned off the pastor. But he said, "I've seen some situations where I have had doubts." He hoped the pastor didn't ask him to elaborate.

"Do you believe in miracles?"

"What, do you mean like Moses and—"

"No. I mean modern-day miracles. Do you believe that God still does miracles?"

Liskey's answer was quick and sharp, almost as if it didn't come from him. "I believe you're a miracle."

"What do you mean?"

"You got shot with a sniper's high-powered round at a relatively close distance, and you live to tell. That's gotta be a miracle."

Pastor Lyons nodded and even managed a half-smile. "Yes, it was. A blessing indeed." He paced the room. "You likely know me as a man who's been fighting for racial reconciliation for two years now. I've been very passionate and deliberate about it."

Liskey listened carefully, taking a sip of tea to soothe an encroaching dryness in his throat. He was grateful that his last answer seemed to quell the pastor's interrogation, at least for now.

Pastor Lyons returned to his chair. "Truth is, it's not the only thing I'm passionate about."

"What do you mean?" Williams asked.

"I'll tell you." The pastor shifted in his chair. "It all started about two months ago."

CHAPTER TWELVE

The Regency

Two months before
Atlanta, Georgia

"What I'm about to say may upset some of you."

Pastor Lyons stood behind an oak lectern with its emblazoned logo *Ambrosia Hotel and Conference Center* temporarily covered with a felt banner that read *2nd Annual Racial Reconciliation Conference*. Most of the 500 people in the room stopped their idle chit-chat and munching on hors d'oeuvres and focused their eyes on him. He had gotten their attention.

"This should be the last time we have this conference."

Silence.

"We in the Christian community are addicted to conferences. We love to meet. We love to talk and converse. We love to declare that God showed up at these meetings because we've learned a few things, or we took home a few great anecdotes. But unless this meeting results in sustained and substantial efforts to effect change, we are wasting our time and might as well go home."

The crowd piped up with a few *amens*.

"What do I mean by sustained and substantial efforts?" The pastor grabbed the microphone out of its holster and stepped to the left of the podium. He was about to get to the main course of his speech and saw that all the ministers, of various races, hung on his every word.

At that moment one of his aides walked on the stage, quietly and quickly handed him a note, and walked off. Lyons, glancing at the folded and taped yellow note, thought it might have been a reminder to acknowledge someone he had forgotten during his opening remarks, or maybe a notification that someone had left their lights on in the parking lot. Before opening the note, he asked the crowd to give a hearty *God Bless you* to the choir that had preceded him. As they applauded, Lyons read the note:

> *Need to meet with you as soon as possible. I need to tell you something that is endangering the church at large, and you seem to be a man of considerable influence. I am not a crazy person; this is real. I was once a pastor myself. Give me just 15 minutes of your time. I will be in room 540 all day today whenever you would like to meet. I am the man standing to the left of the doors in the back.*

Lyons quickly slipped it in his pocket and met eyes with a young man standing near the doors at the rear of the room. The man cordially nodded at Lyons, then slunk out the doors and was quickly out of sight.

Three hours later, during a break in the conference, Lyons took an elevator to the Ambrosia Hotel's fifth floor. He sauntered toward Room 540, the black and burgundy Berber carpet drowning out his footsteps. Stopping in front of the door, he watched it for a moment, as if it would magically speak and give him clues on what agenda the man inside had for him. He was more curious than fearful of what awaited him, but to be on the safe side, he had told his adjutant to come get him if he was not back on the conference floor within 30 minutes.

Lyons lifted the brass door knocker and let it fall against the door; he repeated it two times. Within seconds the door opened, and a young man with perfectly coiffed brown hair wordlessly beckoned Lyons inside.

"Good morning." The man stepped aside as the pastor entered

his room. "Thanks for meeting with me."

Lyons turned to the man as he shut the door. "Who are you?"

The man turned toward Lyons and extended his hand. "My name is Gary Walls. I am an attorney. I used to be the pastor of Neal Memorial Faith Church here in Atlanta up until a year ago."

Lyons gave Gary Walls' a firm handshake. "Nice to meet you. Are you a part of the conference?"

"Not officially." Walls walked past Lyons farther into the room. "But I have my own ministry, of sorts."

Lyons checked his watch, his way of informing Walls that his time was limited, and that Walls needed to get to the point. "What's that?"

"My mission is to make the church aware of a grave threat to its existence. You are the twelfth pastor I have told about this, and I will continue to inform influential people in the body of Christ until there is no longer a threat."

Lyons gave the man a dubious stare. Lyons had been a pastor for over twenty years, and there was one thing he knew, if nothing else: there was *always* a threat to the Christian church. "What type of threat?" he asked, ready to walk out if the man's answer was not compelling enough to deserve his attentions during this busy conference.

"I want you to know that I have been heavily convicted before the Lord and have already repented for what I'm about to tell you," Walls said. "It's the reason I resigned from my pastoral duties. I didn't feel fit to be a pastor after what I had done."

Lyons continued to listen, still standing, resigning himself to sit only if invited and only if what the man had to say called for him staying longer than his allotted 15 minutes.

Walls continued. "About two years ago, I lost my wife and my only son on the same day."

Lyons' expression softened, remembering his own son. "I'm sorry to hear that."

"Hmm. They were shot during a home invasion. I came home from a preaching engagement and found them slaughtered in the basement. My son was only four years old."

"Heavens."

"After that, it was hard to pray, hard to believe God was really looking out for me. I let my grief slip into depression, and it invaded my mind to where I still believed in God, but I no longer believed God had any interest in our suffering on this planet. Yes, God may still be involved in nature and such, but when it came to humankind, God was detached. If He wasn't, my wife and son, the most beautiful and kind people on this earth, would not have died so soon, at least not like that."

Lyons nodded his understanding. He had heard this same story countless times and always found it tragic whenever someone lost their faith because of tragedy. He was on the verge himself on more than one occasion.

"I still continued to preach, but my preaching was lifeless. I really didn't believe much of what I was saying. I lost a lot of my congregation because of it. And unfortunately, I had no one speaking into my life to set me straight."

Lyons nodded again. "Pastoring; one of the loneliest professions in America."

"Don't I know it." Walls moved to an armchair near the window and sat. "It was that reason I was so drawn to this woman that came into my church one Sunday and attended the service. This was a couple of months after my wife passed."

Lyons didn't wait for an invitation, but he sat on the edge of the queen-size bed.

"She was beautiful, kind of favored J.Lo a little bit." Walls looked out the window as if the heavens were inspiring his words. "Rachel asked me out to dinner after church, and I accepted. Long story short, we started seeing each other, and she tried to convince me that the practice of Christianity, as we know it, was faulty and no longer relevant. She said that Christianity is an extended form of slavery, with its rules and regulations and moral codes. She said God didn't intend this, that God intended for us to be free. She started to convince me that Christianity and the Bible were invented by the ruling class to control men."

The scripture from 2 Corinthians 11:14 came to Lyons' mind. *"And no marvel; for Satan himself is transformed into an angel of light."* In this case, that *angel of light* just happened to look like J.Lo. Lyons humored Walls with a question he wasn't sure he needed the answer to. "I assume she presented some evidence of this?"

"Oh, yes." Walls turned away from the window and faced his guest. "She's a member of a very secret, but dangerous group. They are experts at causing doubt about Christianity, the Bible, and everything that Christians believe. In their meetings, they focus on presenting compelling evidence that the Bible, and the practice of Christianity in general, is a fraud. They believe God wants us to live our lives out of our own conscience, free from any rules or codes that enslave us. And I fell for it."

"What's the name of this group?"

"They call themselves *The Regency*."

"Never heard of them."

"Of course, you haven't. And that's the way they like it," said Walls. "Now, Rachel was one of the recruiters for the group, but she never revealed it until about a year and a half ago. I guess she figured I had been brainwashed enough and she could finally get to her real agenda."

"Which was?" Lyons asked.

"Like I told you, I am an attorney. I used to work in the government relations department of a major law firm here in Atlanta. Somehow, the Regency knew this, and sent Rachel to work her considerable feminine charms to get me on their side. She wanted me to join the lobbying department of a law firm connected to the Regency. Of course, that connection exists nowhere on paper, and if anyone were to audit the law firm, they would find no signs of the Regency anywhere, even though the Regency funneled almost 5 million dollars a year into the firm. There were three lobbyists on the team, including myself, each making almost 200 thou a year."

"Nice bit of cheese," Lyons studied Walls. He saw no pride in

Walls, but instead, sensed encroaching shame. "What d'you have to do for the money?"

Almost as if he had expected the question, Walls walked over to the desk, opened a black vinyl folder, removed a set of stapled papers, and handed them to Lyons. "I assume, being a crusader for racial justice, that you are familiar with the Bob Jones University case from 1983?"

"Can't say that I am," Lyons responded, scanning the papers.

"Well, back in the 70s, Bob Jones University had a policy which prohibited interracial relationships on campus. The IRS found out about it and revoked their tax-exempt status, based upon the fact that the interracial policy was contrary to fundamental public policy. Now, Bob Jones eventually got the tax-exempt status back, but they had to drop the interracial rule to get it."

All Lyons could manage was a faint "Hmm" while he read the papers.

"So, the Regency is using that case as a foundation. They say that if the IRS can revoke the tax-exempt status of a religious private school for practicing racial discrimination, the same standard should apply to churches that have policies contrary to established public policy. So, they did a study and discover that there were many churches that had policies and teachings contrary to same-sex marriage, to Roe vs. Wade, to the legalization of marijuana, to interracial marriage, to women's rights, and the government didn't have the resources to properly police these churches to ensure their compliance with public policy."

"Those teachings are like law in many churches," Lyons noted.

"Exactly. And then there are the so-called tax-exempt churches that no longer operate as churches, but still benefit from the tax-exemption. Some guy decides to pray with and have Bible study in his basement with a handful of people each week, and suddenly he's tax-exempt. So, the Regency is making the case that the system is fundamentally flawed and needs to be abolished."

Lyons dropped the papers, removed his glasses, and looked up at Walls. "You mean getting rid of the tax-exemption for churches? That'll hurt a lot of churches."

"Yep. Contributions to churches will no longer be tax deductible. Churches will have to pay property taxes for all their real estate holdings. Ministers will have to pay social security taxes, whether they disagree with social security or not."

"You think they'll actually get away with that? With the conservative majority in Congress and on the Supreme Court?"

"As we speak, this law firm has guys on Capitol Hill working with the members of the House Ways and Means Committee to introduce and support bills that would eliminate the tax exemptions for churches and ministers. That was my responsibility when I was with the law firm—to persuade lawmakers to pass these bills by any means necessary."

"What do you mean by that?"

"By what?"

"By any means necessary."

"Just that. If simple persuasion didn't work, I would throw money at them, throw women at them, whatever it took. We were urged to find out any juicy tidbits about lawmakers so we could use them against them later. For instance, if we knew someone was cheating on his wife, we would threaten them with exposure in exchange for his vote. Well, I wouldn't, but the Regency would send somebody to take care of that. Of course, we never had any connection to that. All I know is that sometimes, lawmakers would go home intending to vote no, but would come back in the office the next day with a sudden change of mind."

"They were threatened."

"And not just with skeletons in the closet. Sometimes, the Regency would threaten them or their family members with death if they didn't get on board."

"You're telling me this group would kill?"

"They would. And they have."

Lyons drew in a breath. "You're telling me they've killed Congressmen?"

"Nobody with that high a profile yet. Usually it's a cousin, or uncle, someone whom nobody cares about except the lawmaker. There was one congressman who intended to vote against something the Regency wanted passed. His nephew was found in a dumpster."

"Lord."

"Now they don't use that method all the time; they don't want to draw any unnecessary scrutiny to themselves. But it is a play in the playbook. Mostly they try to change policy the traditional way, which is to throw money behind candidates for office they know will be sympathetic to their cause, or to bully politicians out of office they know are sympathetic to Christian causes. But have no doubt, they are very dangerous.

"This group is twice as powerful as AARP or the NRA. They have thousands of members stretched all over the country, and no one uses their real name when associating with the group. They are not listed on any piece of paper in any government agency. They rarely ever come together as a group nationally, yet they are extremely close-knit. Most of the members are rich, so the group as a whole is very well-funded. Its leader — no one has ever seen him face to face. He communicates through the dark web and has never shown his true face or used his real name, but he is so influential that people all over this country want to follow him. And this group exists for one reason."

"What's that?"

"To eradicate God from American society. They call it a God slaughter campaign."

Lyons scoffed. "You think that will actually happen? With the number of God-fearing, praying people in this country?"

"The fact is, a lot of evil things have happened in this country right under the nose of the church. Will it happen today? No. Will it happen this year? Likely not. But they are going to nibble at the elephant that is the church in America until there is nothing left. And a lot of churches are allowing it to happen. So, my mission is to wake up the church and let them know this is happening. As you were saying in your remarks today, it's one thing to believe something and constantly talk about it. It's another thing to do something about it. Well, I'm doing something, at considerable risk to my life."

"You're telling me they want to kill you, too?"

"I went along with everything they wanted to do, until I heard they will go as far as murder to achieve their goals. That's where I got off the boat. Now I'm a hunted man."

"What about your girlfriend Rachel?"

"She was assigned to keep me in line. When she failed…" Walls let his words trail off, hoping Lyons would get his point.

Lyons picked up the hanging thread. "Don't tell me they killed her."

"I don't know. But I haven't heard from her since I left the group, and she moved out of her apartment shortly after I defected from the law firm."

"How do you know they're after you?"

"Hmm. I knew my decision to leave the group wouldn't go, uh, unchallenged. So, I leased another apartment a few blocks away and stayed there, without giving up my old apartment. I felt safer that way. About a week after I defected, my landlord called to tell me that someone had broken into my old apartment."

"Could have been just a burglary," Lyons reasoned. "How do you know it was somebody after you?"

"The neighbors described the intruder."

"And?"

"They said he was an intense looking, tall white man."

***

"Of course, that was just one branch of what the Regency was involved in," Pastor Lyons said to the detectives as he recounted his story, pacing around the room. "There are many others, not just involving government. But government is their focus. Now, are they going to get rid of every church in America? Probably not. Are they going to stop people from praying and exercising their faith? Definitely not. But this group recognizes something that many churches don't. In America, it isn't God that has the power. It's the government. They realize that just the swipe of a legislator's pen can create a league of persecution against the church. The influence of biblical principles and the word of God is gradually eroding in this country. This group is shaking the sea bed, and that tsunami is threatening to engulf the church."

"So, what did Walls want you to do?" Liskey asked.

"He wanted me to use my influence, spread the word around about this group to my circle of churches." Lyons continued to pace. "That night, after the conference sessions were done, I called a meeting in my hotel suite and invited all of my coalition leaders. At the meeting, I told them what Walls had told me. I told them we need to organize and put together some type of resistance to this Regency group. It wasn't long after that that I started getting death threats."

"How did they know you knew about them?" Williams asked.

For the first time since the detective's questioning began, Pastor Lyons' face took on a sour look, and he hesitated for a moment. He walked toward the bay window in the living room, looked out briefly, and then turned back toward the detectives. "I think someone in my coalition of pastors is a member of the group."

"Why do you think that?" asked Liskey.

"The threats started the day after I had the conversation with Gary Walls. No one except the men in my coalition were privy to that conversation, and I am sure no one talked out of school."

"Why would a pastor be a member of a group of atheists?"

The pastor walked back toward them. "Oh, they're not atheists. From my understanding, many people in this group claim Christianity."

Williams hung his head low. "That makes no sense."

Pastor Lyons' perked up his voice, relishing the opportunity to teach. "Oh, but it does, detective. You notice I said, 'claim Christianity.' Doesn't mean they practice biblical righteousness. They have lifestyles that counter the word of God, and they are tired of the church challenging their way of life. They believe the biblical way is irrelevant for our times. And we're not just talking about LGBT issues and drugs here. We're talking about racism, sexism, the right to bear arms, war, amassing wealth, relying on science rather than faith, all of which the traditional church has, in many ways, spoken out against. They believe the church has been ineffective against many of the ills of the day, which, to them, is further proof that it is time to abolish God. They will tell you, with pride, that there are over 380,000 churches in the United States, that we are more religious than almost every other country, yet we have significantly more mass murders than any other country. If God is really among us, would Columbine have happened? What about Sandy Hook, Charleston, Fort Hood, the Pulse shooting, Virginia Tech, Las Vegas? And what scares me the most about this group is that so many of their members function as practicing Christians."

Williams was not entirely satisfied with the pastor's answer. "How can a pastor get away with destroying the church?"

"They rely on one simple theory." Pastor Lyons exchanged glances between Williams and Liskey. "As humans, we are more attuned to things outside of ourselves that can destroy us, than things within us. This group understands that. They insert their members inside churches; some of them even plant churches, because they know that when it comes to spiritual warfare, churches and ministers will be more likely to defend against things outside of the church than threats from within. Meanwhile, they are gradually eroding the church from within with a fake gospel that ensures that the people of God are never effective at building God's kingdom. For instance, there's this gospel of inclusion that this famous preacher got branded a heretic for. Well, he's not the only one preaching it. Everybody in this group is. You go to their churches, and you hear nothing about sin and repentance. They preach a gospel that results in condemnation for everyone who dares to believe it."

Liskey set his donut on a plate on the table and stood, facing the pastor. "So, that's why you were shot, because of your knowledge of the group?"

"I believe so," the pastor said. "Now, I had already started planning for the racial reconciliation rally, so I wasn't about to stop just because I was getting threats. So, I prayed to God and asked for His protection. And detectives, the Lord gave it to me."

Liskey smiled. "I'd say. You're still alive, even though you got shot at relatively close range with a 308."

"Yes. God protected me. In fact, just before I passed out, I saw something which convinced me of that."

"What?"

Pastor Lyons took a glance at Williams, then turned to face the window, taking several seconds before turning back to Liskey. "One day, I'll tell you. Now is not the time."

"So, what does all this have to do with Justin and Celia Rayburn?" Liskey asked.

Pastor Lyons nodded. "I'm about to tell you."

CHAPTER THIRTEEN

Truth Emerges

All Marjorie could think about was her family. Where were they? What were they being told about her? Two hours before, Marjorie had made her peace with the possibility she might die, and she had prayed that she could handle whatever would come. If it was her time to die, then there was no sense fretting about it. She made her peace with God and prayed that her family, and particularly Celia, would be okay.

She had been laying there for four hours since she awakened, and she had not seen the tall man for almost eleven hours. Maybe he had left her there and went on his way. She was a little nauseous and weak from the sweating and heat, but maybe she could make enough noise. It was Saturday morning, and most people in the neighborhood were at home. If she screamed for help, maybe someone would hear her. Just as she was thinking about doing just that, a better idea sprang to mind.

She flipped on her side so she was facing the back of the van seat. She worked her hands between the seats. It was easy to do since the ropes that bound her snaked between the bottom and top seat cushions and were tied somewhere underneath. She fished around, ignoring the pennies, sticky candy, and crumbs, and moved her hands around. She was looking for something sharp—a pencil, a long lost key, a paper clip. Anything.

Her hands found something long and straight. She gasped in delight. A pen.

She grabbed the pen, a ballpoint with a metal tip. She quickly dug the pen into the upholstery, near the rear of the van bench, making a hole. Using her fingers, she dug into the hole, tearing out fabric and foam padding, until the hole was almost as big as a dinner plate. She kept digging, flinging the foam padding to the side, coughing from the dust. Finally, she reached the metal frame.

Pulling as hard as she could, she shoved her hands down into the hole until the rope met the semi-sharp edge of the metal frame. The handcuffs bit into her wrists, causing her to wince in pain, but she pulled until she had enough play to grind the rope back and forth across the edge of the frame. She stopped twice, taking a break to relieve herself of the pain, and then went back at it again, grinding the rope until the metal of the handcuffs broke the skin on her wrists. That only intensified the pain, but Marjorie kept going, bolstered as she saw strands of the rope breaking. After ten agonizing minutes, the rope finally broke. Marjorie pulled her hands out and then swung around and sat on the bench. She could now see into the garage through all the van windows, and she noticed no one around. She paid attention to the door leading from her garage to the side hallway of the house that ran alongside the stairway. It was partially open.

With her hands still bound in the cuffs, Marjorie climbed in the front driver's seat. She worked her hands in the door latch to open the driver's side door, all the while staring at the side hallway door. She quickly and quietly stepped out of the van, gently closing the driver's side door until it joined with the door jamb but did not latch.

The door leading to the side yard was only fifteen feet in front of her. She knew once she got out that door, she was only seconds away from being quickly noticed by a neighbor, as a half-naked black woman wearing handcuffs would definitely draw sharp attention in Forest Hill.

She took a deep breath and then charged for the door, holding her hands out in front of her. Just a foot away from the door, Marjorie saw a shadow in her peripheral vision and turned. The punch came hard and fast, landing on her jawbone and sending her careening to the floor. Without her hands to break the fall, she landed on her tailbone. A sharp pain shot through her pelvis, and she screamed.

The tall man ignored the screams, grabbed the chain between the handcuffs, and dragged her along the concrete floor toward the side hallway door. Once he reached the door, he pulled up, hoisting her partially to her feet, and jerked her up the two steps at the side hallway door and into the hallway. Once they had cleared the door, the tall man slammed it shut with his foot.

Ahead of them were stairs leading to the basement. The tall man dragged Marjorie down the stairs, her panties rolling down, exposing her derriere. Between the handcuffs digging into her wrists and the pain in her tailbone worsening by being dragged, Marjorie almost wished that he would inject her again.

The tall man pulled her into the family room and tossed her on a couch. Marjorie buried her hands between her knees, using her knees to press against the handcuffs so she could slide her wrists forward and move the metal away from the injuries on her wrists. She kept her eyes on the tall man, hoping that he would leave her as she was and walk out of the room, even for only a minute. In the next room was the hidden entrance to the safe room, and it would take her only a few seconds to get to it.

The tall man pulled the marble coffee table away from the couch and sat on the table facing Marjorie. He removed his pistol from his waist and set it on his lap as a way of reminding Marjorie he still had control of her. He didn't move, but merely looked at her with eyes of stone. Marjorie moved her arms together in front of her, covering her nakedness as best she could.

Her body trembled as she returned the tall man's intent stare. She cleared her throat. "Excuse me, I know what you told me about talking, but could I ask you something?"

The tall man merely stared at her.

Marjorie took his silence and dead-eyed stare as consent. "Why are you doing this to me? What do you want from me?"

Without batting an eye, the tall man glared at her, calmly and coldly. "I want your daughter to die."

"You mean Celia?"

The tall man said nothing.

"What has she done?" Marjorie's voice shook with every syllable.

"It is not my concern. I do what I am paid to do. No more, no less."

Marjorie took a deep breath, then looked down at herself. "Please let me put some clothes on?"

The tall man continued his hard stare, opting not to answer. In his profession, there were two things he had learned. One of them was not to engage in conversation with a mark; it might humanize them and make them more emotionally challenging to kill. The other was to always strip hostages to humiliate them and to keep them from hiding weapons and contraband.

"Please…"

The tall man gripped his gun. "Say no more to me." He stood. "Shortly, your voice will have a greater audience."

Marjorie frowned. *What exactly did that mean?* Her question would go unanswered as the tall man turned his back to her. He walked into a room next to the family room—the same room with the hidden entrance to the safe room—and retrieved her iMac computer. Suddenly a chilling thought came to her mind, and she hoped—against all hope—that the tall man was not planning to do with that computer what she thought he was going to do.

***

Liskey paced the room, not sure how much of the pastor's story was real and how much were the ramblings of a hyper-religious mind. A secret terrorist society that uses intimidation and murder to change public policy affecting churches? A leader who shepherds thousands with no one ever seeing him? A mole inside Pastor Lyons' preacher coalition? All of it seemed far-fetched to him, and he had a boatload of follow-up questions. But now, he hoped, Pastor Lyons was about to tell him how Celia was connected to this mess, but he had little confidence that any of it would make any sense.

"What I am about to tell you is second-hand information," the pastor stated. "I can't verify or refute any of it."

"Second-hand from whom?" Liskey asked.

Pastor Lyons acknowledged the question with a nod, but did not answer at once. "I woke up in the hospital four hours after I was shot. My wife was there. She told me that the bullet went into the soft tissue and muscle but did not pierce any organs or major arteries. She said the reason I was out for so long was because of the force of my head hitting the stage, rather than the bullet wound itself. But I do remember that bullet hitting me. It felt like a ton of bricks."

Liskey nodded, waiting for him to continue.

"Now, I had my suspicions who was the mole in my coalition, although I never mentioned to anyone in the group that I suspected a mole. I never even mentioned it to my wife. But my wife told me that the man I suspected was at the hospital when the police came by, and of course, he was trying to get information from them in the name of trying to help me. Your reporter also came past."

"Wynn Delano?"

"Yes. He wanted statements from the cops and also from

anyone involved with my coalition. I also understand that he spoke with the mole. Now, what happened after that, I am not clear on. But based on the news that Detective Anderson gave me this morning about Mr. Delano, I'm sure the mole had something to do with it."

Liskey furrowed his eyebrows. "You think the mole arranged Delano's murder?"

"I can't prove it, but I'm certain he did. Along with your girl's husband, I'm afraid."

Liskey heard the ringing of a telephone in a far room, but that only momentarily distracted him from a furious rush of thoughts. "Pastor Lyons?"

"Yes?"

"What you're telling me makes no sense."

"Really?"

"You want me to believe that a secret group is trying to destroy Christianity. As a part of that, they plant a mole in your pastor's coalition, try to assassinate you, kill a reporter, and then go after a woman, killing her husband along the way. And why? What do these two innocent people have to do with any of this?"

Pastor Lyons pressed his fingers together into a steeple. "Something happened in that meeting with Delano and the mole. Now, I don't know what that was. But all I know is that shortly after that meeting, two murders occurred. I wasn't at the meeting, so I don't know what was said or done. The only reason I know about the meeting is because my wife saw the two of them talking in the ER. She said their conversation looked very intense."

"You think he was killed shortly after that?" Williams asked.

"According to Detective Anderson, it could have been about two hours later."

"So, what do you think they were talking about?" Liskey asked.

"I don't know. That's for you guys to figure out."

"Fine with us. Just need you to tell us who this mole is."

Pastor Lyons traded glances between Liskey and Williams as if to make certain they were ready to hear what he had to say. Finally, the name slipped from between his lips. "Jonathan Newberry."

Williams looked over at Liskey. "Who's that? Sounds familiar."

Liskey answered, but kept his eyes on Pastor Lyons, seeing a genuine sadness. "Pastor of the megachurch over in PG County, close to National Harbor."

"The pastor that's on TV all the time? He just built a church from scratch three years ago?" Williams said.

"Yep. Has to be the fastest growing megachurch on the East Coast. They think in a couple of years, it'll be one of the biggest in the country."

"He's connected all over town," Pastor Lyons chimed in. "He's got friends in Annapolis, downtown D.C., Richmond. His church has got more than 35,000 attending weekly, including politicians, celebrities, you name it."

"And you're telling me this guy, who's connected like that, is trying to destroy Christianity?" Liskey said incredulously.

"If my assumptions and beliefs are correct, yes sir." Pastor Lyons stood and approached Liskey, stopping within three feet of him, revealing deep pain in his eyes. "Of course, he has the cover of being the pastor of one of the biggest churches in the D.C. area."

"What made you suspect him?" Williams stood.

Pastor Lyons scoffed, realizing he could give no substantive answer to that question that would satisfy a natural thinker. "I'm a man of the Spirit. God has given me an unction to discern good and evil. I knew by the Spirit that this man was likely the mole."

"Yet you let him stay in the coalition?" Liskey asked.

"As Michael Corleone would say, 'Keep your friends close, and your enemies closer.'"

Liskey often relied upon Ramon Williams to give him a read on persons they were interviewing—usually, Liskey could tell the truth by the look on his partner's face. It worked well, even though Williams was often the more skeptical one, the Scully to his Mulder. This time, as Liskey studied Williams' face, he could tell that Williams didn't believe a word of what Pastor Lyons was saying. Even Liskey had a lot of questions, and he wanted to talk to Lyons' wife, but held off until he consulted with his partner.

"Okay, Pastor Lyons, you've given us a lot of information, and we appreciate it." While he spoke, Liskey removed a card from his jacket pocket. "My partner and I will need to talk and figure out where we go from here. I hope we can follow-up with you at a later time."

Pastor Lyons nodded. He took the card from Liskey but did not offer one of his own. "No problem with me. I'll be here. As you can see, I'm kind of a shut-in these days."

"Why is that?" Liskey asked as they walked toward the door. "I mean, if this group is what you say it is, they'll just hire someone else once we catch this guy. You surely don't plan on being in hiding forever."

"No, I don't." Pastor Lyons walked them to the door. "How and when I come out will depend on the Lord's leading, and the good work of you gentlemen."

The brawny guard opened the door for them. Liskey and Williams walked out and met Detective Anderson halfway down the walkway.

"He tell you anything good?" Anderson asked, walking behind them as they headed to their car.

Liskey kept walking, trying to decide how much information he wanted to share with Detective Anderson. Pastor Lyons was right about that, at least—this information, put in the wrong hands, might get ridiculed and ignored, or worse, used to destroy any chances of discovering why Celia was targeted. When he got to the car, he turned to Anderson. "He told us quite a bit, but I'm not sure how much of it makes any sense. We need some time to process it, run it up the flagpole. I'm sure we'll be in touch with any information that could help your case."

Detective Anderson's face suddenly turned gloomy. "So, what is so important about you, that he talks to you, but not the D.C. police?"

"We have some things in common." Liskey left it at that. He removed the security guard's gun and clip from his pocket. "The pastor's security guard had an unregistered concealed weapon." He handed the weapon and clip to Anderson. "I'll leave it up to you how you want to handle that."

"C'mon, dude," Detective Anderson protested. "I help you out, and you leave me hanging like that? You can't tell me *anything* he said?"

"I'll call you later. We'll talk then." Liskey hoped that statement kept the detective at bay for a few hours, but he knew he eventually had to share with Detective Anderson some of what he had heard. But solving both their cases seemed to be mostly in Liskey's wheelhouse.

Liskey got in his car and, with Williams, drove off.

***

"Lisk, that had to be the weakest interview I've ever seen you do," Williams commented once they were in the car and were driving up Wisconsin Avenue toward Bethesda.

Liskey nodded gently. He agreed, but to spur Williams' thoughts, he asked, "What do you mean?"

"Man, a sinister group that's trying to wipe out Christianity through murder? You believe that?"

"It's not that hard to believe. There are plenty of groups around the world that attack Christians. This is no different."

"Yeah, but we're getting this hearsay from an alleged defector whose name we don't even know. For all we know, he's some kind of nut, if I believe he exists, which I'm not sure I do."

"Why would the pastor make up such an elaborate story?"

"Because he's trying to distract us away from the real story."

"Which is?"

"I don't know. He's probably into some dirt, and that's why he was targeted. He didn't want to tell the real story, and so he made up this fake story and threw Jonathan Newberry in the mix. I've heard Jonathan Newberry on TV. I've seen him preach. He's got politicians going to his church. There's no way this guy is in bed with people trying to wipe out Christianity. And the reason it was important for *you* to be a Christian, so to speak, was because he knew you wouldn't challenge him."

"Really?" Liskey waited eagerly for Williams' insight.

"Yeah. Most Christians have a high level of respect for pastors. So, he knew you wouldn't come at him hard, but throw those powder-puff questions at him. That's why he didn't tell the D.C. Police that story. Anderson is a bulldog that would have ripped that story to pieces. There are all kinds of holes in it. He claims he got death threats. Why would a group that is so secret make threats? Why didn't they just kill him without making threats? And then you didn't ask to talk to the wife. She's a direct witness of what happened between Delano and Newberry."

Liskey scoffed. "So, what about my victim? If the pastor was into some dirt, and he was targeted because of it, what does that have to do with my victim? With Celia? With the reporter?"

"Because they were witnesses, Lisk."

Liskey voice escalated. "Ramon, there were hundreds of witnesses down there. People on the Plaza. People looking through windows. People recording it on their cell phones. Why would he go after these two people?"

Ramon let out a high sigh. "Because they're on record, Lisk. Delano recorded the shooting, and Celia gave an interview to Delano. Everyone else at the Plaza scattered like roaches, and Delano and Celia were down there in front of a camera. He probably followed Celia home, noted where she lived, and then went back for Delano before he came after Celia."

"And why would he do that? Celia never saw the shooter. He was never at risk. The shot came from a hotel, from a room above the sixth floor; D.C. police already figured that out. No way Celia could have been a threat."

Williams voice escalated a few notches. "Lisk, you told me she was in that same building for a job interview. In the same building as the shooter. How do we know she didn't see him at some point? How do we know she didn't know him? Man, for all we know, she might have helped set up the shooting, and now the killer is trying to tie up loose ends. You ever thought about that? Face it, Lisk, you've gone soft. You let this girl get your heart. And you can't do that, not and be a murder police. I mean, for heaven's sake, you even got the girl living with you."

Liskey pulled to the side of the road and stopped, leaving the car in drive. "Ramon, this girl is innocent." He paused and looked Ramon straight in his eyes, letting his words sink in. His voice carried a conviction that surprised even him. "Pastor Lyons is innocent. I can't tell you how I know that. I just know. You know, gut feelings are just as important as facts in this job. How many times have we played off a gut feeling and solved a case?" He waited for an answer from Ramon, but the younger detective just looked away.

Liskey took Ramon's silence as agreement. "Well, I got a

gut feeling about this case. I think the pastor is telling us the truth, and it's an ugly truth. I'd rather hope that your theory is true rather than face the fact that there are pastors trying to kill other pastors because of some New Age agenda. That's some scary stuff, man."

Williams continued to look ahead, stone-faced.

Liskey appeased his partner. "Tell you what. You let me pull out this last dangling string. If nothing comes of it, we'll play it your way. We'll look into Celia and Pastor Lyons hard, find out what connection they have to Roth."

Williams finally responded. "Should have done that to begin with, man."

"If I'm wrong, beers are on me for a full month."

"I just hope that Roth doesn't hurt this girl and her family."

Liskey merely looked at Williams.

A smile grew out of the corner of Williams' mouth. "Better be Heineken, not that Bud Light swill you drink."

Liskey smiled, then made a U-turn and headed south on Wisconsin Avenue.

"Where are we going?" Williams asked.

"George Washington University Hospital. I want to see their parking lot footage."

CHAPTER FOURTEEN

Drawing out of the shadows

11:02 a.m.

The waiting and isolation were perilous. Liskey had warned Celia not to make any attempts to contact her family, as the killer seemed rather sophisticated and could likely trace her attempts. Now, waiting to hear word on her mother's status, of her father's whereabouts, of how her brothers and sisters were coping with this, exasperated Celia to the point of exhaustion. As she was accustomed to cell phones and social media, living this way was worse than prison. She tried to sleep, the best way she could think of to pass the time without being consumed with worry, hoping by the time she woke up, there would be good news. But sleep evaded her, and she spent the time in her bed, staring at the ceiling, tortured with anticipation.

Just as she was about to turn over and try to sleep again, her cell phone rang from the dresser across the room. Celia practically jumped out of bed and hurried over to the phone, checking its caller ID. *Her parents' home number*. With glee, she answered the phone, hoping to hear her mother's voice, or perhaps one of her siblings.

What Celia heard was a German-inflected droll. "Good morning, Celia."

Celia checked the caller ID again, then got back on the

phone. "Who's this?"

"I think you know."

"I don't know. That's why I asked."

"Your mother's here with me. She asked me to tell you hello."

Just then Celia realized whom she was talking to. The tall man's voice frightened her yet filled her with uncertain promise. If he was calling her on the phone, perhaps she could reason with him. But first things first. "Please don't hurt my mother."

"I already have."

Roth's ominous tone sent a chill through her. "What do you mean by that? Is she alive?" Celia asked.

"She is. But not long if you don't do what I tell you."

"I wanna talk to her." Celia tiptoed to the back of the bedroom door, retrieved the sky-blue terry-cloth robe hanging there on a hook, and slipped it on, trying not to alert the tall man to the sound of her movements.

"She's indisposed at the moment. She's in a lot of pain. It took a lot to convince her to give me your new telephone number. Unfortunately, it cost her something."

"Cost her what?"

"A part of her body."

"Oh, Jesus." The frustration, dire concern, and anger came out in a blast of Celia's voice. "Let me talk to my mother now!" She hoped Marian was somewhere nearby and heard her screaming.

"I'm not going to do that. But you *will* listen to me."

"Why are you doing this to me? What do you want from me?"

"Your mother asked me the same question. And I will give you the same answer I gave her. I want you *dead*."

"Why?" Celia opened the bedroom door. She could faintly hear Marian and Graham downstairs, probably in the family room. Judging by their laughter, it was clear they did not hear her.

"That is not my concern."

Celia shook her head, hoping this phone call was a nightmare. She spoke in a loud voice, intended to alert Marian. "Please listen to me…"

The tall man cut her off with a burst of his voice. "No, you listen to me! You will follow my instructions exactly. If you don't, I will leave your mother's pretty head in the middle of Connery Road."

Celia scrambled downstairs, her bare feet almost sliding along the carpet in her haste. "Please don't hurt my mother anymore. I will do whatever you say."

"Do you have a passport?"

Celia hesitated for a moment, trying to remember where she had left her passport. *Oh, yes.* In the glove compartment of her car. "Yes, I do."

"I want you to come to Toronto. How you get here is your concern. At 4 o'clock Toronto time, I will post on your mother's Facebook page and tell you where to meet me. If you are not there in exactly thirty hours from now, I will kill your mother. If you involve any police, or anyone else, I will kill your mother. Do you understand me?"

Celia froze in her tracks. The tall man's statement about police gave her pause. She had intended to alert Marian that her pursuer was on the phone, and she knew, expected, that Marian would alert Liskey right away. Celia was just a few steps away from the family room, and the sounds of Marian and Graham laughing at a TV program were almost at a level that the tall man could hear. She turned and went in the opposite direction toward the basement stairs.

"Do you understand me?" the tall man repeated in a tone that suggested he would not ask that question again.

"Yes." Celia was not sure how she would keep that commitment. But, given the tall man murderous tendencies, it was the only answer she was sure would keep her mother alive for at least another thirty hours.

"If you think I am joking, look at *your* Facebook page."

Celia then heard a click on the other end.

Facebook page? Celia noted the time on her phone, and then, without hesitation, scurried down to the basement.

Celia knew Liskey had given Marian strict instructions not to allow her to leave the premises, use the house phone or use the computer. According to Liskey, any of those actions could cause the tall man, who had shown himself to be technologically savvy, to find her and put her and his family in danger. But Celia didn't see how looking at something on her Facebook page would cause any harm.

The laptop sat on a desk in the open area, surrounded by two neatly stacked piles of paper and magazines. *Please, no password*, Celia thought as she approached the laptop. She tapped a key, and Graham's Instagram page popped up. No password. *Perfect.*

Celia listened to make sure that Marian and Graham were still in the family room, then sat down at the laptop. Within a few keystrokes, she was on her Facebook page. She scrolled down, reading all the updates from her friends, most of whom had no idea what was going on with her. Then, she stopped, drew back, gasped, and then leaned in to make sure she was seeing what she was seeing. The photo, posted on her mother's Facebook account on Celia's timeline, was of a naked woman, bound, a pillowcase over her head. The tall man stood next to her. He held a large knife to her throat, and it looked as if he had drawn blood. It looked like one of those terrorist photos they took just before they beheaded someone. But as Celia read the caption, the photo became all too real:

Come to me within 30 hrs of this writing, or I will take off her head. No polizei, or else.

There was a crude blood-soaked bandage wrapped around Marjorie's left hand. The background, a generic field of daisies, was Photoshopped into the picture.

"Oh, Jesus, Momma." Celia's hand went to her gaping mouth, and tears streamed down her trembling face. "Don't worry, Momma. I'm coming. I'm gonna get you out of there."

Celia stared for a moment at the man who had disrupted and terrorized her life. He did not cover his face, which chilled Celia because he had no fear of being identified. Had she seen him on the street, she would not have guessed he was capable of such evil. He could have passed for a corporate exec if not for the intensity of his eyes.

She deleted the post, logged off the Facebook page, and walked back upstairs. Marian and Graham were still in the family room. She crept across the living room and hurried upstairs. It took five minutes for Celia to get dressed in blue jeans, a T-shirt, and sneakers. She grabbed her purse and cell phone and headed back downstairs, hoping this time that no one saw her. She tiptoed through the kitchen, gently opened the kitchen door so it didn't creak as it usually did, and walked out to the driveway. Looking at the house windows to make sure she wasn't being watched, Celia hurried out of the yard and to the sidewalk, finding herself on Bradley Boulevard. She walked two blocks until she found a Montgomery County Ride-On bus stop. She waited there, hoping the bus would take her to a major road, where she could catch a taxi to her apartment and get her car.

While waiting, Celia prayed for her mother, and for God's grace and mercy, that whatever happened 30 hours from now, both she and her mother would come out of it alive.

***

Liskey and Williams arrived back at Headquarters at 4

p.m., carrying a small boxful of DVDs holding surveillance videos from George Washington University Hospital security cameras covering a four-hour period after Pastor Lyons was wheeled into the emergency room following the shooting. They planned to spend most of the rest of the evening reviewing the footage, trying to verify any part of Pastor Lyons' story. Ramon Williams got on the phone to order Chinese carryout while Liskey dialed his wife on his desk phone.

"Hey, sweetie," Liskey said to his wife, hoping she had not yet started dinner.

"Hey to you," Marian answered.

"What you doin'?"

"Just got finished reorganizing the garage, and now I'm working on supper."

"Well, it looks like I'm not gonna be able to make supper. Still trying to find this guy that has Celia's mother. I got a ton of surveillance videos to review."

"I understand, honey. Graham's at a friend's house, so I guess it's just me and Celia here tonight."

"How's she?"

"She's been in her room all day. I haven't bothered her, like you told me."

"Let me talk to her. I have a few things to share with her about my conversation with Pastor Lyons today."

"Hon', can you call her on her cell phone? I'm mixing batter for the cake, and I can't stop right now."

"No problem, honey. I'll call you later." Liskey hung up, then dialed Celia's number. It went straight to voice mail.

He called Marian again.

"Honey, she didn't pick up the phone. Could you go up there and grab her for me?"

"Okay. Hold on."

While on hold, Liskey thought about how special his wife was. These late-night forays at the office broke up many cops' marriages. Staying late at the office was often used as a cover for infidelity, which often made wives so insecure they doubted the stability of the relationship. Fortunately, Marian never complained, which meant that she either trusted him, or she understood his job and married him with managed expectations. Liskey thought it was a little of both. He appreciated it and would have to show it by bringing her a box of fancy chocolates home, which, next to roses, was her preferred gift. He would have to stop by the Godiva boutique at Montgomery Mall on the way home.

Marian came back on the phone with a voice of urgency. "Lisk, Celia's not here."

Liskey switched the phone to the other ear. "What do you mean she's not there?"

"She's not here. I knocked on her door. I went in her room. She's not there. Her purse and cell phone are gone. She's not anywhere in the house."

"The backyard?"

"No. Nowhere."

"Maybe she stepped out for a minute."

"But why would she do that without telling me? I've been home all day. And Graham was home until about an hour ago."

"I'll try to reach her on her cell again. I'll call you back." Liskey hung up the desk phone, then pulled his cell phone out of his jacket phone to check for Celia's cell number. Having seen no incoming calls from her, he dialed her, but got her voice mail again. He left a message, hung up, and turned to Williams, but his partner was still on the phone.

To avoid ravaging himself with worry, Liskey tried to put a positive spin on Celia's disappearance. Isaac Roth was hundreds of miles away in Toronto, being hunted for the attempted murder of a police officer and for kidnapping. Every border station in Canada had since elevated their security protocols, ensuring that Isaac Roth would not get out of Canada anytime soon. Celia likely felt she was no longer in danger and went to take a walk. Being cooped up like she was the past few days would make anyone stir-crazy, and Liskey understood her need to get out of the house. Had she told Marian her intentions, Marian would likely have tried to convince her to stay inside, which was why Celia never said anything. Her cell phone and purse were gone, which meant she likely left intentionally. Based on his reasoning, Celia was likely safe, but it still made him nervous.

When Williams got off the phone, Liskey said to him, "Celia's gone. Left the house."

"Yeah?" Williams responded. "Voluntarily?"

"Looks that way."

"Well, you know there's not much we can do about it. She's a free woman. Probably felt that since Roth is in Canada, she's in no danger."

"To be honest, I'm surprised she stayed with us as long as she did."

"Maybe she went back to her apartment."

"Possible. I'll ride over there in a bit and check it out."

"Gotcha."

Liskey popped the first of the DVDs in his computer. He wanted to find out if Jonathan Newberry was at the hospital and if he had any contact with Wynn Delano. If so, that would verify at least part of Pastor Lyons' story and increase his suspicion of Newberry, since the minister would have been one of the last people to talk to the reporter before he was killed.

***

Photographed nude. The distal phalanges of her left pinky finger cut off because she dared to defy Isaac Roth by not immediately providing him with Celia's new cell number. A small laceration on her neck because Roth pressed the knife too firmly while making his sordid photographs. The only thing that lessened Marjorie's humiliation was the possibility that the photo posted on Facebook would engender a rescue for her. But even that hope was being dashed, as the tall man was moving her yet again.

The throbbing fire in what was once a complete finger intensified as the tall man pulled and dragged her, bound, across the basement floor, up the stairs, and back into the garage. He seemed to pull her along almost effortlessly, which meant that the tall man was incredibly strong or she was way too skinny. He opened the side door of the van and pushed her. Marjorie's legs connected with the bottom door jamb and she tripped and fell forward onto the van floor, her torn clothing cushioning her fall. The tall man grabbed Marjorie's legs, swung them forcefully inside the van, and shut the door.

Marjorie lay quietly on the floor, listening. She heard the garage door opening and saw an opportunity. It was a sunny and mild Saturday afternoon in Forest Hill, which meant there were people out gardening, jogging, walking, and talking with neighbors. Kids were at play in backyards. Husbands were in open garages, working on honey-do lists. Marjorie knew she could scream right now and someone would probably hear her, especially since the window of the van was still cracked open. But the sharpness of the pain in her finger and the sting of the wound in her neck brought her back to reality. This was the type of man that would kill her in a blink if she made one more wrong move.

After three minutes, Roth climbed in the driver seat, tossed his duffel bag on the passenger's seat, and backed out of the garage. Marjorie lay quiet and still, trying not to do anything that would raise her captor's ire, but hoping and praying that someone in the neighborhood would find something suspicious about a gray van pulling out of their garage and would call the police.

They didn't drive far, it seemed to Marjorie. She was certain they were still in Forest Hill when the van stopped, perhaps even still in the same block. The tall man put the van in park and rummaged through his duffel bag, producing a syringe and the vial of thick, white liquid. Marjorie knew the tall man was about to put her asleep again.

But given the pain tearing through her body, and her increasingly frequent bouts of nausea, and little hope of being rescued soon, Marjorie welcomed the relief from the pain and fear that the medicine inside that syringe would give her.

***

Celia thought she would never return here, but now that she was about to turn herself over to the hands of a murdering maniac, her sense of nostalgia forced her to come upstairs to apartment 1021.

The first thing she saw upon approaching the apartment was the summons for failure to pay rent taped to her door. *My husband gets killed, but they still want their rent*, Celia thought. She briefly read the summons, noticing that the rent was behind almost $6,500. She would have her parents pay the back due, but she knew she would never live here again.

Celia unlocked the door and pushed it open, standing just outside the threshold. Someone had cleaned the apartment since the last time she saw it. No glass on the floor. They had put the furniture back into place. The section of the carpet where her husband had fallen was dislodged from the wall and folded over. The blood had been cleaned up. There was a weird, lingering chemical smell, which told her that they had recently cleaned, perhaps within the past 24 hours.

Celia walked into the apartment, looking into every room. Except for the laptop, she noticed nothing missing, which surprised her. Surely some unscrupulous building mainte-nance employee, a police officer, or a member of the crime scene cleanup crew could have helped themselves to some of the gold and diamond jewelry on the dresser, or a pair or two of Justin's still fresh designer sneakers, or the $75.00 in Justin's wallet on the nightstand. But everything was pres-ent and accounted for, and everything was in place, almost as if nothing had happened.

Not that it would have mattered to Celia if any of it was missing. There was once a time when she walked into this apartment and beamed with pride at all the possessions they had. Now, with the gravity of what she was facing, all of it was just stuff—things that provided no comfort, no hope, unimportant, irrelevant. None of it could help her now. None of it could calm her fears or soothe her pain. They could only dislodge memories, tell about the potential of a life to come. But for Celia, that life was now gone. If she were still alive on the other side of this mess, she would likely start over, live with her parents, and help take care of her mother, as it was clear from the photo on Facebook she had serious injuries.

She removed the $75.00 from Justin's wallet, leaving the ID and credit cards. She figured most of the credit cards had been canceled for nonpayment anyway.

Her next stop was the walk-in closet. About three-quar-ters of it was filled with her clothes, with Justin's taking up the remaining space. Justin had been happy with a ward-robe comprising jeans and T-shirts, with sweatshirts in the winter. Celia fondly remembered trying to get him to up-date his wardrobe and even tried to buy him a few outfits from Macy's. Those outfits still hung in the closet, barely worn.

Celia sighed and tried to fight a tear. There was death or grief on the other side of her trip to Toronto, and neither choice was acceptable to her. The apartment had a stillness and loneliness that worsened her despair. She had to get out of there. She had to get to Toronto, find her father, talk to her sisters and brothers, and hug them all before she reported to Isaac Roth.

Celia closed the closet door and walked toward the front door. She took one more look at the apartment before she turned and walked out. Her car was the only possession she wanted to take from this place.

Celia checked her watch. It was 1:05 p.m. She had a little over 28 hours before Isaac Roth's deadline.

CHAPTER FIFTEEN

If they were going to spend half a shift staring at boring hospital surveillance videos, then they intended to be comfortable while doing it. Liskey and Williams had removed their jackets, neckties, and soft-soled black Oxfords. They had propped their feet on chairs borrowed from the cubicles of the detectives they knew wouldn't be reporting in until the 8 pm to 6 am shift. They cradled Asian takeout boxes filled with steaming shrimp lo mein while watching the videos on Liskey's computer screen. The shift supervisor had left for the day; nonetheless, with no danger of them being discovered, they still hid the Heinekens in their bottom desk drawer, retrieving them only when they took the occasional sip.

They had retrieved Wynn Delano's description and were now watching cameras mounted at the entrance of the hospital emergency room. They didn't have the exact time of Wynn Delano's visit, so they had to watch footage from about a half hour after Pastor Lyons' shooting. Minutes quickly turned into an hour, and an hour into two hours, with Williams drifting off at one point, and Liskey having to make a few trips to the bathroom because of the beer. Finally, after two-and-a-half hours of watching over a hundred people enter through the ER's doors, Williams noticed a man with a blue sport coat and shiny black hair pad urgently through the doors.

"Wait, is that him?" Williams drew Liskey's attention from the texts on his cell phone.

Liskey looked up, then quickly pressed pause on the video application. "That looks like him."

"Yeah, that's him."

"Let's hope he doesn't leave the waiting area. They got no cameras in the treatment area. And I just got a text from Detective Sergeant Jim Peeks. Wants me to give him a call."

"What's the matter? They can't afford long distance?" Williams restarted the video feed.

"Figured it's my case, we should pay the dime," Liskey guessed. He picked up the phone and dialed. If a Toronto detective was texting him at seven in the evening, it must be important.

When the Toronto detective picked up, Liskey left out any greeting and said merely "Jim."

"You guys hear the latest greatest?" Jim's voice was high-pitched and almost squeaky.

"No."

"Okay, so I'm in my office. It's my brother's birthday, and I got reservations at Jacob's. I'm getting ready to plunk down a day's salary on his birthday meal. Just when I'm about to head to the restaurant, I get a call from my CO. He got a call from the FBI field office in Palo Alto, because they got a call from the folks at Facebook. Looks like somebody posted a photo on Marjorie's Wise Facebook account. A very graphic photo. I'm going to send it to your email now because Facebook took the post down about an hour ago."

Liskey heard the chime on his computer; *incoming email.* He paused the video on his computer screen, to Williams' chagrin, as he was trying to track Wynn Delano's movements. Liskey pulled up his email and clicked on the message from Jim.

"Oh, my God." Liskey examined the photo.

Williams leans in, almost dropping a forkful of lo mein.

"Is that Celia's mother?"

"Hard to say for sure," Jim responded. "Based on the photos of her we got from her husband, it's the same body type, same complexion. And that's definitely our guy Roth."

"Why is she naked?"

"I don't know. Some kinky thing he likes to do, maybe."

"He's even showing his face," Liskey printed out the photo and slipped it into a file of papers on his desk. "He's either got to be the cockiest sunnavabitch I know, or he really thinks he's invincible. He obviously wanted Celia to see this post. How does he know she would see it?"

"If she's like every other person under 50 on this continent, she's probably checking her page twenty times a day. But I got another story to tell you."

Liskey scoffed. Peeks really got a kick out of telling his stories. "Lay it on me."

"Last night, I get a call from the police service in Hamilton. It is a city about an hour away from Toronto. They got a 9-1-1 call saying that someone had just dumped a van in one of their neighborhoods, and the guy, a tall white guy, that dumped it was walking down the street with a black woman who was wearing no shoes."

"Do they know about Roth?"

"Every police service in Ontario knows about Roth. We got posters, TV, social media, the whole nine, both him and Mrs. Wise. Anyway, HPS takes the call very seriously, as they should have. They blocked off every street and laneway within a mile radius. They had officers on the ground going door-to-door. They called in the K-9s. They found the van, and they knew right away Roth had dumped it."

"How?"

"For one, it was stolen from Tobin's Mechanical. It's a plumbing company in Toronto. The second thing is they found one of Marjorie's shoes in the van, and it matches the shoe they found at the school. But there's a problem."

"What?"

"The engine in the plumbing van is as cold as a brick. They figured it had been sitting there for at least ninety minutes before the 9-1-1 call came in, but the people who called it in claimed it had just showed up there. So, they go at the people who made the call. They live about three blocks down from the spot where the van was found. They couldn't answer any detailed questions. Finally, they confessed that their son, who was supposed to be home from work at 9:30, called them about an hour later from an unlisted number, told them he had been kidnapped by the guy the police were looking for, and told them to call the police and say that the van had just been dropped off. This was at ten thirty."

Liskey already knew this story would not end with the capture of Roth. Otherwise, Roth would not have been able to post a Facebook photo. "Roth got an hour head start before the call came in."

"Looks that way."

Something clicked in Liskey's head, and his face went flush. "Jim, when was this photo posted?"

"At exactly 11:04 a.m."

"Thanks, Jim. I'll call you back." Liskey hung up and then prepared to dial again. Before he did, he turned to Williams. "Tell me we have a description of Celia's car and her license plate number on file."

"Yep," Williams answered. "We got that information when we searched it."

"Get it to Jim Peeks."

"What's going on? What are you headed with this?"

Liskey turned back to the phone and dialed his wife's number. "What if Celia saw that picture and now she's headed to Toronto? If she is, it's the worst thing she could do. We have to make sure she doesn't get past the border."

***

It was thirty minutes to midnight when Celia rolled her red Dodge Charger into Detroit, Michigan. Now only four hours away from Toronto, a conflict in her heart was getting the best of her. She wanted desperately to save her mother, but her own fear of dying stirred up a soulish agony in her. It was everything in her not to head back to Silver Spring, turn herself over to Liskey, and hope and pray that he had a plan to protect her and save her mother. But even now, with the stress producing palpitations and a mild headache, she couldn't trust the police. It was a remnant of living many years in a crime-ridden neighborhood in Detroit where many of the citizens did not trust law enforcement and often dealt with their crime issues on their own. But she didn't trust Roth either, so it was a matter of choosing between the lesser of two evils. And since Roth seemed to be holding all the cards, Celia didn't want to bet against him.

She could have kept straight on the highway to Canada but waxed nostalgic by driving through her old stomping grounds. Her trip down memory lane brought her past Hutzel Women's Hospital, where she and her eldest sister were born. She remembered working there as a filing clerk during the summer of 1999, her first summer job. She recalled everyone talking about Y2K as if it was Armageddon, and how all the hospitals in the city would shut down on January 1, 2000. She also remembered sitting in a room by herself, filing, with almost no contact with anyone. It bored her silly, but she stuck it out, hoping to use the money to buy new school clothes, as all the school kids in Detroit had to look fly on their first day of school.

She turned onto Grand Boulevard Avenue. Just a few blocks up, and she would be just five blocks away from her childhood home. Grand Boulevard was the virtual fence she couldn't climb over, the line she couldn't cross, when she was a pre-teen. Her father had warned her that she could venture as far as Grand Boulevard, but never cross it. The only exception was when she was being accompanied by an older sibling. Her mother was even more restrictive, recommending she go no farther than the McMichael Middle School, which was only one block away from their home.

She turned off Grand Boulevard and approached Alpheus Street, the one-block neighborhood where she grew up. Riding down Alpheus Street, Celia could tell, even in the dark, that the neighborhood had not changed in five years. There were only a few houses on the block, and half of them were vacant, including an apartment building that sat on the corner, beer bottles standing like sentries on the sills of broken windows. Many houses had been vacant for as long as she could remember. One lone streetlight flickered at the end of the block. She saw a few people in the shadows of the porches, the only thing giving them away was the glow on their cigarettes as they took a drag. Alleyways and many houses were almost entirely shrouded by overgrown shrubbery, rusting shopping carts, and rotting tires. A few suspicious-looking young men wearing white T-shirts, jeans, and baseball caps worn in reverse eyeballed her as she passed.

To the casual outsider, this distressed and impoverished neighborhood was not the place to be caught in at night. But to Celia, it was home. Most residents were decent, upstanding citizens, but there were a few, on this block and on those surrounding it, that were as shady as they come.

Celia stopped in front of the address that had formerly served as her home for twenty-seven years. The modest three-bedroom bungalow had white siding and a covered porch just large enough to accommodate opening the front door and not much else. Another family had moved in, erected a chain-link fence around the property, and seemed to take pride in its upkeep. Her father had screened the buyer well, as he didn't want just anyone buying his former house. For the sake of his neighbors, some of whom he knew and loved, the people living there had to contribute to the well-being of the community, not destroy it. Celia sat there and looked at the house for a few minutes, wishing she could somehow return to the simplicity of days there.

Suddenly she heard a loud knock on her driver's side window. She jumped and spun.

"Malik!" she exclaimed, recognizing the person rapping on her window. Smiling, she stepped out of her car and wrapped her arms around the man whose mother had named him Anthony Sharp at birth. In his teens, he had adopted the name "Malik" as a form of cultural identification, following a general trend for some black men to adopt Islamic or Muslin names, whether or not they were Muslim.

Malik hugged her back, then held Celia in front of him. Celia checked him out, admiring his toned, tattooed biceps and his pectoral muscles bulging beneath a white A-shirt. Celia was 22 years old when she first met Malik, who occasionally visited his 65-year-old uncle on Alpheus Street. He had tried on more than one of his visits to hit on her. Celia, very attracted to Malik, would hang out with him whenever he came to visit Alpheus Street. But Celia's overprotective father would have none of it. George Wise would often tell Malik to stay away from his daughter. This worried Celia, because Malik was a hothead. There had been rumors that Malik took a teen into one of the abandoned buildings and beat him to within an inch of his life over a drug deal. Since that rumor surfaced, Celia's passion for Malik waned, and she followed her father's advice by staying away from him. But in her mind, Malik was exactly the type of guy she wanted, a hardened thug who would protect her from the mean streets of upper west Detroit. He was a far cry from the Bible-quoting Clarke Sanders that her parents wanted her to date.

"Baby girl, what's up with you?" Malik reluctantly released his hold on her while scanning her up and down. "You look kinda rough."

Celia gave him a look of offense, then lightened up. "Yeah, it's been a rough few days."

"Talk to me, girl. What's going on with you?"

Celia looked at him for a moment, not sure how much of the past few days she wanted to share. Malik would have been the perfect guy to have by her side during this crisis. Malik would have likely tracked the tall man down and pushed him off the Woodrow Wilson Bridge. But with a little over 17 hours to go before the tall man's deadline, there was nothing that Celia had to lose by telling Malik her troubles.

Malik sensed her indecision and motioned his head toward his grandfather's house, a two-story Cape Cod with white siding and a porch that extended across the entire front of the house. "Come on over here and holla at me for a minute."

Celia followed Malik to the porch and sat in one of the two rusting metal folding chairs on the porch. Malik sat on the other, turning it so he was at a ninety-degree angle to her. "What's going on?"

Celia looked forward, wringing her hands, but said nothing.

Malik tried to prime the pump. "I heard you hooked up with a white boy and moved down to chocolate city."

Celia looked at Malik with silent contempt, which gave Malik his answer. Celia would have vehemently denied it if it weren't true.

"So, how's that going?" Malik inquired.

Celia looked forward again, then let out a long sigh. "My husband is deceased."

To be polite, Malik said, "Oh, man, sorry to hear that." But he was not the least bit sorry. He was angry when he heard Celia had gotten married and moved to D.C. He harbored resentment in his heart for Justin for many years, a sentiment which dissipated with time. Now, he was glad for another chance with her, given she showed up on Alpheus Street unannounced at almost midnight. "How'd it happen?"

Celia tried to fight the memory, which she knew would bring forth tears. "He was shot."

"Oh, man. Was he robbed, or what?"

"The police don't know."

"So, that's why you're back in Zone 8?"

"Kinda sorta."

"Well, baby girl, I'm here for you."

Celia continued to look directly across the street, at her old home, conjuring memories of the good days there so she could crowd out memories of her husband's violent death.

"You got someplace to stay?"

That question from Malik snapped Celia out of her memory zone. She was tired, but there was no way she would lay her head at Malik's grandfather's house, which she knew was what Malik was implying. She felt almost hypocritical for being so cautious, especially since was certain the tall man would kill her in 17 hours. What could Malik and his grandfather do to her that was worse than what had happened over the past few days and what was about to happen? But making herself that vulnerable to a man of dubious character grated on her nerves, although back in the day, she might have welcomed such an invitation.

"I'm okay. Thanks," Celia muttered.

"C'mon, girl. I ain't gonna do nothin' to you," Malik said. "You can crash on the couch."

"Actually, I'm on my way to Toronto," Celia told him.

"Your Dad's place?"

"Yes."

"Baby girl, that's another four, five hours drive." Malik

motioned his head toward his front door. "Get some rest. Head out in the morning."

Eager to skip the subject, Celia pointed her chin toward her former house. "Who lives there now?"

Malik sighed. "Some older lady. She got a couple of grandkids that live with her. They don't come out much. Big Poppa's been tryin' to get with her, but she ain't tryin' to play ball. He don't get out much either, and it ain't like it's a whole lot of people 'round here to him to be kickin' it with, know what I'm sayin'?"

Celia looked at Malik. "What happened to Mee Maw?"

"She passed two years ago," Malik reported. "You ain't heard?"

"No."

"Big Poppa been strugglin' to deal with it, too. That's why I been spending more time over here, tryin' to make sure he all right."

"You've always been good to him."

"He's like a dad to me, more than my own pops."

"Your pops still up at Oaks?"

"Yeah. They gave him a double deuce. No parole. Gonna be there for a minute."

They sat in silence for a few minutes while Malik lit and dragged on a half-spent Black & Mild lying on the living room windowsill. Finally, Malik looked straight ahead. "You sure you don't need a place to crash? Wouldn't recommend sleepin' in your car. Not around here."

Celia sighed. "No, but there is something you can help me with."

"What's that?" Malik said eagerly.

"You got any charges? Any paper on you?"

"Naw, girl. I'm clean."

"You ever been to Toronto?"

***

Liskey lay in his bed, his topless body covered with 1500 thread count Egyptian cotton sheets. Marian had turned to her side and gone to sleep an hour before, but confusion, frustration, and guilt kept Liskey's eyes open. It bothered him that Isaac Roth had possibly coaxed Celia out of hiding and made her come straight to him, and now he wished he had done a better job at protecting her. Maybe turning her over to witness services would have been a better idea.

He had done everything he could to track down Celia. Patrol in neither district reported seeing her or her car. Every one of his calls to her cell phone went straight to voice-mail. He had given Detective Sergeant Jim Peeks instructions to contact Border Services and detain her if she tried to cross into Canada. Later, Ramon Williams talked him out of it, reasoning it would be better to allow Celia to cross the border, but track her every move, hoping that she would lead them to Isaac Roth.

Although Liskey agreed and took Ramon's suggestion, he had little hope it would work. Isaac Roth was crafty, and Liskey doubted that Roth would reveal his whereabouts to Celia in a phone call, allowing every cop in town to pounce on him. *No.* Roth would not reveal where he would meet Celia until the last possible moment, giving the police little time to organize and capture him. So, he agreed that the Toronto police should track Celia indiscriminately from the border and report back to Liskey, and their own units, her whereabouts. He had to trust them. He had no other choice.

However, Liskey doubted that Roth would be anywhere near the location that Celia would be told to go. Roth was a trained sniper. He could take her out with the same 308 Winchester rounds he had shot the pastor with. With those rounds, he could be three blocks away, gun her down, and then be gone before anyone knew where the bullet came from. Liskey made sure Jim Peeks knew this and Roth's MO: Roth would likely set up in a hotel, or an apartment building, someplace where he could work in private and have a line of sight to wherever he would lead Celia. Liskey urged Peeks to have special ops teams ready to deploy to any hotel or apartment building within a three-block radius of the location, once they discovered where it was. He asked Peeks to alert him as soon as Celia tried to cross the border.

Liskey wanted to wake his wife for a little intimacy, which always took his mind off things. But he decided against it, as he had already talked her ear off about the developments — or lack thereof — in the case. Violating his cardinal rule not to discuss work at home, Liskey had needed a sounding board, and his wife was ready and willing. Besides, this was different. Both Liskey and Marian had grown fond of Celia, and to have her leave the house like this left them flabbergasted.

Liskey needed a plan B in case tracking Celia from the border did not work. Shortly after looking at the hospital videos with Williams, Liskey knew what that plan would be.

In the videos, Jonathan Newberry was clearly meeting with Wynn Delano just outside the visitor's lounge. After the meeting, Newberry went back into the lounge and made a phone call while Wynn talked with other witnesses. Two hours after that meeting, the same man who had tried to kill Pastor Lyons killed Wynn. It was too coincidental. Newberry had to be involved, which meant that Pastor Lyons' story — the most sensible parts, anyway — was credible.

Liskey looked over at his wife as she slept peacefully. He didn't know how much sleep he would get tonight. But one thing he knew. In the morning, Marian would go to her church and worship, in the name of Jesus.

Liskey would also go to church, for the first time in a while. But it wouldn't be to worship.

Chapter Sixteen

Losing Hope

"Let me understand this." Malik lit another cigarette and stood to lean on the banister surrounding the porch, facing Celia as she stood near the door. "This dude killed your man, killed a reporter, and now he's got your mother and is trying to kill you? And you wanna walk right into his hands?"

"If you have a better idea, I'll hear it." Now that Celia had told Malik about the past few days goings-on, she felt a burden lifted somewhat. She sipped on a Vernors that Malik had brought her from the kitchen.

"And you can't go to the police?"

"He said no police. I can't take any chances that the police will mess this up. So far, the cops haven't even been able to catch him."

"Oh, I ain't got no love for the po po, baby, so don't sweat that. But I'm sayin', you just gonna give up your life like that?"

"That's my mom, Malik. She gave me life. I'm not gonna let anybody kill her, although I'm sure she would be willing to die for me, just like I am for her."

"But he might kill both of you."

"Rather that, than live with the guilt of knowing I could have saved my mother, and I didn't."

Malik sucked his teeth. "That's bold, girl."

"Well, I don't really have any other choice."

"So, that's how it's gonna be, huh?"

"That's how it's going to be." Celia looked down, bristling at the finality of those words. "Besides, if I don't do this, he'll kill my mom, and then he'll still come after me. Maybe he'll kidnap my father this time, or maybe one of my brothers and sisters. He's been at my dad's house. He probably knows everything about my family. It has to end."

"Do your father, or your brothers and sisters, know what you about to do?" Malik asked.

Celia looked down and shook her head.

"So, what do you want *me* to do?"

Celia wrung her hands together. "I don't know. I guess I just want somebody with me."

Malik frowned at the morbid suggestion. "Baby girl, I got mad love for you and all, but I ain't fittin' to go up to Canada and watch you get dropped."

"You won't. You can go back about an hour before the deadline. You can take my car."

Malik hung his head. "I don't know, girl."

"Malik, I have maybe 17 hours to live. If there is anything that can be done to get me out of this and save my mother, I don't want to do it alone."

"You got heart, girl. I'll give you that. Where are you s'posed to meet this dude, anyway?"

"I don't know. He's gonna post the location on my mom's Facebook page at 4 o'clock in the afternoon."

Malik scoffed. "You know this is a straight setup, right? I mean, this dude ain't gonna come to that location and shake your hand. He's gonna probably drive by, put you down, and keep on movin'. And then, how do you know he's gonna let your mother live? He might kill her out of spite. It's like you've died for nothing."

"Yes, but then it'll be over for the rest of my family."

"But how do you know that? You don't even know why he got beef with you. If it's because of something you know, how do you know he won't still come after your family in case you told *them*?"

Celia sighed. "Malik, you're starting to bum me out here."

"I don't care about that." Malik caught his voice escalating and toned it down. "I mean, this don't make no sense."

Celia took a few steps closer to Malik and lightly placed her right hand on his shoulder. She breathed, "I know there are no guarantees, but this is the best chance I have to save my family. I *also* know that I don't want to spend the rest of my life in guilt because I had a chance to save my mother, and I didn't."

Malik searched her eyes and saw the earnestness there. "Girl, back in the day, I would have done anything for you."

"That's because you were trying to get some." Celia's eyelids batted flirtatiously.

"Baby girl, half the cats on the westside was tryin' to sleep with you. They used to say them church girls was the biggest freaks and they had the best stuff."

"Is that why you wanted to sleep with me?"

Malik scoffed again. "I ain't gonna front. Hell, yeah."

Celia nodded, respecting his honesty.

"But with you," Malik continued, "I think it would have been a lot more." He paused, looking away as Celia regarded him. "That is until you went and got jungle fever."

Celia playfully shoved him. "Shut up."

After responding with a laugh and a smile, Malik said, "Aw-ight, tell you what. We gonna do this, aw-ight? But the only reason why is because we gotta figure out how to get you out of this mess. You a good girl. You a Christian girl, and you ain't goin' out like that. You don't deserve that."

"My mother doesn't either."

"Well, let's hope we can save both y'all." Malik stepped past her and opened the front door. "Let me get my passport."

Celia looked at him quizzically. "*You* got a passport?"

Malik nodded. "Went up there for a job interview once."

"Make sure that's all you get."

"What you mean?"

Celia gave Malik a deadpan stare.

"You kiddin', right?" Malik shot back.

"I'm serious. We can't risk getting caught at the border with a Glock in the trunk."

Malik clicked his teeth, then deferred to her wisdom. "Aw-ight. I hear you. But I sure hope you got a plan to get one once we get across."

Celia smiled. "I do."

***

1:30 am, Sunday

Liskey had just drifted off to sleep when his cell phone rang. He looked over at his wife, who did not stir. She was so used to Liskey's phone going off during the night that she had learned to tune it out, even when she was asleep.

Liskey reached for his phone on the nightstand. He saw Jim Peeks' number and answered quickly. "Hey, Jim."

"Detective Liskey. Sorry to wake you."

"Wasn't really sleeping well. What's up?"

"Your girl just crossed the border at the Ambassador Bridge. She had some guy with her."

"Who?"

"His name is Anthony Sharp."

"Who's that?"

"Passport said he's from Detroit. Couple of priors. Probably a friend she picked up along the way. Anyway, the CBSA pulled them into secondary and searched the car. They didn't find anything. They put the GPS tracker on the car. They're headed east on 401 now. If they don't stop, they should be in Toronto in about three and a half hours."

"Call me when they get there."

"You got it."

***

Marjorie was feeling worse than someone thrown into a terrorist prison cell. She had awakened six hours ago, finding her mouth taped and gagged, and a blanket wrapped around her, and noticed they were in yet another cargo van. Marjorie wondered why he suddenly went through the extra step of covering her. Maybe he was getting bothered by her nakedness.

The burning in her body was more intense now due to the drugs coursing through her system, and it didn't help that the tall man had given her nothing to eat or drink since he had captured her. Her finger was now throbbing and swollen with infection. Marjorie had fasted before—her church called for a community fast at least once per year. But the heat and lack of water were weakening Marjorie such that she no longer had the strength to fight for her own survival.

She looked at the tall man, who was still sitting in the driver's seat looking out the window. It had to be four in the morning, Marjorie thought. *When did this guy ever go to sleep?* Sheets covered the van's rear windows, making it impossible for anyone to look in, or for Marjorie to look out. Therefore, Marjorie had no idea that she was still in her neighborhood, still parked a block and a parkette away from her house.

Since she could neither talk nor move, she sat on the van floor, waiting for whatever fate befell her. She hoped her daughter got the Facebook message and, if so, would stay put and ignore the tall man's order not to call the police. She knew her daughter had a history of making bad decisions and hoped that her response to the tall man's threat would be an exception.

All she could do now was pray that the Lord would intervene mightily. But she felt, deep in her spirit, that she was about to die, no matter what.

***

8:00 am

George Wise could never sleep in strange beds. Add to that the worry and fear of knowing his wife and daughter were in danger, and there was no way he could sleep, despite having tried for eight hours to get some shut-eye. George got out of bed and looked out the open window, enjoying a view of mature northern pines against a sea-blue sky. He stood there for a while, expecting the beauty of nature to take his mind off his wife, then heard the crunching of gravel in the driveway. He put on a pair of shorts and a T-shirt and headed toward the front room. As George entered, he saw that Detective Hall had already come inside, turned around and left again. Two bags of fast food sat on the dining room table, along with the detective's cell phone.

George had an instant temptation. He wanted to pick up the phone, call one of his kids, and find out if they had heard anything about what was going on. He knew the detectives had advised him not to contact anyone, but he didn't see how contacting his daughter, who was a TV reporter in Detroit, would cause any harm.

George was certain the detective didn't go far without his cell phone. He went to the dining room window and peered out. At the end of the driveway, Detective Hall was chatting up a pretty blonde wearing a sports bra and a pair of ultra-high cut shorts. *He's gonna be a minute,* George thought.

He grabbed the phone from the table and stood close to

the dining room window, where he could keep Detective Hall in his sights, yet ensure that the detective did not see him. He dialed his daughter's number from memory. A pitch-perfect newscaster's voice answered. "This is Meagan Wise."

"Oh, my God, Meagan. It's so good to hear your voice."

"Dad?"

"Yes, honey. Listen, I don't have a lot of time. I..."

"Dad, what the hell's going on? What's going on with Mom?"

George checked on the detective. Still engaged with the blonde. "I guess you've heard about your mother and Celia."

"Yes. It's all over Facebook. I've been trying to reach you since yesterday."

"What do you mean it's all over Facebook?"

"Dad, you didn't see the photo with Mom?"

"No."

"Oh, my goodness, Dad. There was a photo of Mom on my Facebook feed yesterday. She was butt naked, with this white guy holding a knife to her throat. It looked like he had cut her up. And the message said that he would take off her head if someone didn't come to him within 30 hours."

George turned away from the window. "Are you serious?"

"Dad, why would I *not* be serious about something like that? I called the police as soon as I saw it."

"What time did you see it?"

"I dunno. A little before noon yesterday, I think. Where are you? Whose number are you calling from?"

"Honey, I can't talk long. I'm using someone else's phone." George turned to the window and peered out. No sign of the girl or the detective.

Then the front door opened.

George quickly pressed the button to end the call. He

tossed the phone back on the table just before Detective Hall walked in, turned and noticed him. George innocently pointed to one of the fast food bags. "I assume one of these is for me."

"Absolutely." The detective approached the table, grabbed his phone and slipped it in his pants pocket. He sat at the table with George as they devoured their breakfast sandwiches. "Man, you would not believe this chick I just got finished talking to. She was hot. Legs from here to Saskatchewan. D'ya see her?"

"I caught a glimpse."

"Too bad she was married. I don't understand husbands that let their cute wives run around half-naked like that."

"Well, we're in the boondocks. Not like anyone's gonna see her."

"Point for you."

Midway through a bite, George asked, "Any update on my wife?"

Without looking up, the detective shook his head. "Nothing yet."

George stopped chewing. "You sure about that?"

Detective Hall also stopped eating and looked up at George. "Your tone implies that I know something I'm not telling you."

"Well, do you?"

Detective Hall leaned back and gave George a stern expression that eventually morphed into a smile. "Mr. Wise, as a detective involved in a criminal investigation, there are many details about a case that we are not privy to share with…"

"Oh, don't spew me the company line!" George retorted.

"Well, what do you want me to say?" the detective shot back.

George stood, his palms firmly on the table. "I want you to tell me about that photo of my wife on social media yesterday."

The detective pursed his lips and nodded slightly. "How d'you know about that?"

George turned away from the table. "You should never leave your cell phone lying around."

"So, you called somebody on my phone? Who d'you call?"

"My daughter."

"Celia?"

"No. My daughter in Lansing. She's a TV reporter."

"You called a family member, even though we told you it could jeopardize the case?"

George turned around, his eyes burning with fire. "My beloved wife was on social media yesterday naked with a knife to her throat. Half of Michigan probably knows about it. Now, tell me how a phone call to my daughter from a detective's phone is going to hurt your case."

The detective stood. "You had no right to use my phone."

"Well, then lock me up. Send me to jail." George scoffed. "Oh, that's right. I'm already *in* jail."

"Well, Mr. Wise, if you can't appreciate the efforts we are making to keep you and your family safe..."

A blast of George's voice startled the detective. "Safe? Safe?"

For a minute, there was silence in the room, permeated only by the ticking of a clock on the dining room wall. Finally, George spoke up. "Detective, how many kids do you have?"

The detective almost ashamedly answered, "I have none."

"Then you can't possibly know what I'm feeling right now, that the only way to know if my family's safe is if they are right here in my arms." George crossed his arms and stared glumly out the dining room window. "It's my job to keep them safe. Not deferring to a wet-behind-the-ears childless detective who likes to flirt with sexy blondes while on duty."

Detective Hall merely glared at George, having no other visible reaction to George's insult.

Another minute passed before George spoke again. "My apologies. I'm just very frustrated right now."

Detective Hall nodded. "I understand."

Both men sat back down at the table.

"I have to leave this in God's hands. I need to pray. But before I do, I have a favor to ask."

"What's that?"

"I want to see that photo."

"Why?"

"Humor me."

"Mr. Wise, I know you're older than me. But now it's time for me to give you a little advice."

"Which is?"

Detective Hall held his head down and pondered his words before speaking. "I don't know how all of this is going to end. And I pray that it ends well, and we are working to ensure that it does. But if it doesn't, that photo is not the last image you want to see of your wife."

George nodded. "You may be right."

"It's just not a good idea."

"But I want to see it anyway. Who knows? I might know the guy."

"I doubt that."

"Try me."

"It's confidential."

"Detective, it's my wife. There's nothing I haven't seen before. And as for the creep holding her, my guess is you have his picture all over half of Canada by now. And if you don't, then you're not doing your job."

Detective Hall reached into his pocket for his cell phone. "You need to prepare yourself for this. It's not pretty."

With pursed lips and eyebrows furrowed, George gently

nodded. Detective Hall loaded the photo on his phone, then pushed the phone toward George with the screen upward.

"Oh, God." George squeezed his eyes shut to keep the tears from falling, but he was unsuccessful. "Oh, Marjorie. Why would he do this to my sweet Marjorie? That woman never hurt a fly. Why would he do this? Oh, Lord." His shock quickly took a turn into anger. He slammed his hand hard on the table, causing the centerpice to jump and almost topple. "I swear if I get my hands on this—"

Detective Hall quickly interrupted. "Isaac Roth posted that photo on your wife's page yesterday. We caught it and took it down shortly after, but we think Celia saw it already. Long story short, she's on her way to Toronto. In fact, she may be there now."

"And you're going to find her and stop her, right?"

"Right," the detective lied.

George looked at the photo again. "My sweet Marge. Why did he have to take her clothes off? Why did he hurt her like this? What have we done to this guy that he would do this?"

Detective Hall said nothing.

George craned his neck forward, concentrating on something in the photograph. "Wait a minute. Does anybody know where this photo was taken?"

Detective Hall suddenly perked up. "We don't know. We're looking into that."

"The pillowcase over my wife's head. It looks like the same pillowcases my wife bought about a week ago for the basement bedroom. That taupe grid pattern. That's got to be the same pillowcase."

Detective Hall leaned in to check out the photo. "You sure?"

"Yeah. We got 'em from this linen place over on Yonge Street. What's the chance he took my wife somewhere where they have the same pillowcases? Even that knife looks like it came from my wife's kitchen. I don't care about that fake background. He took this picture in my house!"

Detective Hall had his walkie-talkie off his belt within seconds.

George held up his hand. "Wait a second."

"Why?"

"Get me a laptop."

"For what?"

"I have a way to check the inside of my house without anyone knowing."

9:30 am

Ramon Williams, dressed in a tan suit, sat in his car in the parking lot of Harbor Christian Cathedral, near the National Harbor in Prince George's County, just across the D.C. border. He stared in amazement at the church, an almost oval two-story monolith that stretched across nine square blocks, with tinted windows and a steeple portico that rose sixty feet in the air. People came in droves, half of them attending the nine-a.m. service, while the other half were arriving early for the main eleven a.m. service.

Liskey arrived at 9:45 wearing a black suit, tie, and his leather-soled Oxfords rather than the comfort soles he normally wore to work.

Williams regarded him as he approached. "Your idea of getting dressed for church is to just change your shoes? Remember, Lisk, we need to blend in and not scare this guy away by looking like cops on the prowl."

Liskey looked around. "I'm a white guy in a PG County megachurch. How much blending in do you think I'm gonna do? Besides, we don't have time to wait until after the eleven o'clock service is over. We have to talk to him now."

"In the middle of service?" Williams was confused. "The guy's in the pulpit, Lisk."

"No, he's not," Liskey responded. "I called Pastor Lyons last night. Newberry usually doesn't preach the nine o'clock service. He's in the building, but he lets one of his associate ministers preach that service. So, we have just enough time to pull his coat before the next service starts."

Williams let out a hard, exasperated breath. "I thought we planned to go in, act like normal church folk, blend in, observe things, and see if we can hook up with the pastor after service."

"Lyons said that wouldn't work," Liskey told him. "This church isn't like the old country churches I grew up with, where the pastor says goodbye to everyone at the front door. No. At these megachurches, many of the pastors disappear right after they preach. Besides, we don't have time for that. Celia's probably in Toronto as we speak. Naw, we gotta go straight up."

"So, what's the plan? We got no warrant, and if everything Pastor Lyons says about this guy is true, then he's not gonna want to talk to any cops."

Liskey spent five minutes telling Williams his plan. Once he got Williams' buy-in, they started across the massive parking lot toward the front door of the church. When they were halfway there, Liskey's phone rang. Liskey signaled Williams to stop and then answered the phone.

"Sergeant Peeks," Liskey said loudly so that Williams could hear whom he was talking to. "Thought you were going to call me when they hit town. They should've hit town hours ago."

Jim Peeks sleepy-sounding response was low and gruff. "Nope. They stopped off at a Ho Jo's in Beechwood. Didn't move an inch until seven this morning. Kinda scared us for a minute. We thought maybe she was meeting Roth there."

"I doubt it."

"Why do you say that?"

"If he's smart, he's not gonna do her when there's a possibility of cops being around. Too much risk."

"Well, they just crossed the Mississauga city limits, still headed northeast on 401. They'll be in Toronto in about fifteen minutes."

"Where do you think they're going?"

"If I were to wager a guess, I'd say her parents' home. They live in Forest Hill, only about a couple of miles from the expressway. But here's the deal, Liskey. I just found out about ten minutes ago that the Facebook photo Isaac Roth took probably was in Marjorie's own house."

"What?"

"Yeah. This guy, rather than stay as far away from Toronto as he could, holds up in Marjorie's house."

"How do you know? Looks like he edited the real background out of the photo."

"We showed the photo to Marjorie's husband. He recognized the pillowcase over Marjorie's head. Go figure."

"Didn't you have anybody watching the house?"

"Yeah. But we pulled them off once Hamilton told us they had Roth cornered."

"You think he's still in the house?"

"Doubt it. He's savvy enough to know that we can track the IP address from where that photo was posted and use it to get the physical address. He's probably long gone by now."

"What if he isn't?"

There was a long pause before Jim Peeks finally said, "You think he's still there?"

"Maybe not in the house. But certainly close by. He took that picture in Marjorie's house for a reason. He probably knows Celia would show up there. I'll bet that's where he's gonna do it."

"Kinda hard to get a line of sight in certain areas of Forest Hill. But I'll send a couple of units to check it out."

Liskey blurted out an emphatic "No."

Peeks asked, "Why not?"

"Beat cops aren't gonna be enough. You need tactical for that."

"Liskey, you make this guy sound like he's the Taliban or something. He's only one man."

"But one guy with a *hostage*. He's already killed two people, shot two more, and crashed through your border like it was made of toilet paper." Liskey switched the phone to his other ear and gave a signal to a seemingly impatient Williams that he would be off the phone shortly. "You can't just send cops in there. If he sees them, he will kill that hostage. He won't need her anymore. He used her to pull Celia out of hiding. If you send cops in there with chests out, you will have two murders on your board."

Jim Peeks sighed on the line. "Okay, so we stop Celia before she gets to her parents' house. That's something we could have done at the border, but—"

"Yeah, but I didn't think she'd be running into him before the deadline. I didn't know he was anywhere near her parents' house. That changes things."

There was another long pause, then, "Detective Liskey, with all due respect, maybe you should let us handle this."

Once Peeks' statement sunk in, Liskey said, "Jim, she's my witness. I want to be involved."

"Yes, but she's in my city. Now, this guy shot a cop and kidnapped one of our most respected citizens. If we screw this up, I don't want to tell my boss it was because we were following orders from someone outside our jurisdiction."

Liskey's face looked as if someone had eaten a piece of pie he had been waiting all day for. "So, you're cutting me out?"

"No. We'll keep you apprised. But we're going to call the shots on this. I'll call you as soon as we know something." Jim Peeks hung up before Liskey could challenge his decision.

Williams noticed Liskey take the phone from his ear. "What's going on?"

Liskey slipped the phone into his pocket. "Jim Peeks thinks I'm an idiot. And he might be right."

"How so?"

"Long story. I'll explain on the way out of here." Liskey and Williams continued their walk toward the front doors of the church. "Right now, we need to talk to Pastor Newberry and find out who is paying Isaac Roth."

CHAPTER SEVENTEEN

Safe Room

10:18 a.m.

Celia took the exit to southbound Ailen Road and then peered over at Malik, who sat in the passenger's seat gazing out the window. He had been quiet since they left the Howard Johnson's motel. That was all right with Celia because she needed the time to think. But now that they were in Toronto, she needed Malik on point.

"You okay?" Celia asked.

"I'm aw-ight," Malik responded sullenly, without looking away from the window.

"You sure? You're not upset because I wanted separate rooms, are you?"

"Naw, I ain't thinking about all that. Besides, that should be the last thing on your mind."

"Well, we're only ten minutes away from my mom and dad's house."

"You sure this dude ain't there?"

"I don't know. I don't think so." Celia looked over and saw that for the first time since they left the hotel, Malik was looking at her, his eyes congested with concern and worry. "Don't tell me Malik, the toughest guy in Zone 8, is getting cold feet."

"Baby girl, if I was dealing with a dude from around the

way, I'd be okay, 'cause I kinda know what to expect. But this dude, he's been ghostin' people for years, and ain't nobody laid a hand on him. I'll be straight up with you, girl. I ain't feelin' this at all, 'specially since I ain't tooled up."

"Well, don't worry. I have a plan."

Malik turned to her enthusiastically. "What's that?"

"My house is not your normal, everyday house."

Malik watched as Celia made a turn and drove with reduced speed down a tree-lined street with large palatial well-kept homes. "I see."

"That's not what I meant." Celia turned down another street, ignoring the instructions of the GPS. "When my Dad bought his house, he said it used to belong to some big old-timey actress that I never heard of. I think her name was Trudy something or other. She was so paranoid that she paid to have the basement of her house reconstructed."

"What does all that mean?"

"You'll see."

Celia turned down another street which dead-ended at a public playground and park. The backyards of several homes lined the park, cordoned off by wooden privacy fences and dense trees behind them. Celia parked at the end of the street, then turned off the engine. She pointed to a barely visible gate in the wooden fence.

"That gate leads to the back of the pool house in my mom and dad's backyard," Celia reached into the armrest compartment for a set of keys. She opened her door. "Come on."

Malik reluctantly opened his door and got out of the car. They stood there, close to the car, looking around, studying every parked car, every pedestrian. Satisfied that they were not being watched, they walked across an expanse of grass and drew closer to the gate. Malik could see a rooftop over the fence. "Is that the house?"

"No," Celia responded. "That's the pool house." She used one of her keys to unlock the gate.

"And you're sure he's not in the house somewhere?" Malik asked.

"We'll find out." Celia opened the gate to reveal a brick walkway leading to the rear of the beige siding pool house about five yards away. The pool house was broad enough to block the view of most of the backyard and of the main house, and the trees were thick on the lawn between the pool house and the fence. Celia walked through the gate first and waited for Malik to enter before she quietly closed the gate. The walkway ended at a flight of stairs leading up to a terrace and a sliding French glass door at the rear of the pool house.

As they drew closer to the pool house, Malik could see another flight of stairs, below the terrace, leading down to another door directly below the French doors. A red sign with white letters read, "Pool Equipment Closet. High Voltage." Malik followed Celia down the steps and watched as she used the same key to unlock the door, this one made of steel. Celia pulled the door open, causing the metal to scrape against metal. Dead leaves swished loudly against the floor of the areaway, and dust and dead bug carcasses fell off the upper part of the door. It was clear to Malik no one had opened this door in a while.

"Where are we going? Why are we going to the pool closet?" Malik asked, following Celia inside. Ahead of him was a long hallway, lined with painted and sealed concrete block, lit by fluorescent bulbs that switched on automatically in response to the motion in the hallway.

Celia did not answer at once, but allowed Malik to step past her while she lingered behind to close the metal door. She was enjoying this game of suspense she was playing with Malik, withholding information and allowing him to guess and wonder what she was up to and why there was a hallway beneath the grounds of their house. She recalled this was exactly how her father introduced her to this little-known feature of the home.

They walked along the hallway for what seemed like a full minute, enduring the stifling heat and humidity, before they reached another door, this one also made of steel. Celia used another key to unlock this door, then pushed it open and invited Malik inside.

Malik found himself inside a 25-foot square room, with walls and ceiling encased in reinforced concrete. There were three additional doors—one leading to a restroom in the farthest corner, and two others, made of steel, resembling bank vault doors. Two davenports sat at 90-degree angles to each other in another corner of the room. A portable climate unit and a refrigerator occupied the third corner. On the wall near one door were a telephone, a first aid cabinet, and a fire extinguisher. An enormous flat tv screen hung on the wall opposite the davenports, and an Apple computer sat on a hutch just below the monitor. On the floor were sturdy but plush carpet tiles.

After taking everything in, Malik asked, "Is this the basement?"

"Part of it." Celia walked over to the climate unit and turned it on, causing cold air to flow from the ceiling vents. "This is our safe room. It's where the family goes if there is a tornado, or some other dangerous situation, like a home invasion. Notice how heavy the doors are, and the locks?"

"Yep."

"Once those doors are locked from the inside, nobody on the outside is getting in, even if they set off an explosive outside the door."

"Yeah?"

"And there are three ways in and out of here. There's the way we came in, or—" Celia pointed to one of the steel doors "—this door leads to stairs where you can enter on the first floor and from my parents' bedroom on the second floor. And this door—" Celia pointed to the remaining door

"—leads to my dad's study. But if you were in the study right now, you'd never know the door was there."

"How so?"

"This door is attached to a bookshelf in my dad's study. There are panic buttons all over this house that will automatically open the door if they are pressed. See, I have one on my keychain."

Malik looked around in amazement. "How much did all of this cost?"

"My dad says about a million."

Malik scoffed. "Rich people, I swear. I ain't mad at'cha, though. Wish I had one of these down in the 313."

"I can only *imagine* what you'd do with one of these in the 313." Celia turned on the computer, and a few seconds later, live images from eight cameras showed up on the TV screen. Celia studied the footage, then turned to Malik. "There are hidden cameras all over the house, including one outside of each of the entry doors. I don't see anyone else in the house. That doesn't mean he won't come back, though."

Malik tried not to let Celia hear his sigh of relief. "Man, you'd think Tony Montana lived in this joint."

"We probably should just stay in here, just to be safe, until we can think of what to do next."

"I got an idea." Malik walked over to one of the davenports and flopped down on it. "You in Toronto now. Why don't you just call the cops, tell them we're here, and tell them what's up? I ain't all that fond of the boys, girl, but they gotta be better at this than we are."

Celia walked over and sat down on the other davenport. "I remember when Detective Liskey in Silver Spring first interviewed me. He told me he didn't want me in the witness protection program because he was afraid the person who killed my husband was connected to the police somehow. Well, I've been thinking about that. How did this guy know where to find my apartment? How did he know where to find the reporter? How is this guy able to go from D.C. to Silver Spring, to here, and nobody catches him? Maybe he *is* connected to the police somehow. And if we call the police, he'll know that. I just don't know who to trust."

"But if he is hooked up like that, how come he didn't get you at the detective's house?" Malik argued. "How come he didn't stop you at the border or get you at the motel? Girl, if he had that kind of juice, he could have been got to you."

Celia sat quietly for a moment before she buried her head in her hands. "Malik, I don't want to die." She trembled and wept.

Malik walked over, sat next to her, and drew her into his arms. He held her closely and tightly, feeling hours and hours of fear and grief pour out onto his chest. He wanted desperately to save her from this, to save her family, and he wanted to let out a cry of his own for not having any ideas how to do it. Maybe comforting her until the moment of *whatever* was all he could reasonably do under the circumstances. So, he sat there, holding her for another five minutes, until the phone on the wall rang.

Celia jerked out of Malik's arms and sat watching the phone as if it would give clues who was calling.

"Ain't you gon' answer it?" Malik asked.

Celia did not move. The number on that phone was separate from the rest of the house, and no one knew the number outside of the family. After the shock of hearing the phone ring had deteriorated, she hurried to the phone and picked it up. "Hello?"

"Hello, Pookie."

Celia could not believe what she was hearing. "Dad?"

CHAPTER EIGHTEEN

The Church and the Cops

Joy punctuated George Wise's voice upon hearing his daughter's voice. "Yes, baby. Are you okay?"

"Dad, I'm in Toronto. Where are you?"

"Sweetie, the police have me under lock and key somewhere out in the country. I know you're in the safe room."

"How did you know?"

"I'm looking at you now. The cameras in the house have remote access capability. I can watch everything going on in the house through the web."

Celia broke down into tears again. "Dad, what am I going to do?"

"Honey, I need you and Malik to stay in that safe room. Do not come out. The police are going to handle everything. They think that the hitman is still somewhere in the neighborhood. So, you're safe as long as you don't come out of that room."

"But Dad, Mom—"

"I know about your mother, honey. And I know what you are trying to do, and I love you for that. But baby, I ask you to please let the police handle it. There's nothing you can do that they can't."

"But Dad, he asked me not to get the police involved."

"That was just his way of smoking you out. Think about it. This guy kidnapped my wife and then shot a cop. He knows the police are involved. He knows that if you contact the police, they'll tell you to stay put. And then he has nothing."

Celia was silent.

"Baby, one thing I had to learn through all this was to trust God," George said. "You know me. Nobody wants more than me to go out there and deal with this guy. But sometimes you should humble yourself and realize you are not the be-all-and-end-all of everything. Baby, you there?"

"Yeah, Dad," Celia said with the deflated tone that she gave whenever she lost an argument with her parents.

"Pookie, just stay in that room and pray that everything will work out alright. Use your spiritual weapons that I taught you how to use. You and Malik pray for God's grace, mercy and protection on this family, especially your mother."

Prayer. It sounded so ineffectual, so feeble. Justin had told her that prayer was what people do when they can't come up with real solutions. To Celia, prayer felt like defeat. Prayer felt like giving up. She had prayed in Liskey's family room when she first heard about her mother's kidnapping. Since then, Roth had seriously injured her mother, and things were not any better than they were before she prayed. She thought if God were going to do something, He would have done it by now. Maybe He would do it for anyone else but *her*, she thought.

"Baby, the police are here with me. They are listening in on the call. They want to know where Isaac Roth was going to meet you."

"Uh, he didn't say," Celia responded. "He said he was going to post a message on Mom's Facebook page."

"When?"

"At four p.m."

"What else did he say to you?"

"That's all. Other than he would kill Mom if I didn't show up at the meeting place by 5:30."

"Okay, honey. I have to go. But you stay in that room. I mean it. I don't want to lose you or your mother." George Wise gave her Detective Jim Peeks private cell phone number. "You need anything else, or have any other information, you call that number. Okay?"

"Dad?"

"Yeah, honey."

"I love you so much."

George hesitated. "You're saying that like this is the last time I will talk to you."

"No. I'll stay put."

"Good. I love you more. The Lord loves you, too. You hang in there."

"I will."

Once Celia had hung up the phone, she looked over at Malik, who had slumped his body into the cushions on the Davenport.

"Since it looks like we're gonna be in here for a minute, tell me you got some beer in that fridge and HBO on that TV." Malik smiled.

***

Having discussed and agreed that Liskey's interview with Pastor Lyons was sedate, Liskey and Williams agreed that Williams should handle the interview with Newberry. That worked just fine for Liskey, as Williams possessed a sharpness that Liskey often used to his advantage.

Welcoming the detectives at the front door of the church were a blast of air conditioning and a smile and a warm handshake from a clean-shaven thirty-something black man wearing a badge on his crisp black suit that read *Harbor Christian Cathedral, Myron Simms, Greeter*.

"Welcome to Harbor Cathedral," Myron said with such spry enthusiasm it had to be genuine. "Are you here for the nine-a.m. service, or the eleven o'clock service?"

"Neither." Williams flashed his badge. "We're here to see Pastor Newberry."

Myron's megawatt smile went down a few lumens. "Uh, I'm sorry, but Pastor Newberry does not take visitors at this time. Might I suggest you make an appointment with his secretary?" Myron's eyes unintentionally and quickly cut over to a tall, attractive woman talking in a circle with three other people.

Williams looked at the secretary for a couple of seconds, then returned his attention to Myron, looking at his badge. "Myron, I'm Detective Williams, and this is Detective Liskey. We're from the Montgomery County Police Department. It's important that we see Pastor Newberry right now, because lives could be at stake."

Realizing this situation was well beyond his training, Myron waved his hand to get the attention of the secretary, who held a walkie-talkie in her hand. When that failed, he called to her with a voice barely loud enough to rise above the din of conversation in the foyer. "Sister Brooke!"

After two tries, Brooke Saunders heard the greeter, excused herself, and sauntered over. Her black pantsuit hugged her ample curves tightly, and her long black hair and fair skin with Latin features captivated Williams on sight. "Yes, Brother Myron."

"These men are police officers. They want to talk to the Pastor."

"I'm afraid that won't be possible," Brooke told them with a voice equal parts sensuous and authoritative. "He's in a meeting with some guest pastors, and then he has to pray before the service. I'd be glad to set you up with an appointment with him."

Only a few minutes in the door of this church and Liskey felt he might have made a mistake. He could feel Williams' resolve melt at the sight of this stunning woman standing before him. He stood ready to step in should Williams falter.

With a smile and a large helping of charm, Williams said, "Dear heart, an appointment won't quite do. We're trying to save a life here, and the sooner we talk to Pastor Newberry, who may have information we need, the better."

Not missing a beat, Brooke smiled back. "I appreciate that, officers, but we cannot interrupt the flow of the service today, and the pastor cannot be disturbed. Maybe you can wait until the end of service."

Liskey shot an eye over to Williams, hoping he had a comeback, something like *Listen, you pompous patsy. We just told you we are trying to save a life. Either you lead us to the pastor, or we'll tear this church apart trying to find him.*

Instead, Liskey heard a relatively calmer "All we need is a few minutes, sweetie" from a still-smiling Williams.

"I'm sorry, officers, but I have my instructions."

"Detectives, actually," Liskey blurted out sternly, drawing Brooke's attention away from Williams. "It's like this, Sister Brooke. You either show us to the pastor, or we act like cops and find him ourselves. But we're *going* to speak to this man sometime before the benediction of this service. Your choice."

Williams looked at Liskey as if he had lost his mind.

Brooke would not budge. "Detectives, this is a house of God, and it is private property. You're welcome to stay and worship with us. But anything other than that, I must insist that you leave if you don't have a warrant."

Williams gave Liskey the stink-eye, upset his partner had likely quashed his opportunity to flirt with Brooke.

"Would a house of God be so callous to the needs of others?" Liskey argued. "Sister Brooke, my partner just told you that we are trying to save a life. I would think that this urgent piece of police business would trump your holy protocol. Unless you have something to hide."

Brooke merely glared at him.

Liskey drew closer to her, his eyes intensely boring into hers. "And if I leave here thinking you have something to hide, I start looking into matters maybe you don't want me to. I'll get a warrant and start checking phone records, church financial files, and travel records. I'll be right outside that door at every service, interviewing church members. I'll squeeze him, and I'll squeeze him hard. All because you won't give me five minutes with your exalted leader."

Brooke looked away for a moment, then looked back at Liskey as if it disgusted her to do so. "Give me a second." She walked back over to her circle of three, whispered a few words, and then started down the corridor, beckoning the cops to follow her. Williams watched her hips sashay almost the entire way.

Five minutes later, they were on the second floor and inside of an office that required a key pass to enter. Brooke Saunders' nameplate and a computer sat prominently on the mahogany desk. The décor in the room indicated a strong liking of pastels and flowers, and the sweet odor of lilacs hung in the air, though not overbearingly so. "Give me a minute." Brooke went through a heavy wooden door on the opposite side of the room and closed it behind her. Liskey could hear conversation and laughter from several people as the door opened.

"You still upset I ruined your chance?" Liskey asked Williams quietly.

"I dunno, man. She kinda turned into the ice princess at the end, there," Williams commented.

"She's dirty," Liskey said. "Any normal secretary would have caved after the second request, particularly after you said this was life or death. She was protecting him. She's probably sleeping with him, too."

"What makes you think that?"

"Something in her vibe." Liskey peered around the office, looking for anything suspicious or incriminating. Unfortunately, he saw nothing more interesting than the Egg McMuffin sitting half-eaten on Brooke's desk.

The detectives waited for another three minutes before Brooke walked back into the office, holding the door. "He'll see you now, detectives."

Liskey walked into the pastor's office without one look at Brooke. Williams gave Brooke a slight smile and hoped that Liskey was wrong about her on all counts.

Jonathan Newberry stood facing them, his back to a large window overlooking a vast swath of land dotted with trees and small detached homes. Liskey sized him up quickly. Newberry's appearance was not what he had expected. Liskey had envisioned a tall man, perhaps six feet two, husky, beard, maybe bald, harsh and ominous looking. What stood before him was Blair Underwood's twin brother. The man was strikingly handsome, short black hair, almost flawless olive skin tone, wearing a crisply tailored Joseph Abboud suit. If this man didn't survive as a pastor, he could always be that lone black male model in any fashion catalog. Liskey wondered had happened to the people that the pastor had been in the office with. Then he noticed an elevator door at the end of a short hallway.

Once the detectives were inside, Brooke shut the door but did not leave. She stood beside the door, like a sentry, ready to take whatever dubious action or orders her boss would give to her.

Newberry spoke first. "Good morning, detectives." His smile and handshakes were as fake as silk flowers. Once the detectives introduced themselves, Liskey stepped back and allowed Williams to begin the questioning.

"Pastor, we're investigating the murder of a young man." Williams flipped open a notepad he had pulled from his inside jacket pocket. "We believe that the man who killed him was also responsible for the death of a reporter in D.C. and the shooting of Pastor Benjamin Lyons. You were one of the last people that the reporter spoke to. Can you tell us what you talked about?"

"Um, he was just interviewing people who were present at Freedom Plaza when Pastor Lyons was shot. I was one of the members who helped organize the rally, so naturally, he was interested in my take on the events."

"So, you know what reporter I'm taking about," said Williams.

"Uh, yeah," Newberry said. "The one that was at the rally, right?"

"What *was* your part in the rally exactly?"

"Mostly helping to get the word out. Sat in on a couple of meetings with guest speakers. Arranged for churches around the area to attend."

"How long did you speak with the reporter?"

"I dunno. Maybe a couple of minutes."

Williams heard Liskey's phone buzz. He turned just as Liskey was removing the phone from his jacket pocket.

Looking at the caller ID, Liskey excused himself and left the room.

Williams continued feverishly writing in his notepad, angling it so Newberry couldn't see what he was writing. "Where did you meet with him?"

"In the lobby."

"So, two minutes and done?"

"About that much, yeah."

"There were other pastors at the rally. Any of them there with you?"

"No. Just me."

"Why? A man like Pastor Lyons gets shot, and you're the only pastor at the hospital?"

"I can't really speak to that. A deficit of decency of their hearts, I guess."

"You consider yourself a decent man?" Williams flipped his notepad shut.

"That's something that persons other than me would have to determine."

"What did you do after talking with the reporter?"

"I took the escalator up to the ER waiting room, waiting to hear news on Pastor Lyons. I made a few phone calls. When his wife came out to tell us all was okay and that Pastor Lyons would survive, I went home."

"What time was that?"

"I dunno. Around two o'clock, I guess."

"Who did you call?"

"Huh?"

"Who did you call? You said you made a few phone calls while you were in the waiting room. Who did you call?"

Newberry's eyes shifted. "I don't know. I called my wife, a few friends."

"Can you verify that?"

"Verify what?"

"Verify who you made the calls to. A quick check of your cell phone will clear that right up."

Brooke stepped forward. "I'm sorry, detective, but Pastor Newberry's phone is actually registered to the church. And we actually disabled his service a couple of days ago. He's getting a new phone."

"I see. But you still have the old phone?"

"No. We had to trade it in to get the new one," Brooke answered.

"Trade it in where?"

Both Newberry and Brooke looked at each other before Newberry answered, "She meant she threw it away."

"Hmm." Williams put away his notepad. He was done asking softball questions, as Newberry and his sexy protégé would only lie. Newberry had already told two of them. Based on the hospital surveillance footage, Pastor Newberry had spoken to Wynn Delano for more than two minutes, and most of the conversation had happened in a hallway adjacent to the ER, not in the lobby. And he heavily suspected Newberry was lying about throwing away the cell phone.

Yep, Pastor Newberry was hiding something. The question was how to get at it. Normally Williams would take the pastor in for questioning, but he had no police powers in Prince George's County. Technically, he and Liskey were private citizens riding on the respect and consideration afforded them by having badges. But he couldn't press too hard, because if the pastor knew his rights, he could kick the cops out of his church without an ounce of repercussions.

Fear would have to be his friend. Fear would make a man tell things to a cop he would only tell God. Pastor Newberry had a lot to lose. This seat on the pinnacle of religious power in one of the most church-laden counties in the D.C. area had to be a proud and momentous achievement he dared not let easily let slip from his grasp. The potential for shame, financial ruin, and the ostracization of the community would be enough to make a man drop all pretense. Williams had to play into that, even if it meant revealing details about the investigation, which he had been trained never to do, especially with a suspect. But Celia and Marjorie's lives were at stake. He needed information, and he needed it fast.

Williams was prepared to try again with Pastor Newberry, but his cell phone buzzed. He pulled it from his pocket, checked the text he had received, then shoved the phone back into his pocket.

Liskey walked back into the room. Bolstered by the presence of his partner, Williams tried again. "Pastor Newberry, I don't have a lot of time, so let's stop playing with each other here. You're connected to the guy that's been doing these killings, and I need to know how and where to find him. Now, my partner and I are gonna leave this church in about ten minutes. Before we do, I need to know everything that's gonna help us find this guy and find him, now. If I—"

Newberry raised his hand to stop Williams from talking. "Detective, let's get something straight, and then I'm going to ask you to leave a lot sooner than the ten minutes you suggested. I have nothing to do with those murders. Until now, no police officer from any investigating jurisdiction has come to me asking me any questions about it, and I am appalled that you would think I am involved." His voice became louder, sharper. "This is a church, a house of God. I have men and women of power and position sitting under my ministry. Do you think I would be involved in murder? Come now, detective. I have a service to prepare for, and I'm sure you have other people to interrogate who are more deserving of your attentions." He nodded to Brooke. As if on cue, Brooke opened the door and stood aside.

The detectives made no effort to leave. Instead, Williams approached Newberry until their faces were only fifteen inches away from one another. Newberry appeared uncomfortable with having his personal space invaded. He drew his head back slightly but kept his eyes on Williams.

"You know that text I got a couple of minutes ago?" Williams kept his voice calm and steady, the voice of a man who had trapped his prey, and the prey could do nothing about it. "That was my partner texting me from the other room. He got a call from a detective in Toronto, where the guy we're chasing is holed up right now."

Newberry scoffed and turned his head to the side. "Detective..."

Undaunted, Williams continued. "Yesterday, there was a disgusting picture posted on Facebook of this guy and my victim's stepmother. Turns out the IP address from where that picture was posted also communicated with an IP address associated with this church."

Liskey spoke up. "And I just verified the church IP address on the computer outside."

Brooke quickly shut the door and swung her head angrily

toward Liskey. "You had no right to do that! You shouldn't be touching anything in here without a warrant!"

Liskey ignored her. Williams never took his eyes off Newberry, whose eyes no longer focused on his.

"That means that this guy was doing some digital chit-chat with someone in this church," Williams told him. "And I'm willing to bet you know who that person is. And denials to the contrary are not going to hold any water with me. You've already lied to me twice during this interview. Lie to me again, and I might have to act like the kind of cop you won't like."

Brooke was now livid. "Detectives, please get out of this church, before I report you for illegally accessing my computer without a warrant."

"What are you gonna do? Call the police? Call them." Liskey looked directly at Brooke. "But we're not going any-where. If we don't get the information we came here for, and my girl and her mother wind up dead, I'm gonna tem-porarily forget I'm a Montgomery County homicide detec-tive. I'm gonna be on the trail to destroy a Prince George's County minister. And I won't have any conflicts about that, because after that phone call I just got, and the information we have about you so far, you're about as fraudulent and fake as they come. You give a bad name to ministers in this county. Now, normally, that's none of my business. I'm a murder cop. But if we don't get the information we need, and we don't find this guy, I'll make it my business."

Liskey walked over until he was almost shoulder to shoulder with Williams. "I've got buddies on the PG Coun-ty force. I'll work with them and get warrants. I'll check your phone records, your credit card records, your tax re-cords. I'll pull records from every place you've done busi-ness with. Wonder what I'll find there? Wonder what your wife will say about what I find there?" He cut an eye over at Brooke. Brooke responsively darted her eyes away, a gesture of shame if Liskey had ever seen one.

Liskey returned his glare to Newberry. "Now, you're not a stupid man. A stupid man couldn't have built all this." Liskey waved his hand around to indicate the church building. "This is the nicest church I've ever been in. So, you probably have some degree of separation from the killer. You have plausible deniability. But you know who is paying this guy. And I need to know what you know, or you're gonna make an enemy of every cop on the Montgomery County police force. And trust me, you *don't* want that to happen."

Newberry pasted a sly smile on his face — *not* the reaction that Liskey was expecting. Newberry walked away from the detectives and stood behind his desk. "You're right, detectives. I am a smart man. And a smart man wouldn't have built all this without a little help. Help in county government, state government, federal government." He picked up the handset of the phone on his desk. "I pick up the phone and call one of those friends, and your bosses in Montgomery County will pull you off this faster than green grass through a goose. So, don't come into my church trying to intimidate me." He nodded to Brooke.

Brooke, whose expression had morphed from annoyed to worried in the span of a few minutes, slowly, almost reluctantly, opened the door.

Liskey cracked a slight smile and headed for the door. Williams lingered.

"Okay, so that's how you want to play it." Williams backed toward the door. "But we're going to catch this guy. The question is whether we catch him with one body, or three. If that doesn't bother you morally, then I hope, being the *smart* man that you are, you'd help us now and not add two more bodies to whatever sentence you get for your complicity in all this."

Newberry gave the detective a blank stare.

"I guess not." Williams turned and walked with Liskey

out the door. Once Brooke had closed the door behind them and they were in the outer corridor, Williams turned to Liskey. "Hey, did you see the look on Sister Brooke's face?"

"Yeah, I did." Liskey tore a page from his notepad and handed the page to Williams. "Get with Weirick, see what you can find out about that IP address. Also, do a check on Brooke. Her social is on there."

"How d'you find that out?"

"Her purse was in her desk drawer. I took a peek inside."

"If Brooke finds out you did that..."

Liskey dismiss Williams' comment with a shrug. "I'm gonna stick around and work Brooke."

Williams pursed his lips. "I guess you don't want *me* to do that?"

"I'm trying to get information. *You're* trying to get digits. Besides, you already have a girl." Liskey started walking down the corridor.

"It's for the case," Williams said, half-smiling, following Liskey. "No telling what secrets she'll tell during pillow talk."

"Shut up," Liskey said.

CHAPTER NINETEEN

Venturing Out

Liskey went downstairs and took a seat at the rear of the church for the 11:00 am service. After what Pastor Lyons had told him, Liskey expected the 11 a.m. service to be an aberration of the gospel, a cultish Christianity that distorts the gospel. To his surprise, for one who had not been to church in a minute, the service seemed reasonable, right, even thought-provoking. The visiting preacher, from North Carolina, preached a sermon from Matthew 5:44. The mantra *love your enemies, love your enemies,* continually rang out in his mind even after the service was over.

How could Liskey love a man like Isaac Roth, a dangerous, natural-born killer? How could he love Jonathan Newberry, who was apparently complicit in many crimes but pegged himself as an innocent? He knew that love was the truth of the gospel, but it left him conflicted. He was a cop sworn to put these criminals away, even use violence to stop them. How did that jibe with Godly love? Was being a cop antithetical to being a true Christian? He would have to chat with Pastor Lyons about that when he got a moment.

Williams had checked Brooke Saunders background and texted the details to Liskey's cell phone just before the service ended. As the people filed out of the sanctuary after the service, Liskey lingered along a wall and watched Jonathan Newberry's every move. Newberry hugged all the ministers and officials on the pulpit, stopping to converse with a few. Brooke stood nearby, never far away from Newberry. Newberry didn't seem to notice Liskey was still there. However, Brooke, while glancing over the sanctuary, noticed Liskey and looked at him for all of twenty seconds before she looked away. When Newberry disappeared through a side door, Brooke lingered, greeting guests while still taking occasional glances at Liskey.

It was now or never.

Liskey timed his approach to the pulpit when Brooke and only one minister remained. Brooke eyeballed him as he stopped just shy of the stairs leading up to the pulpit.

"Lovely service, Sister Brooke," Liskey said.

"Yes, very lovely," Brooke countered, a confused look on her face.

"I especially liked what the minister said about being free in Christ. I thought that very appropriate for someone like you."

"Someone like me?"

"Being on paper, and all."

Liskey watched as Brooke's face went from confused to shocked almost instantly. *I got her*, he thought. He pulled a business card from his jacket pocket.

"It occurred to me that I hadn't given you my card while we were talking upstairs." Liskey handed Brooke the card. "You seem like a nice lady, so I hope you're not caught up in all this mess. That wouldn't be good for someone like you." Liskey turned and started to walk away. "But if there's anything I can do...."

As Liskey walked out of the sanctuary, Brooke Saunders stood frozen on the pulpit, the card dangling in her hand.

***

It was 1:30 pm, and most of the cars in the church parking lot had left, but Liskey remained, in the vehicle with

A/C blasting, parked on a side street with a full view of the church's side lot. So as not to be blasphemous, he listened to his wife's Casting Crowns CD rather than the well-worn CD of Simon and Garfunkel. It was 3-1/2 hours until Isaac Roth's deadline, and Liskey knew he had to turn this case around soon or he would lose Celia.

How much longer is Newberry going to stay in the church? Liskey thought, occasionally looking up to see if Newberry had exited the church to his car. Liskey intended to wait only another 15 minutes before he gave up and headed back to Montgomery County, hoping that Weirick could turn up another lead with the IP address.

Ten minutes later his cell phone rang. The caller ID listed an unknown number. Liskey hoped it was good news. He answered the call. "Detective Liskey."

"Detective, this is Brooke Saunders."

"What's up, Miss Saunders?"

"Can we meet someplace?"

"I'm actually still close to the church."

"Not here. Somewhere else."

"You know this area better than I do."

"How about the Harbor, at The Awakening?"

"The Awakening?"

"It's a giant sculpture of a man coming out of the sand. Used to be at Hains Point."

"That'll work."

"Thirty minutes."

"See you there."

After Liskey hung up, he called Ramon Williams, informing him of the new development. After Ramon cursed at himself for not getting the chance to meet Brooke at the Harbor, he told Liskey that Weirick could not get any information on the church's IP address until the next day, when he could call the church's internet service provider and get more information. That would be too late. Another dead end. He prayed that Brooke would give him something useful.

After getting good luck wishes from Ramon, Liskey drove straight to the Harbor, about a five-minute drive. He parked and then walked up National Drive between several restaurants to a clearing, where he could see *The Awakening*, a huge five-piece aluminum statue depicting a man rising out of the sand lining the beach. The statue was a huge draw for kids, who crawled all over it like curious squirrels.

Eschewing the open plaza near the statue, Liskey walked along the buildings until he reached the pier and the shade of several canopies. He could stand there shielded from the hot sun until Brooke arrived.

When she arrived about 20 minutes later, Liskey watched her as she stood near the statue. She was a beautiful woman, and Liskey could see why Ramon Williams had been so smitten with her. He hoped all that beauty on the outside came with a sense of decency on the inside.

After Brooke looked around for him, Liskey recruited a passing teenager to go to the statue and tell the woman in the black pantsuit to come over to him near the canopies. Brooke obeyed, meeting Liskey near the canopies and didn't question why.

"What's up, Ms. Saunders?" Liskey noticed for the first time that Brooke wore a lot of makeup. Maybe it was the bright sun that magnified it. Liskey hoped she didn't look like an ogre under all that paint.

"First of all, I'm sorry for being so abrupt today," Brooke began. "I just have a natural inclination to protect Pastor Newberry."

Liskey could have cared less about her reasons for acting like an ice queen. "Why are we here?"

Brooke nodded. "I need to know that you will keep my name out of this."

"Depends on what you tell me."

"I haven't done anything wrong."

"Then why are you worried?"

"Because I'm on paper. I don't want to get caught up in anything that'll get me sent back."

"How long were you in?"

"Two years in Jessup."

"For what?"

"Embezzled some money from a place where I worked."

Sounds about right, Liskey thought. If this cute, all-together woman had told she was locked up for drugs or something like that, it would have messed up his mind. "How did you get hooked up with Newberry?"

"I was staying in a halfway house. Pastor Newberry came there for a meeting with a woman who was the daughter of someone in his church. He saw me, and he took an interest in me."

"I probably don't need to ask why."

"Yes, but at the time, I didn't care," Brooke said. "He took me in, gave me a job at the church, took care of me. I grew up a foster child, so his attention was special to me. A lot of the girls I jailed with are pushing brooms in nursing homes. Meanwhile, I'm wearing Fendi and Louis Vuitton. So, I guess I got kinda became devoted to him. I started spending so much time with him, our romantic relationship just came naturally. I loved him, and I thought he would eventually leave his wife. But I doubt now that's going to happen."

"Is that why you're coming forth now?"

"No. I don't want to go back to jail because of him, and I also don't want anybody else to get killed. After you mentioned the photo from Facebook and started talking about how you were going to get all up in his business, I got scared. I looked in Pastor Newberry's emails when the pastor was in the pulpit today, and I found the photograph. It was so disgusting I couldn't believe a pastor would endorse such a thing. If you want, I can take you back to the church after everyone has left, and I can show you."

"That would be nice, Ms. Saunders." Liskey accepted the invitation, even though he thought it wouldn't do much good. He could only prove that someone in the church had received the photo, but he still couldn't prove a conspiracy to murder on the pastor's part. Without a confession or a witness, that would be a dead end. But maybe something else would turn up to help locate Roth, and he could get it all without a warrant. Ms. Saunders, a church official, had invited him to snoop around. "What else can you tell me?"

"Please promise me you won't drag me into this."

"Only if you have no connection or culpability to my case. Can you promise me that?"

"Trust me. Pastor Newberry did everything he could to keep me out of it."

"Then, I'll do my best."

***

2:05 p.m.

The pure boredom had gotten to Malik, and he had been asleep for about an hour, but Celia could not sleep, no matter how much she tried. She switched the video system over to the camera monitors and studied each image. There was no movement in the house, no apparent activity. The cameras outside also revealed no activity, and the camera pointed at the front door showed a pile of newspapers on the front doormat. Celia pursed her lips. Her dad was so old-fashioned. He preferred to hold a newspaper in his hands rather than get his news online like many people.

Her curiosity was ferocious. She wanted to know how the tall man had gotten into the house and wanted to secure it in case someone else happened by. For all she knew, a door was wide open somewhere in the house. And despite her father's urging her to stay in the safe room, she could not sit around another three hours and wait for whatever fate befell her. She knew the cops couldn't examine the house because their presence would tip off the tall man if he were watching, and then he would change his plans. But she was already in the house. Maybe she could find clues where the tall man was hiding, or where he planned to meet her.

She sensed no immediate danger. But to be certain, she made sure that Malik was asleep, then pushed open the deadbolt on the door leading to the staircase. Celia looked back again to make sure Malik hadn't awakened and then hurried two flights up a dark, thin, and steep staircase to the top landing. She pushed a button to open the electronic deadbolt, then gently and slowly opened the door. The sunlight smacked her in the face, pouring in through a window with the curtains open. She walked over to the window and looked out. Few people were out, and those that had ventured outside were jogging or lounging in the parkette across the street. Celia quickly pulled the curtains shut so that no one outside could see her inside.

Looking around the bedroom, Celia could tell her mother decorated it. Light blue pastels dominated the room, from the carpet, to the bedspread, to the wallpaper. The birch nightstands and the cream-white pillows added a little contrast. Her father's décor would have been more rustic, more antique flavored. Given his way, he would have had an old hunting rifle and a deer's head hanging on the wall above the headboard.

Speaking of guns.

Celia opened the door to a nightstand and pulled out what appeared to be a wide sewing book. But the inside was hollow, and when she opened the book to the 46th page, the small compartment held a semi-automatic pistol. She cradled the pistol in her hand and replaced the sewing book back in the nightstand drawer. There were no bullets in the gun, and she knew her father kept them in one of two places. She opened the walk-in closet door, switched on the light, and walked to the shelf where her father kept his shoes. Almost all of them were leather dress or casual shoes—her father was not one for sneakers. In a corner was a pair of shoes that were well-worn and that her father didn't wear at all anymore. She reached deep inside one shoe and retrieved the box of bullets inside.

Sitting on the bed, she did what her father had trained her to do. She popped out the magazine, then pulled back the slide to ensure there were no bullets in the chamber. A quick inspection of the barrel verified it was clear, and she checked the hammer, trigger, and safety. Everything worked well. She loaded the weapon, racked the slide, and chambered a bullet, then headed out of the bedroom.

Celia was certain the house was clear, yet her trepidation was evident as she walked down the hallway towards the stairs, keeping the gun in her right hand pointed toward the floor. The blue nylon carpet shielded any noise from her footsteps. When she turned the corner and approached the stairs, she could see half the living room from the top landing, including the front door and the main living room window. From her vantage point, there appeared to be no damage to either. Her confidence building, she crept quickly down the stairs and looked over the living room, and then the dining area, staying away from windows, seeing nothing suspicious or out of place. She noticed that the answering machine, another of her father's old school relics, was unplugged and the phone cord was removed. *Strange.*

Celia moved into the kitchen. A quick examination of the kitchen revealed one pointed and disturbing fact: the meat cleaver was missing from the knife block on the counter. As meticulous as her mother was, Celia knew that the cleaver was not just hanging around somewhere. *Maybe she broke it,* she thought.

Celia moved into the hallway and toward the basement door. On the way there, she saw that the door leading to the garage was open. Since there were no cameras in the garage, Celia wasn't sure whether or not someone was still in there.

Poising the gun straight ahead of her, her left hand supporting her right trigger hand, she crept closer to the door and peered around the corner. Seeing no one, she lowered her weapon and walked down the two concrete steps leading to the garage floor. Looking around the empty garage, she saw nothing unusual, which only increased her curiosity. How did the tall man get into the house? There were no signs of forced entry. Could he have gotten a key from somewhere? Maybe he stole it from her mother. *Maybe my answer is in the basement*, she thought.

She left the garage, crossed the hallway, and headed down to the basement. As she crossed the main room to the glass doors at the rear of the basement, she could see that the doors were intact and locked, with no signs of forced entry. She looked out at the pool and the pool house. No sign of anyone. Walking through the basement and checking the two guest bedrooms, she saw that all the windows in the rooms were intact.

Celia returned to the main room and exhaled in frustration. She couldn't see where the tall man had entered the house. Either he had a key, or he was a master at picking locks. Feeling confident there was no immediate danger, Celia engaged the safety on the gun and stuffed it in the back of her jeans, shielding it with her T-shirt. Then, feeling the need to wash her face with cooling water, she walked into the bathroom next to the main room. Within two seconds of entering, she screamed and quickly stumbled backward out of the bathroom.

For a few moments, she stood there, looking wide-eyed into the bathroom, her hand to her chest, her breathing as pronounced as if she had been jogging for two minutes. Then, once she had gathered herself, Celia ran upstairs to the kitchen, grabbed two freezer bags from a cabinet and some ice from the freezer, and hurried back downstairs. Once in the bathroom, she unwound bathroom tissue from the spool, scooped up her mother's bloody pinky finger from the bathroom sink, and wrapped it in the tissue. She dropped the finger into one bag, sealed it, put ice in the other bag, and placed the first bag inside. Celia then ran back upstairs and put the finger into the refrigerator, hoping that it wasn't too late to save it.

Celia returned to the bathroom and scrutinized it. The sink was streaked with blood. There were several gashes on the top of the sink that Celia was sure were made by a sharp object. She looked down and saw the handle of the meat cleaver sticking out of the wastebasket.

Celia left everything else as it was. She backed out of the bathroom and looked around. She trusted no one had heard her scream, as the bathroom had no windows and thick walls. That was why the tall man likely maimed her mother in the bathroom. When her mother screamed, no one outside of the house would hear it.

Celia suddenly felt lightheaded. Since leaving Silver Spring, she had eaten nothing, and the only thing on her stomach was the Vernors that Malik had given her while in Detroit. She made her way to the rear bedroom and lay on the bed, on her side. She would lay there for a moment until she felt better, and then she would raid the refrigerator and rejoin Malik in the safe room. Her body trembled with palpitations, responding to the dread of the ever-looming deadline, after which her mother would either live or die, if she wasn't dead already.

***

The tall man jerked awake and immediately looked back at Marjorie. She was slumping against the wall of the van, awake, but so weak she couldn't move. The tall man figured she had just awakened from the latest dose of Propofol.

It was two-thirty-six p.m., only three hours before his deadline. The tall man looked around, studying his surroundings, checking to see if anyone was watching him, or if there were any significant changes in the environment since he had fallen asleep. A car parked somewhere not parked there before, anyone staring at the van, or anyone still hanging on the streets since before he fell asleep—all those things would have earned his immediate attention. But the tall man saw nothing out of place.

It amazed him how much his former electrical engineering career had prepared him for this. The same analytical skills, attention to detail, and planning and organization savvy served him well in his new career. And he had to admit, the murder-for-hire business was much more financially lucrative than sitting in front of computers all day.

However, satisfaction would be the only payment for his first kill. The priest that had molested his son gave him a taste and a stomach for blood, and he immediately knew one kill would not be enough. To avenge his son, he had to strike at the heart of the system he felt destroyed his family.

At times, he struggled with how killing Celia was helping to achieve that goal. But he had to push those thoughts aside. He was hired to do a job. And he intended to do it, even if it made no immediate sense.

He grabbed his binoculars and studied the house. It looked as if no one had visited, and there didn't appear to be any changes to the house since he fell asleep. That meant that no cops had happened by. If they had, he would have to put Marjorie out of her misery and then regroup.

He trained his binoculars on the second floor of the house. Satisfied that no one had visited the house, he pulled the binoculars away from his eyes, but then had a fleeting thought and took another look. He was confident that when he profiled that house shortly after he left it, the master bedroom window curtains were wide open.

Now they were closed.

The tall man pulled the binoculars away again and looked around, checking for anyone who looked like a cop. He scanned each car parked nearby to see if someone was sitting in wait. He checked the windows of nearby houses to see if anyone was peering out for longer than usual. Nothing unusual. He used the binoculars to recheck the master bedroom window and kept watching for at least fifteen minutes. There was no activity revealing that someone was in the room. *Maybe he was mistaken about seeing the curtains open*, he thought.

The tall man quickly discarded that thought. Yes, he was tired and functioning off little sleep. But he could not discount his training. That window curtain was open twenty-four hours ago. He knew it. And if that were the case, someone had either been in the house or was still there.

The tall man put the binoculars away and started the engine. Pulling out of the parking space, he cased the house to see if someone was there. But he would have to be careful. If the police were watching, his *driving-by looking suspiciously at the house* might be the tip-off that he was the person they were looking for.

The tall man drove normal speed up Connery Road, using his peripheral vision as he passed the house. He could see that the newspapers in front of the house were still there and had not been disturbed. But he also knew there were other ways inside the house, including the rear basement entrance.

He drove around the neighborhood, covering a three-block radius around the house. He looked for any signs of law enforcement—parked police cars, unmarked vans, cruisers driving around the neighborhood. Satisfied that no police were around, he pulled onto the dead-end street that backed up to a playground and to the rear gate of the Wise property. At the end of the street, he noticed a red Dodge Charger parked at the end of the block. What was distinctive about it was not the model of the car nor the color.

The car had red, white, and blue Maryland tags.

Roth pulled a small disposable phone from his bag. It was a basic cheap burner phone he had bought from a convenience store and was good enough only for making a basic phone call.

Or, in Roth case, calling another burner phone he had planted in the basement, which was plugged into a detonator box rigged to activate 500 grams of Semtex plastic explosive hidden in the basement.

***

Liskey and Brooke walked along National Drive. "What I have to tell you only one other person in my church knows about," Brooke said.

"Newberry?"

"Yes.

"So, what do you know?"

"Well, I'm the church administrator. If the pastor has a meeting connected to the church, I know about it. I schedule them. But he's been having these strange meetings that he keeps off the books. He won't tell me about them. No one else in the church knows about them."

"How do you know about the meetings?"

Brooke sighed, then continued. "One day after a Tuesday night service, I asked him to take me home, which he normally does not have any problem doing since I live right down the street from him. This time he couldn't take me home. When I asked him why, he said he had a meeting to attend. It was nine-thirty at night. What possible meeting could he have at that hour?"

"Pastors are on call all the time."

"No, it wasn't that. I caught a vibe, and I had the feeling he was going to see some other woman."

"You mean, other than his wife?"

"Yes. So, after he left the church, I went up to the office and tracked his cell phone."

"What did you find?"

"He went all the way out in the boondocks in St. Mary's County." Brooke paused for effect. "There wasn't a house around for at least a mile. He was there for about an hour before he drove back to his house."

"Hmm." Liskey thought for a few seconds. "St. Mary's County is at least an hour and a half drive from here. He makes that kind of round trip just to stay an hour?"

"Yeah. Weird, right? So, the next day, I asked him how the meeting went, and he said great. That's all. No elaboration. Usually, he would talk my ear off about his meetings. So, that's when I *really* thought he was seeing some other woman. Now, imagine me, the side chick, getting jealous of another side chick. So, for a few days after that, I keep tracking his phone, and a week later, he's in that area again, same time, same place. So, I figure there's got to be somebody's house there."

Liskey listened intently, not sure if he would get information about his case, or a sordid story about an extra-marital affair. "What happened next?"

"So, I called a few friends who were with me in the half-way house." Brooke's voice got quieter. "I asked them if they knew anyone who lived in St. Mary's County. One of them told me she had a cousin who lived in Leonardtown. She gave the cousin my number, and he called me. I said I would give him fifty dollars if he, when I called him, went to where the pastor was going and find out what was going on."

"Sounds like easy money for him."

"Yeah. You can get to almost anywhere in St. Mary's within 10 to 15 minutes."

"So, I assume you had an occasion to send him on his quest?"

"Yep. About two weeks after that."

"And?"

"When he went, he said there was an unpaved side road off the main road, and there was a man standing there, I guess keeping guard."

"What did your friend do?"

"He kept driving past. But a few days, he called a friend of his who hunts down there. He's got something called a trail camera, some camera that takes pictures remotely."

"Yeah," Liskey said. "Hunters use it to scout hunting areas to see where the best prey is."

"Yeah, so he went back early the next morning and drove down the dirt road. When he got to the end, he saw a clearing where there were Tiki torches set up, and it looks like a fire was burning. He said it looked like a campsite."

"I doubt the pastor was going camping that time of night."

"So, he put the camera out of sight in a tree and set it up to send pictures to his cell phone." Brooke reached into her purse, removed her cell phone, and tapped and swiped the screen. "So, when they met again there two weeks later, this is what he got." She handed her phone to Liskey.

Liskey studied the photos on her cell phone carefully. "Looks like 15 pastors gathered around a campfire and having a meeting. Seems innocent enough." He tried to hand the phone back to Brooke, but she did not extend her hand to take it.

"That's what I thought, and I was just relieved he wasn't seeing another woman." Brooke nodded toward her phone. "But look at who's at the meeting. The guy fourth from the left."

Liskey studied the photo again, and his mouth fell open. "That's Isaac Roth."

"I don't know his name, but he's the same guy that was in that photo I pulled up on the pastor's computer. And that's why I wanted to meet with you. And look at the guy right beside Pastor Newberry, to the right."

Liskey strained his eyes to look at the small screen. "What about him?"

"You don't recognize him?"

"No."

"That's Charles Prender, one of the trustees of our church."

"And?"

"Obviously you don't follow politics."

"Not really."

"Charles Prender is a state senator for Maryland. And I'm sure that he is in charge of whatever Pastor Newberry is hooked up with."

"Why do you think that?" Liskey gave Brooke a look of heightened interest.

"On the same day that Pastor Lyons got shot, I was at the church. I was just walking out of my office headed to the trustee chairman's office when I heard the chairman inside, talking to Pastor Newberry on the phone. I admit I stopped and did a little ear-hustling since he didn't know I was there."

"What d'you hear?"

"He was getting on Pastor Newberry for being stupid for looking up at the hotel window and moving back like he did. He said if the police got a hold of the video, they would know he was involved. Then he said, 'Call our guy and take care of him.' Now I didn't know what any of this meant, but when I saw the photo and heard the things you said in the office, I put the pieces together."

Liskey nodded and thought out loud. "So, Charles Prender gave the order to have Wynn Delano and Celia killed."

"Who are they?"

"The reporter. And Celia is the wife of the man that was killed in my jurisdiction."

"Oh."

"My guess is that they targeted Pastor Lyons and then went after Wynn to clean up their mess. Sounds like Newberry incriminated himself on video, and so Roth went after Wynn and Celia because Celia was on that video."

That meant that Celia was innocent. Liskey remembered the moments he berated her for more information about why Roth was chasing her. He knew he owed her a big-time apology.

His phone buzzed in his pocket. He checked the phone and saw a text from Jim Peeks:

Found Celia. She's safe.

Liskey looked out over the shimmering waves of the Potomac and smiled. He would call Peeks later and get details, but for now, he needed to book a flight to Toronto to check on Celia and work with the Canadian authorities to extradite Roth back to Maryland to face charges after he was caught.

Liskey slipped the phone back into his pocket. "I have to take care of something. I'd like to talk to you again, if possible, and take you up on your offer to look at the church computers, but if you need anything in the meantime..."

"I'll call," Brooke said.

"Please do. I want to hook you up with Pastor Lyons. I'm no expert on this, but he has a pure heart, and I think he would be a better spiritual leader for you than Newberry."

"Thank you, Detective. By the way, I have one more thing, if it would be helpful."

"What's that?"

Brooke removed a cell phone from her purse and handed

it to Liskey. "It's Pastor Newberry's old phone."

Liskey opened the flip phone. "So, you never traded it in or threw it away?"

"No. Sorry we lied about that."

"Does Newberry know you still have it?"

"Yes. He told me to toss it just this afternoon."

"Thank you for this, Miss Saunders. You've been a big help."

"You'll keep my name out of this, right?"

"As far as I'm concerned, this meeting never happened."

CHAPTER TWENTY

To Kill or not to Kill?

With Newberry's old cell phone in hand, Liskey headed back to his car and immediately dialed Jim Peeks.

"Peeks here."

"Liskey. Thanks for the text earlier. Celia is safe, huh?"

"Yeah. She's at her father's house, in a basement safe room. Short of a nuclear warhead, nothing or no one's gonna get to her down there. That Malik fellow is with her."

"Good. Can you guys track a sat phone?"

"We can get some of our tech guys on it. Why?"

"I have the cell phone of a man who might have hired Roth. He made several calls to a sat phone around the time that Wynn Delano was killed."

"We can do it, but we need PC and a subpoena, and we will not be able to get either before Roth's deadline. Why can't your people do it?"

"Same reason. I need a Title 3, and there's no way we're getting that before 5 pm. I was hoping you guys had laws up there that actually let you do police work."

"The only thing we can do is to wait until he posts to social media again and hope he reveals his location."

Liskey sighed. "That probably won't happen. If he does it, he'll do it from a computer that is nowhere near his actual location. That last post of Marjorie Wise was done from a computer in a church in PG County, and he was in Canada at the time."

"Roth's got connections at a church?"

"Long story."

"Hold on."

Suddenly the phone went quiet. Liskey sat there, still in the parking lot of National Harbor, looking at Newberry's old phone. Thanks to privacy laws, he couldn't do anything with the phone before Isaac Roth's deadline, but there was one other thing that crossed his mind. Perhaps if he dialed Roth's sat phone number and spoke directly to the man himself....

He was mulling over that possibility when Peeks got back on the line. "Liskey, we got some developments."

"What?"

"We found a 19-year-old boy shot dead just off Viewmount Park. We think he's the same boy that Roth forced to dial the cops to draw us out to East Hamilton."

"So, Roth killed another one?"

"Viewmount Park is very close to Forest Hill, where Celia is. And that's not all. We checked the cameras in the house. Her friend is in the safe room, but Celia is nowhere to be found."

"What?" Liskey's raised voice bounced off the closed windows in the car.

"She's not in the safe room. She may be in one of the bedrooms where there's no cameras. But she definitely is not in any of the common areas."

"Can you roll back the video?"

"The system doesn't work like that. It doesn't record. Live feed only."

"Well, she's vulnerable, and Roth has been hanging around the neighborhood. Peeks, you gotta get somebody over there now!"

"We already have. I took your earlier advice and sent an ETF team over. They're parked in waiting about five blocks away from the house, and I got two sharpshooters in neighboring houses watching everything. If he approaches, we'll get him. Good news is that Celia didn't leave the house. My guys would have seen it."

"Good. That's good to hear."

3:05 pm

In a house just across the street from the rear of the Wise's home, a plainclothes Toronto emergency task force officer crouched down beneath the sill of a second-floor bedroom window, peering out between an inch of space between two drapery panels. A bolt-action sniper rifle lay on the nearby bed. The walkie-talkie in his hand occasionally chirped and buzzed. From his perch, he had a full-view of the street, playground, and most of the rear yard of the Wise's home.

He was rock still, careful not to make any sudden movements that would shift the curtains and give away his presence. The white cargo van sat at the end of the dead-end street and had been there for at least four minutes, idling. The officer had already radioed in the tags; no one had reported the van stolen. His view was of the passenger side of the van, and it was difficult to make out the person driving. Without a positive ID, he could not radio the rest of his tactical team and have them pounce on the van. He had to be careful; if the driver was Isaac Roth, Marjorie Wise was likely also in the van. One whiff of cops, and Marjorie was dead, if she wasn't already.

Suddenly the van went into reverse. The officer grabbed his binoculars and tried to catch a view of the driver, but the mid-afternoon glare made it next to impossible. *Probably just a lost handyman,* the officer thought, as he watched the van make a U-turn and head up the street from where he came.

***

The tall man, after making a U-turn, drove about three blocks away. It was a safe distance, yet close enough that he could ensure the house exploded and take giddy pleasure in his evil deed.

He shut off the engine, rolled down the window, and poised the phone in his hand, ready to dial the main house number that would trigger the bomb. He had put enough Semtex in the house to blow it and every neighboring home to pieces. It would be weeks before the police could dig through the rubble and find out what happened.

He looked back at Marjorie, who lay in the back of the van groggy and unresponsive. The tall man figured she was dying. *No worries.* His task was just about done. And his escape plan was flawless. He would drive along the Canadian border to the St. Lawrence River, where he would wait until night and then swim the narrowest part of the river into Vermont. Through his underworld connections, he would call upon a trained spotter who would stand on the U.S. border with a pair of binoculars and make sure no border patrol agents were in the area the time the tall man trekked across the river.

Satisfied with his plan, he dialed the house number. The bomb would detonate in only 30 seconds.

***

Celia lay on the bed, staring up at the ceiling, thinking about death. She was young enough, and old-age death so far away, that she had no given one iota of thought about it. Now, as the tall man's deadline loomed, and she knew she would likely die at his hands, she wondered if it would be anything like what she had seen in movies, with a bright light beckoning her to some ethereal realm where God would speak to her from beyond.

But what scared her most was not what would happen

after, but at the moment. How would she die? Would he just shoot her? What would that feel like? How much suffering would she have to endure before that bright light came calling? Or, would the tall man put her through a torturous death, making her suffer until her last breath. *Oh, God, please let this be just a dream.*

But this was not a dream. It was more real than any dream she had ever had. And, as her mind transitioned from thinking about death to how to save herself and her family, she closed her eyes and prayed again, hoping that God would forgive her rebellious and somewhat avant-garde personality and show Himself strong on her behalf.

As she opened her eyes, she heard a faint buzzing in the next room.

Celia sat up and trained her ears to the sound. It sounded like a vibrating cell phone, but it couldn't have been. Her mother and father never left their cell phones at home. Celia continued to listen, heard nothing further, blamed it on her weariness, and laid back down.

*****

After her meeting with Liskey, Brooke Saunders went back to the church, intending to get the Bible she forgot. As she went in the ministers entrance and took the elevator to the second floor, Newberry was there, waiting for her in her office. Normally it would mean a Sunday tryst just before both of them went home. But Newberry, with a scowl on his face that could singe hairs, didn't seem in an amorous mood.

Newberry stood near the door as she entered her office. "How was your meeting?"

Brooke went straight to her desk without looking up. "What meeting?"

"Don't play dumb."

Brooke grabbed her Bible and stuffed it inside her purse. "I wish I knew what you were talking about."

"Your meeting with Detective Liskey. One of the ministers called me. He saw you at National Harbor with him."

Brooke clutched her purse tighter and looked up at Newberry with disgust.

The verge of a sinister smile crept onto Newberry's face. "If you want to have clandestine meetings, you probably shouldn't do it at the Harbor. Everybody in this church goes there for lunch."

"After church, he came to me and threatened to have my parole revoked," Brooke said. "He wanted me to meet him, so I did."

"What d'you tell him?"

"Nothing."

"Nothing?"

"Nothing."

"Hmm." Newberry drew closer to Brooke. "So, was it before or after this *nothing* that you handed him a cell phone?"

Brooke pursed her lips. Although she was tempted to, there was no point in lying any further. Instead, she stepped around him. "I gotta go." She somewhat expected him to grab her as she passed, but when he didn't, she quickened her pace down the hallway toward the stairs.

Newberry stepped into the hallway and yelled after her. "You know what'll happen to you if you told him anything!"

Brooke stopped, paused, and turned just as she opened the door to the staircase. "God will protect me," she declared.

Brooke headed down the stairs, knowing it would be the last time she stepped foot in that church again.

***

Nothing. No loud sonic boom. No smoke. No flash. Nothing. The tall man dialed again. Two rings should have been enough to set off the detonator. After six rings, nothing.

The tall man cursed to himself. Something was wrong. He slipped the phone into his pocket and drove the van back toward the house, pulling up on the street across from the back yard. He studied the house carefully. No fire. No smoke. It was as if the bomb were never there.

He looked back at Marjorie again. She had passed out. Ordinarily he would have given her another shot to make sure she stayed that way, but it didn't matter. If she woke up and escaped, no big deal. She wasn't needed any more. He was about to put this game to an end right now.

The tall man got out of the van, tucked his gun in his waistband at the small of his back, and headed toward the house.

***

There was another noise, faint, almost indiscernible, but was enough to bring Celia to her feet. She reached back for her gun and listened. The sound wasn't just birds at the window or a random creaking of the house. It sounded as if someone were trying to jimmy the basement door leading to the backyard.

Celia felt an intense pang of fear. She cocked the gun, held it in front of her, and advanced out of the bedroom. If someone were trying to break into the house, she had no intention of being cornered in that bedroom.

At the end of the hallway was the main room, but that was two doors away. Celia had to pass another bedroom, and then her Dad's study, where the lower-level safe room door was located. She kept her back pressed against the wall and slid along it. She could see the main room, but the glass doors leading to the backyard and the pool were around the corner.

The sound was clearer now. Someone was definitely trying to break in.

Celia held the weapon in front of her, knowing that at any second, she might have to kill. With the fear and adrenaline pulsing through her, she kicked into survival mode and was ready to pull that trigger, especially if the tall man was waiting when she turned that corner. The entrance to her Dad's study was just to the left of her, and she could have easily retreated inside and isolated herself to the security of the safe room. But the weapon in her hand made her feel powerful, gave her control. For once, the odds between her and the tall man were even, and she could not turn down this opportunity to end this once and for all.

She heard the door opening, the high-pitched squeak of the hinges giving it away. Celia felt the palpitations again, and her body tensed. She squeezed the butt of the gun harder than she needed to, and her index finger pulsed nervously on the trigger. Taking a deep breath, she turned the corner, pointing the gun shoulder-high and directly in front of her. For the first time since he attacked her in Silver Spring, she beheld face-to-face the man who had sent her life into turmoil.

The tall man looked up once he was halfway inside. He froze at the sight of Celia standing near a wall, almost ten yards away, her gun pointed directly at him. He stood there, still and calm as an icicle, sizing her up. Within ten seconds, he had scanned the gun, which jittered unsteadily in her hand. *Bauer. Likely a .25 caliber.* He could survive a shot or two from one of those and still return fire. He glanced at the safety. It was off.

Roth then met her eyes with his. The fear he saw there was not of him, but the fear of what she had to do to stop him. He grinned, a wide, victorious, malevolent one that convinced Celia she was truly dealing with a monster.

With no cover nearby, the tall man reached back and tried

to draw his own weapon, trusting that Celia would not have the nerve to fire.

He was wrong.

Celia, wanting to avert her eyes but wisely managing only a squint, squeezed off three shots from the semi-automatic. The bullets shattered the glass doors, spraying glass onto the concrete patio, but neither bullet hit its target. Flying glass sliced the tall man's left cheek, and he stumbled backward, still trying to bring his gun forward to fire at Celia. Seeing that the tall man had not fallen, Celia screamed in fear, simultaneously firing another three shots, emptying the magazine. This time they connected, sending the tall man stumbling back two steps through the doors before he fell onto the patio. The gun flew out of his hand and landed about two feet away. He flinched, turned on his stomach and tried to get to his gun, but the searing pain in his abdomen caused him to abandon his effort and clutch his stomach, writing from side to side in a widening pool of blood.

Celia's body weakened, and with her back to the wall, she slid down to the floor, the gun still pointed straight ahead. Seconds later, four police officers, dressed in tactical gear, scurried from around the rear of the pool house and approached, using the sides of the house as cover. Their rifles were pointed directly at Celia through the hole in the broken glass door. "Police! Drop your weapon!" they yelled. At that instant, Celia heard a loud bang upstairs and men shouting "police" in both English and French. Celia dropped her gun to the floor just as two tactical officers, their rifles pointed directly at her, descended the stairs.

"Police! Put your hands behind your head!" one of them yelled. Celia quickly obeyed. Two more officers charged down the stairs. One headed down the hallway toward the rear bedrooms, and the other approached Celia. He grabbed the gun lying on the floor, checked it for rounds, then disengaged the empty magazine and left it and the gun on the floor. He ordered Celia to her feet, frisked her, and then put handcuffs on her before leading her to the loveseat.

After the officers searched the basement and yelled "clear," two of the four officers from the backyard poured in and surveyed the scene. Celia watched the officers mill around the tall man's body, then heard another commotion upstairs. Amid the yells of "police" and "don't move," Celia heard Malik's voice urging the officers not to shoot him. She hung her head. She had all but forgotten Malik was downstairs in the safe room. He must have exited through the master bedroom once he heard the gunshots.

About five minutes later, another police officer came downstairs, this one dressed in a gray suit, though he was wearing a bulletproof vest. He greeted Celia but said nothing more. Following him, another group of suited detectives filed downstairs, milled about, inspecting every corner of the basement. The first detective walked outside, stepping carefully over the broken glass and blood, examined the tall man's body, talked briefly with officers, and then walked back inside. He approached Celia and crouched in front of her. He whistled for an officer and ordered him to remove the cuffs from Celia's wrists.

Once he removed the cuffs, the detective said, "Hi, Miss Rayburn. I'm Detective Sergeant Jim Peeks. Are you okay?"

Celia looked directly at the tall man's body. "Is he dead?"

"No," Peeks told her. "He's alive, but it doesn't look good for him. You plugged him really good. Where d'you get the gun?"

"My dad's bedroom," Celia answered quickly. "What about my mom? Where is she?"

Peeks hesitated before answering. "We found her. She was outside, in a van. But she's in bad shape. Paramedics are treating her now, and they're going to take her to a hospital."

"I want to see her," Celia said.

"I know. And you will. But first, we have to figure out what happened here. So, we are going to have to take you down to College Street and ask you a few questions."

"Am I under arrest?"

Peeks spoke calmly. "You just shot a man, so we need to get some information from you so we can understand what happened. We also need to make sure you're okay. You just went through a very traumatic event."

"I want my Dad with me."

Peeks nodded. "We'll see what we can do." He stood to his feet and extended his hand. Celia reluctantly took it and allowed Peeks to pull her to her feet. Together, they walked up the stairs. Halfway up, Celia looked back at the tall man's body and hoped and prayed that the man who had traumatized her for several days was dead. *Very dead.* And those thoughts produced a curious jumble of relief and shame.

***

7:23 p.m.

A half hour before, Liskey had landed at Pearson Airport and, after retrieving his checked baggage containing his service weapon and a change of clothes, took a taxi to Toronto Metro police headquarters on College Avenue. Now he sat alone in an eighth-floor conference room sipping on stale black coffee waiting to see Jim Peeks. While he waited, another detective poked his head in the room. "You the detective from the States?"

"I am." Liskey stood and greeted the detective with a handshake. "Detective Frank Liskey."

"Detective Pierre Hall." Detective Hall pulled out a chair and sat across the table from Liskey. "Peeks will be along shortly, but he wanted me to update you on what's going on with the case."

"Yeah, I heard Isaac Roth is dead."

"Yep. Died right after he got to the ER."

"What'd he get hit with?"

".22 cal. Two gut shots, one in the chest."

"Folly of arrogance, probably."

"Think a guy in his profession would wear a vest."

"Where'd she get the gun?"

"Her father's bedroom, apparently."

"How is she?"

"I'll let Peeks have that conversation with you."

That evasive response worried Liskey, and it showed in his face. Detective Hall noticed it and hastened to another subject, hoping to avoid any further inquiry. "Marjorie Wise is over at Western in critical condition, with several lacerations, an infected amputated finger, bruises and scrapes, and an almost lethal dose of anesthesia coursing through her body. But the doctors expect her to live. Her husband's with her, and I think the kids are coming up."

Liskey nodded and took another sip of his coffee.

Detective Hall broke the ensuing silence with "So, why was this Isaac Roth guy chasing Celia, anyway?"

"She was in the wrong place at the wrong time," Liskey said, and left it at that. He wasn't in the mood to elaborate, and he doubted Detective Hall cared, anyway. The Toronto detectives had solved their cases, but his was still wide open. He had no real evidence that Jonathan Newberry ordered Celia's murder. He had given instructions to Ramon Williams to work on getting enough evidence to indict Jonathan Newberry and Charles Prender for their involvement in the murder plot against Pastor Lyons, Celia, and Wynn Delano. As it stood now, the only thing they knew was that Jonathan Newberry had Roth's telephone number, that Roth, Prender, and Newberry had some strange meetings in the backwoods of St. Mary's County, and that the photo of Marjorie Wise was in Pastor Newberry's email. None of this was enough to prove a murder conspiracy. And though Brooke had given him a lot of information, he doubted she would go on the record with it, which made things more difficult.

Liskey's excuse to his sergeant—that he needed to go to Toronto to extradite Isaac Roth once he was captured and to ensure that Celia got home safe—seemed to appease the sergeant. But Liskey knew the excuse was only partly true. He cared about Celia and wanted to ensure that she was okay and that she got home safely. But since Isaac Roth had died while Liskey was still in the air, extradition would be a moot point.

Liskey pushed his chair back against a wall and leaned his head back against it, the crown of his head just an inch from the bottom of the Toronto police logo hanging on the wall. He was tired, physically and mentally, and rightfully so. The information he got from Brooke was revelatory but also frightened him. Was the day coming where Christians would be hunted like foxes in the brush? Had the day arrived when expressing faith in the Cross could get one beheaded?

Liskey wondered if he was fighting the right battle. He signed up to be a cop because he wanted to put bad guys away, and he enjoyed the power and prestige he had while doing it. But there was not much a decorated cop could do about a spiritual strategy. He could work cases and chase down those who meant others harm. But this was more of a spiritual attack, an attempt to discourage Christian expression in America. No weapon that Montgomery County had issued him could be effective against that kind of attack. And he knew killing Isaac Roth would do little to stop them. And that scared him. But Liskey knew of only one way to deal with his fear, and that was to combat it. He was not one to shirk away from a battle. As soon as he got back to the

States, he would have another talk with Pastor Lyons. He knew the two of them would soon be kindred spirits.

Ten minutes later, Jim Peeks walked in, carrying his own cup of coffee, barely able to meet Liskey's intense stare. He removed his blazer, hung it over the back of a chair, and extended his free hand over the table toward Liskey. "I'm Detective Sergeant Jim Peeks."

Liskey leaned forward, giving the detective a firm but brief handshake. "Nice to meet you, Detective. I'd admit I'd be a lot nicer if you had some good news to share."

Peeks took a sip of his coffee and sat down next to Detective Hall. "I wish I did."

"Celia. What's going on with her?"

"She's being held. She's being charged with second-degree murder and unauthorized possession of a firearm."

Liskey was livid, and the coffee did little to calm him down. "You got her locked up? For defending herself?"

"Canada's a little different from the States," Peeks explained. "We got no stand-your-ground-laws here. You can defend yourself, but that's only if you got no other choice. My boss and the Crown's attorney think Miss Rayburn screwed up, and they want to hold her accountable."

"For what?" Liskey almost raised his voice. "They should pin a medal on her. This guy not only killed two people in my neck of the woods, but he shot one of your cops and maimed one of your citizens and killed another. Now you want to charge her with murder for defending herself against that piece of trash?"

"Let's look at that closely, detective," Peeks hoped that a logical explanation would curb Liskey's anger. "Celia's father urged her to stay in that safe room until Isaac Roth was caught. That safe room is a subterranean fortress. Instead, she comes out for some unknown reason, grabs a gun from her father's room, and rolls downstairs."

"What reason did she give for doing that?" Liskey wanted to know.

"Some nonsense about seeing if Isaac Roth had left any clues in the house to his whereabouts. We had already told her that Isaac Roth was probably in the neighborhood, likely watching her house. That was all she needed to know."

"Celia's spent the last few days cooped up, Jim. She was probably stir-crazy."

Without acknowledging Liskey's last comment, Peeks continued. "So, she finds her mother's finger in the house and puts it in the refrigerator on ice. Based on one of our SOCOs read of it, it had been in the fridge for at least thirty minutes before we arrived. So, that means that even if Celia put the finger in the fridge almost immediately after she came out of the safe room, she was out of that room for at least thirty minutes. We believe it was more like forty-five minutes."

"What's your point, Peeks?"

"The point is that for a girl who was in fear of her life, she was out of that safe room for a very long time. We believe she didn't just come out of that room to find clues. We think she deliberately drew Isaac Roth to that house and set him up to be shot and killed."

"Tell me you're kidding."

Peeks leaned forward. "This girl emptied the clip of a Bauer automatic. Standing ten yards away, she landed three body shots, and another three whizzed by him awful close. The guy was armed, but he barely had a chance to get his weapon out. This wasn't a shooter in panic. She was calm and deliberate."

Liskey scoffed.

"And she was ten yards away from the guy. At that distance, she could have retreated back into the safe room. No need to shoot him at all."

"Except had she done that, he might have retaliated by killing her mother," Liskey pointed out.

"Wouldn't have happened."

"What do you mean?"

"Our tactical teams were watching the house. One of our guys was in a neighbor's house on Connery. When our guy saw Roth approach the house, we stormed it. But Miss Rayburn got to him before we did. Like I said, if she had stayed in that safe room..."

"Yeah, you made your point," Liskey said, annoyed.

"And there was her demeanor after the shooting," Peeks continued. "Most people who kill someone in self-defense are a wreck afterward. Not Miss Rayburn."

"May have something to do with the fact that this guy killed her husband, and maimed her mother," Liskey reasoned. "I'm sure she'll feel it later, but right now, she's probably thanking her lucky stars the guy is dead."

"And that goes to the motive. She wanted vengeance. She even stopped by Detroit to pick up a friend of hers, some guy named Anthony Sharp. Mr. Sharp told us they had plans to rescue Miss Rayburn's mother. And Mr. Sharp has a rap sheet longer than a fat man's grocery receipt."

Liskey drank his coffee again. He was running out of ways to refute this.

"Detective," Peeks stood up, "Isaac Roth was an evil, dangerous man. But he is a human, and we have to investigate his death just as we would any other. It's hard for us to see this as a self-defense shooting when Miss Rayburn could have easily prevented it."

"So, you're gonna lock up the girl who killed the man who tried to take her life? She doesn't deserve this." Liskey stood. "I want to see her."

"You and about a half-dozen other people." Peeks motioned with his head for Liskey to follow him. "C'mon. It's about a half hour drive to Eglinton Avenue."

While on the road, Liskey avoided any conversation with Peeks and stared out the window instead. This was his first time to Toronto, but it surprised him how much it looked like any regular big city. Except for a few red maple leaf flags posed high above concrete streets, this part of Toronto looked like Anytown, U.S.A., with its tower apartment buildings, low-end strip malls, and wide streets.

Liskey heard a buzzing sound that appeared to come from Peeks. Without taking his eyes off the road, Peeks pulled a large device from his blazer pocket that Liskey wasn't sure was a cell phone or a tablet. After looking briefly at the device, Peeks pulled over at the curb in front of a Tim Horton's.

"Excuse me for a moment." Peeks tapped and swiped the device. Liskey glanced at the Tim Horton's, reminded of how hungry he was when the odor of sweet baked goods made its way into the car.

Suddenly, Peeks uttered a curse word, which made Liskey abandon his thought to step out of the car for a few moments to visit the Tim Horton's. "What happened?" Liskey asked.

"You wouldn't believe it if I told you." Peeks laid the device on the floor below him and pulled the car away from the curb and headed west on Eglinton.

"Try me."

"The bomb squad is at the Wises' house. There was about a pound of Semtex in a closet in one of the basement rooms. It was hooked up to some kind of detonator that was plugged into a cell phone."

"Sheesh. That much plastic would have taken out the whole house."

"Probably half the block."

"How'd they find it?"

"They searched Roth's truck and saw remnants of the packaging. They also found another cell phone. Fortunately, one of our guys is an army vet. He put two-and-two together, searched around the house for it and found it in the closet."

Liskey nodded slightly. "So, Roth was going to blow up the house?"

"With Miss Rayburn and her friend in it." Peeks looked only momentarily at Liskey before he returned his attention to the road. "Not even sure the safe room would have protected them with that kind of force. At best, it would have shut off all the electricity and left them trapped down there. Funny thing is, the bomb squad said the primary in the det had already gone off. They said it likely happened sometime before Miss Rayburn shot Roth."

Liskey frowned in confusion. "Maybe the Semtex was inert."

"Nope. It was active."

"And no explosion?"

"Nope. Weird. Try to fathom that."

Liskey didn't need to. He remembered Pastor Lyons' testimony about an angel saving his life. Maybe that same angel had passed out more grace in Toronto. A smile crossed Liskey's face as he looked up to heaven and silently mouthed the words, "Thank you."

***

Ten minutes later, a uniformed officer ushered Liskey into the basement of the 41 Division police station on Eglinton Avenue. They walked along a neutral beige concrete block corridor until they reached a gun locker embedded in the wall just ahead of a metal door leading to the interview rooms. Liskey secured his service weapon inside the locker and then waited as the officer unlocked the door to the interview section. The officer led Liskey inside one of the three very-brightly lit interview rooms, nodded to Liskey, and left. A few minutes later, another officer returned with Celia, who was wearing drab green pants and a green shirt. Celia took one look at Liskey and cast her gaze downward. The officer removed the handcuffs and guided her to a hard-plastic chair across the table from Liskey.

Once the officer left, Liskey said, "How are you doing?"

"Not so good," Celia mumbled.

"I'll bet."

"How's my mom?"

"They tell me she's in the ICU, but she's going to survive. Your family's at the hospital now. They're planning to be at your bail hearing tomorrow morning."

Celia sniffed. "First time I've been locked up."

"Do you have a lawyer?"

"My dad's getting me one. The lawyer's supposed to talk to me before the hearing tomorrow."

"Good."

"Detective, I didn't do what they said—"

Liskey held his hand up, cutting her off. "Don't talk about that. This conversation's not protected, if you know what I mean."

Celia shook her head. "I don't care. I didn't do anything wrong. I just want to tell you what happened."

"Not the time or the place. What until you lawyer gets here."

Celia sighed. "So you think I did something wrong?"

"Yeah, you did."

"What?"

"You left my house. And if I had the opportunity to speak with you before you did so, I would have told you it was Isaac Roth's plan to draw you to your parents' house."

"Really?"

"Yeah. He could have found 900 million places in Toronto to take that photograph, but he takes it in your parents' basement. He knew you would come there. He tells you no cops, and then he draws you right into his trap. That five-thirty meeting to swap you for your mother was never going to take place. He was gonna take you out as soon as you came to the house. Your mother likely would have been killed, too. He was keeping her alive just in case his plan didn't work, and he needed her again. And guess how he was going to kill you?"

"He was gonna shoot me?" Celia guessed.

"Nope. They found a pound of plastic explosive in that house. He was watching that house, and as soon as you showed up, he was gonna blow you and that house to high heaven."

Celia's hand went to cover her mouth. "Oh, my God."

"In fact, he had already set off the bomb. You and your friend *should* be dead right now."

"Are you serious?"

"Yeah. The only reason you're not is because the detonator malfunctioned."

Celia's head went down again. "Oh, goodness."

Celia and Liskey sat in silence for almost a minute while Celia absorbed the news she had just heard. Celia broke the silence with a mere "Why?"

Liskey didn't want to get into it. He responded, "We're still working to find out the truth."

"So, maybe I should have told you about Roth's call, huh?"

Liskey said, "Yeah, that would have been nice. I would have thought you would have trusted me enough to do that."

"I'm so sorry."

"Well, I'm sorry you're in this predicament."

"Maybe you can get me out."

Liskey sighed and stood to his feet. "I wish I could, but I don't have any sway up here. Here, I'm just a visitor with a badge that means nothing."

"So, I guess I'm in real big trouble, huh?"

Liskey avoided a direct answer. He wanted to say some encouraging words to Celia but found them lacking from a legal perspective. On the gun charge alone, Celia would get up to ten years in prison. The unfairness of it all made him angry. Why lock up a girl who was only defending herself?

That was Liskey's challenge with being a police officer. Sometimes he had to arrest people more deserving of leniency, compassion, and understanding; not justice. Occasionally he had to file charges against individuals who had made honest mistakes but had broken the law. It frustrated him that there was not enough wiggle room in the law to allow someone with no ill intent to slip through. And Celia was a classic case of someone who was innocent yet had run afoul of the justice system. And Liskey yearned to help her but was irritated that he could not.

But he wanted to try another approach, one buried deep within that he only pulled up when experiencing extreme emotional or spiritual distress. Liskey knew how to pray, and prayed occasionally, but didn't consider himself a man of prayer, akin to a man who could grill a great steak every now and again but didn't consider himself a chef. Liskey was definitely not a seasoned prayer warrior. Yet he depended on it occasionally, enduring chagrin from his wife who would admonish him for praying only when something crazy was happening in his life. *God wants to hear you talk to Him every day*, she would say. Thinking about prayer now made him hesitant to approach God because it seemed selfish to him. But it was the only thing he could offer to Celia, and he would not hold it back.

"Maybe we should pray," Liskey said almost sheepishly.

Celia's scoff was barely noticeable, and she turned her gaze away. "God doesn't want to hear from me."

"Why do you say that?"

Celia jerked her head toward Liskey and got serious, her voice escalating. "Look at me. My life is a wreck. I'm a battered wife. I'm broke. My husband is dead. My mom was almost killed. I'm in jail. And for what? I still don't understand why I am here. I don't know why this crazy man came after me and my husband. And they are trying to lock me up because I killed him in self-defense. At what point is God gonna come down and see about me?" Tears flowed. "I've prayed, and nothing happened. My mom and dad, almost every time they talk to me, say they are praying for me. With all these prayers going forth, why is my life such a mess?"

Liskey retook his seat. He had to think about how to respond to Celia, but he knew he couldn't let her languish in hopelessness. He wished Pastor Lyons was there, someone who would know what to say to strengthen and appease Celia.

His only solution was to refer to himself. "Y'know, my relationship with God is not the best, so I got no right to be preaching to you," Liskey said. "I pray maybe two days a year, and the other 363 days I act like I don't need God. It's like that father that comes to visit only on your birthday and Christmastime, but you don't see him any other days of the year. You have no real relationship." Liskey leaned forward, feeling his wheels slide back on the rails. "But those times I've prayed, God has answered. And if there's any son-of-a-bitch that God should have ignored, it's me. I haven't been to church in years, except this morning, and then it was only to try to lock a preacher up."

Celia's eyes widened. "You locked up a preacher?"

Liskey thought for a moment. Ordinarily, this would have been an excellent opportunity to tell her about what he had learned from Brooke about Jonathan Newberry. But figuring that his news would likely further discourage her faith, he decided against it. Instead, he replied, "Long story. Anyway, my point is that maybe you shouldn't give up on God. Sometimes, just when you are about to give up, is when God is about to come through for you."

"Sounds like one of my Dad's clichés," Celia laughed. "Right up there with 'God is good' and 'prayer changes things.'"

"Might be a cliché, but it doesn't make it any less true."

Celia just looked at him.

Then, Liskey remembered something.

"Look, right now, you should be blown to bits. You would not have been safe anywhere in that house. Yet, the bomb didn't go off. That's very unusual. You can't tell me that God didn't have a hand in that."

Celia still looked at him, her eyes glistening.

"That's an answer to prayer if I've ever heard one." Liskey extended his hands across the table to her. "C'mon, let's pray."

Celia hesitated for a moment. Realizing she had nothing to lose, she joined hands with Liskey across the table. They bowed their heads and closed their eyes, and immediately a peace not there before filled the room.

Liskey felt the presence and responded, "Dear heavenly Father…"

Chapter Twenty-One

Following Up

6:34 a.m., Monday

Celia had seen her husband murdered, yet even that did not prepare her for the agony of pulling the trigger herself. Guilt poured upon her like a steady rain, and she believed maybe the police were right for arresting her. She could have retreated into the safe room. She could have merely wounded him. But she shot to kill, to end the madness permanently, and now she found that the aftermath was far more traumatic than she had imagined. It was one of those acts easy to do but hell to deal with afterward. Every bit of moral conviction, every Scripture she had ever heard, every memory of hearing "thou shalt not kill" pour from a preacher's lips, morphed together to heap perilous regret on her, and she wished urgently that she could redo that moment.

At least twice that night, lying on a concrete bench with only a blanket between her and the hardness of the bench, Celia saw Isaac Roth; once at the foot of her bed at home she thought she was sleeping in, and again in the basement, replaying the entire event again. Except this time, the gun would not fire, and Isaac Roth would march toward her before she woke up in a sweat, heart thumping, finding herself still inside the holding cell with only 45 minutes since she had drifted off. Afraid to go back to sleep, she spent most of the night sitting on the floor, occasionally entertained by the noise of new arrestees coming into the women's holding cell area. She eavesdropped on the hushed twilight conversation of a fellow inmate who had sneaked a cell phone into the holding cell somehow.

Celia wanted this to go away. She had never been in a jail cell in her life, and this one was worse than the ones she had seen on TV. It was essentially an 8-foot by 10-foot concrete block closet, with a stainless-steel combination toilet-lavatory nestled against one wall and a steel door with a slit for a window occupying the opposite wall. She couldn't imagine a long-term stay in this cell. A person would go crazy being this cramped.

It was then, as the sun rose out of her view and officers were preparing to take her and several other arrestees down the road to the courthouse for the bail hearing, that Celia reconsidered her doubts about God. She had agreed to pray with Liskey only to be cordial, not because she believed anything would happen. But now, with her soul being assaulted with nightmares and the looming knowledge she could not handle being thrown in a cell like this for several hours a day, she yearned for the peace that had eluded her for much of her adult life. The last time she could say she had peace was when she was living with her parents in Detroit, in the middle of one of the least peaceful neighborhoods in the country. There was crime and death all around, yet in the Wise household, there was a tranquility that Celia never appreciated until she was no longer there.

Marrying Justin was supposed to bring her the idyllic lifestyle she had hoped for, free of parental intervention and judgment. But once Justin's drinking and womanizing surfaced, her marriage would not be as rosy as she thought. In those moments, she yearned for the comforts of home, though she would never give her parents the pleasure of knowing that. She wanted to prove to them she could run her own life. Now she felt as if she had run it into the ground.

With all pretense and pride gone and her messed-up life now an open book to her parents and her entire family, she needed the peace and comfort of home. What she enjoyed most about her parents' home was because God was there; that quickly became clear to her. The Wise's music was spiritual and heavenly, their speech devoid of epithets or insults, their appearance fashionable yet demure. Prayer and Bible study were regular activities in the home. Whenever visitors came by, George and Marjorie Wise eventually got around to talking about Jesus, which would transform a thirty-minute conversation about the weather and current events to a four-hour conversation about the goodness of God. While she lived in the household, Celia had grown tired of it, while not realizing how much her soul and spirit had thrived from it.

A jingling of keys at the cell door shook her out of her thoughts. After a few seconds, the door slid open, and a female officer waited there holding handcuffs. "Ms. Rayburn, time to go to court."

Celia stood to her feet. "Oh, Jesus, help me," she whispered, hoping her almost silent plea reached the ears of the One she had not spoken earnestly to in years.

***

9:12 am

After talking briefly with his wife on the phone, Liskey got dressed in a modest tan suit, left his hotel room, and took a taxi to the Old City Hall building, a large 18th-century Romanesque structure taking up an entire city block. The taxi dropped him off at a flight of wide concrete steps and several sandstone arches leading to the entrance. As he walked up the stairs toward the door, he was glad he had left his service weapon at the hotel. He wanted no complications getting through security, and he had only 45 minutes before Celia's show cause hearing was to start.

After passing through security and traversing one more flight of stairs, Liskey was at Courtroom 103. Amid the people milling about in the wide corridor, he noticed a middle-aged man standing near one of the long wooden benches that lined the corridor. Two men and one woman, all of whom favored the man but were much younger, sat on the bench.

Liskey buttoned his jacket and casually approached. "Mr. Wise?"

George Wise pivoted to Liskey. George sized him up quickly. He looked safe and distinguished enough, and he didn't appear to be a reporter or an attorney seeking to latch onto a high-profile case. "Yes?" George responded.

"I'm Frank Liskey. I'm the detective from Maryland that was handling your son-in-law's murder case."

George's sharp inhale showed recognition. "Oh, yes." Their handshake lasted until the end of his next words. "Thank you so much for taking care of my daughter."

"Well, I don't know how much I did," Liskey responded. "She's in this mess."

"I don't blame you for that. Celia's always had a mind of her own and never listens. I told her to stay in that safe room. And she should have never come up here to Toronto like she did."

Liskey nodded gently, then motioned toward the bench. "This your family?"

"Three of my children. I also have a daughter that's on assignment. She's a TV reporter in Lansing. And I have another daughter that is at the hospital right now with my wife."

"How's she doing?"

"My wife? She's stable, but they say she's got a long road ahead of her. They're talking possible kidney and heart damage." George lowered his voice. "To be honest with you, if that lunatic that messed up my wife was still alive, I might be the one waiting for my turn in that courtroom right now."

Liskey eyebrows furrowed. "Not a very Christian thing to say, Mr. Wise."

"Hmm." It took only a few seconds for George to fashion his thoughts into words. "There's a Scripture that says, 'Like a trampled spring and a polluted well is a righteous man who gives way before the wicked.' Now, I'm not a vigilante by any means. But I'm not going to sit around and let someone mess with my family. I think that's very biblical. Celia gets that from me. That's why she did what she did, even though she was advised not to. She just wanted to protect her mom." George gently touched Liskey shoulder to guide him farther away from earshot of his children. "Do you have any idea why all of this happened? What was Celia into?"

"All indications are that your daughter was completely innocent, sir," Liskey reported. "She was just in the wrong place at the wrong time. I can't share much, because I'm not exactly clear on it, but she may have been targeted because she witnessed something when she was in downtown D.C. looking for a job."

"You mean the pastor's shooting? I heard about that."

"Not the shooting itself, but something connected to it. Something that a TV reporter caught on camera. I hope to look into it more once I get back to the States. We think your daughter was the target. Your son-in-law was killed likely because he got in the way."

"Will you keep me posted? On what the reporter caught on camera?"

Liskey nodded reluctantly. "Whatever I am at liberty to share, I'll do so."

"Thank you. And thank you for praying with my daughter."

"Oh, you heard about that?"

"I spoke to her briefly this morning. Yes, she told me. Hopefully, this will be the beginning of a real change in her life."

"I dunno. She seems like such a good girl."

"She *is* a good girl," George agreed. "But even a good girl, if they don't follow the Lord's leading, can get into some very bad situations."

Liskey looked over George's right shoulder and saw a thin man, wearing a gray suit, approach. Liskey nodded toward the man, and George turned around. George then looked back at Liskey. "Excuse me for a minute," and walked off down the hall with the man. Liskey watched them as they walked a few yards down the corridor and talked. *Attorney*, Liskey thought. The cowhide briefcase was a dead giveaway.

Liskey leaned against a banister made up of wrought iron flourishes and admired the stained-glass windows in the far wall, the brown floors accented with yellow striping along the edges, and the marble pillars. He had seen many courthouses, but few had as much old-time charm as this one. It would have been a nice place to visit in better circumstances. The noise level in the courthouse was comparable to a big city indoor mall, and it was difficult for Liskey to eavesdrop on the conversation between George and the attorney, even though they were only a few yards away.

After about ten minutes, the attorney walked away, and George returned to Liskey. "Sorry about that," George said. "That was Celia's lawyer. We just got some great news." He extended his hand and motioned for his family to come over. They came off the bench quickly and gathered around him.

"They're gonna drop the murder charges against Celia," George exclaimed.

A yelp and a whoop came from his kids, and they quickly hugged each other in celebration. After getting a quick hug from each of his children, George got their attention again.

"Now, the charge of unauthorized possession of a firearm is still gonna stick, but the lawyer thinks there'll be no problem for Celia to get bail," George explained. "He's gonna try to get the Crown to move forward on a summary conviction, and that'll get Celia no more than a year in jail, if that much."

George watched as the smiles slowly faded from his kids' faces. "C'mon, y'all, she was facing life in prison before this. This is a blessing from the Lord. There's no guarantee she'll even do a year. She might just get probation. This is a major victory."

One son said, "Dad, she shouldn't have to spend any time in prison for this. She was just defending herself."

George sighed. "I know, son. Let's just pray to the Lord that the judge sees it that way." He turned to Liskey. "You're a man of prayer. I trust you will do the same."

Liskey shook his head. "It's been a while for me. Not sure how much God is gonna listen to me."

George kept his eyes on Liskey. "Every prayer, spoken in earnest, is precious to God. I don't care if you haven't prayed since the days your mom made you say the blessing before your meal. He'll hear you just the same."

Liskey nodded. Since he could do nothing else to affect the decisions made in that courtroom, the least he could do was turn his voice toward God again, appealing on behalf of the young lady he and his wife had grown fond of.

***

8:20 a.m.

Upon returning to Maryland, Liskey walked into his house as tired as he had ever been. Marian, who had been in the kitchen, heard him come him and went to greet him with a kiss.

"You hungry?" Marian asked.

"Just something to drink." Liskey flopped on the living room couch while his wife went to the kitchen and came back with a twelve-ounce can of cold Pepsi. Liskey popped the tab on the can and took a long swig, then placed the half-empty can on the coffee table, remembering to use a coaster to avoid his wife's rebuke.

The living room was dark, but the light from the kitchen cast enough brightness so they could see each other's faces. Marian sat down just inches from Liskey and faced him. "What happened with Celia?" she asked.

"She's out on bail," Liskey explained. "They dropped the murder charges. She's just dealing with the weapons charge now. Her father's gonna be the surety until her trial."

"Surety?"

"It's a person the court holds responsible for making sure Celia comes back to court and meets the requirements of her release."

"Is she coming back to Maryland?"

"No. She's on bail, so they have to keep her in Toronto for a while."

"Probably best. She planned on going back there, any-way."

"Yeah."

"You going back for the trial?"

"I'm told the trial likely won't last fifteen minutes. Prob-ably not worth the trip."

"So, what now?"

Liskey pondered that question long enough that Marian wondered if he had heard her. Just when she was about to ask again, Liskey spoke up. "I still not clear on all of this. Charles Prender and Jonathan Newberry are not talking. We were just lucky to get Isaac Roth's sat phone number on Newberry's old phone, but that doesn't prove Newberry hired Roth. And they're not saying a thing."

"Why not?"

"They don't want to go to jail."

Marian closed the gap between them and held Liskey's hands. "Honey, you solved this case. The murderer is dead. Maybe it's time you let this go."

"No, honey. The murderer is not dead." Liskey stood and walked to the other side of the coffee table. "The murderers are whoever is running that group. Isaac Roth was just their tool. Maybe they'll get someone else and go after Celia again. I have to bring them down before they do this again."

Marian looked away.

Liskey sat back down next to her and gently guided her face toward his. "Honey, this group is trying to destroy the church in America as we know it. As much as you've been trying to get me to go to church, if this group gets its way, there may not be church in America in a few years. At least not the way we've known it. I spoke to Pastor Lyons today, and he said that Billy Graham mentioned once that the United States has never seen persecution toward Christians like other countries. Maybe this is the beginning of persecution in this country, and I have to stop it. But I know I can't do it alone. I need you to stand with me."

"Honey, you know I'll support you in whatever you do. But this—" Marian shook her head. "This scares me."

Liskey grabbed Marian's hands and squeezed them affectionately. "You always prayed that I would find the Lord's will for my life. Maybe this is it. Celia was just the beginning. I'm not through with this yet. And yes, I'm afraid, too. But you know what I fear most?"

Marian met Liskey's eyes. "What?"

"That our son will live in a world where he won't be able to raise his hands in worship without being shot."

Marian laid her head on Liskey's shoulder. Liskey wrapped an arm around her and held her tightly, experiencing a tender moment in contemplation of the fact that his life, and the lives of his family, was about to be taken into a supernatural realm he had never expected.

And that was okay with him.

To be continued with the next book in this series, The Regency.